EDITED BY RICH HORTON

Fantasy: The Best of the Year, 2006 Edition
Fantasy: The Best of the Year, 2007 Edition
Science Fiction: The Best of the Year, 2006 Edition
Science Fiction: The Best of the Year, 2007 Edition
Science Fiction: The Best of the Year, 2008 Edition

FANTASY
THE BEST OF
THE YEAR

2008

**Edited by
RICH HORTON**

COSMOS BOOKS

FANTASY: THE BEST OF THE YEAR

Published by
Dorchester Publishing Co., Inc.
200 Madison Ave.
New York, NY 10016
in collaboration with Wildside Press LLC

Cover design by Garry Nurrish.
Cover painting by Lord Frederick Leighton.

ISBN-10: 0-8439-5926-6
ISBN-13: 978-0-8439-5926-0

The name "Cosmos Books" and the Cosmos logo
are the property of Wildside Press, LLC.

Printed in the United States of America.

CONTENTS

THE YEAR, IN FANTASY 2007

———

Rich Horton

What is fantasy? How is it different from realistic fiction? And how is it different from science fiction?

The answer to the first questions seems obvious: fantasy stories are about things that couldn't happen. How is that different from sf? Well, sf stories are about things that could happen—typically in the future, but also perhaps in alternate pasts or presents, or in different universes. Already we are getting a bit fuzzy here—couldn't alternate universes be where fantasy happens? As to realistic fiction—never forget that those stories are works of imagination as well. Could they have happened? Maybe—but they didn't. In the end all fiction is imagined. And these days much fiction published in the "mainstream" is far from realistic.

That said, it is unsatisfying to imply that there is no important difference between sf, fantasy, and realistic fiction. Most centrally, I think, fantasy stories are set in other worlds. Even when the "other world" is at some level our own. Why so? What is fantasy doing? I have long argued that sf stories can be divided (if very roughly indeed) into two categories—those that explore the "alien," the "other," for their own sake; and those that treat the "alien" as a metaphor for humanity. Bruce Sterling's manifesto for "slipstream" fiction, now a recognized subgenre, suggests a third category. Sterling called slipstream "a kind of writing which simply makes you feel very strange; the way that living in the late twentieth century makes you feel." (Take it as written that in 2007 slipstream might describe the way living in the early twenty-first century makes you feel.) It might be argued that this is just another example of using the "alien" as a metaphor for humanity—for "reality," that is—a way of showing how strange "reality" can be. Still—there seems a difference to me—fiction that, usually, purports to show our world, but stranged; as opposed to fiction that shows another world; which may be a strange version of ours.

So here is a collection of short fantasy stories. I note—with some surprise—that very few of the stories seem "slipstream" to me. This is not out of personal disdain for that subgenre; nor I think does it reflect a decline in the production of that subgenre. It's just the way things fell out. Similarly, there are very few stories that seem set in traditional "fantasy" worlds"—Garth Nix's story probably qualifies, and that's more or less it. Indeed, many of the stories here seem just about—but not quite—set in our world—as with Marly Youmans's "The Comb" or Karen Joy Fowler's "The Last Worders." Or the world might be a fantastical alternate history, as in Matthew Johnson's "Public Safety" and Ian R. MacLeod's "The Master Miller's Tale." Or it might be a fabulist past as with Theodora Goss's "Singing of Mount Abora" and Noreen Doyle's "The Rope." Or the story might begin in our world and go elsewhere, as in "Save Me Plz" by David Barr Kirtley or "A Diorama of the Infernal Regions" by Andy Duncan. Or the world might not be all that tightly specified—one odd aspect highlighted in the story's brief space, as with Rachel Swirsky's story, or Carrie Laben's.

What does this mean? I think, perhaps, that at

shorter lengths writers are staying close to home, fairly often—a point made by Holly Phillips in her afterword to the fine original anthology *Tesseracts Eleven*. Maybe this simply means that at shorter lengths there isn't time to create and populate a wholly new world. But the writers here are certainly creating quite striking ideas and characters—and showing us ourselves in fantastical lights.

On a more practical note, what is there to say about the state of the short fiction field these days? The news is not all good, for sure. The circulation of the major professional magazines continues to decline. But there are optimistic ways to look at things. If print magazines seem to be declining—which this old dinosaur insists on regretting—there is more fiction than ever being published online. Two newer sites that publish a lot of both fantasy and sf are trying to make a go on subscription models: *Jim Baen's Universe* and *Orson Scott Card's Intergalactic Medicine Show*. Both have published some very fine work. A couple of the most promising newer magazines (*Fantasy Magazine* and *Subterranean*) have migrated to the web, and they feature excellent work, as does the venerable *Strange Horizons*. Other online sites of interest include a couple newer ones: *Clarkesworld* and *Coyote Wild*, plus the very interesting *Helix* and such longer running sites as *Chiaroscuro*, *Ideomancer*, *Abyss and Apex*, and *Lone Star Stories*.

And the print magazines are still very high quality. *Fantasy and Science Fiction* and *Realms of Fantasy* are consistently strong. *Weird Tales* has a new editor (Ann VanderMeer) and it looks very good, and is appearing quite regularly at last. After a long hiatus, the fine British magazine *The Third Alternative* has been resurrected under the title *Black Static*. Postscripts also continues in fine fashion. And of course the very small 'zines remain fascinating—*Lady Churchill's Rosebud Wristlet*, of course (and they published a large anthology this year), as well as *Flytrap* and *Electric Velocipede*.

I saw a great many fantasy oriented original anthologies in 2007, of which four in particular stand out: *Wizards*, edited by Gardner Dozois and Jack Dann; *Logorrhea*, edited by *Electric Velocipede*'s John Klima; *The Coyote Road*, edited by Ellen Datlow and Terri Windling; and *Fantasy*, edited by Sean Wallace and Paul Tremblay. Stories from all four of these grace this book. (Of course there was also notable work in combined fantasy·and sf anthologies, such as *Eclipse One,* edited by Jonathan Strahan.)

So while it's not clear to me how economically strong the field of short fantasy fiction is these days (especially the magazines) there is no doubt that it is artistically as vibrant as ever.

Finally I thought to mention a number of those stories that I wanted to include in this volume but couldn't. Call this a brief "Recommend Reading" list, if you will. To begin with, the occasion of putting out a third collection of my choices for the best fantasy stories of the year prompts a little—perhaps too hasty—thinking about the history and trends of my choices. For example—which authors in this collection are repeats? Only four—I've previously used stories by Theodora Goss, Matthew Johnson, Benjamin Rosenbaum, and Holly Phillips. But a number of "my" authors published outstanding stories this year, which were ·definitely on the list of candidates for this volume. (Let me emphasize that I can never quite say that this book has a bright line selection of the very best stories. Sometimes stories aren't included for contractual reasons. Sometimes they don't seem to fit—perhaps literally, if they are too long, or figuratively, if too similar to other stories in the book. I try not to include too many stories from the same source. And I don't use multiple stories by the same author in any one volume. And of course deciding which of two successful works of art is "better" in an objective sense is a dicey job anyway—and there are always stories I desperately wanted to include that just didn't make the cut when I made my final decision—but which would have fit the book just as well as the stories that did make it.)

So, among the outstanding stories I couldn't use this year were: "The Man Who Carved Skulls" by Richard Parks (*Weird Tales*); "The Snake's Wife" by Ann Leckie (*Helix*); "Cryptic Coloration" by Elizabeth Bear (*Jim Baen's Universe*); "The Witch's Headstone" by Neil Gaiman (*Wizards*); "We Never Talk About My Brother" by Peter S. Beagle (*Intergalactic Medicine Show*); "The Dreaming Wind" by Jeffrey Ford (*The Coyote Road*); "Quartermaster Returns" by Ysabeau Wilce (*Eclipse One*); and "The Black Hole in Auntie Sutra's Handbag" by Samantha Henderson (*Lone Star Stories*). Not to mention another story by Marly Youmans, who already appears in this book: "Prologomenon to the Adventures of Child Phoenix" from *Lady Churchill's Rosebud Wristlet*. And another story from Kelly Link, "The Constable of Abal" from *The Coyote Road*. And for that matter further stories from Parks ("Hot Water" from *Realms of Fantasy*, a sequel to "Fox Tails" from last year's volume) and Beagle ("The Last and Only; or, Mr. Moscowitz Becomes French" from *Eclipse One*).

To be sure, many first rate stories came from writers I haven't had the honor to publish yet. For example, Ted Chiang's first long story in a while, "The Merchant and the Alchemist's Gate," which appeared both in *F&SF* and in a chapbook from Subterranean

Press. Also, two delightful novelettes in a new series by the wonderful Fred Chappell ("The Diamond Shadow" and "Dance of Shadows" both from *F&SF*). Add "Limits" by Donna Glee Williams (*Strange Horizons*); "Naming Day" by Patricia McKillip (*Wizards*); "A Wizard of the Old School" by Chris Willrich (*F&SF*); and "A Dirge for Prester John" by Catherynne M. Valente (*Interfictions*). Speaking of Valente, it is incumbent on me to mention her wonderful diptych *The Orphan's Tales*. Volume I (*In the Night Garden*) appeared in 2006, and Volume II (*In the Cities of Coin and Spice*) came out in 2007. These are cunningly intertwined stories, modeled to an extent on *One Thousand and One Night*, but quite original, quite lovely, and so interlaced that they are not quite individual stories and not quite a novel but something in between.

Fantasy is perhaps as diverse a field as it has ever been. There is a great deal of excellent short fantasy being published—and the best of it follows immediately!

UNPOSSIBLE

———

Daryl Gregory

Two in the morning and he's stumbling around in the attic, lost in horizontal archaeology: the further he goes, the older the artifacts become. The stuttering flashlight guides him past boxes of Christmas decorations and half-dead appliances, past garbage bags of old blankets and outgrown clothing stacked and bulging like black snowmen, over and around the twenty-year-old rubble of his son's treasures: Tonka trucks and science fair projects, soccer trophies and summer camp pottery.

His shoulder brushes against the upright rail of a dissassembled crib, sends it sliding, and somewhere in the dark a mirror or storm window smashes. The noise doesn't matter. There's no one in the house below him to disturb.

Twenty feet from the far wall his way is blocked by a heap of wicker lawn furniture. He pulls apart the barricade piece by piece to make a narrow passage and scrapes through, straws tugging at his shirt. On the other side he crawls up and onto the back of a tilting oak desk immovable as a ship run aground.

The territory ahead is littered with the remains of his youth, the evidence of his life before he brought his wife and son to this house. Stacks of hardcover books, boxes of dusty-framed elementary school pictures—and toys. So many toys. Once upon a time he was the boy who didn't like to go outside, the boy who never wanted to leave his room. The Boy Who Always Said No.

Against the far wall, beside a rickety shelf of dried-out paint cans and rusting hardware, a drop cloth covers a suggestive shape. He picks his way through the crowded space. When he pulls aside the cloth, he grunts as if he's been elbowed in the stomach—relief and dread and wrenching sadness competing for the same throat.

Dust coats the Wonder Bike's red fenders, rust freckles its handlebars. The white-walled tires are flat, and stuffing sprouts from cracks in the leather saddle. But it's still here, still safe. And the two accessories he most needs, the things he'd almost convinced himself he'd imagined, are fastened to their places on the swooping crossbar: the five-pronged gearshift like a metal hand; and the glass-covered compass, its face scuffed white but uncracked.

The bike's heavier than he remembers, all old-fashioned steel, more solid than anything they'd bother to make today. He heaves it onto his shoulder and makes his way toward the attic door, handlebars snagging on unseen junk, errant wheels triggering miniature avalanches. Sweat pours down his back. He thinks about heart attacks. He's fifty-six now, a middle-aged man if he lives to a hundred and twelve. People younger than he die all the time. All the time.

The weight of the bike drags him down the attic stairs. He wheels it whinging down the hall, then out the front door and across the frostcrackled lawn, aiming for the realtor sign. The sweat on his neck turns cold. Along the street his neighbors' houses are all dark. The moon stays tucked into its bed of clouds. He's grateful for the privacy. He lifts the front wheel and runs over the FOR SALE sign, flattens it.

In the garage he sets to work removing the accessories. The screws are rusted into place, so he puts aside the screwdriver and plugs in the power drill. The shifter comes free, but the screws holding the compass are stripped, spinning uselessly. He can't risk hammering it off, so he works a hacksaw blade between the handlebars and the bottom of the device and cuts it free. Gently he sets the Wonder Bike against the garage wall and gets into the car.

It takes much less time to attach the accessories to the dash. He screws them directly into the plastic, side by side above the radio.

He starts the engine and stares out the dirt-streaked windshield, trying to remember what to do next. It used to be automatic: pedal hard, thumb the gears, follow the compass. But something happened when he turned thirteen. He lost the knack and the bike stopped working for him. Or maybe, he's been thinking lately, he stopped working for the bike.

He sets the DeShifter to NOT RECOMMENDED. He taps the glass of the UnCompass and the needle quivers, stuck between UNFAMILIAR and UNKNOWN.

Sounds about right, he thinks.

Even with the compass it takes determination to get lost. He drives south out of town, past the tangle of interstate exchanges, toward the green empty parts of the map. He turns down the first road he doesn't recognize. He pays no attention to street names; he looks away when signs appear in his headlights.

Soon there are no signs. Forest swallows the highway. Switchbacks and the skulking moon conspire with him to disguise his direction.

Don't look in the rearview mirror, he tells himself. No trail of bread crumbs. As soon as he thinks of the road behind him, he realizes he left the front door of the house

wide open. Maybe by morning robbers will have emptied
the place. That would make it easier on the real estate
agents. Too much clutter, they'd told him. They couldn't
see that the home had been gutted a year ago.

He rolls down the window and lets the cold wind
buffet him. When did he fall out of love with speed?
He'd had adventures once. He'd rescued the Pumpkin-
head Boys, raced the moto-crows, reunited the shards
of the Glass Kingdom. His quick thinking had out-
witted the Hundred Mayors of Stilt Town.

He nudges the DeShifter past INADVISABLE to
ABSOLUTELY NOT and accelerates. The road ahead
doesn't exist until it appears under his headlights; he's
driving a plow of light through the dark, unrolling the
road before him like a carpet.

A tiny yellow sign flashes past his right fender, too
fast for him to read. He glances sideways—nothing but
the dark—and turns back to the road just as the little
purple house appears in his lights like a phantom.

The structure strikes the grille and explodes into a
thousand pieces. The windshield pocks with white
stars. He stomps on the brake and the car bucks, slides
sideways. He jerks the wheel back to the right and suddenly the car's off the road, jouncing across ground.
He bounces against the roof, ragdolling, unable to
hold onto the wheel. The car bangs sideways against
something invisible and immovable and then everything stops.

He stares out the cratered windshield. The engine
coughs politely, shudders, and dies.

The DeShifter shows COMPLETELY OUT OF THE
QUESTION. The UnCompass needle points straight at
UNPOSSIBLE.

Later—he's as unsure of time as he is of
location—he forces the car door open, pushing against
tree limbs and thick brush, and climbs out and down.

The driver-side wheels are two feet in the air. Trees surround the car as if they'd grown up around it.

He walks up a slight incline to the road, his pulse driving a headache deeper into his temples. The muscles of his neck burn; his chest aches where the seatbelt cut into him.

The surface of the road is littered with shattered plywood—and bits of silver. He stoops, drumming fresh pain into his head, and picks up a dime. There are coins all over the roadway.

The only thing remaining of the tollbooth is another of the child-sized yellow signs, miraculously erect: PLEASE HAVE YOUR DESTINATION IN MIND.

He drops the dime into his pocket and starts walking.

A farmhouse squats in the middle of the highway like a great toad, filling both lanes. He walks toward it in the inconstant moonlight, horrified. If he hadn't struck the tollbooth, he'd have slammed into the house at eighty miles per hour.

On closer inspection the house looks like it's been dropped there from a great height. Walls are askew, their wooden siding bowed, splintered, or blown out completely. Roofs cant at contrary angles.

He steps onto the porch and floorboards creak and shift under his weight like unstable ice. High-pitched barking erupts from inside. He knocks on the door and waits, hunched and shivering. A minute passes. The dog—a small, hyperactive thing by the sound of it—barks and barks.

He crouches next to the closest window but gauzy curtains obscure the view. He makes out a lamp, the suggestion of a couch, a dark rectangle that could be a bookshelf or a wardrobe. His teeth are on the edge of chattering.

He knocks again and sends the dog into fresh vocal frenzy. He considers trying the doorknob. It's warm in there. There could be a phone. How big can the dog be?

He backs off the porch and walks around the side of the house. It's nearly pitch black back there; the roof blocks the moon, and the windows at the back of the house, if there are windows at all, are unlit. He can't even tell if the road continues on the side. He moves in what he thinks is an arc, feeling for the scrape of pavement under his shoes, when suddenly he bangs his toes against something low and hard and stumbles forward. He catches his balance—and freezes, realizing where he's standing. He's in the middle of train tracks.

He doesn't hear anything, doesn't see anything but the eye-swallowing dark. Slowly he steps back over the rails, a chill in his stomach even though he'd see a train coming for miles.

The dog resumes barking, and the sound is different somehow. He circles around to the front of the house and sees that the front door is open now, light spilling around some dark shape filling the doorway.

"Hello?" he says. He holds out his hands as he steps toward the door. "I—I had a slight accident. A couple miles down the road."

"You came by car?" A woman's voice, low and rasping.

"I had an accident," he says again. "If you've got a phone, I could call someone . . . "

"The road's closed to your type." He's not sure if she's warning him or merely stating fact. Her shadow recedes. After a moment he approaches the door.

The dog, a tiny black terrier with an age-whitened snout, lies in a towel-lined wicker basket a few feet from the door. It bares its teeth at him and growls, but makes no move to leave its bed. He steps inside the room.

The woman's already sitting, leaning back in an old leather armchair the color of dried mud. The light is behind her so again her face is in shadow. She crosses her legs, sharp white shins over blood-red slippers. She pulls a foil pack from the pocket of her blue-checked housedress and taps out a cigarette.

He folds his arms across his chest and tries to stop shivering. At least the house is warm. He looks around for a phone but knows he won't find one—it's not that kind of house. It's been a long time, but the old instincts are coming back. He smiles thinly. "And what type would that be, ma'am?"

"Storm-chaser," she says. "Wardrobe-jumper." She flicks a cheap plastic lighter and holds the flame to the cigarette. "Mirror shards sticking to your coat, twigs in your hair. Little hard to squeeze that big ol' man-body through the hedgerow, eh?"

"You don't know me. You don't know who I am."

"Oh my goodness, you must be the *special* one," she says in mock recognition. "You must be the only traveler to see *lands beyond*." She taps cigarette ash onto the braided rug. "Let me guess—enchanted sail-boat? Magic choo-choo train? Oh, that's right, you're a driver—electric kiddie car, then. The tollbooth boy."

"I had a bicycle," he says. "The most wonderful—"

She groans. "Spare me." She inhales on her cigarette, shakes her head. "At least you got rid of it. Most of you can't find your way back without the props." She sees his frown and laughs. Smoke spills from her mouth and hazes the lights.

"You think you're the first one to try to sneak back in?" she says. "You're not even the first one *tonight*." She laughs again. "Boo-hoo-hoo, my wife left me, whaaa, my daughters hate me. Life is meaningless, I'm gonna kill myself."

"I don't have a daughter," he says. "And my wife didn't leave me." But of course she had. She left him in the most absolute way, leaving behind a note like a set of driving directions, like a travel brochure to an exotic country. Two years later to the day, their son followed her. Tonight, come to think of it, is the anniversary of their deaths.

He takes a breath. "I'm just looking for a way back."

"Please. You couldn't find your shadow if it was stapled on. You think you can just waltz right back in there nursing your disappointments and diseases, your head stuffed full of middle-age sex fantasies and mortgage payments? You'd ruin everything. You'd stink the place up."

"You don't understand," he says. "I only need—"

"Stink. It. Up." She makes a tired shooing gesture. "Go home, you greedy little boy. No second helpings. You ought to be ashamed of yourself."

This is a test, he thinks. She's trying to throw him off, weigh him down with doubt and discouragement. He's met such trials before, and persevered. Once upon a time he was The Boy Who Always Said No.

As if in confirmation he hears a distant bell, a cheery *ding ding!* He recognizes that sound. He strides out of the room, into the dark kitchen, and flips open the hook to the back door.

"You'll never get on!" the woman calls. The dog begins to bark.

The dark, to his light-adjusted eyes, seems almost solid. He stops a few feet from the house and listens. The trolley must be close by. The little bell sounds again, but he can't tell if it's growing closer or more distant.

He moves forward slowly, arms out, feet sliding forward. The track is only a few yards from the house, he's sure of it. His feet drag through the unseen grass.

After a few minutes he glances back, but now the house is gone as well. He turns in place, eyes wide. There's no sound, not even barking. A dank, dead-fish scent twists in the air.

When he completes his circle he notices a dark, fuzzed shape in the distance, barely distinguishable against a black sky edging toward indigo. It's the first hint since he left the attic that the night is not endless. He doesn't know what it is in the distance, but he recognizes the shape for what it is: unfamiliar, unknown.

The little boat lies at the bottom of the empty seabed, abandoned midway between the shore and the island. Sandy mud sucks at his shoes. He walks toward it, past stacks of smooth-headed boulders and stinking salt-water puddles in the shape of great clawed feet. He walks under a sky the color of pencil lead.

The island is shaped like a bowler hat. If not for the trees—a handful of curve-backed palms with outrageously broad leaves—and for the hunched figure silhouetted at the very crown of the hill, he'd have thought the island was huge but miles away. Instead he can see that it's ridiculously small, like a cartoon desert island.

He reaches the boat and rests a hand on the gunwales. The inside of the boat is an unmade bed, a white pillow and blue blankets and white sheets. Foot-shaped holes, human-size, stamp away from the boat toward the island. He follows them across the drained sea to the rim of the island, where his predecessor's mud-laden feet begin to print the grass. The trail leads up the slope, between bushes tinged yellow and brown. Only a few of the palm trees are standing; dozens of others are uprooted and lying on the ground, or else split and bent, as if savaged by a hurricane.

He climbs, breath ragged in his throat. The man at the top of the hill is facing away, toward the lightening sky. On his back is some kind of white fur shawl—no, a suit like a child's footie pajamas, arms tied around his neck. The yawning hood is a wolf's head that's too small for his grownman's head.

He's huffing, making a lot of noise as he approaches, but the man with the wolf suit doesn't turn around.

When he's caught his breath he says, "Beautiful, isn't it?"

Above them the sky is fitful gray, but across the vast, empty sea in the land beyond, sunlight sparkles on the crystal minarets of the Glassine Palace. A great-winged roc dangling a gondola from its claws flaps toward its next fare. The rolling hills beyond the city are golden and ripe for harvest. It's all as he remembers.

"Look at those wild things go," the man in the wolf suit says. Who knows what he's seeing?

The sun crawls higher, but the clouds above the hill refuse to disperse. He glances at the man in the wolf suit, looks away. Tears have cut tracks down his muddy and unshaven face. The wolf man's older than he, but not by much.

What did the woman in the house say? *Not even the first one tonight.*

He nods at the man's wedding ring and says, "Can't take it off either?"

The man frowns at it. "Left me six months ago. I had it coming for years." He smiles faintly. "Couldn't quite stop making mischief. You?"

"She died a few years ago." But the damage hadn't stopped there, had it? He tilts his head, a half shrug. "Depression runs in her family."

"Sorry to hear that." He slowly shakes his head,

and the upside-down wolf's head wags with him. "It's a disaster out there. Every day like an eraser. Days into months, months into years—gone, gone, gone." The man in the wolf suit stares at him without blinking. "Tell me I'm wrong. Tell me you were having a happy ending."

"No." He almost grins. "Not even close." But was that true? He'd had a dozen happy endings. A score of them.

Together they stare across the ocean of mud and squint into the brightness beyond.

"We can't get back in there," he says to the man with the suit. He's surprised by his certainty. But he can't imagine tracking that muck across the crystal streets. "And we can't stay here." He rubs a hand across his mouth. "Come with me."

The man doesn't answer.

"I could make you leave."

The man in the wolf suit laughs. "Don't you know who I am?" he says. "I'm their king!"

"No," he says. "Not anymore." He grips the edges of the white fur and yanks it over the man's head and off, quick as a magic trick. "I'm the king now."

He runs down the hill holding the suit above his head like a flag. The man roars a terrible roar. It's a chase down to the sea's edge and then they're tumbling in the muck, wrapped up and rolling like bear cubs, choking and half-blinded in mud. Hands claw for the suit. They tug it back and forth, the cloth rasping as threads stretch and tear. Then the zipper snaps and they fall away from each other, splash down on their asses.

They look at each other, too winded to get up.

The man clutches the scrap of fur he's regained. It's not white anymore. "Why'd you *do* that?" he says.

He's not sure. He flicks mud from his hands, wipes

a hand clean on the inside of his shirt, runs a knuckle across his mouth. "It was the only thing I could think of."

The man looks at him. A smile works at the corners of his mudspattered mouth. He makes a sound like a cough, and then he's laughing, they're both laughing. They sit in the mud, roaring.

Eventually they help each other out of the muck. "We screwed it up," the man says. "How did we screw it up?"

He's been wondering that himself for a long time. "I don't think we were supposed to keep them safe," he answers. He hands him the remnant of the suit. "This, the bed, the Wonder Bike—all that stuff. We weren't supposed to *hoard* them."

The man looks stricken. "What?"

"We were supposed to give them away."

"Oh my God," the man says quietly. "Oh my God."

They begin to trudge across the drained sea. They trade stories about their adventures. The man with the wolf suit takes out his wallet and shows him pictures. He has a granddaughter he's never met, six years old, a real hellion by all accounts. "She lives three states away," he says.

A dozen yards from the shore they see the trolley. The little car glides smoothly around the perimeter of the lake and stops in their path. It rolls a few feet forward, a few feet back. *Ding ding!*

They approach it carefully and without speaking, as they would a deer at a watering hole. It trembles as they step up onto the gleaming sideboards. They sit on the polished wooden benches. It's a shame their clothes are so filthy.

The trolley doesn't move.

"Wait," he says, and the man in the wolf suit watches him dig into his pocket. The dime he found on the roadway is still there. The coin clinks into the tin fare box and the car jerks into motion. Soon they're zipping across the plain toward the forest and the black ribbon of highway.

"And yourself?" the man with the suit says.

"No grandchildren," he says. "No children. Not anymore."

The man frowns and nods. "We'll find someone for the bike," he says. "The world is full of children."

LIGHT

——

Kelly Link

two men, one raised by wolves

The man at the bar on the stool beside her: bent like a hook over some item. A book, not a drink. A children's book; dog-eared. When he noticed her stare, he grinned and said, "Got a light?" It was a Friday night, and the Splinter was full of men saying things. Some guy off in a booth was saying, for example, "Well, sure, you can be raised by wolves and lead a normal life but—"

Lindsey said, "I don't smoke."

The man straightened up. He said, "Not that kind of light. I mean a *light*. Do you have a *light*?"

"I don't understand," she said. And then because he was not bad-looking, she said, "Sorry."

"Stupid bitch," he said. "Never mind." The water-color illustration in his book showed a boy and a girl standing in front of a dragon the size of a Volkswagen bus. The man had a pen. He'd drawn word bubbles coming out of the children's mouths, and now he was writing in words. The children were saying—

The man snapped the book shut; it was a library book.

"Excuse me," she said, "but I'm a children's librarian. Can I ask why you're defacing that book?"

"I don't know, *can* you? *Maybe* you can and *maybe* you can't, but why ask me?" the man said. Turning his back to her, he hunched over the book again.

Which was really too much. She opened her shoulder bag and took out her travel sewing kit. She palmed the needle and then jabbed the man in his left buttock. Very fast. Her hand was back in her lap and she was signaling the bartender for another drink when the man howled and sat up. Now everyone was looking at him. He slid off his stool and hurried away, glancing back at her once in outrage.

There was a drop of blood on the needle. She wiped it on a bar napkin.

At a table behind her three women were talking about a new pocket universe. A new diet. A coworker's new baby: a girl, born with no shadow. This was bad, although, thank God, not as bad as it could have been, a woman—someone called her Caroline—was saying.

A long, lubricated conversation followed about over-the-counter shadows—prosthetics, available in most drugstores, not expensive and reasonably durable. Everyone was in agreement that it was almost impossible to distinguish a prosthetic shadow from a real one.

Caroline and her friends began to talk of babies born with two shadows. Children with two shadows did not grow up happy. They didn't get on well with other children. You could cut a pair of shadows apart with a pair of crooked scissors, but it wasn't a permanent solution. By the end of the day the second shadow always grew back, twice as long. If you didn't bother to cut back the second shadow, then eventually you had twins, one of whom was only slightly realer than the other.

Lindsey had grown up in a stucco house in a scab-raw development in Dade County. Opposite the house had been a bruised and trampled nothing. A wilderness that grew, was razed, then grew back again. Banyan trees dripping with spiky epiphytes; tunnels of coral reef

barely covered by blackish, sandy dirt that Lindsey—and
her twin, Alan, not quite real enough, yet, to play with
other children—lowered herself into, to emerge skinned,
bloody, triumphant. Developers' bulldozers made
football field–size depressions that filled with water
when it rained and produced thousands and thousands
of fingernail-size tan toads. Lindsey kept them in jars.
She caught blue crabs, Cuban lizards, yellow-pink
tobacco grasshoppers the size of toy trucks. They spat
when you caged them in your hand. Geckos with their
papery clockwork insides, ticktock barks; anoles whose
throats pulsed out like bloody fans; king snakes coral
snakes *red and yellow kill a fellow, red and black friendly
Jack corn* snakes. When Lindsey was ten, a lightning
strike ignited a fire under the coral reef. For a week
smoke ghosted up. They kept the sprinklers on but the
grass cooked brown. Alan caught five snakes, lost three
of them in the house while he was watching Saturday-
morning cartoons.

Lindsey had had a happy childhood. The women in
the bar didn't know what they were talking about.

It was almost a shame when the man who had
theories about being raised by wolves came over and
threw his drink in the face of the woman named
Caroline. There was a commotion. Lindsey and the
man who had theories about being raised by wolves
went for a walk on the beach. He was charming, but
she felt his theories were only that: charming. When
she said this, he became less charming. Nevertheless,
she invited him home.

"Nice place," he said. "I like all the whatsits."

"Most of it belongs to my brother," Lindsey said.

"Your *brother*. Does he live with you?"

"God, no," Lindsey said. "He's . . . wherever he is."

"I had a sister. Died when I was two," the man said.
"Wolves make really shitty parents."

"Ha," she said, experimentally.

"Ha," he said. And then, "Look at that," as he was undressing her. Their four shadows fell across the bed, sticky and wilted as if from lovemaking that hadn't even begun. At the sight of their languorously intertwined shadows, the wolf man became charming again. "Look at these sweet little tits," he said over and over again as though she might not ever have noticed how sweet and little her tits were. He exclaimed at the sight of every part of her; afterward, she slept poorly, apprehensive that he might steal away, taking along one of the body parts or pieces that he seemed to admire so much.

In the morning, she woke and found herself stuck beneath the body of the wolf man as if she had been trapped beneath a collapsed and derelict building. When she began to wriggle her way out from under him, he woke and complained of a fucking terrible hangover. He called her "Joanie" several times, asked to borrow a pair of scissors, and spent a long time in her bathroom with the door locked while she read the paper. "Smuggling ring apprehended by___ . Government overthrown in___ . Family of twelve last seen in vicinity of___ . Start of hurricane season___ ." The wolf man came out of the bathroom, dressed hurriedly, and left.

She found a spongy black heap, the amputated shadow of his dead twin and three soaked, pungent towels, on the bathroom floor; there were stubby black bits of beard in the sink. The blades of her nail scissors were tarry and blunted.

She threw away the reeking towels. She mopped up the shadow, folding it into a large ziploc bag, carried the bag into the kitchen, and put the shadow down the disposal. She ran the water for a long time.

Then she went outside and sat on her patio and

watched the iguanas eat the flowers off her hibiscus. It
was 6:00 A.M. and already quite warm.

no vodka, one egg

Sponges hold water. Water holds light. Lindsey was
hollow all the way through when she wasn't full of
alcohol. The water in the canal was glazed with light,
which wouldn't hold still. It was vile. She had the
beginnings of one of her headaches. Light beat down on
her head and her second shadow began to move, rippling
in waves like the light-shot water in the canal. She went
inside. The egg in the refrigerator door had a spot of
blood when she cracked it into the pan. She liked vodka
in her orange juice, but there was no orange juice and no
vodka in the freezer, only a smallish iguana.

The Keys were overrun with iguanas. They ate her
hibiscus; every once in a while she caught one of the
smaller ones with the pool net and stuck it in her
freezer for a few days. This was supposedly a humane
way of dealing with iguanas. You could even eat them,
although she did not. She was a vegetarian.

She put out food for the bigger iguanas. They liked
ripe fruit. She liked to watch them eat. She knew that
she was not being consistent or fair in her dealings, but
there it was.

men unlucky at cards

Lindsey's job was not a particularly complicated
one. There was an office, and behind the office was a
warehouse full of sleeping people. There was an agency
in DC that paid her company to take responsibility for
the sleepers. Every year, hikers and cavers and construction workers found a few dozen more. No one
knew how to wake them up. No one knew what they
meant, what they did, where they came from.

There were always at least two security guards on

duty at the warehouse. They were mostly, in Lindsey's opinion, lecherous assholes. She spent the day going through invoices, and then went home again. The wolf man wasn't at the Splinter and the bartender threw everyone out at 2:00 A.M.; she went back to the warehouse on a hunch, four hours into the night shift.

Bickle and Lowes had hauled out five sleepers, three women and two men. They'd put Miami Hydra baseball caps on the male sleepers and stripped the women, propped them up in chairs around a foldout table. Someone had arranged the hands of one of the male sleepers down between the legs of one of the women. Cards had been dealt out. Maybe it was just a game of strip poker and the two women had been unlucky. It was hard to play your cards well when you were asleep.

Larry Bickle stood behind one of the women, his cheek against her hair. He seemed to be giving her advice about how to play her cards. He wasn't holding his drink carefully enough, and the woman's neat lap brimmed with beer.

Lindsey watched for a few minutes. Bickle and Lowes had gotten to the sloppy, expansive stage of drunkenness that, sober, she resented most. False happiness.

When Lowes saw Lindsey he stood up so fast his chair tipped over. "Hey now," he said. "It's different from how it looks."

Both guards had little, conical, paper party hats on their heads.

A third man, no one Lindsey recognized, came wandering down the middle aisle like he'd been shopping at Wal-Mart. He wore boxer shorts and a party hat. "Who's this?" he said, leering at Lindsey.

Larry Bickle's hand was on his gun. What was he

going to do? Shoot her? She said, "I've already called the police."

"Oh, fuck me," Bickle said. He said some other things.

"You called the police?" Edgar Lowes said.

"They'll be here in about ten minutes," Lindsey said. "If I were you, I'd leave right now. Just go. It isn't as if I can stop you."

"What is that bitch saying?" Bickle said unhappily. He was really quite drunk. His hand was still on his gun.

She took out her own gun, a Beretta. She pointed it in the direction of Bickle and Lowes. "Put your gun belts on the ground and take off your uniforms, too. Leave your keys and your ID cards. You, too, whoever you are. Hand over your ID and I won't press charges."

"You've got little cats on your gun," Edgar Lowes said.

"Hello Kitty stickers," she said. "I count coup." Although she'd only ever shot one person.

The men took off their clothes but not the party hats. Edgar Lowes had a purple scar down his chest. He saw Lindsey looking and said, "Triple bypass. I need this job for the health insurance."

"Too bad," Lindsey said. She followed them out into the parking lot. The third man didn't seem to care that he was naked. He didn't even have his hands cupped around his balls, the way Bickle and Lowes did. He said to Lindsey, "They've done this a couple of times. Heard about it from a friend. Tonight was my birthday party."

"Happy birthday," she said. She watched the three men get into their cars and drive away. Then she went back into the warehouse and folded up the uniforms, emptied the guns, cleaned up the sleepers, used the dolly to get the sleepers back to their boxes. There was a bottle of cognac and plenty of beer. She drank steadily. A song came to her, and she sang it. *Tall and tan and young and drunken and—* She knew she was getting the words wrong. *A midnight pyre. Like a bird on fire. I have tried in my way to be you.*

It was almost 5:00 A.M. The floor came up at her in waves, and she would have liked to lie down on it.

The sleeper in Box 113 was Harrisburg Pennsylvania, a young boy. The sleepers were named after their place of origin. Other countries did it differently. Harrisburg Pennsylvania had long eyelashes and a bruise on his cheek that had never faded. The skin of a sleeper was always just a little cooler than you expected. You could get used to anything. She set the alarm in her cell phone to wake her up before the shift change.

In the morning, Harrisburg Pennsylvania was still asleep and Lindsey was still drunk. She'd drooled a little on his arm.

All she said to her supervisor, the general office manager, was that she'd fired Bickle and Lowes. Mr. Charles gave her a long-suffering look, said, "You look a bit rough."

"I'll go home early," she said.

She would have liked to replace Bickle and Lowes with women, but in the end she hired an older man with excellent job references and a graduate student, Jason, who said he planned to spend his evenings working on his dissertation. (He was a philosophy student, and she asked what philosopher his dissertation was on. If he'd said "Nietzsche" she might have terminated the interview. But he said, "John Locke.")

She'd already requested additional grant money to pay for security cameras, but when it was turned down she went ahead and bought the cameras anyway. She had a bad feeling about the two men who worked the Sunday-to-Wednesday day shift.

as children, they were inseparable

On Tuesday, there was a phone call from Alan. He was yelling something in LinLan before she could even say hello.

"*Berma lisgo airport. Tus fah me*?"

"Alan?"

He said, "I'm at the airport, Lin-Lin, just wondering if I can come and stay with you for a bit. Not too long. Just need to keep my head down for a while. You won't even know I'm there."

"Back up," she said. "Where are you?"

"The airport," he said, clearly annoyed. "Where the planes are."

"I thought you were in Tibet," she said.

"Well," Alan said. "That didn't quite work out. I've decided to move on."

"What did you do?" she said. "Alan?"

"Lin-Lin, please," he said. "I'll explain everything tonight. I'll make dinner. House key still under the broken planter?"

"*Fisfis meh*," she said. "Fine."

The last time she'd seen Alan in the flesh was two years ago, just after Elliot had left for good. Her husband.

They'd both been more than a little drunk and Alan was always nicer when he was drunk. He gave her a hug and said, "Come on, Lindsey. You can tell me. It's a bit of a relief, isn't it?"

The sky was low and swollen. Lindsey loved this, the sudden green afternoon darkness as rain came down in heavy drumming torrents so loud she could hardly hear

the radio station in her car, the calm, jokey pronounce-
ments of the local weather witch. The vice president
was under investigation; evidence suggested a series of
secret dealings with malign spirits. A woman had given
birth to a dozen rabbits. A local gas station had been
robbed by invisible men. Some religious cult had
thrown all the infidels out of a popular pocket universe. Nothing new, in other words. The sky was
always falling. U.S. 1 was bumper-to-bumper all the
way to Plantation Key.

Alan sat out on the patio behind her house, a bottle
of wine under his chair, the wineglass in his hand half
full of rain, half full of wine. "Lindsey!" he said.

"Want a drink?" He didn't get up.

She said, "Alan? It's raining."

"It's warm," he said and blinked fat balls of rain
out of his eyelashes. "It was cold where I was."

"I thought you were going to make dinner," she
said.

Alan stood up and made a show of wringing out his
shirt and his peasant-style cotton pants. The rain
collapsed steadily on their heads.

"There's nothing in your kitchen. I would have
made margaritas, but all you had was the salt."

"Let's go inside," Lindsey said. "Do you have any
dry clothes? In your luggage? Where's your luggage,
Alan?"

He gave her a sly look. "You know. In there."

She knew. "You put your stuff in Elliot's room." It
had been her room too, but she hadn't slept there in
almost a year. She only slept there when she was alone.

Alan said, "All the things he left are still there. Like
he might still be in there too, somewhere down in the
sheets, all folded up like a secret note. Very creepy, Lin-
Lin."

Alan was only thirty-eight. The same age as

Lindsey, of course, unless you were counting from the point where he was finally real enough to eat his own birthday cake. She thought he looked every year of their age. Older.

"Go get changed," she said. "I'll order takeout."

"What's in the grocery bags?" he said.

She slapped his hand away. "Nothing for you," she said.

close encounters of the absurd kind

She'd met Elliot at an open mike in a pocket universe near Coral Gables. A benefit at a gay bar for some charity. Men everywhere, but most of them not interested in her. Elliot was over seven feet tall; his hair was canary yellow and his skin was greenish. Lindsey had noticed the way that Alan looked at him when they first came in. Alan had been in this universe before.

Elliot sang the song about the monster from Ipanema. He couldn't carry a tune, but he made Lindsey laugh so hard that whiskey came out of her nose. He came over and sat at the bar. He said, "You're Alan's twin."

He only had four fingers on each hand. His skin looked smooth and rough at the same time.

She said, "I'm the original. He's the copy. Wherever he is. Passed out in the bathroom, probably."

Elliot said, "Should I go get him or should we leave him here?"

"Where are we going?" she said.

"To bed," he said. His hair was feathers, not hair. His pupils were oddly shaped.

"What would we do there?" she said, and he just looked at her. Sometimes these things worked and sometimes they didn't. That was the fun of it.

She thought about it. "Okay. On the condition that

you promise me that you've never fooled around with Alan. Ever."

"Your universe or mine?" he said.

Elliot wasn't the first thing Lindsey had brought back from a pocket universe. She'd gone on vacation once and brought back the pit of a green fruit that fizzed like sherbet when you bit into it and gave you dreams about staircases, ladders, rockets, things that went up and up, although nothing had come up when she planted it, although almost everything grew in Florida.

Her mother had gone on vacation in a pocket universe when she was first pregnant with Lindsey. Now people knew better. Doctors cautioned pregnant women against such trips.

For the last few years Alan had had a job with a tour group that ran trips out of Singapore. He spoke German, Spanish, Japanese, Mandarin Chinese, passable Tibetan, various pocket-universe trade languages. The tours took charter flights into Tibet and then trekked up into some of the more tourist-friendly pocket universes. Tibet was riddled with pocket universes.

"You lost them?" Lindsey said.

"Not all of them," Alan said. His hair was still wet with rain. He needed a haircut. "Just one van. I thought I told the driver Sakya but I may have said Gyantse. They showed up eventually, just two days behind schedule. It's not as if they were children. Everyone in Gyantse speaks English. When they caught up with us I was charming and full of remorse and we were all pals again."

She waited for the rest of the story. Somehow it made her feel better, knowing that Alan had the same effect on everyone.

"But then there was a mix-up at customs back at

Changi. They found a reliquary in this old bastard's luggage. Some ridiculous little god in a dried-up seedpod. Some other things. The old bastard swore up and down that none of it was his. That I'd snuck up to his room and put them into his luggage. That I'd seduced him. The agency got involved and the story about Gyantse came out. So that was that."

"Alan," she said.

"I was hoping I could stay here for a few weeks."

"You'll stay out of my hair," she said.

"Of course," he said. "Can I borrow a tooth-brush?"

more like Disney World than Disney World

Their parents were retired, living in an older, established pocket universe that was apparently much more like Florida than Florida had ever been. No mosquitoes, no indigenous species larger than a lapdog, except for birdlike creatures whose songs made you want to cry and whose flesh tasted like veal. Fruit trees that no one had to cultivate. Grass so downy and tender and fragrant that no one slept indoors. Lakes so big and so shallow that you could spend all day walking across them. It wasn't a large universe, and nowadays there was a long waiting list of men and women waiting to retire to it. Lindsey and Alan's parents had invested all of their savings into a one-room cabana with a view of one of the smaller lakes. "Lotus-eating," they called it. It sounded boring to Lindsey, but her mother no longer e-mailed to ask if Lindsey was seeing anyone. If she were ever going to remarry and produce children. Grandchildren were no longer required. Grandchildren would have obliged Lindsey and Alan's parents to leave their paradise in order to visit once in a while. Come back all that long way to Florida. "That nasty place where we used to live," Lindsey's mother said. Alan had a theory that their parents were not telling them everything. "They've become nudists," he insisted. "Or swingers. Or both. Mom always had exhibitionist tendencies. Always leaving the bathroom door open. No wonder I'm gay. No wonder you're not."

Lindsey lay awake in her bed and listened to Alan make tea in the kitchen. Alan hanging up his clothes in Elliot's closet. Alan turning the television on and off. At two in the morning, he came and stood outside her bedroom door. He said, softly, "Lindsey? Are you awake?"

She didn't answer and he went away again.

In the morning he was asleep on the sofa. A DVD was playing; the sound was off. Somehow he'd found Elliot's stash of imported pocket-universe porn, the secret stash she'd spent weeks looking for and never found. Trust Alan to turn it up. But she was childishly pleased to see he hadn't found the gin she'd hidden in the sofa.

When she came home from work he was out on the patio again, trying, uselessly, to catch her favorite iguana. "Be careful of the tail," she said.

"Monster came up and bit my toe," he said.

"That's Elliot. I've been feeding him," she said. "Probably thinks you're invading his territory."

"Elliot?" he said and laughed. "That's sick."

"He's big and green," she said. "You don't see the resemblance?" Her iguana disappeared into the network of banyan trees that dipped over the canal. The banyans were full of iguanas, leaves rustling greenly with their green and secret meetings. "The only difference is he comes back."

———

The next morning Alan drove her to work and went off with the car. In the afternoon Mr. Charles came into her office. "Bad news," he said. "Jack Harris in Pittsburgh went ahead and sent us two dozen sleepers. The new kid, Jason, signed for them down at the warehouse. Didn't think to call us first."

"You're kidding," she said.

"'Fraid not," he said. "I'm going to call Jack Harris. Ask what the hell he thought he was doing. I made it clear the other day that we weren't approved with regards to capacity. He'll just have to take them back again."

"Has the driver already gone?" she said.

"Yep. Maybe you could run over to the warehouse and take a look at the paperwork. Figure out what to do with this group in the meantime."

There were twenty-two new sleepers, eighteen males and four females. Jason already had them on dollies.

"Where were they before Pittsburgh?" she asked.

Jason handed over the dockets. "All over the place. Four of them turned up on property belonging to some guy in South Dakota. Says the government ought to compensate him for the loss of his crop."

"What happened to his crop?" she said.

"He set fire to it. They were underneath a big old dead tree out in his fields. Fortunately for everybody his son was there too. While the father was pouring gasoline on everything, the son dragged the sleepers into the bed of the truck, got them out of there. Called the hotline."

"Lucky," she said. "What the hell was the father thinking?"

"People your age—," Jason said and stopped.

Started again. "Older people seem to get these weird ideas sometimes. They want everything to be the way it was. Before."

"I'm not that old," she said.

"I didn't mean that," he said. Got pink. "I just mean, you know . . . "

She touched her hair. "Maybe you didn't notice, but I have two shadows. So I'm part of the weirdness. People like me are the people that people get ideas about. Why are you on the day shift?"

"Jermaine's wife is out of town so he has to take care of the kids. What do we do with the sleepers now?"

"Leave them on the dollies," she said. "It's not like it matters to them."

She tried calling Alan's cell phone at five thirty, but got no answer. She checked e-mail and played solitaire. She hated solitaire. Enjoyed shuffling through the cards she should have played. Playing cards when she shouldn't have. Why should she pretend to want to win when there wasn't anything to win?

At seven thirty she looked out and saw her car in the parking lot. When she went down to the warehouse he was flirting with Jason while the other guard, Hurley, ate his dinner.

"Hey, Lin-Lin," Alan said. "Come see this. Come here."

"What the hell are you doing?" Lindsey said. "Where have you been?"

"Grocery shopping," he said. "Come here, Lindsey. Come see."

Jason made a don't-blame-me face. She'd have to take him aside at some point. Warn him about Alan. Philosophy didn't prepare you for people like Alan.

"Look at her," Alan said.

She looked down at a sleeper. A woman dressed in a way that suggested she had probably been someone important once, maybe hundreds of years ago, somewhere, probably, that wasn't anything like here. Versailles Kentucky.

"I've seen sleepers before."

"No. You don't see," Alan said. "Of course you don't. Hey, Lin-Lin, this kind of haircut would look good on you."

He fluffed Versailles Kentucky's hair.

"Alan," she said. A warning.

"Look," he said. "Just look. Look at her. She looks just like you. She's you."

"You're crazy," she said.

"Am I?" Alan appealed to Jason. "You thought so, too."

Jason hung his head. He mumbled something. Said, "I said that maybe there was a similarity."

Alan reached down into the container and grabbed the sleeper's bare foot, lifted the leg straight up.

"Alan!" Lindsey said. She pried his hand loose. The prints of his fingers came up on Versailles Kentucky's leg in red and white. "What are you doing?"

"It's fine," Alan said. "I just wanted to see if she has a birthmark like yours. Lindsey has a birthmark behind her knee," he said to Jason. "Looks like a battleship."

Even Hurley was staring now.

The sleeper didn't look a thing like Lindsey. No birthmark. Funny, though. The more she thought about it the more Lindsey thought maybe she looked like Alan.

not herself today

She turned her head a little to the side. Put on all the lights in the bathroom and stuck her face up close to the mirror again. Stepped back. The longer she looked the less she looked like anyone she knew.

Alan was right. She needed a haircut.

The kitchen stank of rum; Alan had the blender out. "Let me guess," he said. "You met someone nice in there." He held out a glass. "I thought we could have a nice, quiet night in. Watch the Weather Channel. Do charades. You can knit. I'll wind your yarn for you."

"I don't knit."

"No," he said. His voice was kind. Loving. "You tangle. You knot. You muddle."

"You needle," she said. "What is it that you want? Why are you here? To pick a fight?"

"*Per bol tuh*, Lin-Lin?" Alan said. "What do *you* want?" She sipped ferociously. She knew what she wanted. "Why are *you* here?"

"This is my home," she said. "I have everything I want. A job at a company with real growth potential. A boss who likes me. A bar just around the corner, full of men who want to buy me drinks. A yard full of iguanas. And a spare shadow in case one should accidentally fall off."

"This isn't your house," Alan said. "Elliot bought it. Elliot filled it up with his junk. And all the nice stuff is mine. You haven't changed a thing since he took off."

"I have more iguanas now," she said. She took her rumrunner into the living room. Alan already had the Weather Channel on. Behind the perky blond weather witch, in violent primary colors, a tropical depression hovered off the coast of Cuba.

Alan came and stood behind the couch. He put his drink down and began to rub her neck.

"Pretty, isn't it?" she said. "That storm."

"Remember when we were kids? That hurricane?"

"Yeah," she said. "I probably ought to go haul the storm shutters out of the storage unit."

"That kid at your warehouse," he said. His eyes were closed.

"Jason?"

"He seems like a nice kid."

"*Kid* being the key word. He's a philosophy student, Lan-Lan. Come on. You can do better."

"Do better? I'm thinking out loud about a guy with a fine ass, Lindsey. Not buying a house. Or contemplating a career change. Oops, I guess I am officially doing that. Perhaps I'll become a do-gooder. A do-better."

"Just don't make my life harder, okay? Alan?"

"He has green eyes. Jason. Really, really green. Green as that color there. Right at the eye. That swirl," Alan said, draining his third rumrunner.

"I hadn't noticed his eyes," Lindsey said.

"That's because he isn't your type. You don't like nice guys." He was over at the stereo now. "Can I put this on?"

"If you want to. There's a song on there, I think it's the third song. Yeah. This one. Elliot loved this song. He'd put it on and start slithering all over the furniture."

"Oh yeah. He was a god on the dance floor. But look at me. I'm not too bad either."

"He was more flexible around the hips. I think he had a bendier spine. He could turn his head almost all the way around."

"Come on, Lindsey, you're not dancing. Come on and dance."

"I don't want to."

"Don't be such a pain in the ass."

"I have a pain inside," she said. And then wondered what she meant.

"It's such a pain in the ass."

"Come on. Just dance. Okay?"

"Okay," she said. "I'm okay. See? I'm dancing."

———

Jason came over for dinner. Alan wore one of Elliot's shirts. Lindsey made a perfect cheese soufflé, and she said nothing when Jason assumed that Alan had made it.

She listened to Alan's stories about various pocket universes as if she had never heard them before. Most were owned by the Chinese government and, as well as the more famous tourist universes, there were ones where the Chinese sent dissidents. Very few pocket universes were larger than, say, Maryland. Some had been abandoned a long time ago. Some were inhabited. Some weren't friendly. Some pocket universes contained their own pocket universes. You could go a long ways in and never come out again. You could start your own country out there and do whatever you liked, and yet most of the people Lindsey knew, herself included, had never done anything more venturesome than go for a week to someplace where the food and the air and the landscape seemed like something out of a book you'd read as a child; a brochure; a dream.

There were sex-themed pocket universes, of course. Tax shelters and places to dispose of all kinds of things: trash, junked cars, murder victims. People went to casinos inside pocket universes more like Vegas than Vegas. More like Hawaii than Hawaii. You must be this tall to enter. This rich. Just this foolish. Because who knew what might happen? Pocket universes might wink out again, suddenly, all at once. There were bestselling books explaining how that might happen.

Alan began to reminisce about his adolescence in a way that suggested it had not really been all that long ago.

"Venetian Pools," he said to Jason. "I haven't been there in a couple of years. Since I was a kid, really. All those grottoes that you could wander off into with someone. Go make out and get such an enormous hard-on you had to jump in the water so nobody noticed and the water was so fucking cold! Can you still get baked ziti at the restaurant? Do you remember that, Lindsey? Sitting out by the pool in your bikini and eating baked ziti? I heard you can't swim now. Because of the mermaids."

The mermaids were an invasive species, like the iguanas. People had brought them back from one of the Disney pocket universes, as pets, and now they were everywhere, small but numerous in a way that appealed to children and bird-watchers. They liked to show off and although they didn't seem much smarter than, say, a talking dog, and maybe not even as smart, since they didn't speak, only sang and whistled and made rude gestures, they were too popular with the tourists at Venetian Pools to be gotten rid of.

Jason said he'd been with his sister's kids. "I heard they used to drain the pools every night in summer. But they can't do that now, because of the mermaids. So the water isn't as clear as it used to be. They can't even set up filters, because the mermaids just tear them out again. Like beavers, I guess. They've constructed this elaborate system of dams and retaining walls and structures out of the coral, these elaborate pens to hold fish. Venetian Pools sells fish so you can toss them in for the mermaids to round up. The kids were into that."

"They sing, right?" Lindsey asked. "We get them in the canal sometimes, the saltwater ones. They're a lot bigger. They sing."

"Yeah," Jason said. "Lots of singing. Really eerie stuff. Makes you feel like shit. They pipe elevator music over the loudspeakers to drown it out, but even the kids felt bad after a while. I had to buy all this stuff in the gift shop to cheer them up."

Lindsey pondered the problem of Jason, the favorite uncle who could be talked into buying things. He was too young for Alan. When you thought about it, who wasn't too young for Alan?

Alan said, "Didn't you have plans, Lindsey?"

"Did I?" Lindsey said. Then relented. "Actually, I was thinking about heading down to the Splinter. Maybe I'll see you guys down there later?"

"That old hole," Alan said. He wasn't looking at her. He was sending out those old invisible death rays in Jason's direction; Lindsey could practically feel the air getting thicker. It was like humidity, only skankier. "I used to go there to hook up with cute straight guys in the bathroom while Lindsey was passing out her phone number over by the pool tables. You know what they say about girls with two shadows, don't you, Jason?"

Jason said, "Maybe I should head home." But Lindsey could tell by the way that he was looking at Alan that he had no idea what he was saying. He wasn't even really listening to what Alan said. He was just responding to the vibe that Alan put out. That *come hither come hither come a little more hither* siren song.

"Don't go," Alan said. "Stay a little longer. Lindsey has plans, and I'm lonely. Stay a little longer and I'll play you some of the highlights from Lindsey's ex-husband's collection of pocket-universe gay porn."

"Alan," Lindsey said. Second warning. She knew he was keeping count.

"Sorry," Alan said. He put his hand on Jason's leg. "*Husband's* collection of gay porn. She and Elliot, wherever he is, are still married. I had the biggest hard-on for Elliot. He always said Lindsey was all he wanted. But it's never about what you want, is it? It's about what you need. Right?"

"Right," Jason said.

———

How did Alan do it? Why did everyone except for Lindsey fall for it? Except, she realized, pedaling her bike down to the Splinter, she did fall for it. She still fell for it. It was her house, and who had been thrown out of it? Who had been insulted, dismissed, and told to leave? Her. That's who.

Cars went by, riding their horns. Damn Alan anyway.

She didn't bother to chain up the bike; she probably wouldn't be riding it home. She went into the Splinter and sat down beside a man with an aggressively sharp cologne.

"You look nice," she said. "Buy me a drink and I'll be nice, too."

there are easier ways of trying to kill yourself

The man tried to kiss her. She couldn't find her keys, but that didn't matter. The door was unlocked. Jason's car still in the driveway. No surprise there.

"I have two shadows," she said. It was all shadows. They were shadows too.

"I don't care," the man said. He really was very nice.

"No," she said. "I mean my brother's home. We have to be quiet. Okay if we don't turn on the lights? Where are you from?"

"Georgia," the man said. "I work construction. Came down here for the hurricane."

"The hurricane?" she said. "I thought it was headed for the Gulf of Mexico. This way. Watch out for the counter."

"Now it's coming back this way. Won't hit for another couple of days. You into kinky stuff? You can tie me up," the man said.

"Better knot," she said. "Get it? I'm not into knots.

Can never get them untied, even sober. This guy had to have his foot amputated. No circulation. True story. Friend told me."

"Guess I've been lucky so far," the man said. He didn't sound too disappointed, either way. "This house has been through some hurricanes, I bet."

"One or two," she said. "Water comes right in over the tile floor. Messy. Then it goes out again."

She tried to remember his name. Couldn't. It didn't matter. She felt terrific. That had been the thing about being married. The monogamy. Even drunk, she'd always known who was in bed with her. Elliot had been different, all right, but he had always been the same kind of different. Never a different kind of different. Didn't like kissing. Didn't like sleeping in the same bed. Didn't like being serious. Didn't like it when Lindsey was sad. Didn't like living in a house. Didn't like the way the water in the canal felt. Didn't like this, didn't like that. Didn't like the Keys. Didn't like the way people looked at him. Didn't stay. Elliot, Elliot, Elliot.

"My name's Alberto," the man said.

"Sorry," she said. She and Elliot had always had fun in bed.

"He had a funny-looking penis," she said.

"Excuse me?" Alberto said.

"Do you want something to drink?" she said.

"Actually, do you have a bathroom?"

"Down the hall," she said. "First door."

But he came back in a minute. He turned on the lights and stood there.

"Like what you see?" she said.

His arms were shiny and wet. There was blood on his arms. "I need a tourniquet," he said. "Some kind of tourniquet."

"What did you do?" she said. Almost sober. Putting her robe on. "Is it Alan?"

But it was Jason. Blood all over the bathtub and the pretty half-tiled wall. He'd slashed both his wrists open with a potato peeler. The potato peeler was still there in his hand.

"Is he okay?" she said. "Alan! Where the fuck are you? Fuck!"

Alberto wrapped one of her good hand towels around one of Jason's wrists. "Hold this." He stuck another towel around the other wrist and then wrapped duct tape around that. "I called 911," he said. "He's breathing. Who is this guy? Your brother?"

"My employee," she said. "I don't believe this. What's with the duct tape?"

"Go get me a blanket," he said. "Need to keep him warm. My ex-wife did this once."

She skidded down the hall. Slammed open the door to Elliot's room. Turned on the lights and grabbed the comforter off the bed.

"*Vas poh!* Your new boyfriend's in the bathroom," she said. "Cut his wrists with my potato peeler. Wake up, Lan-Lan! This is *your* mess."

"*Fisfis wah*, Lin-Lin," Alan said, so she pushed him off the bed.

"What did you do, Alan?" she said. "Did you mess with him?"

He was wearing a pair of Elliot's pajama bottoms. "You're not being funny," he said.

"I'm not kidding," she said. "I'm drunk. There's a man named Alberto in the bathroom. Jason tried to kill himself. Or something."

"Oh fuck," he said. Tried to sit up. "I was nice to him, Lindsey! Okay? It was real nice. We fucked and then we smoked some stuff and then we were kissing and I fell asleep."

She held out her hand, pulled him up off the floor. "What kind of stuff? Come on."

"Something I picked up somewhere," he said. She wasn't really listening. "Good stuff. Organic. Blessed by monks. They give it to the gods. I took some off a shrine. Everybody does it. You just leave a bowl of milk or something instead. There's no fucking way it made him crazy."

The bathroom was crowded with everyone inside it. No way to avoid standing in Jason's blood. "Oh fuck," Alan said.

"My brother, Alan," Lindsey said. "Here's a comforter for Jason. Alan, this is Alberto. Jason, can you hear me?" His eyes were open now.

Alberto said to Alan, "It's better than it looks. He didn't really slice up his wrists. More like he peeled them. Dug into one vein pretty good, but I think I've slowed down the bleeding."

Alan shoved Lindsey out of the way and threw up in the sink.

"Alan," Jason said. There were sirens.

"No," Lindsey said. "It's me. Lindsey. Your boss. My bathtub, Jason. Your blood all over my bathtub. My potato peeler! Mine! What were you thinking?"

"There was an iguana in your freezer," Jason said.

Alberto said, "Why the potato peeler?"

"I was just so happy," Jason said. He was covered in blood. "I've never been so happy in all my life. I didn't want to stop feeling that way. You know?"

"No," Lindsey said.

"Are you going to fire me?" Jason said.

"What do you think?" Lindsey said.

"I'll sue for sexual harassment if you do," Jason said. "I'll say you fired me because I'm gay. Because I slept with your brother."

Alan threw up in the sink again.

"How do you feel now?" Alberto said. "You feel okay?"

"I just feel so happy," Jason said. He began to cry.

not much of a bedside manner

Alan went with Jason in the ambulance. The wind was stronger, pushing the trees around like a bully. Lindsey would have to put the storm shutters up.

For some reason Alberto was still there. He said, "I'd really like a beer. What've you got?"

Lindsey could have gone for something a little stronger. Everything smelled of blood. "Nothing," she said. "I'm a recovering alcoholic."

"Not all that recovered," he said.

"I'm sorry," Lindsey said. "You're a really nice guy. But I wish you would go away. I'd like to be alone."

He held out his bloody arms. "Could I take a shower first?"

"Could you just go?" Lindsey said.

"I understand," he said. "It's been a rough night. A terrible thing has happened. Let me help. I'll stay and help you clean up."

Lindsey said nothing.

"I see," he said. There was blood on his mouth too. Like he'd been drinking blood. He had good shoulders. Nice eyes. She kept looking at his mouth. The duct tape was back in a pocket of his cargo pants. He seemed to have a lot of stuff in his pockets. "You don't like me after all?"

"I don't like nice guys," Lindsey said.

There were support groups for people whose shadow grew into a twin. There were support groups for women whose husbands left them. There were support groups for alcoholics. Probably there were support groups for people who hated support groups, but Lindsey didn't believe in support groups.

By the time Alan got back from the hospital it was Saturday night; she'd finished the gin and started in on the tequila. She was almost wishing that Alberto had stayed. She thought about asking how Jason was, but it seemed pointless. Either he was okay or he wasn't. She wasn't okay. Alan got her down the hall and onto her bed and then climbed into bed too. Pulled the blanket over both of them.

"Go away," she said.

"I'm freezing," he said. "That fucking hospital. That air-conditioning. Just let me lie here."

"Go away," she said again. "*Fisfis wah.*"

When she woke up, she was still saying it. "Go away, go away, go away." He wasn't in her bed. Instead there was a dead iguana, the little one from the freezer, on the pillow beside her face.

Alan was gone. The bathtub stank of blood and the rain slammed down on the roof like nails on glass. Little pellets of ice on the grass outside. Now the radio said the hurricane was on course to make land somewhere between Fort Lauderdale and Saint Augustine sometime Wednesday afternoon. There were no plans to evacuate the Keys. Plenty of wind and rain and nastiness due for the Miami area, but no real damage. She couldn't think why she'd asked Alberto to leave. The storm shutters still needed to go up. He had seemed like a guy who would do that.

If Alan had been there, he could have opened a can and made her soup. Brought her ginger ale in a glass. Finally, she turned the television on in the living room, loud enough that she could hear it from her bedroom. That way she wouldn't be listening for Alan. She could pretend that he was home, sitting out in the living room, watching some old monster movie and painting his fingernails black, the way he had done in high school. Kids with conjoined shadows were supposed to be into all that Goth makeup, all that music, so Alan was into it. When Alan had found out that twins were supposed to have secret twin languages, he'd done that too, invented a language, LinLan, and made her memorize it. Made her talk it at the dinner table. *Ifzon meh nadora plezbig* meant *Guess what I did? Bandy Tim Wong legkwa fisfis, meh* meant Went all the way with Tim Wong. (Tim Wong fucked me, in the vernacular.)

People with two shadows were *supposed* to be trouble. They were supposed to lead friends and lovers astray, bring confusion to their enemies, bring down disaster wherever they went. (She never went anywhere.) Alan had always been a conformist at heart. Whereas she had a house and a job and once she'd even been married. If anyone was keeping track, Lindsey thought it should be clear who was ahead.

Monday morning Mr. Charles still hadn't managed to get rid of the sleepers from Pittsburgh. Jack Harris could shuffle paper like nobody's business.

"I'll call him," Lindsey offered. "You know I love a good fight."

"Good luck," Mr. Charles said. "He says he won't take them back until after the hurricane goes through. But rules say they have to be out of here twenty-four hours before the hurricane hits. We're caught between a rock—"

"And an asshole," she said. "Let me take care of it."

She was in the warehouse, on hold with someone who worked for Harris, when Jason showed up.

"What's up with that?" Valentina was saying. "Your arms."

"Fell through a plate-glass door," Jason said.

"That's not good," Valentina said.

"Lost almost three pints of blood. Just think about that. Three pints. Hey, Lindsey."

"Valentina," Lindsey said. "Take the phone for a moment. Don't worry. It's on hold. Just yell if anyone picks up. Jason, can I talk to you over there for a moment?"

"Sure thing," Jason said.

He winced when she grabbed him above the elbow. She didn't loosen her grip until they were a couple of aisles away. "Give me one good reason why I shouldn't fire you. Besides the sexual harassment thing. Because I would enjoy that. Hearing you try to make that case in court."

Jason said, "Alan's moved in with me. Said you threw him out."

Was any of this a surprise? Yes and no. She said, "So if I fire you, he'll have to get a job."

"That depends," Jason said. "Are you firing me or not?"

"*Fisfis buh*. Go ask Alan what that means."

"Hey, Lindsey. Lindsey, hey. Someone named Jack Harris is on the phone," Valentina said, getting too close for this conversation to go any further.

"I don't know why you want this job," Lindsey said.

"The benefits," Jason said. "You should see the bill from the emergency room."

"Or why you want my brother."

"Ms. Driver? He says it's urgent."

"Tell him one second," Lindsey said. To Jason: "All right. You can keep your job on one condition."

"Which is?" He didn't sound nearly as suspicious as he ought to have sounded. Still early days with Alan.

"You get the man on the phone to take back those six sleepers. Today."

"How the fuck do I do that?" Jason said.

"I don't care. But they had better not be here when I show up tomorrow morning. If they're here, you had better not be. Okay?" She poked him in the arm above the bandage. "Next time borrow something sharper than a potato peeler. I've got a whole block full of good German knives."

"Lindsey," Valentina said, "this Harris guy says he can call you back tomorrow if now isn't a good time."

"Jason is going to take the call," Lindsey said.

everything must go

Her favorite liquor store put everything on sale whenever a hurricane was due. Just their way of making a bad day a little more bearable. She stocked up on everything but only had a glass of wine with dinner. Made a salad and ate it out on the patio. The air had that electric, green shimmy to it she associated with hurricanes. The water was as still as milk, but deflating her dock was a bitch nevertheless. She stowed it in the garage. When she came out, a pod of saltwater mermaids was going out to sea. Who could have ever confused a manatee with a mermaid? They turned and looked at her. Dove down, although she could still see them ribboning there, down along the frondy bottom.

The last time a hurricane had come through, her dock had sailed out of the garage and ended up two canals over.

She threw the leftover salad on the grass for the iguanas. The sun went down without a fuss.

Alan didn't come back, so she packed up his clothes for him. Washed the dirty clothes first. Listened to the rain start. She put his backpack out on the dining room table with a note. *Good luck with the philosopher king.*

In the morning before work she went out in the

rain, which was light but steady, and put up the storm shutters. Her neighbors were doing the same. Cut herself on the back of the hand while she was working on the next to last one. Bled everywhere. Jason's car pulled up while she was still cursing, and Alan got out. He went into the house and got her a Band-Aid. They put up the last two shutters without talking.

Finally Alan said, "It was my fault. He doesn't usually do drugs at all."

"He's not a bad kid," she said. "So not your type."

"I'm sorry," he said. "Not about that. You know. I guess I mean about everything."

They went back into the house and he saw his suitcase. "Well," he said.

"*Filhatz warfoon meh*," she said. "*Bilbil tuh*."

"*Nent bruk*," he said. No kidding.

He didn't stay for breakfast. She didn't feel any less or more real after he left.

The twenty-two sleepers were out of the warehouse and Jason had a completed stack of paperwork for her. Lots of signatures. Lots of duplicates and triplicates and fucklipates, as Valentina liked to say.

"Not bad," Lindsey said. "Did Jack Harris offer you a job?"

"He offered to come hand me my ass," Jason said. "I said he'd have to get in line. Nasty weather. Are you staying out there?"

"Where would I go?" she said. "There's a big party at the Splinter tonight. It's not like I have to come in to work tomorrow."

"I thought they were evacuating the Keys," he said.

"It's voluntary," she said. "They don't care if we stay or go. I've been through hurricanes. When Alan and I were kids, we spent one camped in a bathtub under a mattress. We read comics with a flashlight all night long. The noise is the worst thing. Good luck with Alan, by the way."

"I've never lived with anybody before." So maybe he knew just enough to know he had no idea what he had gotten himself into. "I've never fallen for anybody like this."

"There isn't anybody like Alan," she said. "He has the power to cloud and confuse the minds of men."

"What's your superpower?" Jason said.

"He clouds and confuses," she said. "I confuse and then cloud. The order makes a big difference."

She told Mr. Charles the good news about Jack Harris; they had a cup of coffee together to celebrate, then locked the warehouse down. Mr. Charles had to pick up his kids at school. Hurricanes were holidays. You didn't get snow days in Florida.

On the way home all the traffic was going the other way. The wind made the stoplights swing and flip like paper lanterns. She had that feeling she'd had at Christmas, as a child. As if someone was bringing her a present. Something shiny and loud and sharp and messy. She'd always loved bad weather. She'd loved weather witches in their smart, black suits. Their divination kits, their dramatic seizures, their prophecies that were never entirely accurate but always rhymed smartly. When she was little she'd wanted more than anything to grow up and be a weather witch, although why that once had been true she now had no idea.

She rode her bike down to the Splinter. Had a couple of whiskey sours and then decided that she was too excited about the hurricane to get properly drunk. She didn't want to be drunk. And there wasn't a man in the bar she wanted to bring home. The best part of hurricane sex was the hurricane, not the sex, so why bother?

The sky was green as a bruise and the rain was practically horizontal. There were no cars at all on the way home. She went down the middle of the road and ran over an iguana almost four feet long, nose to tail. Stiff as a board, but its sides went out and in like little bellows. The rain got them like that sometimes. They got stupid and slow in the cold. The rest of the time they were stupid and fast.

She wrapped her jacket around the iguana, making sure that the tail was immobilized. You could break a man's arm if you had a tail like that. She carried it under her arm, walking her bike, all the way back to her house and decided it would be a good idea to put it in her bathtub. She went out into her yard with a flashlight. Checked the storm shutters to make sure they were properly fastened and discovered three more iguanas. Two smaller ones and one real monster. She brought them all inside.

By 6:00 P.M. it was pitch-dark. The hurricane was still two miles out at sea. Picking up water to drop on the heads of people who didn't want any more water. She dozed off at midnight and woke up when the power went off.

The air in the room was so full of water she had to gasp for breath. The iguanas were shadows stretched along the floor of the living room. The black shapes of the liquor boxes were every Christmas present she'd ever wanted.

Everything outside was clanking or buzzing or yanking or shrieking. She felt her way into the kitchen and got out the box with her candles and flashlight and emergency radio. The shutters banged away like battle.

"Swung down," the announcer was saying. "How about that—and this is just the edge, folks. Stay indoors and hunker down if you haven't already left

town. This is only a Category 2, but you betcha it'll feel
a lot bigger down here on the Keys. It's 3:00 A.M. and
we're going to have at least three more hours of this
before the eye passes over us. This is one big baby girl,
and she's taking her time. The good ones always do."

Lindsey could hardly get the candles lit; the
matches were that soggy, her hands greasy with sweat.
When she went to the bathroom, the iguana looked as
battered and beat, in the light from her candle, as some
old suitcase.

Her bedroom had too many windows for her to
stay there. She got her pillow and her quilt and a fresh
T-shirt. A fresh pair of underwear.

When she went to check Elliot's room there was a
body on the bed. She dropped the candle. Tipped wax
onto her bare foot. "Elliot?" she said. But when she got
the candle lit again it wasn't Elliot, of course, and it
wasn't Alan either. It was the sleeper. Versailles
Kentucky. The one who looked like Alan or maybe
Lindsey, depending on who was doing the looking.

She dropped the candle again. It was exactly the
sort of joke Alan liked. Not a joke at all, that is. She
had a pretty good idea where the other sleepers
were—in Jason's apartment, not back in Pittsburgh.
And if anyone found out, it would be her job too. No
government pension for Lindsey. No comfy early
retirement.

Her hand still wasn't steady and she was running
low on matches. When she held up the candle, wax
dripped onto Versailles Kentucky's neck. But if it were
that easy to wake a sleeper, Lindsey would already
know about it.

In the meantime, the bed was against an exterior
wall and there were all the windows. Lindsey dragged
Versailles Kentucky off the bed.

She couldn't get a good grip. Versailles Kentucky

was heavy. She flopped. Her head snapped back, hair snagging on the floor. Lindsey squatted, took hold of the sleeper by her upper arms, pulled her down the dark hall, trying to keep her head off the ground. This must be what it must be like to have murdered someone. She would kill Alan. Think of this as practice, she thought. Body disposal. Dry run. *Wet* run.

She dragged Versailles Kentucky through the door of the bathroom and leaned the limp body over the tub's lip. Grabbed the iguana. Put it on the bathroom floor. Arranged Versailles Kentucky in the tub, first one leg and then the other, folding her down on top of herself.

Next she got the air mattress out of the garage; the noise was worse out there. She filled the mattress halfway and squeezed it through the bathroom door. Put more air in. Tented it over the tub. Went and found the flashlight, got a bottle of gin out of the freezer. It was still cold, thank God. She swaddled the iguana in a towel that was stiff with Jason's blood. Put it into the tub again. Sleeper and iguana. Madonna and her very ugly baby.

Everything was clatter and wail. Lindsey heard a shutter, somewhere, go sailing off to somewhere else. The floor of the living room was wet in the circle of her flashlight when she went to collect the other iguanas. Either the rain beginning to force its way in under the front door and the sliding glass doors, or else it was the canal. The three iguanas went into the tub too. "Women and iguanas first," she said, and swigged her gin. But nobody heard her over the noise of the wind.

She sat hunched on the lid of her toilet and drank until the wind was almost something she could pretend to ignore. Like a band in a bar that doesn't know how loud it's playing. Eventually she fell asleep, still sitting on the toilet, and only woke up when the bottle broke when she dropped it. The iguanas rustled around in the tub. The wind was gone. It was the eye of the storm or else she'd missed the eye entirely, and the rest of the hurricane as well.

Light came faintly through the shuttered window. The batteries of her emergency radio were dead, but her cell phone still showed a signal. Three messages from Alan and six messages from a number that she guessed was Jason's. Maybe Alan wanted to apologize for something.

She went outside to see what had become of the world. Except that what had become of the world was that she was no longer in it.

The street in front of her house was no longer the street in front of her house. It had become someplace else entirely. There were no other houses. As if the storm had carried them all away. She stood in a meadow full of wildflowers. There were mountains in the far distance, cloudy and blue. The air was very crisp.

Her cell phone showed no signal. When she looked back at her house, she was looking back into her own world. The hurricane was still there, smeared out onto the horizon like poison. The canal was full of the ocean. The Splinter was probably splinters. Her front door still stood open.

She went back inside and filled an old backpack with bottles of gin. Threw in candles, her matchbox, some cans of soup. Her gun. Padded it all out with underwear and a sweater or two. The white stuff on those mountains was probably snow.

If she put her ear against the sliding glass doors that went out to the canal, she was listening to the eye, that long moment of emptiness where the worst is still to come. Versailles Kentucky was still asleep in the bathtub with the iguanas, who were not. There were red marks on Versailles Kentucky's arms and legs where the iguanas had scratched her. Nothing fatal. Lindsey got a brown eyeliner pencil out of the drawer under the sink and lifted up the sleeper's leg. Drew a birthmark in the shape of a battleship. The water in the air would make it smear, but so what. If Alan could have his joke, she would have hers, too.

She lowered the cool leg. On an impulse, she picked up the smallest iguana, still wrapped in its towel.

When she went out her front door again with her backpack and her bike and the iguana, the meadow with its red and yellow flowers was still there and the sun was coming up behind the mountains, although this was not the direction that the sun usually came up in and Lindsey was glad. She bore the sun a grudge because it did not stand still; it gave her no advantage except in that moment when it passed directly over-head and she had no shadow. Not even one. Everything that had once belonged to her alone was back inside Lindsey where it should have been.

There was something, maybe a mile or two away, that might have been an outcropping of rock. The iguana fit inside the basket on her handlebars and the backpack was not uncomfortably heavy. No sign of any people, anywhere, although if she were determined enough, and if her bicycle didn't get a puncture, surely she'd come across whatever the local equivalent of a bar was, eventually. If there wasn't a bar now, then she could always hang around a little while longer, see who came up with that bright idea first.

THE TEASHOP

Zoran Zivkovic

Miss Greta was delighted to see a teashop across the street from the entrance to the railway station. The train she'd arrived on had been a quarter of an hour late, but the train she was meant to take for the rest of her trip had left on time. The next possible train wouldn't leave for around two-and-a-half hours. She could have spent that time reading in the waiting room, but that didn't seem very appealing. She'd never liked waiting rooms, and then what would she have to read on the train? About eighty pages were left in her book, just enough to shorten the last part of the journey. It would certainly be much nicer in the teashop. And in any case it was time for her afternoon tea.

She stood at the main entrance to the station for a few moments, uncertain about what to do with her suitcase. Although it was heavy, she had only to cross a small square to reach the teashop. Even so, there was no reason to lug it along, particularly since the drizzling rain was now getting harder. She turned this way and that until she found a sign that directed her to the left luggage window. The short, oldish man behind the counter had an extremely red nose, typical of people inclined to tipple, but he didn't smell of alcohol. He lifted the bulky suitcase effortlessly with one hand and gave her a baggage check.

Miss Greta opened a large umbrella with alternating triangles in two shades of brown that matched her coat, shoes and handbag. She waited for two cars to pass so they wouldn't spray her and then headed across the square with swift little steps. Even though she chose carefully where to step, it was inevitable that she got splashed. When she reached the arched roof covering the entrance to the teashop, she turned around and shook out her umbrella, returning a flurry of drops to the rain.

Standing in the doorway, she looked around the long room. The waiter at the counter on the right, a heavyset man in his early forties with bushy sideburns and a pencil-thin moustache, was wearing a white short-sleeved shirt and a green vest. The slender cashier with bright red hair and oversized glasses, writing something down at the cash register, was also dressed lightly, in a white blouse and the same green vest.

There weren't many customers. The elderly man sitting in the corner to the left of the door was reading a newspaper. He raised his eyes briefly when Miss Greta entered, then went back to his reading. A young couple was sitting next to the large window. They were leaning over the table towards each other, their noses almost touching, talking in low voices. At the back of the room was a woman in a navy blue suit wearing a hat of the same color. Her elbows were on the edge of the table and her head was resting in her hands as she looked at the steaming cup in front of her, lost in thought.

Miss Greta headed for an empty table away from the window. She didn't like to expose herself to the gaze of passers-by. She took off her coat, hung it on the coat rack, and put her umbrella in the brass stand underneath it. When she sat in one of the heavy arm-chairs covered in green plush, she seemed to be sucked into it.

She didn't have to open the long, thin menu with a

cover of the same green. In the afternoon she always drank chamomile tea. Suddenly, though, she decided to make an exception. The circumstances were unusual and there were so few deviations from daily routine in her life. She shouldn't have been there at all, but since chance had brought her to the teashop, why not make good use of it? An impish desire filled her to do something reckless in a place where no one knew her. She would order the tea that seemed the most unusual.

The menu had four densely-filled pages. She'd never heard of most of the teas and had tried only a few, even though she'd been drinking this hot beverage in the morning and afternoon regularly since childhood. Reading through the splendid selection, she wondered with a tinge of sorrow why she limited herself to the humdrum. This had once seemed a virtue, but now she could not remember why. She shouldn't be inhibited, at least as far as tea was concerned. Now was the chance to make up a little for what she'd missed, albeit belatedly.

Along with the names of the teas was a description of their beneficial effects. Some astonished her, others brought a smile to her lips, and yet others made her blush slightly. She didn't even know there was tea made of cabbage (a "salutary digestive"), spinach ("relieves the pain of spondylosis") and carrots ("helps fight anemia"). Nettle tea was thought to improve one's memory and moss tea purportedly calmed tense nerves, while papyrus tea rekindled the flames of desire.

The fourth page offered teas that were preposterous. Had circumstances been otherwise, the level-headedness that made Miss Greta proud would have forced her to frown at what she read. Just now, however, it did not seem to be tasteless frivolity. What difference did it make if they were preposterous when they sounded so nice? She could have asked what the teas were really made of, but decided not to because that would only dispel the magic.

Tea made of wind chased away apathy, tea made of clouds brought a yearning to fly, moonshine tea inspired lightheartedness, spring tea made you feel young again, tea made of night led to sinful thoughts, tea made of silence filled you with tranquility, tea made of mist brought great joy, snow tea offered hope. She could have chosen any one of these teas. The best thing would actually be a mixture of them all. She was deficient in everything they promised.

But in the end she didn't order any of them. She chose the last one on the menu—tea made of stories. This was partially influenced by the brief recommendation next to it: "You need this." The decisive element, however, was that she adored stories. She read them every day, as ritualistically as she drank tea. Whenever she was in low spirits, she would scold herself for living a better and fuller life in the world of stories than in the real world, but this dismal conclusion never dissuaded her from reading, and as soon as she got caught up in a story her depression disappeared the same moment. Since she was already determined to try the most unusual tea, this was the right choice.

She closed the menu and put it on the table. That was a signal for the waiter to approach.

"Good day," he said with a smile. "May I take your order?"

"Good day," she replied with a fleeting smile. "Tea made of stories, please."

She didn't say it very loud, overcome by an embarrassment she would not have felt had she asked for an ordinary tea. Even so, in the silence of the teashop her soft words seemed to reach everyone's ears. The cashier stopped writing and turned towards her table. The man next to the entrance looked at her over the top of his newspaper. The young couple with eyes only for each other turned their heads in unison towards her. Even the lady in the navy blue suit stopped staring at the cup on the table and looked at her with interest.

Miss Greta blushed and lowered her head. She felt like she'd been caught committing a crime. She alone was to blame for this predicament. Had she ordered chamomile tea, as she should have, no one would have batted an eyelid. It served her right for having no self-control. Tea made of stories, indeed. What must they think of her?

She was rescued from this discomfort by the waiter. He bowed, his smile broadening.

"Of course, ma'am. Right away."

She didn't raise her head when the waiter left to make her tea. She stared for some time at the folded hands in her lap, almost physically feeling the inquisitive and scornful looks. But when she finally mustered the courage to glance quickly around the teashop, she noted with relief that the others had ceased to be interested in her. They had all returned to what they'd been doing before.

Several minutes later the waiter put before her a white cup in the shape of an inverted bell, its handle resembling a mouse's ear. The tea was the same green color as the vests of the teashop staff. She smiled at the waiter, thanking him with a nod of the head.

Instead of leaving, he stood there next to her table. Embarrassment filled her once again. She didn't know why he was still there or how she should react. In the end she concluded that the best thing would be to act as though he was nowhere near her. She would start to drink the tea. That was why she'd ordered it, right? What else could she do, in any case?

She brought the cup to her lips and blew a little on

the steaming green liquid. She tasted it cautiously, anxious about the heat and the unknown taste. The tea was mild with a suggestion of bitterness. She had the feeling she'd tasted it before, but was unable to identify it. It seemed to be a mixture of almonds, dogwood and something else that escaped her. She put the cup back on the saucer.

"Is it to your liking?" asked the waiter.

"Yes," she replied after a moment's hesitation. "Very much."

"That's nice. So, now we can move on to the stories." He indicated one of the two empty armchairs. "May I?"

She watched in bewilderment as he sat down without waiting for her permission.

"The stories?" she repeated after he had settled in his chair.

"Yes. The stories that go with this tea. You took the tea made of stories, didn't you?"

She wanted to say she hadn't imagined it would be like that, but then it would look like she hadn't known what she was ordering and this would only compound her distress. She had no idea what was to follow, but there was no turning back. Just see what the desire to do something reckless had brought her.

"Of course," she agreed.

The waiter coughed slightly, like an actor clearing his throat before going onstage, and then began.

"Up until the thirty-third execution, the executioner had successfully performed his duty. He belonged to a respected family of executioners that had been doing this responsible job impeccably for six generations. There had never been any complaints about their work; they had even been decorated for their exceptional devotion and diligence during periods of great social upheaval. Families of the convicted would write sometimes and thank them for the skill with which they'd despatched their loved ones from this world with the least possible suffering.

"A veil of secrecy surrounded the reason why the youngest scion of this honorable family tree suddenly decided to break with their glorious tradition. He refused to offer any explanation, thus his reasons could only be surmised. The last execution he'd performed was thought to have influenced his choice, although he couldn't have been particularly affected by the elimination of a baby-faced hardened criminal who had mercilessly killed eleven librarians, first forcing them to put on firefighting uniforms and read the same excerpt from an ancient epic, while he accompanied them on the harp, wearing diving equipment.

"It was also conjectured that the fact that he'd recently joined an association to protect white bear cubs had influenced his decision to leave his profession. This had allegedly dulled the insensitivity that is a characteristic of every good executioner, but that wasn't very convincing either. It is a well-known fact that compassion for animals usually does not go hand in hand with compassion for humans. Haven't most of those who've left the bloodiest trails behind them been remembered for their touching gentleness towards some cat, dog, horse, parrot or crocodile?

"Be that as it may, the executioner withdrew to a tuberculosis sanatorium in the mountains even though he was perfectly healthy. That is when he started to collect rare mountain flora. The head nurse supported him in his efforts, as she herself was an amateur botanist. Sometimes, when she was not on duty, she would take long walks with him across the slopes and peaks and they would return with a multitude of new specimens for their herbariums.

"Rumors about a sentimental attachment between

them inevitably spread through the sanatorium, but they paid no attention, offering no grounds for this gossip in their public behavior. Nothing can be said for sure, of course, as to whether or not anything happened when they were out of the doctors' and patients' sight. If it did, it was very discreet, as befits such a highly dignified institution. Everything might have been disclosed in the end if it weren't for an unfortunate incident that thwarted the would-be lovers.

"When one of the patients, a retired mining professor, found out that in spite of everything there was no hope and he had only a few weeks left to live, he became gravely concerned about the fate of the large hoard of napkins that he'd been collecting since he was a schoolboy. Since he had no heir, he had no one to leave it to. He wrote to various museums, offering his collection free of charge, even including his considerable savings to maintain it. For the most part there were no replies, and those he did receive hurt him with their indifference and often unconcealed disdain.

"In the throes of a nervous breakdown, without considering the consequences, the professor put all his napkins in the middle of his room and set them on fire. The fire blazed into a fury and quickly spread to the neighboring rooms, then engulfed the whole floor and finally the entire sanatorium, an old building without proper fire precautions. In the chaos that ensued, all efforts were focused on saving the helpless patients, so what the executioner did passed almost unnoticed.

"When it was already too late to stop him, he was seen rushing into the flaming building. By some miracle he made his way to his room on the first floor and threw a bunch of herbarium tanks through the closed window. In spite of everyone's exhortations to jump and save himself even at the risk of injury, he went back for the rest of the herbarium tanks, although tongues of fire were already flickering all around him.

"Nothing else came flying out the window and he did not appear at it again. The sanatorium burned to the ground. The remains of eight bodies were found in the charred ruins. This, however, did not agree with the number who had disappeared, which was nine. After great effort, when they identified the burned bodies, it turned out that the only one to disappear without a trace was the executioner. It was concluded that his body had been vaporized in the fire, and he was officially declared dead."

Finishing the story, the waiter bowed briefly. Miss Greta was tempted to applaud, but held back, returning his bow with a smile. This was the kind of story she liked best—romantic and mysterious. True, there had been too much violence in it for her taste, the hero shouldn't have been an executioner exactly, and many people had died in the fire, but she shouldn't grumble. After all, it was only a story.

She was no longer sorry she'd ordered this tea. What a wonderfully clever idea it was to offer a good story along with an equally good drink. The only pity was that it had been so short. She wondered what would happen if she ordered another one. Did the waiter have a new story for every new cup of tea? First she had to finish the one in front of her as it would be inconsiderate not to do so, even though it had most likely cooled off while she was listening to the story. She lifted the cup and took a long sip, surprised to find that it was still quite hot.

"Wonderful," said the waiter when the cup was on the saucer once again. "So now we may continue."

Without giving an explanation, he got up and headed back to the counter. Along the way he passed the cashier, who was headed for her table. Without even asking for permission, the tall woman sat right down in the same armchair as the waiter. She took a green handkerchief from the breast pocket of her vest, removed her oversized glasses and started to wipe them. This made her chestnut brown eyes look smaller. When she put her glasses back on she didn't start the story right away. She gazed at Miss Greta for several moments, as though looking through her.

"After the calamity in the sanatorium, the head nurse decided to change her profession. Not even the avalanche of attractive offers she received after winning recognition for saving the patients from the fire could dissuade her from this decision. She withdrew from the world for several weeks and when she came back she was like a different person. Everything about her had changed: the raven-haired woman had become a blond, her classically-cut dark dresses were replaced by striking leather suits in bright colors, and instead of being modest and gentle she was sharp and gruff.

"But the biggest surprise was her choice of new profession. She became a stuntwoman, showing an acrobatic agility and courage that were unimaginable even to those who knew her best. She was undaunted by the most perilous assignments and soon the best film directors started to ask for her. A brilliant career awaited her, but then something happened that made her cut it short.

"The assignment was to shoot down a dangerous waterfall with two other stuntpeople in a rubber boat. All protective measures were taken and the scene had been gone over in detail, but the security cable snapped during filming. Instead of being held back, the boat and its occupants ended up on the rocks at the bottom of the waterfall. By some miracle, the former nurse was the only one to survive, suffering just minor scratches.

"The investigation that was conducted established that it had not been an accident as first thought. The cable hadn't snapped, it had been cut. Who had done it remained a mystery, although the two people who died turned out to have a motive. They were actually part of a strange love triangle. He was obsessively in love with the new stuntwoman, even though she rejected his advances unrelentingly, while she was jealous of her, convinced that she'd stolen the man she loved so desperately.

"Once again the nurse turned stuntwoman withdrew for a long time and came back drastically changed. Her blond hair was now red, light sportswear replaced the leather suits, and her behavior changed accordingly—she was cheerful and coquettish. The change in profession was also a surprise. She joined a traveling circus.

"First she tried a number of secondary jobs. She took care of the books, looked after the trained animals and was makeup artist for the clowns. She might not have advanced if it weren't for two young illusionists who came to the circus and needed an assistant. They said they were brother and sister, although their behavior was suspicious from the outset. They were demonstratively tender with each other and often held hands, so rumors started to circulate that they were lovers who had a reason to lay low or, worse yet, that they were having an incestuous affair. But since their act soon became the hit of the show, no one made an issue out of it.

"All of their acts were brilliant, but the one in which the former nurse took part won the greatest acclamation. A glass box resembling a sarcophagus filled with water was placed in the middle of the circus ring. The assistant, dressed in a turquoise one-piece swimsuit, would take a deep breath and plunge into the water. The box was closed and locked with huge padlocks and then the two illusionists threw a turquoise cloth over it. The suspenseful moments that followed were accompanied by appropriate tension-inducing music. When the audience was already fidgeting fretfully, the cloth was removed, revealing the empty sarcophagus with the padlocks still in place. That same moment there would be a fanfare of trumpets, the curtain would open and the assistant would run into the ring, completely dry, to the audience's thunderous ovation.

"Unfortunately, after the seventeenth performance this act, along with all the others put on by the young illusionists, was removed from the program. Something inexplicable happened that made them leave the circus. After their departure it was said that just before the strange event relations between the brother and sister had suddenly cooled. They stopped holding hands and were overheard quarrelling in low voices. It was even said that tears were seen in the brother's eyes. These stories, however, were not to be trusted.

"One thing set the seventeenth performance apart from the previous ones. When the fanfare sounded, no one appeared from behind the curtain. Everyone except the illusionists was surprised. They alone remained unruffled, as though everything was perfectly fine. There was another fanfare, but again no one ran out before the audience. The failure might not have been so complete if news about the act hadn't spread, with the result that the audience knew what to expect. The mysterious disappearance of the assistant from the sarcophagus was certainly striking in itself, but her absence at the end caused first a commotion and then a great chorus of whistles. It almost closed the entire show.

"After the show was over, everyone set out in search of the former stuntwoman, but in vain. She had disappeared as though the earth had swallowed her up. The brother and sister were questioned but claimed to know nothing of her fate. They denied having anything to do with the unpleasant event, indicating that the assistant might have been dissatisfied with her secondary role and this had led her to leave.

"The ringmaster briefly thought of notifying the police, but in the end he didn't because this would merely have saddled him with greater worries. His ears were still filled with the whistling; if the police were to start sniffing around the circus his audience would disappear entirely. In any case, no offence or crime had been committed that would require police intervention. Everyone had the right to leave the circus whenever they felt like it. In the end the two illusionists were forced to abandon the troupe. The circus lost a highly popular act, but this was the price that had to be paid."

The cashier bowed at the end just as the waiter had. This time Miss Greta had to clap, although she did it almost soundlessly, barely putting her palms together. The story seemed tailor-made for her—full of romantic suggestions and secrets, without too much violence. True, two of the main characters had died in the stunt episode, but this seemed unavoidable. If it was any consolation, love had guided them to their deaths. Love was also in the background of the circus event. She was curious to find out more about the relationship between the brother and sister, and of course what had happened to their assistant.

She thought of asking the cashier, who remained at the table after the end of the story. There certainly must be a continuation, particularly since the first two stories were connected. And then she remembered that she hadn't had to ask for anything the last time. If she was not mistaken, it had been enough to take a sip of tea to get a new story. Perhaps it might work again. It wouldn't hurt to try. And she had to finish the tea anyway.

Swallowing a new sip, she wondered who would talk this time. Probably the waiter. The easiest thing would be to take turns until the customer drank all the tea. After all, they weren't professional actors accustomed to giving long performances, although they certainly were deserving of praise. They were very skilled at storytelling, letting the listener enter easily into the spirit of the tale. They must have acquired this skill through frequent repetitions. Tea made of stories was undoubtedly a favorite in this teashop.

But when the cashier bowed once again and headed back towards the cash register, Miss Greta had a surprise in store. She watched in bewilderment as the young couple sitting at the table by the window approached her instead of the waiter. Smiling, they sat in the two armchairs without saying a word. There was no time to think about this unusual turn of events because the young man started the story right away.

"After they left the circus, the two illusionists split up. He found work as a cook on a luxury ocean liner. During one of the cruises through tropical seas he met the rich young widow of a notorious arms merchant who had died when a stray golf ball hit him clean in the temple. For some time the tabloids played up the story, claiming it hadn't exactly been an accident, but if there were any conspiracy it was soon covered up.

"The cook attracted the widow's attention with an excellent soup composed of mushrooms, figs and snails that he made from an ancient recipe that was said to have a strong aphrodisiac effect. She asked to meet him, and when he was brought before her he captivated her at first glance. She continued to see him under various pretexts, always leaving large tips, even when there was no reason.

"Her attempts to lure him into her cabin, however, met with failure for a long time. The ship's crew was strictly forbidden from any sort of fraternizing with the passengers, and entering their cabins was considered a particularly serious offence. Nonetheless, on the penultimate evening of the cruise the widow's intentions finally succeeded thanks to her cunning and to alcohol that the young cook was unaccustomed to drinking.

"No one knows for sure what happened that night in the cabin. When the maid entered in the morning she found him sound asleep on the floor, while the widow lay dead in the bed. The ship's doctor established that she had died of a heart attack, so he could not be blamed for her death. Even so, he lost his job on the spot and disembarked at the next port."

At this point, the young man turned towards the girl and nodded. She nodded in return and took up the story.

"After leaving the circus, the sister illusionist found work as a restorer in a museum. She soon caught the eye of the director, who had a bad reputation as a womanizer. Behind him were four broken marriages and seven daughters, as well as numerous adventures, but this did not stop him from new entanglements, even though he was no longer a spring chicken.

"The restorer coldly rejected his advances, but this only made the director more resolute. In the end, when it was clear that he would fail, he resorted to the last means available, something that had yet to let him down. He accused the restorer of doing an unprofessional job and threatened to fire her unless she satisfied his desires.

"She protested, informing him that she had just made a discovery that would not only prove her professionalism but also make her famous. Working on a late Renaissance canvas, she came to the realization that it was some sort of palimpsest. Underneath it was a considerably older work by a famous master from the end of the Middle Ages that had been considered lost forever. She invited the director to be the first one to see this painting under a painting.

"Not suspecting anything, the director rushed to see it, already devising plans on how to take credit for the discovery. But what he saw turned him numb. The original painting portrayed a scene from hell. A monstrous devil was taking great relish in torturing a sinner who had spent his life in vicious debauchery. When he looked at the sinner's face more closely, it was like looking into a mirror. By some miracle the old master had depicted his face to perfection.

"At that moment something seemed to break inside the director. Instead of firing the innocent restorer, he resigned immediately and soon retired to a remote monastery where he lived in extreme abstinence from all physical pleasure, outshining many of the ascetics in this regard. As a sign of recognition, the restorer was offered his position, but she refused without an explanation and left the museum, too."

The young girl and boy nodded to each other once again, then he took up the relay.

"The former ship's cook soon got into trouble in the port. He was sitting by himself at a table in a disreputable tavern when a bunch of noisy, drunken sailors burst in. They started to pester the guests, pouncing in particular on the pretty, young and timid tavern maid. They heckled and pinched her aggressively, and when one of them, who was exceedingly arrogant, grabbed the girl by the hand and pulled her onto his lap, trying to kiss her by force, the former illusionist could no longer sit there indifferently. He jumped up to protect the poor girl.

"Everything happened in a twinkling. Blows were exchanged, jugs and chairs went flying, knives flashed. When the skirmish was over, the arrogant sailor was twitching on the floor in the throes of death, his stomach skewered, while everyone else had fled. The terrified girl begged her savior, who had an oozing wound on his upper arm, to escape as well, even offering to hide him in her room upstairs, but he refused and waited for the police to arrive.

"Although the girl and all those who witnessed the tavern brawl testified in his defense at the trial, he was still found guilty of murder and sentenced to twelve-and-a-half years of hard labor. In prison he was put in a cell with an older convict who was soon to be released after being locked up almost a quarter of a century. A crime of passion had put him there. He'd found his wife in bed with his best friend and in a moment of blind rage killed them both with one single shot from a crossbow.

"The old man turned out to be very well-read. Since the young convict was also proud of his erudition, the two of them began spending long hours in stimulating conversation, amazing each other with their knowledge and sagacity. When the day of his departure was quite near, the old man decided to tell his last cellmate, in whom he had infinite trust, something that he had not confided to anyone.

"In the prison library, which was surprisingly well-stocked and contained some truly rare editions, he had come across a book that mentioned a secret society with a strange belief. All creatures capable of thinking were nothing more than cells in the gigantic brain of a cosmos that was striving to grasp its own meaning. The former cook found this very interesting and wanted to read the book without delay. But this, unfortunately, was not possible. The old man told him that the book had disappeared from the library after he'd returned it and all trace of it had been removed even from the card catalogue.

"Luckily, however, the old convict had a photographic memory, so he was able to pass on faithfully everything he'd read, including the part about the complex and dangerous rite of linking with the cosmic mind. Wonderful possibilities opened up for those who survived it, for they would acquire almost divine abilities. The old man admitted, a bit reluctantly, that he had started the ritual once but stopped at the last moment, lacking courage. He asked his cellmate whether he might have the necessary bravery, and he agreed without a moment's hesitation.

"The next morning when the guards came to release the old man, they found him sitting in the corner of his bed, terrified, shaking his head, mumbling something unintelligible. There was a wild look in his eyes and his hands trembled uncontrollably. There was no trace of the other convict. It was impossible to learn what had happened in the cell during the night. The old man never emerged from his stupor, so instead of finally finding himself free he was locked up again, this time in a mental asylum for the poor."

Finishing the story, the young man bowed towards Miss Greta, but there was no time for her to return the bow because the young woman started right away.

"Leaving the museum, the former illusionist and restorer joined an expedition into the jungle, where the ruins of a temple from a previously unknown ancient civilization had been found. The team was led by a famous archeology professor, a tall and learned man with graying hair that only made him more attractive. She fell in love with him immediately, but had to hide her feelings because the professor's wife was present.

She was also a prominent scientist and still lovely, although no longer in her prime.

"On the other hand, suspecting none of this, the professor's two assistants had their eye on the former restorer. They competed for her favor, even though she made it perfectly clear that their efforts were in vain. Who knows where their rivalry might have led—a duel with machetes was only avoided by a hair—if it weren't for a discovery that pushed their aching hearts into the background. Underneath the temple they found a network of underground passages filled with priceless treasure. In addition, unknown hieroglyphics covered the walls.

"They all threw themselves enthusiastically into their work, but not for long. The three male members of the team soon came down with a mysterious disease that brought shivering, high fever, exhaustion and vomiting. Something in the stale air of the passages seemed to affect only the men. The expedition had to be suspended so the ailing men could be taken urgently to the hospital.

"Although the professor tried to dissuade the two ladies, mentioning in his delirium an ancient curse, they decided to take their last chance and go down below the temple one more time before the helicopter arrived. Just as they reached the passage, everything around them started to tremble and give way. It looked like a strong earthquake, but it turned out later that the trembling had not been natural. They rushed for the way out, but only the professor's wife was saved.

"When she had recovered a little from her shock, she confided to the professor alone what had happened in her last moments underground. Both of them could have been saved, but just when they reached the stairs there was a powerful flash of light in the chaos behind them. She was blinded an instant; when she regained her sight she saw the young woman going back down again. She screamed at her to come back, the passages were liable to collapse at any moment, but she paid no attention. She continued, arms stretched out in front of her as though spellbound. There was no time to try to rescue her because that's when the granite walls around her started to crack as though made of plaster. She was barely able to make it to the surface."

Just as the young man had done before her, the girl bowed after she had finished. This time Miss Greta applauded without the slightest hesitation, unconcerned that she was disrupting the silence in the teashop. She had to express her delight and in return received one more bow in unison from the two young people. The other stories had been wonderful, but these surpassed them. Particularly the girl's—so full of passion, tension, mystery. She didn't like the episode in the prison very much in the boy's story. It had been interesting, but she was bothered by the absence of female characters, although she knew it would be hard to have them in a men's prison. The episode in the tavern, though, had been perfect in all respects.

Not only were the stories superlative, they had also been told with such inspiration. These two could not be just customers in the teashop, as she'd mistakenly assumed. They were most certainly professional actors. Only actors were capable of presenting events so skillfully and convincingly, as though it had all happened to them, each one picking up where the other left off. She felt like clapping again when she realized this. It was beyond all expectations: keeping two actors on standby just so one of the customers would be able to order tea made of stories.

And then a thought made her stiffen. She hadn't

paid attention to the price of the tea she'd ordered. She hadn't thought it necessary. Tea didn't cost very much. But there was no way that this one could be inexpensive. Perhaps the waiter's and cashier's stories had been free, but actors had to be paid. Who would perform and hang around wasting time between performances without remuneration?

Unable to control her impatience, she opened the menu again with a mixture of dread and embarrassment, even though she was not alone at the table. She hoped that the two actors sitting there smiling at her would not figure out what she was doing. Her eyes flitted down the fourth page. What she saw brought relief along with confusion. The only place where the price was not listed was for tea made of stories.

She closed the menu and in her bewilderment, almost unconsciously, just to occupy her hands, raised the cup and took one more long drink that emptied it. The color seemed to have turned a darker green and it was now tepid, but strangely enough this did not lessen the flavor. On the contrary, it seemed to have acquired an additional quality. As she lowered the cup, the young couple stood up, bowed one last time and returned to their table by the window.

Miss Greta wasn't sure whether the performance that went with the tea made of stories was over or not. It seemed to her somehow unfinished. Perhaps the waiter or cashier would return to the stage, or both of them together. It wouldn't be surprising. What did happen, though, was the last thing she expected. A new couple headed towards her table: the woman in the navy blue suit and the man who had been reading a newspaper.

He bowed, she smiled, and then they settled into the armchairs. There was no introduction. The woman started her story at once.

"The archeologist's wife left him soon after he recovered from his fever. The illness seemed to have changed him. He blamed her without letup for what had happened when she'd gone underground for the last time. He seemed to regret the loss of his assistant more than the disappearance of an ancient civilization's shrine. She felt doubly betrayed: as a wife and an expert.

"She gave up archeology and joined a charitable organization that sent its members to different parts of the world, where they helped the unfortunate. Her first assignment took her to a desert region hit by starvation and contagious disease. There she met a handsome missionary who helped her get accustomed to the terrible conditions. Working selflessly with him day in and day out, she started to feel an attraction for him, although he could almost have been her son.

"She would have kept this secret to herself, of course, if the young missionary had not contracted the disease. Its course was unremitting: it led first to blindness and then death. Conscious of the fact that there was nothing to be done, he refused to go to hospital, wanting to stay in the mission until the end. She never left his side, particularly after he lost his sight. When his end drew near, she finally confessed her love for him.

"He, however, refused to believe her, claiming that she only felt compassion because of his condition. Overcome by despair, she thought of catching the disease herself in order to prove her love, but failed in this intention because death was faster. The missionary died in her arms, unconvinced of her love, and she, totally crushed, decided to return home."

There was no pause. As soon as the woman in the navy blue suit finished, the man adroitly picked up the thread.

"The old man spent three and a half months in a mental asylum for the poor. He finally recovered, although it was impossible to get anything out of him about what had happened that fatal night in the cell. A free man at last, he found work as a cemetery guard in a small town in the provinces. He soon caught sight of a young woman who came every Monday morning right after eleven when there were usually no other visitors.

"Dressed in elegant mourning and always wearing sunglasses, she would go to the spot where a retired ornithologist had lain in rest for more than eighty-five years. She would spread out a gray blanket on the grave, sit on it and then take a chess set out of her bag. She would line up the pieces, always putting the white ones in front of her, and the match would begin. After she made her move, she would look towards the tombstone and then, as if receiving instructions, play a black chess piece. Sometimes the games were drawn out. Once it was almost five before she left the cemetery.

"The old man was a devoted chess player himself, so it was no wonder that he was compelled by the unusual rivalry. In the beginning he kept his distance, watching surreptitiously, but since his eyesight was already poor, he gradually came closer, though fearing that the woman in mourning might chastise him for disturbing her. But there was no word of reproach, not even when he approached quite close and stood right behind her back.

"He was rather surprised to learn that this was not amateur chess, as he'd expected for some reason. These were sophisticated matches between players of equal stature. They always ended in a draw, which was reached after a great battle. Each time before she left, the woman would take a queen's chess piece made of marzipan out of her bag and put it on the tombstone. The birds would devour it by morning.

"Several months passed before the cemetery guard mustered the courage to ask the woman in mourning if she would play a game of chess with him. He was convinced she would refuse, but she agreed without a moment's hesitation. Without a word, she indicated that he was to sit on the blanket across from her. Three hours and forty-two minutes later he got up from there the loser. Even worse than the defeat was the fact that he was certain he hadn't made any mistakes.

"Then, for the first time, the woman took off her sunglasses and spoke. She told him that if he wanted to live he should never play chess again, he should quit his job at the cemetery and leave town. He hesitated not a moment as to whether to do as she said. He went straight to the cemetery office and resigned, then went to his rented apartment, packed his few belongings, and headed towards the train station. He bought a ticket to the farthest destination that could be reached by the next train."

"All that remained was for her to take a train on the last part of her arduous trip from the desert regions and the dismal memories that tied her to them. She was alone in the compartment for a long time, and then she acquired a traveling companion at the station in a small town with a pretty cemetery next to the track, full of tall cypress trees.

"She was pleased to see that the elderly man kept to himself. He greeted her politely, sat next to the window and gazed out pensively. She certainly would not have liked to engage in small talk. She went back to reading the archeological journal that she'd bought at the airport."

"Two stations later another passenger entered the compartment. He was on the brink of middle age, heavyset, with bushy sideburns and a thin mustache. He bowed and sat down next to the door without a word. Silence reigned in the compartment until they stopped unexpectedly in a tunnel. An announcement came over the P.A. system that there had been a rockslide nearby and the rails would be cleared in about fifteen minutes. No one got up to turn on the light nor did anyone suggest it."

"When the train came out of the tunnel, only the passenger who was last to arrive was sitting in the compartment. He was in the same place, staring straight ahead. The darkness had hidden what had happened to the other two passengers. There was no trace of them, not even their luggage."

"The passenger got out at a large station where several lines intersected. Just as he stepped onto the platform, out of the blue he made the most important decision of his life. He would no longer be an executioner. He would interrupt the family tradition of the past six generations. And he would not tell anyone why. It was none of their concern, after all."

"As he left the train station he almost ran into a woman who suddenly started to turn this way and that, looking for the left luggage window. Although she hadn't noticed him, he mumbled something in apology and then continued on his way."

The stories were over, but Miss Greta did not clap. She sat there without moving, watching the woman in the navy blue suit and the older gentleman stand up, nod briefly and return to their seats. When they sat down, she lowered her eyes to the empty cup in front of her.

She stayed like that, staring for some time, as though seeing something on the bottom that other eyes could not discern. She finally turned towards the coat rack, reached into her coat pocket and took out the baggage check she'd received at the left luggage window. She turned it over several times and then raised it a little as though wanting to show it to everyone. Then she tore it up. She was delighted to receive the resounding applause that greeted her after she placed the pieces of paper on the saucer next to the cup.

THE ROPE: A NEW TALE OF THE ANTIQUE LANDS

Noreen Doyle

The rope was braided out of common halfa-grass, as many ropes are in the Antique Lands. It trailed from a low and broad basket, made of doum-palm fibers but unworthy of further remark. Some length of the rope lay coiled beside this basket. The other end of the rope, which had to be thought of as the far end, stood at present some fifteen yards distant. And this, as will be seen, was worthy of remark indeed.

The rope had been displayed in the Lower Ópetian port town of Noofr for five days now. Late each morning the blind old man who owned the basket set it in a broad sort of plaza that periodically filled up with tradesmen and merchants, forming near the ice manufactory an ephemeral *sooq* of goats, bitumen, fish, rice, and other regional produce. This place was more than broad enough for the rope to have been laid straight out in any direction without touching the wall of the native town, or that of the manufactory, had its owner chosen to do so. The old man, whom the people of Noofr came to call the little khedeev (that is, the little "ruler of Ópet"), chose not to do this.

The effect of this location, likely unintended by the old man, was also to keep the rope some distance from any building whose roof or window might have facilitated a closer inspection of the far end. The residents and visitors to the *sooq* were much inclined to attempt this, because from its coil beside the basket the rope rose straight into the air. And there was no yardarm or balloon tethered anywhere along its length.

Rope-charming is a profession not unknown in this part of the world, but it has never been a common one. Most rope-charmers will use cordage, thin rope or often ordinary cotton twine, not longer than five or six yards. (The precise length of the little khedeev's rope had not been determined, but its diameter was in excess of two inches.) Some rope-charmers use drums, and others reed pipes, to "draw up" the rope. The little khedeev used a side-blown ivory horn. From the embouchure of this unsophisticated instrument he forced a curious series of notes. These were themselves worthy of as much remark as the rope, on account of their duration, tonal achievements, and charming effects.

He also had a boy with him, as rope-charmers sometimes do. The boy was seven or eight years of age, black-haired, brown-skinned, and slender, a good Upper Ópetian type one might expect to see on a photographic cabinet card. Each day the boy swarbled up the rope. With him he dragged the attention of the crowd, away from the dusty street, away from their chores and labors. Away from the recently depopulated harbor, away from their worries about the real khedeev, who was very unpopular.

The khedeev was, in fact, so unpopular that two weeks prior to this day, while he visited abroad—and specifically on the very day he toured *L'Exposicion Grand* in Lutet—a minor uprising had disturbed Noofr. Several buildings had been set afire and certain people were beaten, threatened, or killed. This had precipitated both the departure of most of the foreigners by means of the tourist steamers operated by Baker & Son, and the arrival of a contingent of the khedeev's army, which had quickly brushed through and removed the offenders like nits on a louse-comb. These occurrences had left things in such a state that even the local population did not know what might happen next. Ever since, to whatever extent possible, the foreigners had stayed away, visitors and ex-patriates alike. A nebulous sense of worry hung over the town, except here in this plaza. The rope and the boy and the old man had become a sort of holy trinity, granting a bright daylight hour of relief from worldly cares.

Such ease of heart notwithstanding, rope-climbing boys do fall now and then, before they have had a chance to run away or grow too large in their proportions or be stolen away by some family member or slave-dealer. A bad note or rhythm from the rope-charmer's instrument, or a slip of a clumsy hand, can pluck him from the sky and send him back down, haste post haste, to the street. In such cases gravity proves the greater magic. Much more rarely, a boy neither descends the rope nor plummets from it. Now and then, it is said, a boy climbs up and up and up into the glare-gold of the sun, and never returns. It is supposed to be a rare and marvelous thing for a boy to be so pretty and so virtuous as catch the fancy of God. (It being usually difficult to maintain both states simultaneously.)

But in the event that this boy fell, he would not lie on the streets to be picked over by thieves. In the shadow of a mendicant eye-surgeon's awning, a young woman of Lower Ópet named Iánheh tá-Heybesi waited, ready to fetch his body to Temple servants who would properly entomb him. This was not her usual employment. She was, in fact, the vaccinator's daughter, although Iánheh herself had no deep interest in the science of inoculation and these days earned a modest income as a dragoman, guide and interpreter for foreigners who found themselves in Noofr. Her current role of jackal was occasioned by the recent events. These had deprived Iánheh of her customary clientele, and few of the local population knew quite what to do with her (her father being in Lutet with the khedeev at the time). During the minor uprising, which earned several column inches in local and foreign newspapers and half-tones in those that had the apparatus, the vaccinator's house had burned down.

The servants of the Temple did not particularly care about Iánheh's politics (they were anyway awaiting the return of the great eminence called the Sole of God), or even her religion (she wore the white and yellow *qafiyeh* that marked her as one of the *kópees*, who worship a multiplicity of powers rather than exclusively the sun, which is called God in the Antique Lands). In return for the boy's body, and thereby his soul which the servants of God would press into duty, they would give her something to eat.

By this time, Iánheh had come, somewhat unhappily, to the conclusion that the boy was not going to be providing her dinner. At least it was fortunate for him. But Iánheh had waited five days for his consequences and, as her own consequence, had gone rather hungry.

There was today other game afoot here, and Iánheh finally decided to pursue it. Like Iánheh, the other people of Noofr had been watching this performance for five days and had grown just a little tired of it. More strangers, for whom the rope remained yet a novelty, made up the crowd now. While there were no foreigners from beyond the Antique Lands, the various nations (if they may be so called) within the Antique Lands, and the forty-two provinces of Upper and Lower Ópet, were well-represented. Someone might need a desert guide, when the performance was finished. Iánheh knew the routes. She had followed her father's inoculation rounds for many years.

A well-bearded man of Qinahni found himself in her aim. He had crossed the Crocodile Canal (Noofr stands at its northern entrance) into Ópet, and had earlier remarked to the eye-surgeon that he was bound next for Qáriyá, grandest city in Ópet and, by certain accounts, in all the world.

"*Yá sáyeed*," Iánheh said, approaching, "the roads from Noofr are not as felicitous as those that bring a man here. A *móteneet* would smooth your path, keep dogs from your shadow, ensure water for your horse, or find you a horse if you have none." She used a common word for desert guide in the language of the *kópees*, who are famed and prized for remaining loyal to their employers.

Her lineage and its accompanying reputation did not impress the Qinahnite. He continued to stare in the direction of the boy, pulling in the flowing sleeve of his embroidered cotton robe so that it did not stray too near her body. "Where are your foreign masters gone off to, girl? Swim after them!"

Attempts upon several others likewise brought rejection, if not so cruelly. Iánheh's usual services were evidently of no greater use today than her unusual ones. She said to herself, "My father will return from Lutet soon. But not so soon that I can wait for him without eating."

She had one last salvaged morsel, a fig, slightly charred. Before making a meal of it, she made it vanish and appear at turns by sleight-of-hand. Her father had taught her these tricks, for the amusement of those children to whom he administered in his inoculation duties. The fig walked the back of her hand, was reborn from an old woman's ankle ("Here is your last-born, *sáyeeda*! May it grow to bear you many fruit that those who crouch in your shade might share!"), disappeared into thin air—O no, there it was, beneath Iánheh's *qafiyeh*.

Was the honest *leger-de-man* of this female adept any less wonderful than the tricks of the rope-climbing boy? Taking away the wonder of the rope and installing him upon an ordinary pole of no great height, certainly not. Regarding more passive aspects of their presentations, ornamental as the boy was, Iánheh was herself a reasonably attractive specimen of a Lower Ópetian type (with even a few red hairs among her dark brown ones, barely numerous enough to suggest a latency of mischief to anyone who came close enough to notice them). But as this boy was now, a pretty Upper Ópetian appended to an untethered rope that had risen to a very respectable height, he was a creature of air, an occasion of contemplation and joy. Iánheh might as well have been a snake in the dust of the earth, the bystanders accorded her such notice.

"How high the boy has climbed! O God! O God!" one onlooker remarked to the next. "How marvelous the little khedeev's magic is! Will it happen today? Will God take him?"

From their hands rained *báqsheesh* in the form of coins and, among them, a copper bracelet, these puddling before the crossed legs of the blind rope-charmer. The bracelet was thin and green with age. Iánheh thought, "That is nothing more than a scrap, an insult, a bruise upon the flesh of his poor purse! What will the old man do with such a thing? But I know the sort of foreigner who'd buy it. The foreigners will come back. Their winters will grow cold again and they'll forget about the uprising—even if I won't—and remember only Ópet's warm breezes and *anteekehs*."

The bystanders craned their necks heavenward, looking holy in contemplation of God as the Temple horologues sang the noon hour. By now the boy had gone higher than they had ever before seen any boy climb on such a rope. He had to be nearly at the far end, the very end. Everyone—Iánheh not excepted—drew a loud breath. The boy fumbled for his hold as he had never done before, and was pendant from the rope by one hand only. Everyone—even those who had grown bored with the performance—watched now.

As their breaths came out filled with urgency and prayer timed to the rapid cadence of their hearts, O God! O God!, their hands went out, collectively. Everyone—Iánheh not excepted—tipped or flicked their wrists or bent down to put their hands before the old man. The little pile of *báqsheesh* grew, despite all things, larger than before. But their eyes still attended the boy. Now Iánheh was excepted, because she was examining the copper bracelet she had pinched from among the coins. And her neighbors ululated.

Iánheh leapt up. The rope stood there still, but the boy was gone from the end of it. Iánheh said to herself, "Where has he fallen to?" but the ululation was of overwhelming joy.

The boy was gone. He had climbed straight up to the sun. "O God! O God! God be praised! His presence fills my heart! O God! O God! What a blessed boy! What a fortunate boy, to be taken away by God! O God! O God!" People departed amid self-congratulations, saying, "Did you see? Yes? O how wonderful for you and your family, and me and mine. Yes, it is a blessing to witness such a miracle with one's own eyes, to have such manifestation of God's love to sate one's heart." They went away, thanking the little khedeev with gifts of even more coins.

Iánheh squinted into the sun as it continued on its way, her fingers feeling the edges of the bracelet. Foreigners would return for it. They would return for her, and her father would too and the khedeev would come back and everything would be as it had been, except for the house, which had burned to the ground.

She wondered if the boy might also return. She said to herself, "Did the sun god come for him as the unblinking eye of a falcon, or as a ball pushed along by a beetle, or as a golden boat? Or maybe, as the Temple servants say, as a flawless orb of light." And she wondered too, "Will the boy fall?"

After a time spent scraping the coins into a small cotton sack, and calling "Boy! O for a boy!" (to no effect except that in Noofr mothers attended their sons a little better from that time forward), the old man tucked in his legs. His spine jerked, and one might argue next whether his legs lifted him or whether something hauled him up by the shoulders. It was very much like watching a puppet as he wrenched himself from the ground. This, and his blindness, were why the bystanders of Noofr had named him the little khedeev.

The little khedeev set the ivory horn upright in his basket. Around it he proceeded to guide the rope into a coil. With the little sack inside too and the lid pinned into place, he shouldered this burden.

Iánheh ran before him, bowing. "*Yá sáyeed! Yá sáyeed!*" Then, in the language of the *kópees*: "*Ha niboo! Ha niboo!*"

"*Yá! Yá!*" said the little khedeev fearfully. Into his palm she pressed her last fig.

"Your boy is gone, *sáyeed*, taken by your God, and all the other boys have been all taken away by their mothers."

His long fingers curled around the scorched fruit. He squatted in the shadow of a house with no windows and, there, devoured it. "*Yá!* Sit here, sit here, *kópeet.* No one sits with me." The little khedeev rocked back and forth. "Do you think that a blindman among the sighted is like a foreigner among real people, needful of a dragoman? O I can discern what's about me, girl, very well indeed! I know what is in people's hearts and, most of all, what they lack. I hear it, I smell it, I feel it, I taste it. I provide it. In my yesterdays I had this horn and nothing else with which to accomplish this. From sooq to sooq I traveled—O I might have had a donkey from time to time, but that is all."

"No boy?"

"Not so much as a monkey!" He was smiling now, squinting as if to see something distant and bright. "Yesterday," the little khedeev said, "the rope danced along the ground. People came to marvel at it! For a long time this brought me *báqsheesh.* But then there came a day when nobody's heart was filled by this anymore. I pleaded, 'What displeases you, *sáyeed* and *sáyeeda?*' The reply was, 'Up the road is a foreign tsampouna-player who claims to have fitted his pipes to the bladder of the infidels' Good Lord, which he himself dug up out of a tomb. He's playing up his Lord's ___ ! But your rope! It might as well be a snake!' I said, 'Well, who is to say that it will remain a snake?'"

"People watched for a little while in hopes that something else might happen, then, when it didn't, went on to the tsampouna-player, or else to a man who served wine from the horn of the foreigners' Devil, or even to a woman who kept a lock of hair from our very Sole of God braided among her own. Then, one day as I played, the rope rose from the ground. People stopped to watch it for a while. In time it reached into the sky. People came from near and far to behold this rope emerging from its basket, drawing up and up and up! O how they loved this. For many years, so many years, this filled their hearts and my purse. But today! It is not yesterday anymore. Today most any creature with lips on his face and breath in his lungs may send string or cord or length of catgut into the air. People will gape and stare for a little while, but only if you put a monkey or, better, a boy on the rope. You might think that this satisfies them, and I forgive you for it, but they are not amazed, not by what they once were."

His legs thrust the rest of his body up again. He gathered the basket onto his back, and the sack of coins within it changled. "Enough of this place!"

"Where are you going, *sáyeed*?"

"Everywhere! Qáriyá, to Qáriyá."

Iánheh walked beside him, warding dogs and sheep from his path. "You'll need a *móteneet*, surely, at least for a little while. And what will you do without a boy? I believe that nobody in Noofr will give you one. Who will stare at your rope and toss coins to you now?"

The little khedeev cracked a smile around his yellow teeth. "O but you are a girl. Would you make a pretty, virtuous thing for God to snatch away, leaving me as I am now?"

"Virtuous? O *sáyeed*," Iánheh tá-Heybesi replied, cupping the copper bracelet at her wrist, "there is no danger of that."

The vaccinator's daughter led the little khedeev to a ferryboat that took them southward down the Crocodile Canal to Renáriyá. Thence westward by rail to Qáriyá, because he had the coinage to let them spaces in a mostly empty cattle car. Qáriyá is said by certain writers to be the greatest city on earth, and in terms of antique wonders this can hardly be doubted, although the city was deficient (though not altogether lacking) in manufactories, mills, telegraph wires, and other modern fixtures so common in the west.

Many of the foreigners who had fled Noofr had come to Qáriyá. Such an influx greatly pleased those in the business of letting rooms, but, because this was also a festival season during which pilgrims journey to honor their ancestors (westward of Qáriyá lie suburbs of the dead), it meant that the little khedeev and Iánheh had to camp in an alley near one the eastern entrances. Little traffic passed them by after the horologues sang the city's seventy-two gates shut at the first hour of night. When Iánheh suggested that he take advantage of their relative solitude to send the rope into the night sky, so that she might discreetly climb it once or twice and become accustomed to its peculiarities, the little khedeev laughed until he coughed. "Girl! Who would see you then? Whose heart could you satisfy in the darkness? Would you have the moon or the stars carry you away? Such middling ambitions!"

In the morning they went into a certain broad crossroads of several *sooqs*, principally devoted to produce-sellers and to makers of shoes, boots, and slippers. He had Iánheh identify a well-stocked fruit-seller at a corner and near this woman's narrow cell he settled. As he opened the basket, a carrion odor wafted out. "A mouse crawled in and died last night," Iánheh said, settling some of its heavy coils on the ground. "Or maybe a night or two before." The little khedeev thrust his nose over the basket and took a deep breath. He shook his head and waved her off to perform *leger-de-man*.

Small coins disappeared from the hands of large men and reappeared as large coins from the ears of small children. One orange—honestly paid for—became two and then three, to the consternation of the fruit-seller who sat queenly upon her *mustubeh* (a brick bench), smoking a *nargeleh*. The woman cried from around the mouth piece of her pipe, "If fruit can be so easily come by, I'll cut down half my grove and sell the wood to some rich man!"

"*Yá sáyeeda,*" said Iánheh as she passed to her the oranges, "you should have more faith in the order of the world as ordained by your God!"

And the fruit-seller then saw that one of her bags had collapsed, half-empty. She called people to witness this juggler with her poor blind *sáyeed*, to marvel at the pretty *kopeet's* tricks, to pity the old man's condition—and O might not someone be a little hungry too?

With fingers sticky from the fruit-seller's produce, onlookers applauded Iánheh's *leger-de-man*, thankful that this nimble-fingered monkey was kept in plain sight, else they would surely lose their purses. (This stung Iánheh's pride, because, copper bracelet aside, she was really not much inclined toward casual thievery.) A coin fell, then two. She forgave them then their stings and barbs.

Very soon a restlessness grew among them. The call of a child or husband, a foreman's cry to some member of his gang, a shopkeeper summoning his messenger, donkey-driver, or gatekeeper, tugged at them. Just as a few began to wander away, the little khedeev blew a wheezing gale through the embouchure.

The ivory horn blasted everything else in the crossroads into silence. And, beneath that tempestuous insufflation of noise, like a whisper in a storm came a hush-rustle from within the basket. The rope extended to sway against the morning breeze. Its far end, its frayed head knotted to the size of a strongman's fist, held at the height of the awning that shaded the fruit-seller's *mustubeh*. The little khedeev's breath reverberated through the horn, whose note was no longer so loud. The crowd regained its voice, the rope crawled higher. Joined to the air by an umbilical cord of halfa-grass, the unremarkable basket became the navel of the world.

The buildings around this certain crossroads were not so tall as those about that plaza in Noofr. None stood more than two stories. A few were capped with pigeon towers which sufficiently enterprising youths might have scaled, but the young men had come down to the street to view Iánheh earthbound more closely. The rope had gone a little higher now, to the level of the rooftop of the nearest building plus two yards. As this building happened to be a single story, it was therefore not very far to climb. Even so, she hesitated to touch the rope. Boys fell even from such heights. Most of these unfortunates broke a wrist, arm, ankle, spirit, thus ending their careers. Others were even less fortunate. She had, once or twice, delivered their bodies and their souls to the servants of the Temple.

"Up! Up! Up, you pretty monkey!" said the fruit-seller. A child threw pebbles at her feet, and some of the youths challenged her to climb higher than their heads, that they could get a good look at her from below.

Iánheh bowed to them and up the rope she swarbled, badly, arms and shoulders shaking with effort, heels kicking for some absent purchase on the halfa-grass fibers, the cotton-sheathed flesh of her thighs and knees pinching the rope like gloved forefinger and thumb. (She wore that immodest eastern type of female trouser, which is not considered an acceptable garment beyond the Antique Lands.) She did not succeed in her climb, but nor did she fail. The best that may be said is that she attempted.

She said to herself, "Well, this must annoy my *sáyeed*, but I never promised him that I was a good rope-climber. And anyway, the bystanders don't seem to mind."

The bystanders did not, as it happened, mind at all. Girls are rarer rope-climbing specimens and, therefore, something to stare after, no matter how ill they fare. She hung in midair, clutching the rope with an evident desperation, mere yards above their heads. Ululations from below, especially from the older youths. (Her performance happened to occur along a route commonly taken to the Polytechnic Institute, a foundation of the unpopular khedeev's brother.) Until she could hold no longer, in which time she slipped down the rope, hands burned. Her feet came to rest upon a carpet of coins. They slipped beneath her, so she fell undignified to the dust.

Such was her presentation for the first day, and the second. By the third, although the rope was somewhat higher than it had been previously, she had accustomed herself to its sways and ripples, which originated, it seemed to Iánheh, from the basket, or flowed, or pulled, at least, upward from some point below her. She began to experiment with the strength of the crook of each arm, and with wrapping the rope around a lower leg and pressing upon it with a foot, thus standing one-legged on the braid of halfa-grass and surveying the rooftops and pigeon towers. By the sixth day Iánheh could rely on a hand and a foot only, which was fortunate because now the bystanders were becoming bored with her swarbling up and, once she climbed as far as she dared, clutching the rope like a frightened infant at its mother's leg. To their credit, they had maintained their interest notably longer than the people of Noofr, who had been presented with a superior performance by the boy.

She did, it must be emphasized, but a single one of

these performances each day, as the boy had done and as rope-charmers do in most places. While the magic is not especially difficult to achieve, it is excessively difficult to maintain. Using a rope of any weight or making it bear a burden only complicates matters. Some rope-charmers will work in bouts of several minutes. The little khedeev preferred a sustained exhibition and had perfected it to last nearly an entire hour.

At her *sáyeed's* suggestion, after the sixth day Iánheh performed an unshodding. This met with the distinct approval of the nearby footwear-makers, who, for a certain sum given to the old man, arranged to have examples of their craft highly displayed. She began her ascent wearing a pair of sandals, boots, or slippers, whatever was given to her that day. The little khedeev had Iánheh devise a series of tricks that would keep the bystanders' gaze at her ankles for a period of time before she went too high. Juggling was good for this, and pulling coins and fruit from her footwear even better. Then she kicked off her slippers or what-had-she, to the delight of boys and certain more ambitious men, who jostled to catch them. Foreign men—tourists and businessmen—were not quite so bold as the Ópetians. They stared wondering at indecently naked female toes and ankles, a common enough sight in Ópet if very seldom from below. (Afterwards, many of them bought slippers to send home as presents for their wives, but never for their daughters.)

The crossroads choked with bystanders then of all races and nations and professions. The police from the local guard-house kept watch and found no offense on which to arrest anyone. The *bashaw-ruzool*, or chief of bailiffs, came himself to inspect the situation and could identify no reason to issue a warrant. Nor could clerks from the khedeeval palace, even after returning to the archives which house all manner of ancient and dehydrated law. Try as they might, the officials could not define the assembly as an unruly mob because its constituents did not act in any way in concert and were, in any case, entirely passive. The assembly lasted no more than one summer daylight hour. There was nothing of a *"secret"* nature that the girl could have seen from her height. The magic itself was of an entirely legal variety and the little khedeev (whom they did not refer to as such in Qáriyá, for reasons too obvious to require elaboration) paid the appropriate fees and taxes on his collections. Many clerks spent some days puzzling over this, fascinated to the point where they took their pots, pestles, and other apparatus of a coffee service, and their *nargelehs*, into the archives and enjoyed their afternoon leisure there. (This self-indulgence resulted in the unfortunate loss of a small stack of very ancient texts, and damage to a slightly larger stack, none of which would have had any bearing on this particular case.) A few of the clerks even went back to the *sooq* to observe the display, thus giving tacit sanction to the performances.

After all this time, what the clerks, the *bashaw-ruzool*, and any other bystander expected, and came, to see was something like this: the girl did *leger-de-man* of the sort that tended to amuse small children until the old man blew his horn. The rope rose. When it was a certain height, the girl leapt to the rope. With visible effort she hauled and crawled up to a not very great height, though this improved day by day. Here, she played with her sandals (or boots or slippers) before sacrificing them to the onlookers below. A little higher, she juggled an orange the fruit-vendor had given to her. Heel to hand to knee again, to elbow, to palm. A leg and an elbow dedicated to the rope, the rest of her to the crowd. Then, a little higher.

The crowd ululated, loudly and joyously, and dropped coins from their fingers. Their tongues braided praise for Iánheh—"What a virtuous girl! What a pretty girl! O God! O God!"—which rose from their gaping mouths. If below she was a snake, above she was a swallow, lifted in an updraft.

Soon the rope became a little slack. Iánheh felt a familiar sensation, a ripple, a tremble. Both she and the crowd had come to anticipate the end of the hour and to equally dislike it. She missed the sweet breeze, the ululation of praise, the prayers of O God O God that almost, but only almost, filled a painful hollowness in their hearts.

On one of these days, as she descended, a tensity rippled up and then down the rope as it released the sky. Iánheh began to slide, the rope biting her hands, knees, ankles. The crowd shouted and cried. Horrified mothers turned their children away, while keeping watch themselves. The Polytechnic youths argued how best to catch her, coming to no timely decision. The horn slipped from the little khedeev's mouth. The rope withdrew into a hasty coil.

Iánheh dropped the last three yards. The impact drove her thighbones hard into her hips and rattled her jaw. She did not otherwise fall, this time.

"O! O!" the crowd exclaimed. They threw more coins than they had before and drifted away, as if, like the rope, they had shrugged themselves free of the little khedeev's spell.

Then came another particular day that began like those before it. On his way from their camp in the alley to the *sooq*, the little khedeev gleaned good-mornings from clerks and Polytechnic students, and broke fast with the fruit-vendor. But this morning, as Iánheh and the old man crouched, eating raisins, no one stopped to inquire if they were to perform today. The fruit-vendor hailed passers-by. People paused, bought her dates and raisins and oranges, glanced at the little khedeev, and went on their way.

"What are they doing?" the old man asked, and Iánheh told him. "Do not squat in the dust," he said, slapping her but lightly. "Give a tidbit for their hearts, that they will linger, or there will be no more sky for you!"

Iánheh juggled the fruit-vendor's produce and returned it unbruised. Passers-by awarded her only flat gazes, if they looked at her at all. Even the youths, deciding her to be untouchable, found other amusements (perhaps other girls who would toss their slippers from windows rather than from ropes), and the foreigners had seen enough of her naked heels (and many went off to touch the real thing in a bath-house).

"O this I have seen, many times," one clerk said to another, who was visiting from Upper Ópet. Iánheh recognized the former and bowed, favoring both with a smile and a proffered fig, no, two figs.

"But I have not," said the Upper Ópetian clerk, who began to reach for the fruit.

"It is nothing," the first clerk answered. He picked two oranges from a sack and paid the fruit-vendor for them. "You may see it any day, for they are always here, the blindman and his monkey-girl, and she goes up, up, up. It has been this way for, oh, thirteen days? Or thirty nine? Long enough, long enough!" Both passed by.

The horn-blast signaled the end of Iánheh's earthbound antics and signaled away her worried frown. The rope rose. A coin struck the little khedeev's toe. The *bashaw-ruzool* was still amused.

Up, high as she could, to please him. There was a

small gathering now, modest. It stirred, snagging others who might have otherwise passed by. Someone was clapping. She could hear a heavy pounding, rhythmic, encouraging her pace. In trying to keep up with it, her legs slipped from the rope. Below, rumbling impatience transformed into thin ululations (encouragement) and gasps (surprise). It pleased them to see a rope-climbing girl with feet dangling free, fingers-and-palms from plummet. Sensible to this, she indulged them by hauling herself up, hand-over-hand. It had become easier now. The rope, or the air around it, or the little khedeev's notes, or most likely the ardency of the onlookers, buoyed her along on a more palpable current.

The rope had risen far higher than anyone might have thought possible. She now hung fifteen or sixteen yards above the ground, and yards more of the rope stood above her. "Can they see the sweat soaking my trousers, the raw-red skin of my palms?" Iánheh said to herself. "Can they see my eyes?"

They could not, the crowd rooted to the dirt, not with their own eyes. She had become something too high to be reached, too distant to be real any longer to anything other than their hearts.

"I must be something to them yet, anyway," Iánheh said. "They still stare. Others pause, stop, and they gape like the rest, like baskets, braiding pretty strands of words that they send up to me. I can hear their O God O God. Higher, then, just a little higher, just for you. Maybe this will sate you."

The higher she climbed, the sweeter the breeze, the stronger the current. Then came a point at which it seemed that she might have passed through an invisible membrane, which hitherto she had but hung below. Here, the ting of each coin hitting the dirt echoed, as did the old man's phlegmatic breath passing through the horn, and, above all, the rhythmic hearts of the crowd.

Below, the crowd said, "Is she gone? O God! O God! Will you take her? O God! O God! Be kind, O God! O God! Be generous to our hearts, O God! O God!"

Iánheh drew the ambrosial air—stuff surely held back from the dusty earth by this membrane—into her lungs and held it there. The rope too was making a noise. It was like the noise one hears in one's own ears, amid even completest silence. It was like a rushing, pulsing stream through a hose, which she could feel pushing upward or drawn upward, urging, rhythmic, hollow, hungry.

To herself she said, "What will it be like to sail the sky forever? To receive praise and adoration with the sun, sung along by horologues? I will climb the stays of the sun god's boat, dance upon his carapace, balance upon his sphere, juggle before his eye, guide all seventy-two of his sacred forms upon otherworldly roads."

This decided, she turned away from the dust, away from the earth, away from unrest and dissatisfaction, to climb aloft to what was above, boat or beetle, eye or orb. What was above, was not these. It was bloated and glistening, its ruddy surface, mottled and veined, stretching and pulsing, beating faster and faster, in a familiar rhythm O God O God. To it, the rope, an artery. It smelled of boy, of flesh, of blood, of great hunger.

From below, a joyous ululation, overwhelming, and their hearts beating faster and faster, swelling in hope and anticipation O God O God.

She knew their desires. She knew what would sate them. So had the boy. Up! Up! Up, you pretty monkey! O God! O God!

Iánheh uncurled her fingers.

"O God! O God! What a blessed girl! O God! O God!
What a virtuous girl! O God! O God! Fill our hearts
with your presence! O God! O God!" Until their joyful
ululation changed its pitch and into silence. Then, after
a moment, bitter sighs among them. Passers-by
consoled the little khedeev with a coin or two. They
might have given more, they said, but after all, the girl
had only fallen.

Iánheh tá-Heybesi awoke on a rooftop, knowing that
one arm was broken and that a little boy was stripping
the copper bracelet from her wrist. Then he took her
qafiyeh, her tunic, and her trousers. Iánheh huddled
naked in the shadow of a pigeon tower until nightfall,
then crept away from Qáriyá in stolen clothes.

She stowed away among goats in a crowded livestock car to Renáriyá, thence limped barefoot home to
Noofr. Her father the vaccinator had returned, as did,
sometime later, the unpopular khedeev. Her father contracted for a new house and meanwhile Iánheh's arm
mended. Foreigners came again, in ways Iánheh could
never have anticipated. She resumed her customary
employment as dragoman, in which she had any
number of interesting encounters, none of which have
much to do with the present tale.

However, during these she occasionally met the
little khedeev again. He had this rope-climbing boy
one time, that rope-climbing boy another. Iánheh never
stopped to observe them perform tricks that she could
neither have imagined nor attempted, and she
cautioned her *sáyeeds* to do likewise. But the little
khedeev had become quite famous. Many people
gathered about him and his rope and his boy, asking,
"Will God take the boy? O God! O God!"

Until one day people realized that now all of the boys disappeared at the end of the rope. Then, when the little khedeev put the embouchure of the ivory horn to his lips and sounded his perfect notes and the rope rose from the basket into the sky and the boy swarbled up and up and up, they said, "O we've seen the likes of this so many times before! This boy will dangle by his toes and snare a pigeon flying in mid air before he disappears, just like the last one. It is nothing special. God takes them all the time. It is nothing at all."

Iánheh tá-Heybesi passed them by, muttering only, "It is not God. It is not God." Of course, no one listened. And so she abandoned them all, to whatever new tricks the old man would invent for that which waited at both ends of the rope.

BUTTONS

———

William Alexander

Everything is connected. This is what my eight-year-old daughter tells me, and it terrifies her, and I'm not sure what to do about it. She won't let me touch the coffee maker, and the lack of caffeine is beginning to make my skull shrink.

Two days ago she whimpered when I pushed a crosswalk button. I was walking her to school, and we were both late. The light didn't change. I whacked the button again a few times. She started crying.

"I'm sorry," I said automatically, without taking my eyes off the traffic light or having the slightest idea what I was sorry for. This was bad. This was insensitive of me, so I looked down and tried again. "Sorry," I said, shrugging. "I hate being late. And I know the button doesn't actually do anything. It's just there to give us something to do. The people who hate waiting, I mean."

"You're wrong," she said. She didn't say it like she was arguing with me. She said it with conviction. Argument didn't matter; I would still be wrong.

"Oh?"

"They do something. They don't change the light, but they do do something."

"They doo-doo something?"

She didn't laugh. I waited.

"Okay," I said, giving in. "What do the buttons do?"

"Kill people," she told me, her face to the ground and her eyes on her shoes.

"Excuse me?"

"They kill people. They make the executions happen. Nobody wants to be an executioner, and anybody who does want to be one shouldn't be allowed, so whenever somebody is sentenced to die they wire up the lethal injections to crosswalk lights. It's so we never know who did it, because we all did. It's always like that. Firing squads put blanks in some of the guns so no one would know who really did the shooting. It's the same when we drop bombs only they use elevator buttons for that."

She raised her head. Her face was wet, but she wasn't sniffling anymore.

"What the hell kind of television have you been watching?" I asked.

"I don't watch TV," she whispered. "Not anymore." Her shoulders shook, and I couldn't tell if she was more afraid of the TV shows or the on/off switch on the television. "And we missed the crossing light."

We waited for another one. I pressed the button when she wasn't looking, and I sipped from my extra-large, xmas-present travel mug, and eventually I managed to walk her to school. This was two days ago. This was before she screamed when I tried to turn on the coffee maker, and just kept shaking her head when I asked why. I don't know if the button secretly injects shampoo into the pried-open eyes of laboratory rabbits, or if it green-lights prisoner torture in faraway cells, or else systematically eradicates all dolphins and kittens from the face of the globe, one cup of coffee at a time.

My head hurts, and she's still screaming upstairs. I don't know what she's screaming about.

BROTHER OF THE MOON

———

Holly Phillips

Our hero wakes in his sister's bed. Last night's vodka drains through him in sluggish ebb, leaving behind the silt of hangover, the unbrushed taste of guilt. He rolls onto his stomach, feeling the rumpled bed wallow a little on the last of the alcoholic waves, and opens his eyes. His sister sleeps with her curtains open. The tall window across from the bed is brilliant with a soft spring sunlight that slips past crumbled chimneys and ornate gables to shine on his sister's hands. She has delicate little monkey's paws, all tendon and brittle bone, that look even more fragile than usual edged by the morning light. Sitting cross-legged among the rumpled sheets, touch as an underfed orphan in the undershirt and sweatpants she uses as pajamas, our hero's sister is flipping a worn golden coin. She is a princess. Our hero is a prince.

The coin sparkles in a rising and falling blur. Our hero watches with bemusement and pleasure as his sister's nimble hands catch the coin, display the winning face, send it spinning and winking through sunlight with the flick of a thumb. Our hero's sister manipulates the coin, a relic of ancient times, with a skill our hero would never have guessed. It is the skill of a professional gambler who could stack a deck of cards in her sleep, which is mystifying. Our hero's sister is not the gambling type. Our hero clears a sour vodka ghost from his throat.

"You're up early."

The coin blinks at him and drops into his sister's hand. With her fingers closed around it, she leans over him and kisses his stubbled head.

"You snore."

"I don't," he says. "Are you winning?"

"It keeps coming up kings." Her monkey's hands toy with the coin, teasing the golden sunshine into our hero's eyes. "Who were you with last night?"

Our hero scrubs his tearing eyes with a fold of her sheet. The linen is soft and yellow with age and smells of his sister. "No one special. No one. I forget."

His sister's face is like her hands, delicate, bony, feral. Our hero thinks she's beautiful, and loves her with the conscious, deliberate tenderness of someone who has lost every important thing but one.

"How do you know I snore?" he says. "You're the woman who can sleep through bombs."

This is literal truth. When the New Army was taking the city and the two of them were traveling behind the artillery line, she had proven she could sleep through anything. But she says, "Bombs don't steal the covers," and since our hero is lying on top of the blanket, fully dressed, with his shod feet hanging off the end of the bed, he understands that she was awakened by something other than him. It troubles him that he cannot guess what might have been troubling her. Or perhaps it is a deeper worry, that he can imagine what it might have been. He stretches out a hand and steals the coin from between her fingers. The gold is as warm and silky as her skin. The face of the king has been the same for five hundred years.

"Granddad," our hero says ironically.

His sister sighs and stretches out beside him, stroking his head.

"You need to shave," she says.

People have said they are too close. The new government has cited rumors of incest as one reason to edge our hero out of the public eye. The rumors are false, they have never been lovers. But perhaps it is more honest to say that if they are lovers, they have always been chaste. She rubs her palm back and forth across his scalp, and he knows how much she enjoys the feel of stubble just long enough to bend from prickly to soft, because he enjoys it so much himself. Her touch soothes his headache and he is on the verge of dropping off when a van mounted with loudspeakers rolls by in the narrow street below, announcing the retreat of the New Army—the new New Army, our hero thinks, remembering all the friends and rivals who have died—routed from the border in the south. The invasion has begun. Our hero squints to see the losing face of the coin against the mounting sun. The tree and moon of the vanished kingdom has been smoothed into clouds by generations of uncrowned monarchs' hands.

"One toss," our hero's sister says across the echoes of the retreating van. "If it comes up moons, I'll go."

Dread knots his stomach, but he does as she asks. She is the only person in the world he will obey, not because she rules him, but because he trusts her when he does not himself know what is right. This is often the case these days. Maybe there are no more rights left. Maybe there are only lesser wrongs. He props his head on his fist and flips the coin, catching it in his cupped palm. Moons. He makes a fist before his sister can see, and feels as if he is clenching his hand around his own heart. It's a dreadful duty, a calamity whichever one of them goes, but he would rather be lost than lose her. Before she can pry his fingers open, he tosses the coin high into the golden light and catches it again with a flourish.

"Kings," he says. She looks at him, stricken, heartsick, and he is glad of his lie.

Walking north along the river our hero has the road to himself. No one will evacuate in the advent of this war. It is the last war, the death of the independent state, and in any case, Russia and the West have between them closed the borders: there is nowhere to go. Despite the years of infighting and politics, of failing idealism and the gradual debasement of his figurehead's throne, our hero still reflects with nostalgic pride on the romanticism and ruthless practicality of the mercenary army-turned-government he and his sister had fought for, legitimized, defended. They had been conquerors and puppets. They had driven the unlikely alchemy that transformed an imposed dictatorship into the last true democracy in the world. They had been used and pushed aside when they were no longer useful, but they had been loyal. This seems odd to our hero as he walks north along the blue river. He has always put his loyalty in the service of necessity, hidden it behind a guise of practicality, and now he has to wonder what moral force, what instinct of worth has shaped the meaning of need. What need—whose need—sends him north, leaving his sister behind to wait for the end alone? He loves her more than ever, and hates her a little for believing his lie and letting him go.

Walking in the sunshine intensifies his hangover thirst. He feels gritty and unkempt, with a sour gut and a spike through his temples, but his worn army boots hug his feet like old friends, and it is good to be on the move, good to have a destination and a goal. He hopes the security service doesn't give his sister too much grief when they realize he is gone.

There is little traffic after a year of oil embargoes.

There are pedestrians, a few horse carts, peasant working their fields with mattock and hoe. Peasants who will watch the invasion on satellite feed, who will email reports to relatives in Frankfurt and London and Montreal, who will tell one another with pride and a languorous despair that they are sticking it out to the end. A young man wearing a billed cap with the logo of an American sports team dips his hand into the bag slung across his back and casts his seed with a sweeping gesture, a generous, open-handed gesture that answers the question *why* with a serene and simple *because*. He pauses between casts to raise his hand to our hero passing on the road. Our hero answers with an abbreviated wave and turns his head away, afraid of being recognized, afraid of being seen with tears in his eyes. Settling into the mud of the ditch between the river and the road lies the burned-out carcass of an army jeep, and there it all is, the present, the future, the past. A blackbird perches on the machine gun mount and sings its three note song. It is an image with all the solace of a graveyard.

Our hero walks off his hangover and an old vitality begins to well up through the sluggish residue left by weeks, months, of dissolution. He has relaxed into the journey, and the bolt of adrenaline he suffers when he sees the checkpoint ahead feels like a sudden dose of poison. His stride falters, losing the rhythm of certainty, but he does not stop or turn aside. The checkpoint has of course been sited to give the illegitimate traveler minimum opportunities for escape. He has papers, but he is afraid of being the victim of love or hate. He tells himself he is only afraid of being stopped, but does not believe his own lie.

The soldiers are young, volunteers in the new New Army, dressed in flak jackets and running shoes and jeans. One of them is a woman. She is younger than our hero's sister, with blond hair instead of black, brown eyes instead of blue, but she has a solemn, determined self-sufficiency our hero recognizes with a pang, though his sister is much more casual about her courage now. She is more casual about death, both our hero's and her own, and he suspects she has learned to think historically while he still sees the faces of the living and the dead.

Young woman, he thinks at her in a stern Victorian uncle's voice, *you are becoming historical*, which is a joke that would make her smile.

"Where are you going?" the young sergeant asks.

"North," our hero says.

"Away from the border."

This statement is indisputably true. The peaceableness with which our hero answers the young people's hostility is not.

"Yes," he says mildly, "I have business there."

"Business." The sergeant's sneer is implicit behind the mask of his face. The bland, deadly façade of a brutal bureaucracy comes naturally to the nation's youth, they have been raised to it. It was the look of freedom that had been, briefly, imposed.

Our hero does not respond to the sergeant's echo. His mouth grows wet with a desire for vodka, and he has a fantasy, rich though fleeting, of walking into the shade of the soldiers' APC with his arm around the young woman's shoulders, hunkering down to pass a bottle around, to educate and uplift them with stories of the Homecoming War. That would be so much better than this. He unbuttons his shirt pocket and takes out his identity papers. The sergeant ignores them.

"We know who you are," he says. "What business can you have away from the capital at such a time?"

This is not an easy question to answer honestly. Our hero does not want to lie, yet claiming an urgent war-related mission in the face of no vehicle, no companions, no standing in the government, is impossible. After too long a silence, our hero says, "I am going to the old capital. It is my ancestral home. I will fight my war from there."

He looks deeply into the sergeant's eyes, and for a moment he thinks the old mystique has come alive, the old ideals of courage, nobility, adventure rising between them like a bridge of understanding, or of hope. But this young man was bred with disillusionment in his bones, and the moment dies.

"Give me your papers," the sergeant says with the blunt and sullen anger of disappointment. "I will have to call it in."

As if she is summoned by his need, Colonel Vronskaya appears with a blast of fury for the recruits and a bottle for our hero. She embraces him with a powerful cushioned grip like a farmwife's, and then stands with her hands clenched on his shoulders to study him the strong spring sun. She is not handsome at close quarters, Martiana Vronskaya. Her eyes are too close-set, too deep-set, too small for her flat, spider-veined face. Our hero leans into her regard, reassured by the familiar hard and humorous clarity of the old New Army, practical, piratical, and oddly moral in her amorality.

"Jesus fuck, you seedy son of a bitch," she says, shaking him. "This is the face we followed to victory?"

"Hell no," our hero says, "but it's the same ass."

"I wish I could say the same."

Vronskaya leads him to her car, a Japanese SUV rigged out in scavenged armor plate, and pulls a bottle of Ukrainian rotgut from a pocket of her bulging map case. They sit together on the back seat, passing the bottle between them as they talk. The river eases by, blue riffled by white around the ruins of a bridge.

"That river was like a sewer when we came. Shit brown," Vronskaya says, and our hero braces himself for some heavy-handed nostalgia. But his companion stops there, and he feels a youthful apprehension rising through him. He can feel her tension, and knows she is also braced for something hard. Thinking to make it easier on them both, he nudges her arm with the bottle and says, "You still shooting deserters these days?"

Vronskaya cuts loose with an explosive breath and says, "Hell no, we just kick their asses back to the front."

"It might be easier to tell them to sit down and wait."

"Fuck," Vronskaya says in agreement. She finally takes the bottle and drinks, passes it back. He drinks. She says, "Is that what you're doing? Looking for a good place to wait?"

"Pick your ground and defend it to the end."

"Lousy strategy, my friend. Lousy fucking strategy."

"You have a better one to offer?"

"No."

She drinks. He does. The rotgut burns going down, a welcome heat.

"Go ahead," he says. "Ask your questions."

"What," she says, "you think your crazy sister is the only one who remembers her babya's stories? Okay, okay." He had made a sudden move. "She's not crazy. She's not here, so she's not crazy. But don't tell me this isn't her idea."

"It isn't anyone's idea," our hero says, grandiose with vodka in his veins. "It's fate."

"Sure. Your fate."

"You'd be happy to see us both on this road? You want us both to die?"

"No." Vronskaya speaks with leaden patience. "I don't want you *both* to die."

Our hero slams out of the SUV, startling the checkpoint guards, startling himself. Mindful of weapons in nervous hands he smoothes his hands over his head, feeling the stubble pull at his sunburned scalp. Vronskaya heaves herself out of the car.

"Jesus fuck," she says, "you're serious. You're really going to do this thing."

"If you have any better ideas . . . " our hero says, too tense to give it the right ironic lilt.

"Sure I have better ideas. Fight and die with your old comrades instead of skulking off like a sick dog who's not allowed to die in his mistress's house."

"You never liked her," our hero says.

"No, I never did. Have you ever asked her what she thinks of me? Of any of us?"

"She loves you better than you know," he says, looking into Vronskaya's eyes.

"Me? The country, maybe, I'll grant you that. Me, she doesn't give a shit for, and never has. Or—" But Vronskaya's gaze slips aside.

Or you. But our hero knows that's not true, and knows that Vronskaya knows, so he can let it go. He says, "Will you believe me? This isn't her idea. I was the one who wouldn't let her go."

Vronskaya shrugs, sullen. "So you're the crazy one."

"Maybe. I've always been a gambler, and this is my game to play."

"It's not a game you can fucking win!"

"And yours is? Come on, Martiana, we've already lost. We lost before a shot was fired. You know it, I know it. Those damn kids know it, and so do the soldiers dying in the retreat, and so do the babyas waiting in the capital. We're losing. We've already fucking lost. East and West will meet at the river and swallow us whole." Our hero is shouting, hoarse with years of frustration. Vronskaya, her driver, the checkpoint guards, are all listening with the shame-faced scowl of those caught with their worst fears showing. "We're fucked! We're doomed! *Tell me I'm wrong!*"

In the silence that follows, they can hear a trio of small jets roaring by in the southern sky. The West has promised no civilian populations will be bombed. Even if they keep that promise, everyone knows the Russians won't. Our hero squeezes the back of his neck, then lets his arms fall to his sides.

"I have one card to play, and I'm playing it. What difference does it make where I cash my chips?"

Vronskaya, long-time poker rival, long-time friend, gives him a mournful look and says, "It's bad to die alone."

But our hero won't be alone at the end.

The old capital perches on a high bluff, a forerunner of the northern mountains, like a moth on a wolf's nose. A wing-tattered moth on a grizzled and mangy old half-breed dog, more like, for the hillsides have been logged and grazed, and the ancient town has been starved down to its stony bones. But the river runs deep and fast in a curve around the old walls, white foam clean and bright around sharp-toothed rocks, and the castle high above the slate-roofed town still rears its dark towers against the sky. Jackdaws like winged Gypsies make their livings there. The place might have been a museum once, but now it is not even a ruin, just an empty house with rotten foundations and a badly leaking roof. Our hero and his sister camped there for a time when the New Army was fighting to reach the modern city on the plain, and he remembers the melancholy ache of nostalgia, the romance of the past and the imperfect conviction that that past was his. But he had been younger then, and dangerous, and he could relish the pain.

The town is quiet. No loudspeakers here, just the murmur of radios and TVs through windows left open on the soft spring evening. It has taken our hero three days to walk this far, but the news is the same. Only the names of the towns marking the army's retreat have changed. His old comrades have managed to slow the invasion some, and along with the sting and throb of his blistered feet and the ache of his empty stomach he feels the burn of the shame he would not admit to Martiana Vronskaya, that he has been walking in the wrong direction. There must be some value to this last mad act. He must somehow make it so.

But how will he know if he has succeeded? The thought of dying in uncertainty troubles him more than the thought of death, and he pauses in his climb up the town's steep streets to sit at an outdoor table of a small café. His feet hurt worse once he is off them and he stretches his legs out to prop them on their heels. A waitress comes out and asks him kindly for his order. She is an older woman and he suspects her of having a son at the front: she is too forgiving of our misplaced hero. She brings him a cup of ferocious coffee and bread and olives and cheese. It all tastes delicious, and he looks up from his plate to tell his sister so, only to be reminded that she is not here. He wishes she was. He would like to see this small, cramped square through her eyes. She notices things: the sparrows waiting for crumbs, the three brass balls above an unmarked door, the carved rainspout jutting a bearded chin over the gutter. These things would tell her something about this neighborhood, this town, this world. To our hero, they are only fragments of an incomprehensible whole. The world is this, and this, and this. It is never complete. It is never done.

Oh God, our hero thinks for the first time, I do not want to die.

His feet hurt worse after the rest and plague him as he climbs the steep upper streets to the castle door. It is an oddly house-like castle, with no outer wall, no courtyard, no barbican and gate. The massive door, oak slabs charred black by the cold smolder of time, stands level with the street, and the long stone of the sill has been worn into a deep smiling curve by the passage of feet. Generations of feet, our hero thinks, an army that has taken a thousand years to pass through this door. The gap between door and sill is wide enough for a cat, but not a child, let alone a man. The sun has fallen below the surrounding roofs and the light has dimmed to a clear, still-water dusk. The stone is a pale creamy gray. The sky is as far as heaven, and blue as his sister's eyes. Our hero, hoping and fearing in equal measure, turns the iron latch and discovers that the door is unlocked. The great wooden weight swings inwards with a whisper of well-oiled hinges, and the boy sitting before the small fire in the very large hearth at the far end of the entrance hall calls out, "Grandfather! He's here!" as if our hero is someone's beloved son returning home. He has no idea who these people are.

The old man and the boy share a name, so they are Old Bradvi and Young Bradvi. They stare at our hero with the same eyes, bright and black and flame-touched, like the tower's birds. Our hero has heard the jackdaws returning to their high nests, their harsh voices unbearably distant and clear through the intervening layers of stone. He remembers that sound, the mournful clarity of the dusk return, and misses his old friends, the lover he had embraced in a cold, cobwebbed room, his sister. He misses her so intensely that her absence becomes a presence, a woman-shaped hole who sits at his side, listening with her eyes on her hands. The boy explains with breathless faith that he and his grandfather have been waiting since the invasion began.

They live in the town. "My mother is there, in our house, watching the television, she wouldn't come, but we have been here all the time."

All the time our hero has been walking, this boy and his grandfather have been here, waiting for him to arrive. Despite himself, our hero feels a stirring of awe, as if his and his sister's despair has given birth to something separate and real.

Old Bradvi says, "Lord, we knew you would come." He makes tea in a blackened pot nestled in the coals, his crow's eyes protected from the smoke by a tortoise's wrinkled lids. In the firelight his face is a wizard's face, and our hero feels as though he has already slipped aside from the world he knows, as though he has already stepped through that final door. When the boy takes up a small electronic game and sends tiny chirps and burbles to echo up against the ceiling, this only deepens the sense of unreality. Or perhaps it is a sense of reality that haunts our hero, the sense that this is the truest hour he has ever lived. The old man pours sweetened tea into a red plastic cup and says, "Lord, it is better to wait until dawn."

Who is this man? How does he know what he knows? Our hero does not ask. Reality weighs too heavily upon him, he has no strength for speculation, and no need for it: they have all been brought here by a story, lured by the same long, rich, fabulous tale that has ruled our hero's life, and that now rules our hero's death. At least the story will go on. Stories have no nations, only hearts and minds, and as long as his people live, there will be those. He drinks his tea and listens beyond the sounds of the fire, the game, the old man's smoker's lungs, to his sister's silent voice.

Late in the night he leaves the old man and the sleeping boy to take a piss. Afterward, he wanders the castle in the dark, finding his way by starlit arrow slits and memory. It is a small castle made to seem larger than it is by its illogical design. It seems larger yet in the darkness, and our hero's memory fails. He stumbles on an unseen stair and sits on cold stone to nurse a bruised shin. He wants to weep in self-pity, and he wants to laugh at the bathos of this moment, this life. He curses softly to the mice, and dozes for a moment with his head on his knee before the chill rouses him again. He climbs the stair, and realizes it is the stair to the tower. The floors are wooden here and there is a cold, complex, living smell of damp oak, bird shit, feathers, smoke. He crosses to a window, his muffled steps rousing sleeping birds above his head, and squeezes himself onto the windowsill. There are few streetlights in the town below, but there are windows bright yellow with lamplight or dimly underwater-blue with TV light. There are lives below those sharp, starlit roofs. There is history out there in the cold, clean air. And there is the moon, a rising crescent that hangs in the night sky no higher than our hero's window, as if it means to look at him eye to eye. A silver blade, a wink, a knowing smile, close enough to tempt his reach, far enough to let him fall if he tried.

Sitting above the town with no company but the moon and the sleeping birds, our hero feels alone, apart, and yet a part of all those lives, all that history taking place right now, here and everywhere, with every beat of every heart. The paradox of loneliness is a black gulf within him, a rift between the broken pieces of his heart. The moon casts his shadow into the room behind him, and there, in the moonlit dark, the shadow of his sister's absence puts her arms around his neck and lays her cheek against his stubbled head, and he turns and leans his face against her breast, wraps his arms about her waist, and finally weeps.

When the stars fade and the frost-colored light of day begins to seep back into the world, the old man brings the knife, and the deed is swiftly done.

It is the birds that wake him. Two jackdaws have drifted down on black wings from the rafters and stand about, peering at him with cocked heads, discussing in sarcastic tones whether he is alive or dead. Dead, he tries to tell them, but his throat remembers the iron blade and closes tight on the word. What is this? he wonders. Is he still dying? But he remembers the knife, the sudden icy tear, the taste of blood, the drowning. Air slides into his lungs at the thought, tasting of dust and feathers. What is this? Is he alive? He sits, clumsy with cold, and the birds sidle off, muttering and unafraid. Their claws make a clock's tock against the floor. Our hero's shirt is stiff and evil with blood. What, then, is this running through his veins? He is too bewildered to feel afraid.

At first he cannot see the changes, and he thinks that he has failed, though how he could have failed and yet be alive escapes him. The dissonance between possibility and impossibility is too intense, he is numb and not, perhaps, entirely sane. He stumbles down the stairs, the same spider-haunted stairs, while the birds leave by the windows. They laugh at him as they go, he has no doubt: jackdaws have a black sense of humor. He blunders his way through the half-remembered halls, gets lost, laughs out of sheer uncomprehending terror. When he finds the entry hall, there is a fire burning on the vast hearth, a whole log alight, filling the fireplace with snapping and dancing flames, but he does not pause. The door is wide open, and the air is bright with morning light, although the sun is still below the roofs of the town.

There are bells ringing somewhere below, a shining tin-tanning of bronze, such a happy sound that our hero pulls off his blood-soaked shirt so as not to sully the good day. He walks bare-chested into the town, and no one stares or looks aside, although the streets are almost crowded. The people are not so happy as the bells; many seem as quietly, profoundly bewildered as our hero feels. He stops a woman about his own age, a woman with soft fair hair tousled across her face, and asks what has happened.

"What do you mean?" she says. "Everything has happened. Everything!"

"O God," an older woman says beside them. "O God, do not abandon us. O God, preserve us."

A man across the narrow street is cursing with a loud and frantic edge to his voice. He seems to be haranguing his car which is parked with two wheels up on the pavement, and which is no doubt out of gas after all these months of the embargo. Our hero supposes that the invading armies are near, perhaps at the fragile old walls of the town, and so, although there is something odd about the man's defunct automobile, he continues on down the hill toward the river where he might be able to see what there is to see.

But there are other odd things, and gradually they begin to distract him from the shock of being alive. The streets are wider as they near the archaic boundary of the old wall, and the pavements here are lined with strange statues. Wrought-iron coaches with weighty and elaborate ornaments, brass lions with blunt, dog-like faces and curling manes, horses with legs like pistons and gilded springs. The people clustered around these peculiar artworks are predictably confused, but there are others in the streets who walk with shining eyes and buoyant steps, and some of these people, too, seem odd to our hero. Their clothing is too festive, their hair is strung with baubles, their faces are at once laughing and fierce. One bearded man catches our hero's eye and bows. He sweeps off his jacket, blue velvet stiff with gold braid, and offers it to our hero with another bow. "My lord," he says, and when our hero takes what is offered, the man spreads his arms with a wide flourish, as if to present to him everything: the people, the town, the world.

And then our hero sees, as if before he had been blind. The tired old houses propped up by silver barked trees hung with jewel-faceted fruit. The banners lazily unfurling from lampposts that have moonstones in place of glass. The violets shivering above the clear, speaking stream that runs down the gutter, between the clawed feet of the transformed cars. It is the new world, the ancient world, the world that had faded to a golden dream on the losing face of his sister's hoarded coin. It is the world he died for. He has come home.

It is still a four-day walk back to the new capital, and though it seems both illogical and unfair, our reborn hero's feet still throb and sting with blisters in his worn-out army boots. He is warm enough in his old jeans and the blue velvet coat, despite the clouds that roll in from the east, but he walks with a deep internal chill that only deepens the closer he gets to home. He should have kept his ruined shirt to remind him that there is no such thing as a bloodless victory, a bloodless war. The invaders had penetrated too deeply to be shed with the nation's old skin. Like embedded ticks engorged with suddenly poisoned blood, they—men and women of the East and the West, their weapons and machines—have suffered transformation along with the rest of them, and though harmed, they have not been rendered harmless. There are monsters in this new world. He sees one slain, a tank-dragon with bitter-green scales, a six-legged lizard with three heads and one mad Russian face, in the fields near where he had met the checkpoint guards and Martiana Vronskaya on his way north just a few days ago. Perhaps some of these confused and scrabbling warriors are those same young volunteers with their flak jackets and jeans. The jeans have not changed, nor the fearful determination, but the short spears with the shining blades are new. New, and as old as the world. Our hero leaves them to their bloody triumph on the flower-starred field, and like the veteran he is, continues on his painful way.

The new capital has changed more than the old, its modern buildings wrenched into something too much stranger than their origins. Our hero suspects this will never be an easy place to live, not even the old quarter where his sister lives. Here, 18th-century houses have melted like candlewax, or spiraled up into towers like narwhal tusks and antelope horns, crumbling moldings and baroque tiles bent and twisted out of true. Our hero cannot tell if this new architecture is better or worse than the old, uglier or more beautiful. He is only frustrated that the landmarks have changed, and that he cannot figure out where the house is that once he could find blind drunk and staggering. It seems bitterly unfair. He circles the half-familiar streets, until finally a doorway catches his eye, a pale door like a tooth or a pearl, with above it a wholly prosaic glass-and-iron transom in the shape of a fan. He knows that transom, and now that he is looking, he recognizes a brass-capped iron railing, a graffitoed slogan barely legible among the creeping blue flowers on the pavement at his feet. Tears of gratitude sparking hot and wet in his eyes, he turns the corner and walks to the second door.

His key still works, despite the rubies bursting like mushrooms from the crazed paint on the door. He enters the old-house quiet, breathes in the intimately remembered smell of dry wood and cabbage and sandalwood incense, climbs the crooked, creaking, fern-and-trumpet-vine stairs. He knocks on his sister's door, and she opens it, and she is just the same.

A DIORAMA OF THE INFERNAL REGIONS, OR THE DEVIL'S NINTH QUESTION

Andy Duncan

My name is Pearleen Sunday, though I was always called Pearl, and this is the story of how I met the widow of Flatland House and her 473 dead friends and sang a duet with the Devil's son-in-law and earned a wizard's anger by setting that wizard free.

At the time I did these things, I was neither child nor woman, neither hay nor grass. I was like a cat with the door disease. She scratches to be let in or scratches to be let out, but when you open the door she only stands halfway and cocks her head and thinks deep cat thoughts till you could drown her. Had I been on either side of the door that summer, things might have turned out differently, but I could not decide, and so the door stood open to cold winds and marvels.

I grew up in Chattanooga in Professor Van Der Ast's Mammoth Cosmopolitan Musee and Pavilion of Science and Art. Musee is the French word for museum, and cosmopolitan means citified, and Professor Van Der Ast was born Hasil Bowersox in Rising Fawn, Georgia. Whether his were the quality Bowersoxes, who pronounce "Bower" to rhyme with "lower," or the common Bowersoxes, who pronounce "Bower" to rhyme with "scour," I cannot say, for Professor Van Der Ast never answered to either. The rest of the name of Professor Van Der Ast's Mammoth Cosmopolitan Musee and Pavilion of Science and Art is self-explanatory, although the nature of science and art is subject to debate, and it was not a pavilion but a three-story brickfront, and I would not call it mammoth either, though it did hold a right smart of things.

You would not find the museum if you looked today. It sat in the shadow of the downtown end of the new Walnut Street Bridge across the Tennessee River. Years before, General Sherman had built a bridge there that did not last any time before God washed it away, but He seemed to be tolerating the new one for now.

I was told my parents left me in a hatbox in the alley between the museum and the tobacco warehouse. Two Fiji cannibals on their smoke break took pity and took me inside to the Professor, who made me a paying attraction before I was two years of age. The sign, I was told, read "Transparent Human Head! All Live and On the Inside!" What was inside was me, sucking a sugar tit with a bright lamp behind my head so my little brain and blood vessels could be seen. Every word on the sign was true.

A young girl like myself with no mother, father or schooling could do worse in those days than work in an educational museum, which offered many career opportunities even for girls with no tattoos or beards and all their limbs. Jobs for girls at Professor Van Der Ast's included Neptuna the Living Mermaid, who combed her hair and switched her tail in a pool all day, and the Invisible Girl, who hid behind a sheet and spoke fortunes into a trumpet, and Zalumma Agra the Circassian Princess, Purest Example of the White Race, who when snatched from the slave traders of Constantinople had left behind most of her clothes, though not enough to shut us down. Our Purest Example of the White Race in summer 1895 was my friend Sally Ann Rummage of Mobile, Alabama, whose mother had been a slave, though not in Constantinople. Sally Ann was ashamed of the museum and wrote her parents that she had become a teacher, which I suppose she had.

I had none of those jobs that summer because I was in that in-between age, and the Circassian Princess in particular was no in-between sort of job. No, I was so out of sorts with myself and the world that Professor Van Der Ast cast me entirely from the sight of the paying public, behind our Diorama of the Infernal Regions.

Now a diorama in those days was only a painting, but a painting so immense that no one ever would see it all at once. It was painted on a long strip of canvas 10 feet high, and to see it, you rolled it out of a great spool, like a bolt of cloth in a dressmaker's shop for giants, and as it rolled out of the first spool it rolled back up in a second spool about twenty feet away. In between the spools the customers stood shoulder to shoulder and admired the sights that trundled past.

The spools were turned by an engine, but someone in the back had to keep the engine running and make sure the canvas threaded smooth, without snagging and tearing—for your town may have had a fine new Hell, but Chattanooga's was as ragged and patched as a family Bible. That someone in the back was me. I also had to work the effects. As the diorama moved past, and as Professor Van Der Ast stood on the public side and narrated the spiel, I opened and closed a bank of lanterns that beamed light through parts of the canvas—to make the flames of Hell flicker, and bats wheel through the air, and imps and satyrs wink in and out of existence like my evil thoughts as I sweated and strained like a fireman in a furnace-room. Every day in the spotty mirror over my washstand upstairs, I rubbed my arms and shoulders and wondered what man would ever want a woman with muscles, and what man she might want in return.

Ours was the only diorama I ever saw, but Professor Van Der Ast said that one famous diorama in New York City was a view of the riverbank along the entire length of the Mississippi, from Minnesota to New Orleans. Park Avenue swells in boater hats could lounge in air-cooled comfort and watch it all slide past: eagle-haunted bluffs, woodlands a-creep with Indians, spindly piers that stopped at the overalled butts of barefoot younguns, brawling river towns that bled filth for miles downstream. Professor Van Der Ast himself had been no farther north than Cleveland, Tennessee, but he described New York's Mississippi just as well as he described Chattanooga's Infernal Regions. You felt like you were there.

"Observe, my friends, from your safe vantage point this side of the veil, the ghastly wonders of the Infernal as they pass before you. I say, *as they pass before you!*" (The machinery was old and froze up sometimes.) "First on this ancient scroll, bequeathed us by the Chaldean martyrs, witness the sulfurous vapors of Lake Avernus, over which no sane bird will fly. Here is Briareus with his hundred arms, laboring to drag a chain the width of a stout man's waist, and at the end of that mighty leash snaps the hound Cerberus with his fifty heads, each of his fifty necks a-coil with snakes. Here is the stern ferryman who turns away all wretches who die without Christian burial. Next are the weeping lovers wringing their hands in groves of myrtle, never to be reunited with their soul-mates.

Madame, my handkerchief. Your pity does you honor. Next is the whip of scorpions that flays those who believed their sins concealed in life. Here is the nine-acre giant Tityus, chained at the bottom of the abyssal gulf. Here are sufferers chin-deep in water they are doomed never to drink, while others are doomed to bail the water with sieves."

A weeping schoolmarm might ask: "But what about the realms of the blessed? the Elysian fields? the laurel groves?"

"For such consolations, madam, one must consult canvases other than mine. And here we have the writhing Pandaemonium of pleasure, where all noble and spiritual aims are forgotten in the base fog of sensation and lust. Next is the great—"

"Hey, buddy, could we have a little more light on that there Pandaemonium of pleasure?"

"This is the family show, friend, come back at ten. Here is the great wine-press in which hundreds of the damned are crushed together until they burst. Here are the filthy, verminous infants of ingratitude, which spit venom even as they are hoisted with tongs over the fire. Note, ladies and gentlemen, that throughout this dreadful panorama, the plants in view are all thorny and rank, the creatures all fanged and poisonous, the very stones misshapen and worthless, the men and women all sick, feeble, wracked, and forgotten, their only music Hell's Unutterable Lament! Where all suffer horrid torments not for one minute, not for one day, not for one age, not for two ages, not for a hundred ages, not for ten thousand millions of ages, but forever and ever without end, and never to be delivered! Mind your step at the door, next show 2:30, gratuities welcome."

That was Professor Van Der Ast's side of the canvas, the public side. I told no one what I saw on my side: the patches and the stains, the backward paintings, the different tricks played by the light. I could see pictures, too, but only half-glimpsed, like those in clouds and treetops in leafy summertime. The pictures on my side were not horrible. I saw a man wrestling a lightning rod in a storm; and a great river catfish that sang to the crew in the gondola of a low-flying balloon; and a bespectacled woman pushing a single wheel down the road; and a ballroom full of dancing ghosts; and a man with a hand of iron who beckoned me with hinged fingers; and a farmer who waved goodbye to his happy family on the porch before vanishing and then, reappearing, waved hello to them again; and an angry face looking out of a boot; and a giant woman with a mustache throwing a man over the side of a riverboat; and a smiling man going over Niagara Falls in a barrel while around him bobbed a hundred hoodoo bottles, each with a rolled-up message for Marie Laveaux; and a hound dog with a pistol who was robbing a train; and a one-eyed man who lived in a gator hole; and a beggar presenting a peepshow to the Queen of Sheba; and a gorilla in a boater hat sitting in a deck chair watching a diorama of the Mississippi scroll past; and a thousand other wonders to behold. My Infernal Regions were a lot more interesting than Professor Van Der Ast's, and sometimes they lighted up and moved without my having to do a thing.

My only other knowledge of magic at the time was thanks to Wendell Farethewell, the Wizard of the Blue Ridge, a magician from Yandro Mountain, North Carolina, who performed at Professor Van Der Ast's for three weeks each summer. I never had the chance to see his act because, as the Professor liked to remind us, we were being paid to entertain and not to be entertained, but I was told that at the climax he caught in his teeth a bullet fired through a crystal pitcher of lemonade, and I believe it was so because sometimes when a pinhead was not available, the Professor asked me to go on stage after the show and mop up the lemonade and pick up the sharp splinters of glass.

The tricks I saw the wizard Farethewell perform were done after hours, when all the residents of the museum went to the basement for drinks and cold-meat sandwiches and more drinks. I squirmed my way into the front of the crowd around a wobbly table made of splinters and watched as he pulled the Queen of Hearts out of the air and walked coins across his knuckles and floated dollar bills. "Just like the government," he always said when he floated a dollar bill, and we always laughed. He showed us fifty-seven ways to shuffle a deck of cards and seventeen of the ways to draw an ace off the top whenever one was needed, even five times in a row. "Do this in a gambling hall," he said, "and you'll get yourself shot. Do it among you good people, and it's just a pleasant diversion, something to make Little Britches smile."

That was what Farethewell called me, Little Britches. He was the only one who called me that. Big Fred, who played our What-Is-It?, tried it once, and I busted his nose.

If the night wore on and Farethewell drank too much, he got moody and talked about the war, and about his friend, an older man he never named. "The 26th North Carolina mustered up in Raleigh, and I couldn't sleep that first night, without no mountains around to hold me, so I mashed my face into my bedroll and cried. I ain't ashamed of it, neither. The others laughed or told me to hush, but this man, he said, 'Boy, you want to see a trick?' Now, what boy don't want to see a trick? And after he's seen it, what boy don't want to know how it's done?" As he talked he stared into space, but his hands kept doing tricks, as if they were independent of the rest of him. "At New Bern he taught me the back palm, the finger palm, the thumb palm; at the Wilderness the Hindu Shuffle and the Stodart egg; at Spotsylvania the Biseaute flourish, the Miser's Dream, the Torn and Restored. I learned the Scotch and Soda and the Gin and Tonic before I drank either one; and all through the war, every day, I worked on the Three Major Vanishes: take, put, and pinch." As he said that, three coins disappeared from his hand, one by one. "So that was our war. It kept my mind off things, and maybe kept his mind off things, too. He had the tuberculosis pretty bad, toward the end. The last thing he taught me was the bullet catch, in the stockade at Appomattox, just before he died. I got one of his boots. The rest, they burned. When they turned out his pockets, it was just coins and cards and flash paper. It didn't look like magic no more. It just looked . . . It looked like trash. The magic went when he went, except the little he left to me."

Someone asked, "What'd you learn at Gettysburg?" and Farethewell replied:

"What I learned at Gettysburg, I will teach no man. But one day, living or dead, I will hold the Devil to account for what I learned."

Then he began doing tricks with a knife, and I went upstairs to bed.

My in-between summer came to an end after the last viewing of a Saturday night. As I cranked the diorama back into place, I heard the Professor talking to someone, a customer? Then the other voice got louder: "You ain't nothing but an old woman. She'll do just fine, you watch."

I could hear no more over the winding spool, and I did not want to stop it for fear of being caught eavesdropping. Then the Professor and the wizard Farethewell were behind the diorama with me.

"Shut off that engine, Little Britches. You can do that later. Right now, you got to help me." He had something in his hand, a tangle that glittered in the lamplight. He thrust it at me. "Go on, take it. Showtime was five minutes ago."

"What are you talking about?" It was a little sparkly dress with feathers, and a hat, and slippers with heels. I looked at Farethewell, who was drinking from a flask, and at the Professor, who was stroking his silver beard.

"Pearl, please mind Mr. Farethewell, that's a good girl. Just run along and put that on, and meet us in the theater, backstage." I held the costume up to the light: what there was of the light, and what there was of the costume. "Sukie can't help Mr. Farethewell with the ten o'clock show. She's sick."

"Dead drunk, you mean," Farethewell roared, and lifted his flask. The Professor snatched it away. Something spattered my cheek and burned.

"Get as drunk as you like at eleven," the Professor said. "Pearl, it'll be easy. All you have to do is wave to the crowd, climb into the box and lie there. Mr. Farethewell will do the rest."

"The blades won't come nowhere near you, Little Britches. The box is rigged, and besides, you ain't no bigger'n nothing. You won't even have to twist."

"But," I said.

"Pearl," said the Professor, like there were fifteen R's in my name. So I ran upstairs.

"What's wrong with you?" Sally Ann cried when I burst in.

I told her while she helped me out of my coveralls and my blue denims and into the turkey suit. "What in the world are they thinking?" Sally Ann said. "Hold still, Pearl, if I don't cinch this you'll walk plumb out of it."

"My legs are cold!" I yelled.

The hat was nothing I would have called a hat. In a rainstorm it would have been no cover at all. I finally snuggled it down over my hair and got the ostrich plume out of my face. Sally Ann was looking at me funny.

"Oh, my," she said.

"What?"

"Nothing. Come on, let's go. I want to see this. Clothes do make a difference, don't they?"

"Not to me," I said, and would have fallen down the stairs if she hadn't grabbed me. "Who can walk in any such shoes as this?"

There's no dark like the dark backstage in a theater, but Sally Ann managed to guide me through all the ropes and sandbags without disaster. I carried the shoes. Just inside the backdrop curtain, the Professor made a hurry-up motion. I hopped one-legged to get the shoes back on and peered through the slit in the curtain, but was blinded by the lamps shining onto the stage.

Farethewell was yelling to make himself heard over what sounded like a theater full of drunken men. "And now, my lovely assistant will demonstrate that no cutlass ever forged can cut her, that she can dodge the blade of any cavalryman, whether he be a veteran of the Grand Army of the Republic—"

The crowd booed and hissed.

"—or whether he fought for Tennessee under the great Nathan Bedford Forrest!"

The crowd whooped and stomped its approval.

"Here she is," muttered the Professor, as he held the curtain open.

I blinked in the light, still blinded. Farethewell's big callused hand grabbed mine and led me forward. "Ladies and gentlemen, I give you Aphrodite, the Pearl of the Cumberland!"

I stood frozen.

The crowd continued to roar.

Lying on a table in front of us was a long box like a coffin, open at the top. A pile of swords lay beside it.

"Lie down in the box, honey," Farethewell murmured. He wore a long blue robe and a pointed hat, and his face was slick with sweat.

I walked to the box like a puppet and looked down at the dirty pillow, the tatty blanket inside.

"And if you don't believe me when I tell you how amazingly nimble Aphrodite is, why when I am done shoving cutlasses into the box, those of you willing to pay an additional fifty cents can line up here, on the stage, and look down into the box and see for yourself that this young woman has suffered no injury whatsoever, save perhaps to her costume."

The crowd screamed with laughter. Blinking back tears, I leaned over the box, stepped out of the shoes: first left, then right. I looked up and into the face of a fat man in the front row. He winked.

In my head I heard the Professor say: "This is the family show, friend, come back at ten."

I turned and ran.

The noise of the crowd pushed me through the curtains, past Sally Ann and the Professor. In the sudden darkness I tripped over a sandbag, fell and skinned my knees, then stood and flailed my way to the door and into the corridor beyond.

"Pearl! Come back!"

My cheeks burned with shame and anger at myself and the crowd and Farethewell and the Professor and Sally Ann and those stupid, stupid shoes; I vowed as I ran barefoot like a monkey through the back corridors that I would never wear their like again. I ran as fast as I could—not upstairs, not to the room I slept in, but to the one place in the museum I felt was mine.

I slammed the door behind me and stood, panting, behind the Diorama of the Infernal Regions.

Someone, probably the Professor, had done part of my job for me, and shut down all the lamps. It was the job I liked least, snuffing the lights one by one like candles on a cake. But the Professor had not finished rolling up the canvas. It was backstage dark, but up there on the canvas, at eye level, was a little patch of light, flickering.

I'm sure that when I went missing, my friends thought I had run away, but they were wrong. I was running away from nothing. I was running *to* something, though I did not know what it was. Running to *what* is the rest of my story—is all my story, I reckon.

I walked right up to the flickering spot on my side of the canvas. The tip of my nose was an inch from the paint. When I breathed in, I smelled sawdust and walnuts. When I breathed out, the bright patch brightened just a little. If you blow gently on a flame, it does not go out, but flares up; that's how the canvas was. I almost could see a room through the canvas, a paneled room. Behind me, a woman's voice called my name, but in front of me, I almost heard music, organ music.

I closed my eyes and focused not on the canvas, but on the room beyond.

I stepped forward.

Have you ever stepped through a cobweb? That's how I stepped out of Professor Van Der Ast's Mammoth Cosmopolitan Musee and Pavilion of Science and Art and into a place without a ticket booth, into my own canvas, my own Infernal Regions.

Not a funeral, a ball. The organist was playing a waltz.

I opened my eyes.

I was in a ballroom full of ghosts.

I reached behind to feel the canvas, to feel anything familiar and certain. Instead I felt a cold hard surface: a magnificent stained-glass window that ran the length of the wall, depicting mermaids and magicians and a girl at the lever of an infernal engine. Window and room spun around me. My knees buckled, and I sank onto a beautifully inlaid wooden floor.

The room wasn't spinning, but the dancers were. Fifty couples whirled through the room, the silver chandeliers and mahogany paneling and gold-leaf wallpaper visible through their transparent bodies. I never had seen such a beautiful room. The dancers were old and young, richly and poorly dressed, white and black and Indian. Some wore wigs and knee breeches, others buckskins and fur caps, others evening gowns or tailcoats. They didn't look like show people. All moved faster than their actual steps. No feet quite touched the floor. The dancers were waltzing in the air.

Against the far wall was a pump organ, and sitting at the bench with her back to me was a tiny gray-haired lady, shoulders swaying with the force of her fingers on the keys, her feet on the pedals. I tried to see the sheet music through her but could not. She was no ghost; she was substantial. I looked at my hand and saw through it the interlocking diamond pattern of the floor. That's when I screamed.

The music stopped.

The dancing stopped.

The old lady spun on her bench and stared at me.

Everyone stared at me.

Then the dancers gasped and stepped—no, floated—backward in the air, away from me. There was movement beside me. I looked up to see a skinny girl in a feathered costume step out of the stained-glass window. I screamed again, and she jumped and screamed, too.

She was me, and she also was becoming transparent.

"Five minutes break, please, everyone," trilled a little-old-lady voice. "When we return, we'll do the Virginia Reel."

The second Pearl had slumped onto the floor beside me. A third Pearl stepped out of the stained glass just as the old lady reached us. She wore an elaborate black mourning-dress with the veil thrown back to reveal chubby, ruddy cheeks and big gray eyes. "There, there," she said. "This won't do at all. The first rule of psychic transport is to maintain integrity, to hold oneself together." A fourth Pearl stepped from the glass as the old lady seized my hand and the second Pearl's hand and brought them together, palm to palm. It was like pressing my hand into butter; my hand began to sink into hers, and hers into mine. We both screamed and tried to pull back, but the old lady held our wrists in a grip like iron.

"Best to close your eyes, dear," the old lady said.

My eyes immediately shut tight not of my own doing but as if some unseen hand had yanked them down like windowshades. The old lady's grip tightened, and I feared my wrist would break. My whole body got warmer, from the wrist onward, and I began to feel better—not just calmer, but somehow fuller, more complete.

Finally the old lady released my wrist and said, "You can open your eyes now, dear."

I did, and it was my own doing this time. I stared at my hands, with their lines and calluses and gnawed-to-the-quick nails, and they were so familiar and so *solid* that I started to cry.

The ballroom was empty but for me—*one* of me—and the old lady kneeling beside me, and a single

ghost bobbing just behind her, a little ferret-faced mus-
tached man in a bowler hat and a checked waistcoat
that might have been colorful once, but now was gray
checked with gray.

"Beautifully done," said the floater. "You have the
hands of a surgeon."

"The hands are the least of it, Mr. Dellafave, but
you are too kind. Goodness, child, you gave me a
fright. Six of you stranded in the glass. Good thing I
was here to set things right. But I forget my manners.
My name is Sarah Pardee Winchester, widow of the late
William Wirt Winchester, and this is my friend Mr.
Dellafave." She eyed my costume, reached over and
tugged on my ostrich plume. "Too young to be a
showgirl," she said, "almost."

I shuddered and wiped my nose with the back of my
wonderful old-friend hand and asked: "Am I . . . Are
you . . . Please, is this Heaven or Hell?"

The old lady and the bowler-hatted man both
laughed. His laugh sounded like steam escaping, but
hers was throaty and loud, like a much younger, much
larger woman.

"Opinions differ," the old lady said. "We think of it
simply as California."

She called the place Llanada Villa, which she said was
Spanish for "Flatland House." I had never lived in a
house before the widow took me in, so you might call
Flatland House my introduction to the whole principle
of houses. And what an introduction it was! No house
I've seen since has been a patch on it.

There was the size, to start with. The house covered
six acres. Counting the rooms that had been walled off
and made unreachable except by ghosts, but not
counting the rooms that had been demolished or
merged into larger spaces, the house had a hundred

and fifty rooms, mostly bedrooms, give or take a dozen. "I've slept in only seventy or eighty of them myself," the widow told me, "but that's enough to get the general idea."

Still the place was not finished. Workmen were always in the process of adding rooms, balconies, porches, turrets, whole wings; or in the process of dismantling or renovating what they had built just the month before. The construction had moved far away from the front of the house, where the widow mostly lived, but the distant sounds of saws and hammers and the men's voices calling to one another—"Steady! Steady! Move it just a hair to the right, please, Bill"—could be heard day and night. They worked in shifts around the clock. Once a week the foremen took off their hats and gathered in the carriage entrance for payday. The widow towed from the house a child's wagon full of heavy sacks, each full of enough gold pieces to pay each foreman's workers the equivalent of three dollars a day. The foremen were all beefy men, but even they strained to heft the bags and tote them away. They never complained, though.

"Aren't you afraid?" I asked the widow, that first payday.

"Of what, dear?"

"Of one of those men breaking into the house, and robbing you."

"Oh, Pearl, you are a caution! You don't need to worry about robbers, oh, no. Not in *this* house."

I suppose intruders would have gotten quickly lost, for many parts of the house simply did not make sense. Staircases led to ceilings and stopped. Doorways opened onto brick walls, or onto nothing, not even a balcony, just the outside air. Secret passageways no taller than the widow crisscrossed the house, so that she could pop in and out of sight without warning, as if

she herself were a ghost. The widow told me the front
door had never been opened, never even unlocked,
since its hinges were hung.

I found the outside of the house even more
confusing. If I walked around any corner, I found
arched windows, recessed balconies, turrets and
witch's caps and cupolas with red tile roofs, and miles
of gingerbread trim. If I walked around the next
corner, I found the same thing, only more of it. Many
houses, I'm told, have only four corners to walk
around, but Flatland House had dozens. Looking away
from the house was no help, because no matter what
direction I looked, I saw the same high cypress hedge,
and beyond that, rolling hills of apricot, plum, and
walnut trees stretching to the horizon. I never made it
all the way around the place, but would give up and go
back inside, and where I went inside always seemed to
be the breakfast-room, with the widow knitting in the
wicker chair just where I left her. She always asked,
"Did you have a good trip, dear?"

In all those hundred and fifty rooms was not a
single mirror. Which suited me just fine.

I did get lonely sometimes. Most of the ghosts had
little to say—to the living, anyway—beyond "Lovely
day, isn't it?" The few indoor servants seemed afraid of
me, and none stayed in the house past sundown. The
workmen I was forbidden to speak to at all.

"Do you never have any visitors," I asked the
widow, "other than the workmen, and the ghosts, and
the servants, and me?"

"Goodness, that's enough, wouldn't you say? I
know there are 473 ghosts, not counting the cats, and
Lord only knows how many workmen coming and
going. And don't ever think of yourself as a visitor,
Pearl dear. Consider this your home, for as long as you
wish to stay."

The only ghost willing to spend time with me, other than the cats, was Mr. Dellafave. Three weeks into my stay at Flatland House, during a stroll around the monkey-puzzle tree, I asked him:

"Mr. Dellafave, what did you do before . . . "

His face had the look of someone expecting his feelings to be hurt but game not to let on.

" . . . before you came here," I finished.

"Ah," he said, smiling. "I worked for a bank, in Sacramento. I was a figure man. I added, mostly, and subtracted twice a week, and, on red-letter days, multiplied. Long division was wholly out of my jurisdiction, that was another floor altogether—but make no mistake, I could have done it. I was ready to serve. Had the third floor been swept away by fire or flood, the long division would have proceeded without interruption, for I'd had the training. But the crisis, like most crises, never came. I arrived at the bank every morning at eight. I went across the street to the saloon every day at noon for two eggs and a pickle and a sarsaparilla and the afternoon papers. I left the bank every day at five, and got back to the boarding house for supper at six. Oh, I was a clockwork, I was. 'You can set your watch by Dellafave,' that's what they said at the bank and the saloon and the boarding house and, well, those are the only places they said it, really, because those are the only places where anyone took any notice of me at all. Certainly that streetcar driver did not. He would have rung his bell if he had; it's in their manual. That was a sloppy business all around, frankly, a harsh thing to say but there it is. I know the time had to have been 12:47 precisely, because I walked out of the saloon at 12:46, and the streetcar was not due to pass until 12:49. I was on schedule, but the streetcar was not. I looked up, and there it was, and I flung up my arms—as if that would have helped, flinging up my arms. When I lowered them, I was standing in what I now know as Mrs. Winchester's potting shed. I was never an especially spiritual man, Pearl dear, but I considered myself fairly well-versed on all the major theories of the afterlife . . . none of which quite prepared me for Mrs. Winchester's potting shed. I didn't even bring my newspaper."

"But why—"

He held up a hand, like a serene police officer at an intersection. "I have no idea, Pearl, why I came here. None of us does. And I don't mean to imply that we're unhappy, for it is a pleasant place, and Mrs. Winchester is quite good to us, but our leaving here seems rather out of the question. If I were to pass through that cypress hedge over there, I would find myself entering the grounds through the hedge on the other side. It's the same front to back, or even up and down."

"I guess Mrs. Winchester is the magnet, and you and the others are . . . "

"The filings, yes. The tacks pulled from the carpet. I stand in the tower sometimes—if you can call it standing—and I look over all these rooftops and chimneys, all connected to the same house, and I'm forced to admit that this is more room than I allowed myself in life. If the boarding house were the front door of Llanada Villa, the bank would be at the carriage entrance, and the saloon would be at the third sun porch, the one that's been walled in and gets no sun. Which is such a small fraction of the house, really. And yet the whole house feels such a small part of the Earth, and I find myself wishing that I had ventured a bit farther, when I could."

We walked together in silence—well, I walked, anyway—while I reflected that the owner of the house seemed quite unable to leave it herself. And what about me? Could I leave Flatland House, and were I to leave it, where would I go? Professor Van Der Ast's seemed much farther away than a single continent.

"You'd best get inside, Pearl. The breeze from the bay is quite damp today."

I moved my face toward Mr. Dellafave's cheek, and when he began to blur, I figured I was close enough, and kissed the air.

"Shucks," he said, and dissipated entirely.

I felt no bay breeze, but as I ran back to the house I clutched my shawl more tightly anyway.

The next day, the earthquake struck.

The chandeliers swayed. The organ sighed and moaned. The crystal chittered in the cabinets. One nail worked its way free and rolled across the thrumming floorboards. A rumble welled up, not from below the house, but from above and around the house, as if the sound were pressing in from all sides. The ghosts were in a mad whirl, coursing through the house like a current of smoke overhead, blended and featureless but for the occasional startled face. I lurched along the walls, trying to keep my balance as I sought the exit nearest me, the front door. Once I fell and yelped as my palms touched the hot parquet.

Plaster sifted into my eyes as I stumbled through the entrance hall. I knew my mistake when I saw that massive front door, surely locked, the key long since thrown away or hidden in a far scullery drawer of this lunatic house. If the entire edifice were to shake down and crush me, this slab of swirling dark oak would be the last thing standing, a memorial to Pearl.

The grandfather clock toppled and fell just behind me, with the crash of a hundred heavy bells. I flung myself at the door and wrenched the knob. It turned easily, as if oiled every day, and I pulled the door open with no trouble at all. Suddenly all was silent and still.

A robin sang in the crepe myrtle as the door opened on a lovely spring day. A tall black man in a charcoal tailcoat stood on the porch, top hat in hand, and smiled down at me.

"Good morning," he said. "I was beginning to fear that no one was at home. I hope my knock didn't bring you too dreadfully far. I know this house is harder to cross than the Oklahoma Territory."

"Your knock?" I was too flabbergasted to be polite. "All that was your knock?"

He laughed as he stepped inside, so softly that it was just an open-mouthed smile and a hint of a cough. "That? Oh, my, no. That was just my reputation preceding me. Tell me, pray, might the mistress of the house be at home?"

"Where else would I be, Wheatstraw?" asked the widow, suddenly at my elbow and every hair in place.

"Hello, Winchester," the visitor said.

They looked at each other without moving or speaking. I heard behind me a heaving sound, and a muffled clang. I turned just as the grandfather clock resettled itself in the corner.

Then the widow and the visitor laughed and embraced. She kicked up one foot behind. Her head did not reach his chin.

"Pearl," the widow said, "this is Mr. Petey Wheatstraw."

"Pet-ER," he corrected, with a little bow.

"Mr. Wheatstraw," the widow continued, "is a rogue. My goodness," she added, as if something had just occurred to her. "How did you get in?"

We all looked at the front door. It was closed again, its bolts thrown, its hinges caked with rust. No force short of dynamite could have opened it.

The man Wheatstraw nodded toward me.

"Well, I'll be," the widow said. "She makes as free

with my house as a termite, this one does. Well, you haven't come to see me, anyway, you old good-for-nothing," she said, swatting him as she bustled past. "It's a half-hour early, but you might as well join us for tea."

Wheatstraw offered me an arm and winked. This was far too fresh for my taste, but I was too shaken by the not-quite-earthquake to care. As I took hold of his arm (oak-strong beneath the finery), I felt my muscles complain, as if I had done hard work. I looked over my shoulder at the seized-up door as Wheatstraw swept me down the hallway.

"I heard you were here," Wheatstraw said.

"How?"

"Oh, you're a loud one, Miss Big Feet, clomp clomp clomp." He winked again. "Or is that just your reputation I heard?"

Something was wrong with the corridor, something I couldn't quite put my finger on. Then I realized that it was empty. Everything in the house was back to normal—paintings returned to their nails, plaster returned to the walls—except the ghosts, which were nowhere to be seen. I was so used to them flitting past me and over me and through me, even gliding through my bedroom wall and then retreating with apologies, like someone who didn't realize the train compartment was occupied, that their presence hardly bothered me at all. Their absence gave me a shiver.

"They'll be back after I'm gone," Wheatstraw said.

I laughed. "You telling me you scared off the haints? I mean, are you saying that Mrs. Winchester's, uh, guests don't like you?"

"I'm sure they have nothing against me personally. How could they? Once you get to know me, I'm really a fine fellow, full of learning and grace and wit, a decent dancer, a welcome partner at whist. I never snort when I laugh or drag my shirtsleeves in the soup. No, it must be my business affiliation. The company I represent. The Old Concern. My father-in-law's firm, actually, and my inheriting is out of the question. But these days we all must work for somebody, mustn't we?"

I thought of Sally Ann the Circassian Princess, and of Farethewell's hand on mine. "True enough," I said.

Wheatstraw set down his teacup and saucer with a clatter and said, "Well, enough chitchat. It's question time."

"Oh, Petey," the widow said. "Must you? We were having such a nice visit. Surely that can wait till later."

"I am in no hurry whatsoever, Winchester, but my father-in-law is another story. You might say that impatience rather defines my father-in-law. It is the cause of his, uh, present career. Pearl, please pay close attention."

I said nothing, having just shoved another chocolate cookie lengthwise into my mouth. I never quite realized that I was always a little hungry at Professor Van Der Ast's, until I came to Flatland House.

Wheatstraw rummaged in the inside pocket of his jacket and produced an atomizer. He opened his mouth and sprayed the back of his throat. "La la la la la," he said. "La la la la laaaaa. Pitch-perfect, as ever. Winchester?" He offered her the atomizer. "Don't, then. Now: Pearl."

He began to sing, in a lovely baritone:

Oh, you must answer my questions nine
Sing ninety-nine and ninety
Or you're not God's, you're one of mine
And you are the weaver's bonny.

"Now, Pearl, when I say, 'one of mine,' please understand that I speak not for myself but for the firm that I represent."

"And when you say 'God,' " I said, speaking carefully, "you speak of the firm that you do *not* represent."

"In a clamshell, yes. Now, if you're quite done interrupting—"

"I didn't interrupt!" I interrupted. "You interrupted yourself."

He slapped the table. "The idea! As if a speaker could interrupt himself. Why, you might as well say that a river could ford itself, or a fence jump itself."

"Or a bore bore himself," the widow said.

"You're not helping," Wheatstraw said.

"And I'm not the weaver's bonny," I said, becoming peevish now, "whatever a weaver's bonny is."

"Well," Wheatstraw said, "a weaver is a maker of cloth, such as aprons are made with, and gags, and a bonny is a beauty, a lovely creature, a precious thing."

"I don't know any weavers," I said, "except my friend Sally Ann taught me to sew a button. And I'm not beautiful, or lovely, or precious."

"Granted, that does seem a stretch at the moment," Wheatstraw said. "But we mustn't always take things so literally. When you say, 'I'm a silly goose,' you don't mean you expect to be plucked and roasted, and when you say, 'I'm fit to be tied,' you aren't asking to be roped and trussed, and when you say, 'Well, I'm damned,' you don't mean . . ."

His voice trailed off. A chill crept into the room. The sunlight through the bay window dimmed, as if a cloud were passing.

". . . anything, really," Wheatstraw continued, and he smiled as the sun came out. "So, for purposes of this song, *if no other,* who are you?"

I folded my arms and forced my shoulders as far as I could into the padding of the loveseat and glared at

Wheatstraw, determined to frown down his oh-so-satisfied smile.

"I'm the weaver's bonny," I mumbled.

Am not, I thought.

"Fine and dandy," Wheatstraw said. "Now, where was I? I'll have to go back to Genesis, as Meemaw would say." He cleared his throat.

> *Oh you must answer my questions nine*
> *Sing ninety-nine and ninety*
> *Or you're not God's, you're one of mine*
> *And you are the weaver's bonny.*

Ninety-nine and ninety *what?*, I wondered, but I kept my mouth shut.

> *What is whiter than the milk?*
> *Sing ninety-nine and ninety*
> *And what is softer than the silk?*
> *Oh you are the weaver's bonny*
> *What is higher than a tree?*
> *Sing ninety-nine and ninety*
> *And what is deeper than the sea?*
> *Oh you are the weaver's bonny*
> *What is louder than a horn?*
> *Sing ninety-nine and ninety*
> *And what is sharper than a thorn?*
> *Oh you are the weaver's bonny*
> *What's more innocent than a lamb?*
> *Sing ninety-nine and ninety*
> *And what is meaner than womankind?*
> *Oh you are the weaver's bonny*

It was a short song, but it seemed to last a long time; as I sat there determined to resist, to be defiant and unamused, I realized I wasn't so much listening to it as being surrounded by it, filled by it, submerged in it. I was both sleepy and alert, and the pattern in the parquet floor was full of faces, and the loveseat pushed back and kneaded my shoulders, and the laces of my high-topped shoes led into the darkness like tracks in the Lookout Mountain tunnel. I could not vouch for Wheatstraw being a decent dancer as he claimed (though I suspected *decent* was hardly the word), but the man sure could sing. And somewhere in the second hour of the song (surely, I think now upon telling this, some lines were repeated, or extended, or elaborated upon), Wheatstraw's voice was joined by a woman's, his voice and hers twined together like fine rope. That voice was the widow Winchester's: *And you are the weaver's bonny.*

I sucked air and sat up as if startled from a dream, but felt less alert than a second before. The song was over. The widow pretended to gather up the tea things, and Wheatstraw pretended to study his fingernails.

"That part about womankind is insulting," the widow said.

"I didn't write it," he said. "The folk wrote it."

"Menfolk," she said.

"Eight," I said, and only after I said it did I realize why I had said it.

"Hm?" Wheatstraw asked, without looking up.

The widow held a tipped teacup, looking at nothing, as a thread of tea like a spider's descended to the saucer.

"Eight," I repeated. "Milk, silk, two; tree, sea, four; horn, thorn, six; lamb, kind, eight." I sang, rather than spoke, in surprise at my voice: "*Oh, you must answer my questions nine* . . . It ain't questions nine, it's questions eight. What's the ninth question?"

Wheatstraw looked at the widow, and the widow looked at Wheatstraw. "Maybe that's it," Wheatstraw murmured. " 'What's the ninth question,' maybe that's the ninth question."

"No," I said.

"Why no?" Wheatstraw cooed.

"Because," I said. "Because that would be stupid."

Wheatstraw laughed and slapped his thigh with his hat. The widow slammed two plates together.

"Indeed it would be," she snapped. "Petey, take these plates. Take them, I say. Do a lick of work for once in your lazy son-in-law of a life."

"So what's the ninth question?" I asked again.

"That's for you to tell us," Wheatstraw said.

"To tell *you*, you mean," the widow said, driving him from the room beneath a stack of dishes. "Don't drag *me* into this."

"Oh, excuse me, Lady Astor, whose house is it? The girl's a wizard, Sarah, and you can't stow a wizard in the china-cupboard like a play-pretty, like one of your ghosts, like Mr. Dellafave in there," he shouted as he passed a china-cupboard. Its door trembled, and someone inside squeaked.

"You know the rules," Wheatstraw continued as we all entered the kitchen in a clump. He dumped the dishes into the sink with a crash and whirled to face us. I tried to hide behind the widow, though she was a foot shorter. Wheatstraw pointed at her like he wanted to poke a hole in the air. His gentleman's fingernail was now long and ragged, with something crusted beneath, and his eyes were red as a drunkard's. "Just look at her," he said. "Just stand near her, for pity's sake! She's stoked with magic like a furnace with coal, and the wide world is full of matches. She's in a different world now, and she has got to learn." He turned to me. "Tea party's over, my dear. From now on, it's test after test, and you have your first assignment, your first nine questions."

"Eight," I said.

He threw back his head and roared like a bull. I clapped my hands over my ears and shrieked. Our dresses billowed as if in a strong wind. The cords stood out on Wheatstraw's neck. His hot breath filled the room. Then he closed his mouth, and the roar was gone. "All righty then," he said. "Eight it is. You owe the Old Concern eight answers—and one question." He jammed his hat two-handed onto his head down to his eyebrows, then sprang into the sink. He crouched there, winked, and vanished down the drain with a gurgle. His hat dropped to the porcelain and wobbled in place until it, too, was snatched into the depths. Wheatstraw's voice chuckled through the pipes, and ghosts flowed keening from the faucet.

"Showoff," the widow said. She squeezed my arm. "He's a liar, too. Absolutely terrible at whist."

"When he said I had to answer those questions, was that a lie, too?"

"Ah, no, that part was true enough."

"And the part about me being . . . a wizard?"

The widow smiled. "Truest of all," she said.

"All wizards have much the same talents," said the widow, as she washed the unbroken dishes and I dried them, "just as all carpenters, all painters, all landscapers do. But each wizard also has a specialty, some talent she is especially good at. Some work at the craft for decades before realizing what their specialty is. Some realize what it was only in hindsight, only on their deathbeds, if they ever realize it at all. But other wizards have their talents handed to them, almost from birth, the way we all are granted the earth and the sky.

"I myself was no taller than a turnip when I realized that many of the little friends I played with every day, in the attic and beneath the grape arbor and in the bottom of the garden, were children that others could not see, and I realized, too, that my parents did not like for me to speak of them, to say, 'Oh, Papa, how funny! Little Merry just passed through your waistcoat, as you were stirring your tea.' How cross he became that day."

She wrung dry a dishcloth in her tiny fists. I blew soap bubbles from my palm into the face of a sleeping tabby as it floated past. The bubbles bobbed through the cat, or was it the other way around? The widow had been scrubbing dishes with pumice, so the bubbles were reddish in color and seemed more substantial than the wholly transparent cat. Then the bubbles vanished, and the tabby remained.

The widow continued: "And so I began keeping my talent secret, and once you start keeping your talents secret, why, you're well along the path of the wizard."

"My talents are a secret even from me," I said.

"There now, you see how wrong you can be?" said the widow. She popped my shoulder with the dish-towel. "You play with dead cats. You converse with all my boarders. You unbind the front door and then bind it again without half trying. You come here from Tennessee in a single step, as if the world were a map you could fold. My goodness, that's a step even Paul Bunyan couldn't take, and Paul is a big, big man." After a moment's reverie, she shook her head and with a great splash yanked free the plug. "Well, that's done!" she cried over the rush of the emptying sink. "May it all go down Wheatstraw's gullet." She stood on tiptoe and kissed my cheek. Her kiss was quick, dry, and powdery, like the dab of a cotton swab. "Never you fret, child," she said, taking my arm and leading me down the steps into the garden. "You've got talent to burn, as Mr. Winchester would have said. And now that you've begun to focus, well, you'll tumble across a specialty or three very soon, I daresay."

"Mr. Wheatstraw said I'm in a different world now."

The widow snorted. "Different world, indeed! You can't change worlds like garters, my dear. This is the same world you were born into, the same world you are stuck with, all the days of your life. Never forget that. But the older you get, and the more traveling you do, why, the more of this world you inevitably will see—and inevitably be *able* to see, I daresay."

"Because I walked through the diorama, you mean?"

"That was a powerful bit of traveling, indeed it was. Doubtless it broadened your mind a bit. Who knows? A few weeks ago you might have been as ignorant of the spirit world as my carpenters, might have looked right through Mr. Dellafave without even seeing him, much less being able to converse with him. And what a shame that would have been," she said, not sounding quite convinced.

I considered telling her that Mr. Dellafave was in love with her, but decided she knew that already. Instead, I finally dared to ask a question.

"Mrs. Winchester. In all these years since Mr. Winchester died, has he ever, well . . . visited?"

"Ah, that's sweet of you to ask, child," said the widow, with a sniff and a toss of her head. "No, not yet, though early on I looked for him and listened for him, by day and by night. Especially by night. I confess I even hired a medium or two to conduct a séance—for those were all the rage, a few years ago." She waved absently as we passed a headless brakeman, who raised his lantern to her. "A phantom herd of buffalo might have stampeded through the parlor without those frauds noticing. And the mess! We mopped up ectoplasm for days." She leaned against the trunk of an English yew and stared, not unhappily, into the sky. "I finally concluded that Mr. Winchester—like my Mama and Papa, and my old nurse, and my little dog, Zip, that I had when we were first wed, and my poor child Annie—that I will be reunited with none of them until I'm as insubstantial as that lady in the pond over there."

In silence, we watched the woman as she rose from the water, stood a few moments on the surface, then sank out of sight amid the lily pads, her face unreadable. Her dress was from an earlier time. Where had all her lovers got to, I wondered, and what did she remember of them?

"I'll tell you the puzzle that worries me," the widow Winchester abruptly said, "and it's not Mr. Winchester, and it's not where all the dogs go. What worries me is that in all these years of receiving the dear departed in my home, I have met not one—not one—who was, in life, a wizard."

"Sarah!" the man yelled. "Sarah!"

The widow and I ran to the bay window in the parlor. I knew that voice.

A two-horse wagon had pulled up in front of the house, and a big man in a black suit and black hat was climbing out of it. It was a warm fall day, but his hat and shoulders were dusted with snow, and ice clung to the spokes of the wheels. The wagon was faded blue and covered with painted stars and crescent moons. The side read:

WIZARD OF THE BLUE RIDGE
MAGICIAN OF THE OLD SOUTH
PURVEYOR OF MAGIC AND MIRTH

He removed his hat and called again: "Sarah! I got him! I finally got him!"

It was Mr. Farethewell.

By the time we reached the front door—which the widow opened with a wave of her hand—a horse and rider had galloped up. It was Petey Wheatstraw, dressed like a fox hunter in red coat, white breeches and high boots.

"Winchester, do something!" he yelled as he dismounted. "Farethewell's gone crazy."

"Crazy, nothing," Farethewell said. "He's trapped like a bug in a jar."

"Who is?" the widow asked.

"Old Scratch himself!" Farethewell replied. "Here's your Devil."

He went to the back of the wagon and began dragging out something heavy, something we couldn't yet see.

The widow looked to Wheatstraw. "Is this true?"

He threw up his hands. "Who knows? No one's seen the Old Man in days."

Farethewell dragged the whatever-it-was a little closer to the end of the wagon, and an old boot thumped to the gravel. I stepped closer, out of the shadow of the porch.

"Well, hello, Little Britches," said Farethewell. "Sarah told me you were here. So you decided to pull some magic after all?" He pulled a flask from his jacket, looked at it, then laughed and flung it across the yard. It landed in the rosebushes with a clank.

"She told you?" I cried. I got behind a pillar. Just the sight of Farethewell made me feel flushed and angry. "You *know* each other?"

"Well, he *is* a wizard," Wheatstraw said.

Farethewell stood there, hands on hips, and looked pleased with himself. The widow peered into the wagon.

"Where is he? Is that his boot?"

Farethewell snatched her up and hugged her and spun her around. "That ain't his boot. That's him! He's in the boot! Come look, Little Britches!"

"Don't you call me that," I yelled, but I stepped off the porch anyway. Farethewell took hold of the boot with both rough hands and walked backward, hunched over, dragging the boot toward the house as if he dragged a big man's corpse. The boot tore a rut in the gravel.

"Couldn't be," Wheatstraw said.

"It is!" Farethewell said.

"Blasphemy," the widow said.

"Bad for business, anyway," Wheatstraw said.

Farethewell let go of the boot and stepped back, gasping, rubbing the small of his back with his hands. "I run him down in the Sierras," he said. "He'd a got away from me, if he had just let go of that chicken. Seven days and seven nights we fought up and down them slopes. The avalanches made all the papers. I've had this boot since Appomattox. It's my teacher's boot, hexed with his magic and with his blood. On our eighth day of wrestling, I got this jammed down over the Devil's head, and just kept on jamming till he was all inside, and now the Devil will pay!"

We all gathered around the boot.

"It's empty," the widow said.

Wheatstraw cackled. "Sure is. Farethewell, you are crazier than a moonstruck rat."

I did not laugh. Peering out through the laces of the boot was a face. The two blue eyes got wider when they saw me. The face moved back a little, so that I could see more of it.

It was Farethewell in the boot.

I looked over my shoulder. Yes, big Farethewell stood behind me, grinning. But the tiny man in the boot was Farethewell also, wearing a robe and pointed hat, as I last had seen him at Professor Van Der Ast's.

The little Farethewell hugged himself as if he were cold and began silently to cry.

"What's the matter, child?" the widow asked. I shrugged off her little spindly hand of comfort. It was like twitching free of a spider.

"What you see in there?" Wheatstraw asked.

"Tell them, Little Britches!"

"Don't take on so, dear. What could you possibly see? This has nothing to do with you."

"Maybe it does," said Farethewell. "Who you see in there, girl? What's this varmint to you?"

"What's his name this time?" Wheatstraw asked. "The Old Man answers to more names than the Sears and Roebuck catalog."

I didn't answer. Little Farethewell was backing up, pressing himself flat against the heel of that old floppy boot. I stepped forward to see him better, and he shook so, the whole boot trembled.

"He's scared," I said, more loud and fierce than I meant to sound, for in fact this scared me worse than anything—not that I was faced with a second Farethewell the size of a kewpie you could win with a ball toss, but that I was more fearsome to him than his larger self was. What kind of booger did he take me for? This scared me but made me mad, too. I snarled and made my fingers into claws like Boola the Panther Boy and lunged.

"Yah!"

Little Farethewell twitched so hard the boot fell over. The sole was so worn you could see through it nearly, and a gummy spot at the toe treasured a cigarette butt and a tangle of hair.

"He's ours," big Farethewell hissed into my ear. "Whatever face he's showing you, girl, whoever he once was to you, he is ours now and no mistake. All the way here, off the slopes and down the river and through the groves, it was all I could do to keep him booted and not kicking the boards out of the wagon, but now you got him broken like a pony. And a girl loves a pony. He's mine and yours together now."

"Don't listen," the widow said.

"Sarah. You forgetting what we got in there? You forgetting Gettysburg, Cold Harbor, Petersburg? The tuberculosis that carried off your William, the marasmus that stole Annie from the cradle? Don't you care what this *thing* has done to the world, what it still could do? Ain't you learned nothing?"

"Some things ain't fit to be learned," the widow said, "and some wizards breathing God's free air are cooped up worse than this creature is. Petey, tell him. You've seen worse than Cold Harbor, worse any of us."

Wheatstraw did not answer at once. He did not seem to be listening. He was in the act of dusting a metal bench with his handkerchief. He slowly refolded the handkerchief, then flicked off one last spot of dust and sighed and settled himself on the bench, perched on the edge as if delicacy alone could keep his breeches away from the iron. The moment he sat, a transparent cat jumped onto his lap and settled itself. Wheatstraw scratched between its ears as it sank out of sight, purring, until Wheatstraw was scratching only his leg.

"What I see," Wheatstraw finally said, "is that whatever half-dead thing you dragged in, Farethewell, it ain't yours anymore. It's Pearl's."

"Pearl's!" said Farethewell and the widow, together.

"Pearl's," Wheatstraw repeated. "Otherwise she couldn't see it, could she? So it's hers to do with as she will. And there ain't no need in y'all looking like you just sucked down the same oyster. Folks making up their own minds—why, that's the basic principle of the Old Concern, the foundation of our industry. And besides," he added, as he leaned back and tipped his felt hat over his eyes and crossed his legs at the ankles, "she's done made it up anyhow."

When he said that, I realized that I had.

"No," Farethewell said.

I picked up the boot. It was no heavier for me than a dead foot. The thought made me shiver.

"Wheatstraw," said Farethewell. "What have you done to me, you wretch? I can't move."

"It ain't my doing."

"Nor mine," said the widow.

"Pearl. Listen to me."

I held up the boot and looked at it, eye to eyelet. The trembling shape no longer looked much like Farethewell—more like a bad memory of him, or a bad likeness of him, or just a stain on a canvas that put you in mind of him, if you squinted just right. To whatever it was, I said, "Go home."

Then I swung the boot three times over my head and let it fly.

"*Noooo!*" Farethewell yelled.

The boot sailed over the fence and past the point where it ought to have fallen back to earth and kept on going, a tumbling black dot against the pale sky like a star in reverse, until what I thought was the boot was just a floater darting across my eye. I blinked it away, and the boot was gone.

Mr. Farethewell stared into the sky, his jaw working. A tear slid down his cheek. He began to moan.

"Whoo! Don't reckon we need wait supper on him tonight," Wheatstraw said.

"I knew it," the widow said. She snapped her fingers in Wheatstraw's face. "I knew it the moment she and her fetches stepped out of the ballroom window. Her arrival was foretold by the spirits."

"Foretold by the spirits, my eye," Wheatstraw said. "She's a wizard, not the 3:50 to Los Angeles."

Farethewell's moan became a howl.

I suddenly felt dizzy and sick and my breath was gone, like something had hit me in the gut. I tried to run, without quite knowing why, but Farethewell already had lunged across the distance between us. He seized my shoulders, shook me like a rag, howled into my face.

"I'm sorry!" I cried. "I had to do it. I had to!"

He hit me then, and I fell to the grass, sobbing. I waited for him to hit me again, to kill me. Instead the widow and Wheatstraw were kneeling beside me, stroking my hair and murmuring words I did not understand. Farethewell was walking jerkily across the yard, like a scarecrow would walk. He fell to his knees in the rosebushes and scrabbled in the dirt for his flask, the thorns tearing his face.

I stayed in bed a few days, snug beneath layers of goosedown. The widow left the room only to fetch and carry for me. Mr. Dellafave settled into a corner of the ceiling and never left the room at all.

When she felt I was able, the widow showed me the note Mr. Farethewell had left.

> *I never should have hit you, Little Britches, and I am sorry for it, but you never should have got between me and the Devil. Many women and children in Virginia got between the armies and died. Hear me. Farethewell.*

"His fist didn't hurt you," the widow said.

"I know," I said. "Doing what I did with the boot, that's what hurt me. I need to find out what I did, and how to do it right. Mrs. Winchester?"

"Yes, child."

"When I am better, I believe I shall take a trip."

"Where, child?"

"All over," I said. "It was Mr. Dellafave's idea, in a way. I need to see some of the other things in the diorama, and I need to meet some other wizards. As many as I can. I have a lot to learn from all of them."

She pulled a handkerchief out of her sleeve and daubed her eyes. "I can't go with you," she said.

"But I'll always come back," I said. "And you mustn't worry about me. I won't be alone."

I considered walking back through the ballroom window, but I had been there before. I ran my finger over the pebbled face of the stained-glass girl to say goodbye.

When I walked out the front gate of Flatland House, toting an overstuffed carpetbag, I half-expected to find myself walking in at the back, like Mr. Dellafave. But no, there were the orchards, and the lane leading over the hill to San Jose, and Petey Wheatstraw sitting cross-legged on a tall stump like a Hindu fakir.

I waved. He waved, and jumped down. He was dressed like a vagabond, in rough cloth breeches and a coarse shirt, and his belongings were tied up in a kerchief on the end of a stick.

"You're a sight," I said.

"In the future," he replied, "they'll call it *slumming*. Which way?"

"That way, to the top of the hill, and then sideways."

We set off.

"Also, Mr. Wheatstraw, I have some answers for you."

"Are you prepared to sing them? Anything worth saying is worth singing."

"I am."

"You're so agreeable this morning. It can't last." He sang:

Oh you must answer my questions nine
Sing ninety-nine and ninety
Or you're not God's, you're one of mine
And you are the weaver's bonny

I sang back:

Snow is whiter than the milk
Sing ninety-nine and ninety
And down is softer than the silk
And I am the weaver's bonny.
Heaven's higher than a tree
Sing ninety-nine and ninety
And Hell is deeper than the sea
And I am the weaver's bonny
Thunder's louder than a horn
Sing ninety-nine and ninety
And death is sharper than a thorn
And I am the weaver's bonny
A babe's more innocent than a lamb
Sing ninety-nine and ninety
And the Devil is meaner than womankind
—"*And MAN kind too,*" I said, interrupting myself—
And I am the weaver's bonny.

Wheatstraw gave me a half-mocking salute and sang:

> *You have answered my questions nine*
> *Sing ninety-nine and ninety*
> *And you are God's, you're none of mine*
> *And you are the weaver's bonny.*

Then I asked him the ninth question, and he agreed that it was the right question to ask, so right that he did not know the answer, and together we reached the top of the hill and walked sideways, right off the edge of the world.

Just this year I made it back to Chattanooga. The town was so changed I hardly recognized it, except for the bend in the river and the tracks through the tunnel and Lookout Mountain over everything.

The new bridge is still hanging on, though it's no longer new and carries no proper traffic anymore, just visitors who stroll along it and admire the view and take photographs. Can you call them photographs anymore? They need no plates and no paper, and you hardly have to stand still any time to make one.

At the end of my visit I spent a good hour on the bridge, looking at the river and at the people, and enjoying walking my home city on older, stronger legs and seeing it with better eyes and feeling more myself than I had as a girl—though I'm still not as old-looking as you'd expect, thanks to my travels and the talents I've picked up along the way.

How you'd *expect* me to look at my age, I reckon, is *dead*, but I am not that, not by a long shot.

I wondered how many of these young-old people creeping along with the help of canes, and candy-faced children ripping and roaring past me, and men and women rushing along in short pants, my goodness, their stuck-out elbows going up and down like pistons—how many of them dreamed of the world that

I knew. But what had I known myself of the invisible country all around, before I passed into the Infernal Regions?

Up ahead, sitting on one of the benches along the bridge, was a girl who put me in mind of my old Chattanooga friend Sally Ann Rummage, with her red hair and her long neck and her high forehead like a thinker. Probably about sixteen, this girl was, though it's hard to tell; they stay younger so much longer now, thank goodness. She didn't look very happy to be sixteen, or to be anything. A boy was standing over her, with one big foot on the bench like he was planting a flag, and he was pointing his finger in her face like Petey Wheatstraw was known to do, and his other hand was twisting her pretty brown jacket and twisting her shoulder, too, inside it, and she looked cried-out and miserable. He was telling her about herself, or presuming to, and when he glanced my way—no more seeing me than he would a post or a bird or a food wrapper blowing past—I saw that he was Farethewell. He was high-cheeked and eighteen and muscled, where Farethewell was old and jowly, and had a sharp nose unlike Farethewell, and had nothing of Farethewell's shape or face or complexion, but I recognized him just the same. I would recognize Farethewell anywhere.

I stood behind him, looking at her, until she looked up and met my gaze. This is a good trick, and one that even non-wizards can accomplish.

The boy said to me something foul that I will not lower myself to repeat, and I said, "Hush," and he hushed. Of all the talents I've learned since I left Flatland House, that may be the handiest.

The girl frowned, puzzled, her arms crossed tight to hold herself in like a girl I once knew in a California parlor long ago. I smiled at her and put in her head the Devil's ninth question:

Who am I?

And while I was in there, in a thousand places, I strewed an answer like mustard seeds: *I am the weaver's bonny.*

Then I walked on down the bridge. The sun was low, the breeze was sharp, and a mist was forming at the river bend, a mist only I could see. The mist thickened and began to swirl. The surface of the water roiled. In the center of the oncoming cloud, twin smokestacks cleaved the water, then the wheelhouse, then the upper deck. The entire riverboat surfaced, water sluicing down the bulkheads, paddlewheel churning. I could read the boat's bright red markings. It was the Sultana, which blew up in 1865 just north of Memphis, at the islands called the Hen and Chickens, with the loss of 1,700 men. And my, did she look grand!

At the head of the steps to the riverfront, I looked back—for wizards always look back. Have I not been looking back since I began this story, and have you not been looking back with me, to learn the ways of a wizard? I saw the girl striding away from the boy, head held high. He just stood there, like one of Professor Van Der Ast's blockheads with a railroad spike up his nose. The girl whirled once, to shout something at him. The wind snatched away all but one word: "—ever!" Then she kept on walking. The mustard was beginning to sprout. I laughed as loudly as the widow Winchester, and I ran down the slick steps to the river, as giddy as a girl of ninety-nine and ninety.

HEARTSTRUNG

———

Rachel Swirsky

One, two, three, the needle swoops.

Pamela squirms as the needle cuts into her sensitive heart tissue. "It hurts!"

"Shh," the seamstress says. "It's almost done, honey. Just a few more stitches and you'll be like mommy."

The seamstress bends forward as she presses her needle into her daughter's heart for another stitch, squinting to make sure she sews tight and even. As she pulls the thread taut, she realizes this stitch marks the midpoint—she's now halfway finished sewing Pamela's heart onto her sleeve.

Just yesterday, Pamela's heart lay locked beneath her ribs like a treasure. Then her daddy decided it was time for her to grow up, and now Pamela's heart lies red against the cuff of her pale blue sweater, bright as a cardinal in the summer sky. When the seamstress finishes sewing it on, Pamela will become a woman.

Right now, though, she's just a little girl. The seamstress tries to distract her. "Aren't you excited about the ceremony?"

"Will Beth be there?" asks Pamela. She's asked this question several times in the past few days. The seamstress plays along anyway.

"Beth will be there and so will Uncle Jake and Aunt Mattie," she says. "Everyone's coming for you.

So you have to be good now so you won't disappoint them."

Pamela nods grudgingly. The vinyl chair she's standing on creaks underfoot. The seamstress puts her hand on the back of the chair to keep it from sliding across the linoleum.

"Good girl," she says, slipping her hand underneath the cuff as she sews to make sure that none of the stitches go too deep and prick Pamela's wrist. As the needle goes in, she sees Pamela wince anyway. "Remember how lovely Beth looked after she had it done? Remember when Uncle Jake slapped her across the face at her ceremony and her smile lit up like a light bulb and everyone clapped?"

"Will everyone clap for me?"

"Of course they will, if you just stand still."

Mid-stitch, the needle snaps in two. The seamstress glances at the broken pieces in her palm, then tips them into her apron pocket. As she fumbles for a replacement needle, the broken tip catches underneath the heart on her own sleeve, and the seamstress pauses for a moment to shake it loose.

Rubbing her wet eye with a closed fist, Pamela shifts her weight to take advantage of the respite. "It hurts," she repeats. Pamela's fingers dig into her palm. Her knuckles have turned white.

Seeing this, the seamstress feels a twinge of anxiety. The flare of emotion flicks past her eyes, which remain dry, and past her lips, which stay smiling. The anxiety travels through her bloodstream into her arm, down the plaid sleeve of her sweater, and into the heart which is sewn on her own cuff. The heart absorbs it, as it has absorbed all her strong emotions since she was sewn at thirteen. Only a dull, polite echo of the anxiety remains.

The seamstress grabs a dishtowel from the rack

next to the kitchen sink and dabs at her forehead, then begins sewing up around the curves of her daughter's heart. This part is the trickiest, especially since her needle has a tendency to slip in the loose knit weave.

The seamstress knew the cardigan would be difficult to sew on when she picked it, but she bought it anyway because it's both timeless and attractive. It's cut so that the fabric falls close to the skin without revealing too much of the shape underneath, and the knit is a pretty but not intrusive color. It's the kind of sweater that never seems to go out of fashion.

The seamstress is pleased with the choice. The only thing that worries her is the plastic flower-shaped button that clasps the sleeve. Will Pamela think it's childish to have a flower button on her sleeve when she's in high school? When she makes love for the first time? Marries?

The seamstress glances up at Pamela's face. The little girl is surreptitiously trying to wipe a tear away from her eye. Little girls learn to emulate their sewn mothers long before the stitches make it easy, although Pamela hasn't always obeyed the social rules. A memory overlays the scene: Pamela, at age three, screaming "I won't apologize!" after pinching the arm of a boy she saw in line at the movies. When Pamela's father dragged her by the elbow to the boy's parents, she hurled herself onto the sidewalk. "He's a boy! I won't say I'm sorry!" Her expression was wound up in a red tangle. The tears didn't roll; they detonated one by one like bullets. Her determination not to cry now looks similar.

Remorse spins through the seamstress' mind before vanishing into the heart on her sleeve. Nine years old is so young to be sewn, but it's done younger and younger these days. The seamstress and her husband argued about the timing for weeks, late at night after Pamela had gone to sleep. The seamstress had lain restlessly in bed while they argued, buttoning and unbuttoning the mother-of-pearl clasps on her own sweater. Ultimately, she'd had to concede. Did she want Pamela to be the only girl in her class who hadn't had it done?

The needle swoops. Three stitches left. Two stitches left. One stitch left.

The seamstress tugs on the cuff, examining the heart to make sure none of the stitches are tight enough to pinch or loose enough to come undone.

"Are you done?" asks Pamela.

"I am."

Pamela lifts her sleeve up to her face so she can scrutinize her mother's work more closely. Her surreptitious tears have dried and her fingers have relaxed, leaving faint welts on her palms. Her lips lift upward into a gentle smile—the same smile the seamstress sees on her neighbor's faces, in the expression of the butcher's wife and the grocer's sister, in the mirror.

"Do you feel better now?" the seamstress asks.

"Yes," Pamela says. Her polished smile is as lovely as the recess beneath the summit of a cresting wave.

Another memory emerges: the seamstress was picking Pamela up from school a few years ago. She arrived late and Pamela had spent the time doing gymnastics on the school playground. When Pamela's mother pulled into the circular driveway, Pamela was on the very top of the jungle-gym. When she saw her mother, she leapt down and ran across the playground to her mother's car. Her knees were grass-stained and her chin blotted with dirt. Her grin was both too wide and too full of teeth, one of them crooked, another stained with a smear of strawberry jam.

Pamela will never smile like that again.

The seamstress feels the expected surge of regret—but

it doesn't vanish. Surprised, the seamstress pauses to see if it will drain a heartbeat late, but it doesn't. It stings. Her hands freeze on Pamela's shoulders.

"Should I get dressed now?" Pamela asks.

"Why?" The seamstress stares at Pamela uncomprehendingly. She'd forgotten that regret stings. "The ceremony," she reminds herself. Stiffly, she moves her hands back to her sides. "Yes. Go ahead."

Pamela clings to the back of the chair while she slides down to the floor. Her shoes squeak as she leaves the room and disappears up the stairs.

The seamstress pulls a chair out from the kitchen table and sits down. She doesn't know what to do. Should she call her husband? She probes the edges of the heart on her sleeve to see if it's somehow come loose, but the stitches pull tight and strong. She finds a trickle of blood on her cuff and traces it back to a single loose stitch. Feeling underneath, she discovers the tip of the needle she broke earlier. It must have gotten caught there.

She digs it out and stands to get a new needle and a spool of thread. She needs to sew up her heart before she loses too much blood. The trickle down her sleeve becomes a rivulet in her palm and a drop splashes onto the table. Before long, she'll get dizzy, and her hand will be too unsteady to sew. Best to do it now.

Except, she can't remember the last time she felt regret—at least, felt it long enough for it to settle in her body. The feeling makes exhausts her, but it also captivates her, salves a craving she hadn't known she possessed. She pulls out the chair and sits again.

Suddenly, the seamstress remembers the last time she felt regret, but the memory is no longer distinct on its own. It's bound up with another memory. The second one took place two years ago, when Pamela was seven. While playing with a tea set she'd received for her

birthday, Pamela dropped a cup. All of the cups in the
set were painted with roses and embossed with gold
around the rim, but this one had been lithographed with
Pamela's initials as well, so it was Pamela's favorite.

It was a stormy day. Rain pounded on the windows
behind Pamela as she held up the fragments and
demanded that they be put back together again.

"I can't. It's broken," said the seamstress.

"I broke it!" wailed Pamela, pushing the two pieces
together. She was thinking, no doubt, of the future tea
parties that would be ruined by having only three cups
for four saucers, but Pamela's distress reminded the
seamstress of her own childhood when she'd once left a
little shovel and pail on the beach where they were
washed away by the tide. She'd felt as though she'd
betrayed them; she'd made them lost and lonely, and
how would they ever forgive her?

The seamstress lifted her daughter onto her hip and
walked over to the trash so that Pamela could drop the
pieces of the cup into the bin. She held up Pamela's
hands and examined them to make sure there were no
cuts and when she was sure there weren't, she set
Pamela down and fetched a broom and dustpan to
clean up the rest of the fragments.

"It's okay," the seamstress assured her daughter,
"The teacup broke because there was something
trapped inside. When the glass was made, a tiny air
spirit that flies in the wind crawled into the big oven
where they were cooking the sand. 'What's this?'
thought the air spirit, and she fell asleep in the oven.
When she woke up, she was baked into the teacup.
She's been waiting for someone to let her out."

The seamstress didn't know where she'd found that
idea; she was only following her fancy. Pamela looked
up at her with eyes still half-full of tears. The little girl's
expression was skeptical.

"It's true," the seamstress insisted. "Listen. Can you hear that?"

They listened. Outside, the rain swept droves of leaves onto the deck.

"That's the air spirit playing in the wind. She's so happy to be free that she's knocking on all the branches."

Pamela chewed on a strand of her hair thoughtfully before nodding. "Oh," she said, and went back to playing with the tea set.

The next day, all the cabinets in the kitchen were open and the floor was covered in glass. "I wanted to make sure there were no more air spirits!" Pamela said when her father threatened to spank her. "What have you been telling the child?" the seamstress' husband demanded.

So the seamstress had to explain to Pamela how sometimes stories aren't really true outside, they just feel true inside, and the family bought a new set of dinner dishes.

Pamela's footsteps fall heavily on the stairs. The seamstress pulls her chair back, not wanting to be discovered brooding. Pamela has dressed herself all askew: skirt hitched into her tights, hair tumbling out of her self-made bun.

"How do I look?" Pamela asks, spinning on her heel.

"Beautiful," says the seamstress. "Just let me touch you up."

Pamela's eyes light on the blood spilling down her mother's hand. "Mom!"

"It's all right, honey," the seamstress says, watching her daughter's alarm drain out of her eyes and into her sleeve. "I cut myself while I was making dinner. I'll take care of it."

She wraps her arm in a dishtowel and sets about

straightening her daughter's clothes and pinning up her curls. Wearily, she considers what will happen at the ceremony. She pictures her husband slapping Pamela across the face, and Pamela still smiling, the same bland, perfect smile that all the women wear, and suddenly she can't imagine going.

She smoothes the shoulders of Pamela's dress. "Go back upstairs and wait for your father to come home, honey. He'll take you to the ceremony. I'm not going."

Pamela frowns. "But Aunt Mattie will be there and you bought a new dress and everything."

"I know, but I'm not going."

The seamstress braces herself for a temper tantrum, but there isn't one. A tangle of anger and confusion crosses Pamela's face, then her heart pumps and it drains. Her lips curve upward into a placid smile. Without another word, she turns toward the stairs.

"You know you can talk to me," the seamstress says, haltingly, "If there's anything you want to talk about."

"Like what?"

The seamstress tries to foment her regret into words. They fail to come. "Just . . . things."

"Okay, mom." Without a pause, Pamela waves and leaves. The seamstress chuckles shallowly and feels the heart on her sleeve contract like a clenched fist.

She sinks back into her seat and thuds her elbows onto the table, bowing her head into the bowl of her hands. The heart on her cuff has swollen, red and round as a pomegranate.

With regret heavy in her blood, the seamstress realizes so many things she should have done. She should have told her husband no and spared Pamela for a few more years, even though she knows the little girl would have hated her for not letting her "grow up" like her peers. She should have run away with Pamela into the woods and caught trout bare-handed and built a hut out of sticks. But now it's too late: there's no way to bring Pamela's emotions back without cutting her loose from her heart and starving her body of blood.

A brief fantasy enters the seamstress' mind like a hallucination: she imagines snatching the heart off her sleeve. In her head, the stitches rip free with an immense roar. She imagines slicing open her chest cavity and using the bathroom mirror as a guide while she reattaches her heart to the veins and arteries that have fluttered loose all these years. She knows she would bleed to death long before she could even get to the bathroom.

It's then that the seamstress realizes the end of the air spirit's story. After so long baked in glass, the little thing could never have flown away. When she tried, she would have discovered that her feathers were brittle and broken.

The seamstress listens to the traffic outside. Her husband will be home soon. She feels light-headed. She doesn't know how to judge how much blood she's lost. It looks like a lot, but how much more blood does her body contain? If her husband comes home in time, he might try to rush her to the hospital and save her life, but she's tired of being baked into glass.

Her fingers converge at her throat and unclasp the long row of buttons that line the front of her sweater. She parts the cloth around her neck and pulls it open to her rib cage, her belly, her waist. She pushes the sleeves away from her shoulders. Against pale skin that hasn't been bare for over twenty years, the lukewarm air of the kitchen is shocking, like a swab of alcohol applied to a wound.

Carefully, the seamstress pulls her arm out of the right sleeve. Her heart throbs on the left one, just above the neatly folded cuff. Then the seamstress slides her arm out of that sleeve too. Her elbow slips free, her wrist, her knuckles. The cloth is slack between her fingers. She drops it. Her heart sinks to the floor.

As her blood stagnates in her veins, emotions waft into her brain like mosquitoes rising from a still pool. Each faint tinge feels strong in the body long denied. Fear and desire undulate through her brain, unpleasant and fascinating before she passes out and they slide into oblivion.

In a few minutes, Pamela will hear her father pulling into the driveway and scamper down the stairs in her fancy dress, and yes, she will be the one to find the body. When she sees her mother slumped over the table-top like a statue, she'll feel only a twinge of grief. The emotion will flare and drain away. She will take her father's arm and accompany him to the ceremony. And when he slaps her across the face, she will smile and politely receive her applause.

Outside, rain will knock on the branches, and she will ignore it. Like a grown up.

THE CAMBIST AND LORD IRON

Daniel Abraham

For as many years as anyone in the city could remember, Olaf Neddelsohn had been the cambist of the Magdalen Gate postal authority. Every morning, he could be seen making the trek from his rooms in the boardinghouse on State Street, down past the street vendors with their apples and cheese and into the bowels of the underground railway, only to emerge at the station across the wide boulevard from Magdalen Gate. Some mornings he would pause at the tobacconist's or the newsstand before entering the hallowed hall of the postal authority, but seven o'clock found him without fail at the ticker tape checking for the most recent exchange rates. At half past, he was invariably updating the slate board with a bit of chalk. And with the last chime of eight o'clock, he would nod his respect to his small portrait of His Majesty, King Walther IV, pull open the shutters, and greet whichever traveler had need of him.

From that moment until the lunch hour and again from one o'clock until six, Olaf lived and breathed the exchange of foreign currencies. Under his practiced hands, dollars became pounds sterling; rubles became marks; pesos, kroner; yen, francs. Whatever exotic combination was called for, Olaf arranged with a smile, a kind word, and a question about the countries which minted the currencies he passed under the barred window. Over years, he had built nations in his mind; continents. Every country that existed, he could name, along with its particular flavor of money, its great sights and monuments, its national cuisine.

At the deep brass call of the closing gong, he pulled the shutters closed again. From six until seven o'clock, he reconciled the books, filled out his reports, wiped his slate board clean with a wet rag, made certain he had chalk for the next day, paid his respects to the portrait of the king, and then went back to his boarding room. Some nights he made beans on the hotplate in his room. Others, he would join the other boarders for Mrs. Wells's somewhat dubious roasts. Afterward, he would take a short constitutional walk, read to himself from the men's adventure books that were his great vice, and put out the light. On Saturdays, he would visit the zoo or the fourth-rate gentleman's club that he could afford. On Sundays, he attended church.

He had a reputation as a man of few needs, tepid passions, and great kindness. The romantic fire that the exotic coins and bills awakened in him was something he would have been hard pressed to share, even had he anyone with whom to share it.

Which is to say there could not be a man in the whole of the city less like Lord Iron.

Born Edmund Scarasso, Lord Iron had taken his father's title and lands and ridden them first to war, then to power, and finally to a notorious fame. His family estate outside the city was reputed to rival the king's, but Lord Iron spent little time there. He had a house in the city with two hundred rooms arranged around a central courtyard garden in which trees bore fruits unfamiliar to the city and flowers bloomed with exotic and troubling scents. His servants were numberless as ants; his personal fortune greater than some smaller nations'. And never, it was said, had such wealth, power, and influence been squandered on such a debased soul.

No night passed without some new tale of Lord Iron. Ten thousand larks had been killed, their tongues harvested, and their bodies thrown aside in order that Lord Iron might have a novel hors d'oeuvre. Lord Biethan had been forced to repay his family's debt by sending his three daughters to perform as Lord Iron's creatures for a week; they had returned to their father with disturbing, languorous smiles and a rosewood cask filled with silver as "recompense for his Lordship's overuse." A fruit seller had the bad fortune not to recognize Lord Iron one dim, fogbound morning, and a flippant comment earned him a whipping that left him near dead.

There was no way for anyone besides Lord Iron himself to know which of the thousand stories and accusations that accreted around him were true. There was no doubt that Lord Iron was never seen wearing anything but the richest of velvets and silk. He was habitually in the company of beautiful women of negotiable virtue. He smoked the finest tobacco and other, more exotic weeds. Violence and sensuality and excess were the tissue of which his life was made. If his wealth and web of blackmail and extortion had not protected him, he would no doubt have been invited to the gallows dance years before. If he had been a hero in the war, so much the worse.

And so it was, perhaps, no surprise that when his lackey and drinking companion, Lord Caton, mentioned in passing an inconvenient curiosity of the code of exchange, Lord Iron's mind seized upon it. Among his many vices was a fondness for cruel pranks. And so it came to pass that Lord Iron and the handful of gaudy revelers who followed in his wake descended late one Tuesday morning upon the Magdalen Gate postal authority.

Olaf took the packet of bills, willing his hands not to tremble. Lord Iron's thin smile and river-stone eyes did nothing to calm him. The woman draping herself on Lord Iron's arm made a poor affectation of sincerity.

"Well," Olaf said, unfolding the papers. "Let me see."

These were unlike any currency he had ever seen; the sheets were just larger than a standard sheet of paper, the engraving a riot of colors—crimson, indigo, and a pale, delicate peach. The lordly face that stared out of the bill was Moorish. Ornate letters identified the bills as being valued at a thousand convertible guilders and issued by the Independent Protectorate of Analdi-Wat. Olaf wondered, as his fingers traced the lettering, how a protectorate could be independent.

"I'm very sorry, my lord," he said. "But this isn't a listed currency."

"And how is that my problem?" Lord Iron asked, stroking his beard. He had a rich voice, soft and masculine, that made Olaf blush.

"I only mean, my lord, that I couldn't give an exchange rate on these. I don't have them on my board, you see, and so I can't—"

"These are legal tender, issued by a sovereign state. I would like to change them into pounds sterling."

"I understand that, my lord, it's only that—"

"Are you familiar with the code of exchange?" Lord Iron asked. The dark-haired woman on his arm smiled at Olaf with all the pity a snake shows a rat.

"I . . . of course, my lord . . . that is . . ."

"Then you will recall the second provision of the Lord Chancellor's amendment of 1652?"

Olaf licked his lips. Confusion was like cotton ticking filling his head. "The provision against speculation, my lord?"

"Very good," Lord Iron said. "It states that any cambist in the employ of the crown must complete a requested transfer between legal tenders issued by sovereign states within twentyfour hours or else face review of licensure."

"My . . . my lord, that isn't . . . I've been working here for years, sir . . ."

"And of course," Lord Iron went on, his gaze implacable and cool, "assigning arbitrary value to a currency also requires a review, doesn't it? And rest assured, my friend, that I am quite capable of determining the outcome of any such review."

Olaf swallowed to loosen the tightness in his throat. His smile felt sickly.

"If I have done something to offend your lordship . . ."

"No," Lord Iron said with something oddly like compassion in his eyes. "You were simply in the wrong place when I grew bored. Destroying you seemed diverting. I will be back at this time tomorrow. Good day, sir."

Lord Iron turned and walked away. His entourage followed. When the last of them had stepped out the doors, the silence that remained behind was profound as the grave. Olaf saw the eyes of the postal clerks on him and managed a wan smile. The great clock read twenty minutes past eleven. By noontime tomorrow, Olaf realized, it was quite possible he would no longer be a licensed cambist.

He closed his shutters early with a note tacked to the front that clients should knock on them if they were facing an emergency but otherwise return the next day.

He pulled out the references of his trade—gazetteer, logs of fiscal reports, conversion tables. By midafternoon, he had discovered the location of the Independent Protectorate of Analdi-Wat, but nothing that would relate their system of convertible guilders to any known currency. Apparently the last known conversion had been into a system of cowrie shells, and the numbers involved were absent.

The day waned, the light pouring into the postal authority warming and then fading to shadows. Olaf sent increasingly desperate messages to his fellow cambists at other postal authorities, to the librarians at the city's central reference desk, to the office of the Lord Exchequer. It became clear as the bells tolled their increasing hours that no answer would come before morning. And indeed, no answer would come in time.

If Olaf delayed the exchange, his license could be suspended. If he invented some random value for the guilders, his license could be suspended. And there was no data from which to derive an appropriate equation.

Anger and despair warring in his belly, he closed his station, returned his books to their places, cleaned his slate, logged the few transactions he had made. His hand hovered for a moment over his strongbox.

Here were the funds from which he drew each day to meet the demands of his clientele. Pounds sterling, yen, rubles. He wondered, if he were to fill his pockets with the box's present contents, how far he would get before he was caught. The romance of flight bloomed in his mind and died all in the space of a breath. He withdrew only the bright, venomous bills of the Independent Protectorate of Analdi-Wat, replacing them with a receipt. He locked the box with a steady hand, shrugged on his coat, and left.

Lord Iron, he decided as he walked slowly down the

marble steps to the street, was evil. But he was also powerful, rich, and well connected. There was little that a man like Olaf could do if a man of that stature took it as his whim to destroy him. If it had been the devil, he might at least have fallen back on prayer.

Olaf stopped at the newsstand, bought an evening paper and a tin of lemon mints, and trudged to the station across the street. Waiting on the platform, he listened to the underground trains hiss and squeal. He read his newspaper with the numb disinterest of a man to whom the worst has already happened. A missing child had been found alive in Stonemarket; the diary of a famous courtesan had sold at auction to an anonymous buyer and for a record price; the police had begun a policy of restricting access to the river quays in hopes of reducing accidental death by drowning. The cheap ink left more of a mark on his fingers than on his mind.

At his boardinghouse, Olaf ate a perfunctory dinner at the common table, retired to his room, and tried in vain to lose himself in the pulp adventure tales. The presence of a killer among the members of the good Count Pendragon's safari proved less than captivating, even if the virtuous Hanna Gable was in danger. Near midnight, Olaf turned out his light, pulled his thin wool blanket up over his head, and wondered what he would do when his position at the postal authority was terminated.

Two hours later, he woke with a shout. Still in his nightclothes, he rushed out to the common room, digging through the pile of small kindling and newspaper that Mrs. Wells used to start her fires. When he found the evening newspaper, he read the article detailing the sale of the courtesan's diary again. There was nothing in it that pertained directly to his situation, and yet his startling, triumphant yawp woke the house.

He arrived at work the next day later than usual, with bags dark as bruises under his eyes but a spring in his step. He went through his morning ritual rather hurriedly to make up for the time he had lost, but was well prepared when the street doors opened at eleven o'clock and Lord Iron and his gang of rank nobility slouched in. Olaf held his spine straight and breathed deeply to ease the trip-hammer of his heart.

Lord Iron stepped up to the window like an executioner to the noose. The woman on his arm this morning was fair-haired, but otherwise might have been the twin of the previous day's woman. Olaf made a small, nervous bow to them both.

"Lord Iron," he said.

Lord Iron's expression was distant as the moon. Olaf wondered if perhaps his lordship had been drinking already this morning.

"Explain to me why you've failed."

"Well, my lord, I don't think I can do that. I have your money here. It comes to something less than ten pounds, I'm afraid. But that was all the market would bear."

With trembling hand, Olaf slid an envelope across the desk. Lord Iron didn't look down at it. Fury lit his eyes.

"The *market*? And pray what *market* is that?"

"The glassblower's shop in Harrington Square, my lord. I have quotes from three other establishments nearby, and theirs was the best. I doubt you would find better anywhere."

"What do they have to do with this?"

"Well, they were the ones who bought the guilders," Olaf said, his voice higher and faster than he liked. He also ran on longer than he had strictly speaking intended. "I believe that they intend to use them as wrapping paper. For the more delicate pieces. As a novelty."

Lord Iron's face darkened.

"You sold my bills?" he growled.

Olaf had anticipated many possible reactions. Violence, anger, amusement. He had imagined a hundred objections that Lord Iron might bring to his actions. Base ignorance had not been one of them. Olaf's surprise lent a steadiness to his voice.

"My lord, *you* sold them. To me. That's what exchange is, sir. Currency is something bought and sold, just as plums or gas fixtures are. It's what we do here."

"I came to get pounds sterling for guilders, not sell wrapping paper!"

Olaf saw in that moment that Lord Iron genuinely didn't understand. He pulled himself up, straightening his vest.

"Sir," he said. "When a client comes to me with a hundred dollars and I turn him back with seventy pounds, I haven't said some Latin phrase over them. There aren't suddenly seventy more pounds in the world and a hundred fewer dollars. I buy the dollars. You came to sell your guilders to me. Very well. I have bought them."

"As wrapping paper!"

"What does that matter?" Olaf snapped, surprising both Lord Iron and himself. "If I invest them in negotiable bonds in Analdi-Wat or burn them for kindling, it's no business of yours. Someone was willing to buy them. From that, I can now quote you with authority what people are willing to pay. There is your exchange rate. And there is your money. Thank you for your business, and good day."

"You made up the price," Lord Iron said. "To place an arbitrary worth on—"

"Good God, man," Olaf said. "Did you not hear me before? There's nothing *arbitrary* about it. I went

to several prospective buyers and took the best
offered price. What can you possibly mean by 'worth'
if not what you can purchase with it? Five shillings is
worth a loaf of bread, or a cup of wine, or a cheaply
bound book of poetry because that is what it will buy.
Your tens of thousands of negotiable guilders will buy
you nine pounds and seven shillings because that is
what someone will pay. And there it is, in that
envelope."

Never before in his life had Olaf seen nobility
agape at him. The coterie of Lord Iron stared at him as
if he had belched fire and farted brimstone. The fair-
haired woman stepped back, freeing his lordship's
sword arm.

I have gone too far, Olaf thought. *He will kill me.*

Lord Iron was silent for a long moment while the
world seemed to rotate around him. Then he chuckled.

"The measure of a thing's worth is what you can
purchase with it," he said as if tasting the words, then
turned to the woman. "I think he's talking about you,
Marjorie."

The woman's cheeks flushed scarlet. Lord Iron
leaned against the sill of Olaf's little, barred window
and gestured Olaf closer. Against his best judgment,
Olaf leaned in.

"You have a strange way of looking at things,"
Lord Iron said. There were fumes on his breath.
Absinthe, Olaf guessed. "To hear you speak, the baker
buys my five shillings with his bread."

"And how is that wrong, my lord?" the cambist
asked.

"And then the wineseller buys the coins from him
with a glass of wine. So why not buy the bread with the
wine? If they're worth the same?"

"You could, my lord," Olaf said. "You can express
anything in terms of anything else, my lord. How many

lemon tarts is a horse worth? How many newspapers equate to a good dinner? It isn't harder to determine than some number of rubles for another number of yen, if you know the trick of it."

Lord Iron smiled again. The almost sleepy expression returned to his eyes. He nodded.

"Wrapping paper," he said. "You have amused me, little man, and I didn't think that could be done any longer. I accept your trade."

And with that, Lord Iron swept the envelope into his pocket, turned, and marched unsteadily out of the postal authority and into the noon light of Magdalen Gate. After the street doors were closed, there was a pause long as three breaths together and then one of the postal clerks began to clap.

A moment later, the staff of the postal authority had filled the vaults of their chambers with applause. Olaf, knees suddenly weak, bowed carefully, closed the shutters of his window, and made his way back to the men's privacy room where he emptied his breakfast into the toilet and then sat on the cool tile floor laughing until tears streamed from his eyes.

He had faced down Lord Iron and escaped with his career intact. It was, no doubt, the greatest adventure of his life. Nothing he had done before could match it, and he could imagine nothing in the future that would surpass it.

And nothing did, as it turned out, for almost six and a half months.

It was a cold, clear February, and the stars had come out long before Olaf had left the Magdalen Gate authority. All during the ride on the underground train, Olaf dreamed of a warm pot of tea, a small fire, and the conclusion of the latest novel. Atherton Crane was on the verge of exposing the plot of the vicious

Junwang Ko, but didn't yet know that Kelly O'Callahan was in the villain's clutches. It promised to be a pleasant evening.

He knew as soon as he stepped into the boarding-house that something was wrong. The other boarders, sitting around the common table, went silent as he shrugged out of his coat and plucked off his hat. They pointedly did not look at him as Mrs. Wells, her wide friendly face pale as uncooked dough, crossed the room to meet him.

"There's a message for you, Mr. Neddelsohn," she said. "A man came and left it for you. Very particular."

"Who was he?" Olaf asked, suspicion blooming in his heart more from her affect than from any guilt on his conscience.

"Don't know," Mrs. Wells said, wringing her hands in distress, "but he looked . . . well, here it is, Mr. Neddelsohn. This is the letter he left for you."

The envelope she thrust into his hand was the color of buttercream, smooth as linen, and thick. The coat of arms embossed upon it was Lord Iron's. Olaf started at the thing as if she'd handed him a viper.

Mrs. Wells simpered her apology as he broke the wax seal and drew out a single sheet of paper. It was written in an erratic but legible hand.

Mr. Neddelsohn—
    I find I have need of you to settle a wager.
You will bring yourself to the Club Baphomet
immediately upon receipt of this note. I will,
of course, recompense you for your troubles.

The note was not signed, but Olaf had no doubt of its authorship. Without a word, he pulled his coat back on, returned his hat to his head, and stepped out to hail a carriage. From the street, he could see the faces of Mrs. Wells and his fellow boarders at the window.

The Club Baphomet squatted in the uncertain territory between the tenements and beer halls of Stonemarket and the mansions and ballrooms of Granite Hill. The glimmers behind its windows did little to illuminate the street, perhaps by design. From the tales Olaf had heard, there might well be members of the club who would prefer not to be seen entering or leaving its grounds. The service entrance was in a mud-paved alley stinking of piss and old food, but it opened quickly to his knock. He was bundled inside and escorted to a private sitting room where, it seemed, he was expected.

Of the five men who occupied the room, Olaf recognized only Lord Iron. The months had not been kind; Lord Iron had grown thinner, his eyes wilder, and a deep crimson cut was only half healed on his cheek. The other four were dressed in fashion similar to Lord Iron—well-razored hair, dark coats of the finest wool, watch chains of gold. The eldest of them seemed vaguely familiar.

Lord Iron rose and held his hand out toward Olaf, not as if to greet him but rather to display him like a carnival barker presenting a three-headed calf.

"Gentlemen," Lord Iron intoned. "This is the cambist I mentioned to you. I propose that he be my champion in this matter."

Olaf felt the rictus grin on his face, the idiot bobbing of his head as he made small bows to the four assembled gentlemen. He was humiliated, but could no more stop himself than a puppy could keep from showing its belly to beg the mercy of wolves.

One of the four—a younger man with gold hair and ice-blue eyes—stepped forward with a smile. Olaf nodded to him for what must have been the fifth time.

"I am Simon Cole," the gold-haired man said. "Lord Eichan, to my enemies."

At this, Lord Iron raised a hand, as if to identify himself as one such enemy. The other three men chuckled, and Lord Eichan smiled as well before continuing.

"Our mutual acquaintance, Lord Iron, has made a suggestion I find somewhat unlikely, and we have made a wager of it. He is of the opinion that the value of anything can be expressed in terms of any other valuable thing. I think his example was the cost of a horse in lemon mints."

"Yes, my lord," Olaf said.

"Ah, you agree then," Lord Eichan said. "That's good. I was afraid our little Edmund had come up with his thesis in a drugsoaked haze."

"We've made the agreement," Lord Iron said pleasantly. "Simon, Satan's catamite that he is, will set the two things to be compared. I, meaning of course *you*, will have a week to determine their relative worth. These three bastards will judge the answer."

"I see," Olaf said.

"Excellent," Lord Iron said, slapping him on the back and leading him to a chair upholstered in rich leather. It wasn't until Olaf had descended into the chair's depths that he realized he had just agreed to this mad scheme. Lord Eichan had taken a seat opposite him and was thoughtfully lighting a pipe.

"I think I should say," Olaf began, casting his mind about wildly for some way to remove himself from the room without offending either party. "That is, I don't wish that . . . ah . . ."

Lord Eichan nodded as if Olaf had made some cogent point, then shaking his match until the flame died, turned to face Olaf directly.

"I would like to know the value of a day in the life

day in the life of his majesty the king equates to nineteen and three quarter hours of a prisoner of the crown."

There was a moment's silence. Simon, Lord Eichan blinked and an incredulous smile began to work its way onto his countenance. Lord Iron sat forward, his expression unreadable. One of the judges who had not yet spoken took a meditative puff on his cigar.

"I was never particularly good at sums," the man said in an unsettlingly feminine voice, "but it seems to me that you've just said a prisoner's life is *more* valuable than that of the king?"

"Yes," Olaf said, his belly heavy as if he'd drunk a tankard of lead. The eldest judge glanced at Lord Iron with a pitying expression.

"Let me also make some few observations," Olaf said, fighting to keep the desperation from his voice. "I have met with several physicians in the last few days. I am sorry to report that overindulging in strong liquor is thought by the medical establishment to reduce life expectancy by as much as five years. A habit of eating rich foods may reduce a man's span on the earth by another three to four years. A sedentary lifestyle by as much as eight. Indulging in chocolate and coffee can unbalance the blood, and remove as many as three years of life."

"You have now ceased to preach to the choir," said Lord Eichan. And indeed, the judges had grown more somber. Olaf raised a hand, begging their patience.

"I have used these medical data as well as the reports of the warden of Chappell Hill Prison and the last two years of his majesty's reported activities in the newspapers. I beg you to consider. A prisoner of the crown is kept on a simple diet and subjected to a mandatory exercise period each day. No spirits of any kind are permitted him. No luxuries such as coffee or chocolate. By comparison . . ."

Olaf fumbled with the sheaves of papers, searching for the form he had created. The eldest judge cleared his throat.

"By comparison," Olaf continued, "in the last two years, his majesty has taken vigorous exercise only one day in seven. Has eaten at banquet daily, including the richest of dishes. He regularly drinks both coffee and chocolate, often together in the French style."

"This is ridiculous," Lord Eichan said. "His majesty has the finest physicians in the world at his command. His life is better safeguarded than any man's in the realm."

"No, sir," Olaf said, his voice taking on a certainty that he was beginning to genuinely feel. "We say that it is, much as the embezzler claims honesty and the wanton claims virtue. I present to you the actions, as we agreed. And I would point out that his majesty's excesses are subject only to his personal whim. If he wished, he could drink himself insensible each morning, eat nothing but butterfat and lard, and never move from his seat. He could drink half a tun of coffee and play games with raw gunpowder. Unlike a prisoner, there is no enforcement of behavior that could rein him in. I have, if anything, taken a conservative measure in reaching my conclusions."

A glimmer of amusement shone in Lord Iron's eyes, but his face remained otherwise frozen. Simon, Lord Eichan was fidgeting with his cigar. The eldest judge sucked his teeth audibly and shook his head.

"And yet prisoners do not, I think, have a greater lifespan than monarchs," he said.

"It is impossible to say," Olaf said. "For many criminals and poor men, the time spent in the care of the crown can be when they are safest, best overseen, best clothed, best fed. I would, however, point out that his majesty's father left us at the age of sixty-seven, and the oldest man in the care of the crown is . . ."

Olaf paused, finding the name.

"The oldest man in the care of the crown is David Bennet, aged eighty. Incarcerated when he was sixteen for killing his brother."

He spread his hands.

"Your argument seems sound," the eldest judge said, "but your conclusion is ridiculous. I cannot believe that the king is of lesser value than a prisoner. I am afraid I remain unconvinced. What say you, gentlemen?"

But before the other two judges could answer Olaf rose to his feet.

"With all respect, sir, the question was not the value of the king or the prisoner, but of the days of their respective lives. I was not asked to judge their pleasures or their health insofar as their discomforts are less than mortal."

The effeminate judge lifted his chin. There was a livid scar across his neck where, Olaf imagined from his knowledge of men's adventure, a garrote might have cut. But it was Simon, Lord Eichan who spoke.

"How is it that a king can be more valuable than a prisoner, but his days be less? It makes no sense at all!"

"There are other things which his majesty has," Olaf said. He had warmed to his topic now, and the fact that his own life hung in the balance was all but forgotten. "A prisoner must take his exercise; a king has the power to refuse. A prisoner may wish dearly for a rich meal or a great glass of brandy, but since he cannot have them, he cannot exchange pleasure for . . . well, for some duration of life."

"This is a waste of—"

"Be quiet," the eldest judge said. "Let the man have his say."

"But—"

"Don't make me repeat myself, Simon."

Lord Eichan leaned back, sneering and gripping his wineglass until his knuckles were white.

"It's a choice every man in this room has made," Olaf went on, raising his arm like a priest delivering a homily. "You might all live as ascetics and survive years longer. But like the king, you choose to make a rational exchange of some span of your life for the pleasure of living as you please. A prisoner is barred from that exchange, and so I submit a greater value is placed on his life precisely to the degree that strictures are placed on his pleasure and his exercise of power.

"Gentlemen, ask yourselves this; if I had two sons and saw that one of them kept from drink and gluttony while letting the other run riot, which of them would you say I valued? The prodigal might have more pleasure. Certainly the king has more pleasure than an inmate. But pleasure and power are not *life*."

"Amen," said Lord Iron. It was the first time he had spoken since Olaf had entered. The silence that followed this declaration was broken only by the hissing of the fire in the grate and the rush of blood in Olaf's ears.

"Your reports were accurate, Lord Iron," the drawling judge said. "Your pet cambist is *quite* amusing."

"Perhaps it would be best if you gave us a moment to discuss your points," the eldest judge said. "If you would be so kind as to step out to the antechamber? Yes. Thank you."

With the blackwood door closed behind him, Olaf's fear returned. He was in the Club Baphomet with his survival linked to Lord Iron's, and only an argument that seemed less and less tenable with each passing minute to protect him. But he had made his throw. His only other hope now was mad flight, and the door to the corridor was locked. He tried it.

What felt like hours passed, though the grandfather clock ticking away in the corner reported only a quarter hour. A pistol barked twice, and a moment later Lord Iron strode into the room. The door swung shut behind him before Olaf could make sense of the bloody scene. His gorge rose.

"Well done, boy," Lord Iron said, dropping something heavy into Olaf's lap. "I'll have you taken home in my personal carriage. I have Lord Eichan's sister to console this evening, and I won't be needing horses to do it. And I thought you should know; it wasn't unanimous. If his majesty hadn't taken your side, I think we might not have won the day."

"His majesty?"

Olaf's mind reeled. The face of the eldest judge resolved itself suddenly into the portrait he kept at his desk.

"You did well, boy," Lord Iron said. "Your country thanks you."

Without another word, Lord Iron unlocked the door, stepped out to the corridor, and was gone. Olaf looked down. A packet of bills squatted in his lap. Five hundred pounds at a guess, and blood smeared on the topmost bill.

He swore to himself in that moment that he would never answer another summons from Lord Iron, whatever the consequences. And, indeed, when the hour arrived, it was Lord Iron who came to him.

The weeks and months that followed were if anything richer in their tales of Lord Iron. While traveling in the Orient, he had forced a barkeep who had fallen into his debt to choose between cutting off one of his infant daughter's toes or three of his own fingers in lieu of payment. He had seduced six nuns in Rome, leaving two of them with child. He had ridden an ostrich down the streets of Cairo naked at midnight. Of the untimely death of Lord Eichan there was no word, but apart from removing the portrait of the king from his desk, Olaf took no action. The less he personally figured into the debaucheries of Lord Iron, the better pleased he was.

Instead, Olaf plunged more deeply than ever into his work, his routine, and the harmless escapism of his men's adventure novels. But for the first time in memory, the perils of the heroines seemed contrived and weak, and the masculine bravery of the heroes seemed overstated, like a boy who blusters and puffs out his chest when walking through the graveyard at dusk.

Clifford Knightly wrestled an alligator on the banks of the great Nile. Lord Morrow foiled the evil Chaplain Grut's plan to foul the waters of London. Emily Chastain fell gratefully into the mighty arms of the noble savage Maker-of-Justice. And Olaf found himself wondering what these great men would have done at Club Baphomet. Wrested the gun from Lord Iron? From Simon, Lord Eichan? Sternly spoken of God and truth and righteousness? Olaf doubted it would have had any great effect.

Winter passed into spring. Spring ripened to summer. Slowly, Olaf's discontent, like the nightmares from which he woke himself shouting, lessened. For weeks on end, he could forget what he had been part of. Many men who came to his window at the postal authority had traveled widely. Many had tales to tell of near misses: a runaway carriage that had come within a pace of running them down in the streets of Prague, a fever which had threatened to carry them away in Bombay, the hiss of an Afghan musket ball passing close to their head. These moments of real danger were more convincing than any novel Olaf had ever read. This was, in part, because he had tales of his own now, if he ever chose to share them.

And still, when autumn with its golden leaves and fog and chill rain also brought Lord Iron back into his life, Olaf was not surprised.

It was a Tuesday night in September. Olaf had spent his customary hours at the Magdalen Gate postal authority, come back to his boardinghouse, and eaten alone in his room. The evening air was cool but not biting, and he had propped his window open before sitting down to read. When he woke, he thought for a long, bleary moment that the cold night breeze had woken him. Then the knock at his door repeated itself.

His blanket wrapped around his shoulders, Olaf answered the door. Lord Iron stood in the hall. He looked powerfully out of place. His fine jacket and cravat, the polished boots, the wellgroomed beard and moustache all belonged in a palace or club. And yet rather than making the boardinghouse hall seem shabby and below him, the hallway made Lord Iron, monster of the city, seem false as a boy playing dress-up. Olaf nodded as if he'd been expecting the man.

"I have need of you," Lord Iron said.

"Have I the option of refusal?"

Lord Iron smiled, and Olaf took it as the answer to his question. He stepped back and let the man come through. Lord Iron sat on the edge of the bed while Olaf closed his window, drew up his chair and sat. In the light from Olaf's reading lamp, Lord Iron's skin seemed waxen and pale. His voice, when he spoke, was as distant as a man shouting from across a square.

"There is a question plaguing me," Lord Iron said. "You are the only man I can think of who might answer it."

"Is there a life at stake?" Olaf asked.

"No," Lord Iron said. "Nothing so petty as that."

When Olaf failed to respond, Lord Iron, born Edmund Scarasso, looked up at him. There was a terrible weariness in his eyes.

"I would know the fair price for a man's soul," he said.

"Forgive me?" Olaf said.

"You heard me," Lord Iron said. "What would be fit trade for a soul? I . . . I can't tell any longer. And it is a question whose answer has . . . some relevance to my situation."

In an instant, Olaf's mind conjured the sitting room at the Club Baphomet. Lord Iron sitting in one deep leather chair, and the Prince of Lies across from him with a snifter of brandy in his black, clawed hands.

"I don't think that would be a wise course to follow," Olaf said, though in truth his mind was spinning out ways to avoid being party to this diabolism. He did not wish to make a case before that infernal judge. Lord Iron smiled and shook his head.

"There is no one in this besides yourself and me," he said. "You are an expert in the exchange of exotic currencies. I can think of none more curious than this. Come to my house on Mammon Street in a month's time. Tell me what conclusion you have reached."

"My Lord—"

"I will make good on the investment of your time," Lord Iron said, then rose and walked out, leaving the door open behind him.

Olaf gaped at the empty room. He was a cambist. Of theology, he knew only what he had heard in church. He had read more of satanic contracts in his adventure novels than in the Bible. He was, in fact, not wholly certain that the Bible had an example of a completed exchange. Satan had tempted Jesus. Perhaps there was something to be taken from the Gospel of Matthew. . . .

Olaf spent the remainder of the night poring over his Bible and considering what monetary value might be assigned to the ability to change stones to bread. But as the dawn broke and he turned to his morning ablutions, he found himself unsatisfied. The devil might have tempted Christ with all the kingdoms of the world, but it was obvious that such an offer wouldn't be open to everyone. He was approaching the problem from the wrong direction.

As he rode through the deep tunnels to Magdalen Gate, as he stopped at the newsstand for a morning paper, as he checked the ticker tape and updated his slate, his mind occupied itself by sifting through all the stories and folk wisdom he had ever heard. There had been a man who traded his soul to the devil for fame and wealth. Faust had done it for knowledge. Was there a way to represent the learning of Faust in terms of, say, semesters at the best universities of Europe? Then the rates of tuition might serve as a fingerhold.

It was nearly the day's end before the question occurred to him that put Lord Iron's commission in its proper light, and once that had happened, the answer was obvious. Olaf had to sit down, his mind afire with the answer and its implications. He didn't go home, but took himself to a small public house. Over a pint and a stale sandwich, he mentally tested his hypothesis. With the second pint, he celebrated. With the third, he steeled himself, then went out to the street and hailed a carriage to take him to the house of Lord Iron.

Revelers had infected the household like fleas on a dying rat. Masked men and women shrieked with laughter, not all of which bespoke mirth. No servant came to take his coat or ask his invitation, so Olaf made his own way through the great halls. He passed through the whole of the building before emerging from the back and finding Lord Iron himself sitting at a fountain in the gardens. His lordship's eyebrows rose to see Olaf, but he did not seem displeased.

"So soon, boy? It isn't a month," Lord Iron said as Olaf sat on the cool stone rail. The moon high above the city seemed also to dance in the water, lighting Lord Iron's face from below and above at once.

"There was no need," Olaf said. "I have your answer. But I will have to make something clear before I deliver it. If you will permit me?"

Lord Iron opened his hand in a motion of deference. Olaf cleared his throat.

"Wealth," he said, "is not a measure of money. It is a measure of well-being. Of happiness, if you will. Wealth is not traded, but rather is generated by trade. If you have a piece of art that I wish to own and I have money that you would prefer to the artwork, we trade. Each of us has something he prefers to the thing he gave away; otherwise, we would not have agreed on the trade. We are both better off. You see? Wealth is *generated*."

"I believe I can follow you so far," Lord Iron said. "Certainly I can agree that a fat wallet is no guarantor of contentment."

"Very well. I considered your problem for the better part of the day. I confess I came near to despairing; there is no good data from which to work. But then I found my error. I assumed that your soul, my lord, was valuable. Clearly it is not."

Lord Iron coughed out something akin to a laugh, shock in his expression. Olaf raised a hand, palm out, asking that he not interrupt.

"You are renowned for your practice of evil. This very evening, walking through your house, I have seen things for which I can imagine no proper penance. Why would Satan bother to buy your soul? He has rights to it already."

"He does," Lord Iron said, staring into the middle distance.

"And so I saw," Olaf said, "you aren't seeking to sell a soul. You are hoping to buy one."

Lord Iron sighed and looked at his hands. He seemed smaller now. Not a supernatural being, but a man driven by human fears and passions to acts that could only goad him on to worse and worse actions. A man like any other, but with the wealth to magnify his errors into the scale of legend.

"You are correct, boy," he said. "The angels wouldn't have my soul if I drenched it in honey. I have . . . treated it poorly. It's left me weary and sick. I am a waste of flesh. I know that. If there is no way to become a better man than this, I suspect the best path is to become a corpse."

"I understand, my lord. Here is the answer to your question: the price of a soul is a life of humility and service."

"Ah, is that all," Lord Iron said, as if the cambist had suggested that he pull down the stars with his fingers.

"And as it happens," Olaf went on, "I have one such with which I would be willing to part."

Lord Iron met his gaze, began to laugh, and then went silent.

"Here," Olaf said, "is what I propose . . ."

Edmund, the new cambist of the Magdalen Gate postal authority, was by all accounts an adequate replacement for Olaf. Not as good, certainly. But his close-cropped hair and clean-shaven face lent him an eagerness that belonged on a younger man, and if he seemed sometimes more haughty than his position justified, it was a vice that lessened with every passing month. By Easter, he had even been asked to join in the Sunday picnic the girls in the accounting office sponsored. He seemed genuinely moved at the invitation.

The great scandal of the season was the disappearance of Lord Iron. The great beast of the city simply vanished one night. Rumor said that he had left his fortune and lands in trust. The identity of the trustee was a subject of tremendous speculation.

Olaf himself spent several months simply taking stock of his newfound position in the world. Once the financial situation was put in better order, he found himself with a substantial yearly allowance that still responsibly protected the initial capital.

He spent his monies traveling to India, Egypt, the sugar plantations of the Caribbean, the unworldly underground cities of Persia. He saw the sun set off the Gold Coast and rise from the waters east of Japan. He heard war songs in the jungles of the Congo and sang children's lullabies in a lonely tent made from yak skin in the dark of a Siberian winter.

And, when he paused to recover from the rigors and dangers of travel, he would retire to a cottage north of the city—the least of his holdings—and spend his time writing men's adventure novels set in the places he had been.

He named his protagonist Lord Iron.

SOMETHING IN THE MERMAID WAY

Carrie Laben

As fall crept on and the storms got worse, the supply of monkeys ran low.

At first, we actually prospered, because we were able to use the monkeys that the other shops could not. The best monkeys for making into mermaids, by most standards, were the suckling young—their skins were pliant and they were of a size that matched well with many common fish. But my mother, in her youth, had developed a process that let her shrink the larger monkey skins—even the full-grown monkeys who often died in defense of their young and whose rough pelts the hunters would part with for small coins—down to an appropriate size, without drying them out too much to work with.

Thus we had survived ten years ago when the monkeys had been exterminated from Isla Scimmia, turning the name into a cruel joke that outlanders used to taunt the inhabitants for our dark coloring and the heavy hair on our arms. More than half of the families who made mermaids then had since left the island altogether, some for Rome, some for the New World or parts still more exotic. One notable family, a husband and wife and five daughters ranging from a twenty-five-year-old spinster to a toddling child, had all drunk arsenic.

Mother was disgusted. She'd held the family in high regard before; along with her own, they'd been among the few original mermaid-making families to survive when the mermaids themselves went away, to weather the early storm of competition from Fiji, to cope with the way the fish seemed to shrink every year and the fickleness of the sailors who were always looking for some new novelty. The eldest daughter had been her particular friend.

But these days, according to Mother, everyone was a degenerate. She announced it loudly as she ducked into the workshop, shaking the rain out of her loose dark hair. "Degenerates! Think they can sell me stinking half-rotten monkeys for twice, three times the usual price. They'd try to sell a shell to an oyster and ask for pearls in payment."

She held two packages—by the smell of them I could tell that she'd managed to find a few acceptable monkeys. She almost always did, even when Annagrazia and I came home empty-handed. I took one of the packets, wrapped in coarse oiled cloth, and untied the ends to reveal one of the small grey North African monkeys.

"You got the good kind," Annagrazia said, unwrapping the other bundle and laying it on the table beside her knives.

"Too big," Mother said, and fished out a packet of glass eyes from the pocket of her cloak. "It will take days to shrink them properly." The shrinking process was Mother's pride and our salvation, and she hated it—it was long, tedious, it produced smells that gave her headaches. To hear her talk she'd as soon never do it again. But she laughed at the women who came to try to buy the secret from her.

Annagrazia picked up her knife and tried the blade carefully against the inside of a coarse-haired leg. The lower half of the monkey would be discarded, of course, but there was no need to cut it to ribbons—the fur could still be used to line boots or collars. "I like these grey ones though. They look the most like real mermaids."

"Like those white-eyed idiots at the docks would know a real mermaid from a hole in the fence."

"I don't care if they know. I know." She slid the knife along the inside of the leg, skirted the groin, and split the belly. I thought for a moment that she had cut too deep and the rotting intestines would spill, but the knife glided along and left the muscles in place. "Which reminds me. Did you get brown eyes?"

"Blue eyes. The sailors like blue."

"There never was a mermaid with blue eyes," Annagrazia said, as she had so many times before.

"There never was a mermaid that was actually half monkey and half salmon either."

When Annagrazia finished skinning the monkey, I took the body away to clean and bone and see if any meat could be salvaged.

Just before the storms finally broke, I noticed that Annagrazia was looking pale and sick. The quality of her work was falling off a bit too—not enough that I could see it, but enough that she cursed and wept at her tools before Mother patted her hand and told her it was good enough, it would still sell.

Annagrazia threw her needle across the workshop and ran to the kitchen.

Three days later, Mother sent me to the apothecary for pennyroyal.

"You've left it too late," she was scolding when I got back.

"I haven't. I had an idea. I can make a mermaid that looks real, Mama, when you see . . . "

"And your plan required fucking some sailor boy from the docks?"

"A man from one of the island families would have been better, but it makes no nevermind. Our blood is thick. Anyway, my stupid sailor boy was able to give me some brown glass eyes."

"You and those eyes!" I thought for a moment that Mother might slap her. But Mother never slapped Annagrazia. She shook her head and snatched the pennyroyal from me and went for the kettle.

The baby slipped out in a mess of bloody unnamable fluid, and never drew a breath before it was out of the world. Tradition called those babies the happy ones.

"Let me hold it," Annagrazia said, and I placed it in her arms. "There, look. The hair is so fine on the arms, and the eyes are brown."

Mother smiled. "You're right. Our blood is strong. No sailor boy in that."

Annagrazia reached for the knife she'd kept by the bedside in readiness.

When the mermaid was finished, it was indeed perfect.

"The spitting image of my grandmother," Mother said triumphantly. "This is the finest mermaid that has ever come out of any shop on this island since our ancestors died out. The price we can put on this—we could fool a ship's doctor with it."

"We can't sell it," Annagrazia said. "It's too perfect. This is the best thing I will ever do. I will keep it."

Then Mother did raise her hand to slap her, but Annagrazia was holding her skinning knife and they stood staring at each other for a long time.

"I will keep this one," Annagrazia said with a smile, "but I can make more."

PUBLIC SAFETY

———

Matthew Johnson

Officier de la Paix Louverture folded Quartidi's *Père Duchesne* into thirds, fanning himself against the Thermidor heat. The news inside was all bad, anyway: another theater had closed, leaving the *Comedie Francaise* the only one open in Nouvelle-Orleans. At least the *Duchesne* could be counted on to report only what the Corps told them to, that the *Figaro* had closed for repairs, and not the truth—which was that audiences, frightened by the increasing number of fires and other mishaps at the theaters, had stopped coming. The *Minerve* was harder to control, but the theater-owners had been persuaded not to talk to their reporters, to avoid a public panic. No matter that these were all clearly accidents: even now, in the year 122, reason was often just a thin layer of ice concealing a pre-Revolutionary sea of irrationality.

On the table in front of him sat his plate of beignets, untouched. He had wanted them when he had sat down, but the arrival of the group of gardiens stagieres to the cafe made him lose his appetite. He told himself it was just his cynicism that caused him to react this way, his desire to mock their pride in their spotless uniforms and caps, and not the way they looked insolently in his direction as they ordered theirs cafes au lait. Not for the first time Louverture wondered if he should have stayed in Saint-Domingue.

The gardiens stagieres gave a cry as another of their number entered the café, but instead of heading for their table he approached Louverture. As he neared, Louverture recognized him: Pelletier, a runner, who despite being younger than the just-graduated bunch across the room had already seen a great deal more than they.

"Excuse me, sir," Pelletier said. Though it was early, sweat had already drawn a thick line across the band of his cap: he must have run all the way from the Cabildo. "Commandant Trudeau needs to see you right away."

Louverture nodded, glanced at his watch: it was three eighty-five, almost time to start work anyway. "Thank you, Pelletier," he said; the young man's face brightened at the use of his name. "My coffee and beignets just arrived, and it seems I won't have time to enjoy them; why don't you take a moment to rest?" He reached into his pocket, dropped four deci-francs in a careful pile on the table.

"*Thank* you, sir," Pelletier said; he took off his cap, revealing a thick bristle of sweat-soaked blond hair.

Louverture tapped his own cap in reply, headed for the west exit of the Café du Monde; he lingered there for a moment, just out of sight, watched as Pelletier struggled to decide whether to sit at the table he had just vacated or join the group of young gardiens who were, assuming that out of sight meant out of hearing, now making sniggering comments about café au lait and creole rice. When Pelletier chose the empty table Louverture smiled to himself, stepped out onto Danton Street.

It had grown hotter, appreciably, in the time since he had arrived at the café; such people as were about clung to the shade like lizards, loitering under the awnings of the building where the Pasteur Brewery made its tasteless beer. Louverture crossed the street at a run, dodging the constant flow of velocipedes, and braced himself for the sun-bleached walk across Descartes Square. He walked past the statue of the Goddess of Reason, with her torch of inquiry and book of truth; the shadow of her torch reached out to the edge of the square, where stenciled numbers marked the ten hours of the day. He doffed his cap to her as always, then gratefully reached the shadows of the colonnade that fronted the Cabildo, under the inscription that read *RATIO SUPER FERVEO*.

"Commandant Trudeau wishes to see you, sir," the gardien at the desk said. The stern portrait of Jacques Hébert on the wall behind glowered down at them.

Louverture nodded, went up the stairs to Trudeau's office. Inside he saw Trudeau at his desk, looking over a piece of paper; Officier de la Paix Principal Clouthier was standing nearby.

"Louverture, good to see you," Trudeau said. His sharp features and high forehead reminded those who met him of Julius Caesar; modestly, Trudeau underlined the resemblance by placing a bust of the Roman emperor on his desk. "I'm sorry to call you in early, but an important case has come up, something I wanted you to handle personally."

"Of course, sir. What is it?"

Trudeau passed the paper to him. "What do you make of this?" It was a sheet of A4 paper, on which were written the words *Elle meurt la treizième*.

" 'She dies on the thirteenth,' " Louverture read. "This is a photo-stat. There is very little else I can say about it."

"Physical Sciences has the original," Clouthier put in. His round face was redder than usual, with the heat; where Trudeau let his hair grow in long waves, Clouthier kept his cut short to the skull, like a man afraid of lice. "They barely consented to making two copies, one for us and one for the Graphologist."

"And Physical Sciences will tell you it is a sheet of paper such as can be bought at any stationer's," Louverture said, "and the ink is everyday ink, and the envelope—if they remember to examine the envelope—was sealed with ordinary glue. They will not tell you what the letter smells like, or the force with which the envelope was sealed, because these things cannot be measured."

"Which is why we need you," Trudeau said. "Concentrate on the text for the moment: the other parts will fall into place in time."

"I take it there was no ransom demand?" Louverture said; Trudeau nodded. That was why they had called him, of course: his greatest successes had been in finding the logic behind crimes that seemed, to others, to be irrational. Crimes they thought a little black blood made him better able to solve.

"No daughters of prominent families missing, either, so far as we know," Clouthier said. "We have gardiens stagieres canvassing them now."

Louverture smiled, privately, at the thought of the group at the café being called away on long, hot velocipede rides around the city. "Of course, the families of kidnap victims often choose not to inform the police—though rationally, they have much better chances with us involved. Still, I do not think that is the case here: if a kidnapper told the family not to involve the police, why the letter to us? Tell me, Commandant, to whom was the letter addressed? Did it come by mail or was it delivered by hand?"

"By hand," Clouthier said before Trudeau could answer. "Pinned on one of the flames of Reason's torch—a direct challenge to us."

"Strange, though, that they should give us so much

time to respond," Trudeau mused. "The thirteenth of Fructidor is just under two décades away. Why so much warning? It seems irrational."

"Crimes by sane men are always for gain, real or imagined," Louverture said. "If not money, then perhaps power, as a man murders his wife's lover to regain his lost power over her. The whole point may be to see how much power such a threat can give this man over us. Perhaps the best thing would be to ignore this, at least for now."

"And let him think he's cowed us?" Clouthier said.

"The Corps de Commande is not cowed," Trudeau said gently. "We judge, sanely and rationally, if something is an accident or a crime; should it be a crime, we take the most logical course of action appropriate. But in this case, Officier Louverture, I think we must respond. If you are correct, ignoring this person would only lead him to do more in hopes of getting a response from us. If you are incorrect, then we certainly must take action, do you agree?"

"Of course, Commandant," Louverture said.

"Very good. I have the Lombrosologist working on a composite sketch; once you have findings from him, Graphology, and Physical Sciences, the investigation is yours. I expect daily reports."

Louverture nodded, saluted the two men, and stepped out into the hall. Clouthier closed the heavy live-oak door after he left, and Louverture could hear out his name being spoken three times in the minute he stood there. He hurried down the steps to the cool basement where the scientific services were and went into the Lombrosology department, knocking on the door as he opened it.

"Allard, what do you have for me?" he called.

"Your patience center is sorely underdeveloped," a voice said from across the room. "Along with your minuscule amatory faculty, it makes for a singularly misshapen skull."

The laboratory was a mess, as always; labeled busts on every shelf and table, and skulls in such profusion that without Allard's cheerful disposition the place would have seemed like a charnel house. Instead it felt more like a child's playroom, the effect magnified by the scientist's system of color-coding the skulls: a dab of red paint for executed criminals, green for natural deaths, and a cheery bright blue for suicides. In the corner of the room Allard sat at the only desk with open space on it, carefully measuring a Lombroso bust with a pair of calipers and recording the results.

Louverture picked up a skull from the table nearest him; it had a spot of red paint and the words *Meurtrier—Nègre* written on it. "It is not my skull I am concerned with today," he said.

"But it is such a fascinating specimen," Allard said in full sincerity. He had asked Louverture repeatedly to let him make a detailed study of his skull: on their first meeting he had, without introduction, run his hands over Louverture's head and pronounced that he was fortunate to have the rational faculty of the Frank and the creativity of the Negro.

"Could we stick to the matter at hand?" Louverture said.

"Of course, of course." Allard put down his calipers, turned his full attention to Louverture. "My sketch won't be ready for an hour or so, though."

"Never mind that. What can you tell me about the man who wrote the letter?"

Allard picked up the notes he had been consulting, peered through his pince-nez as he flipped through them. "He is most likely not a habitual criminal, so he will lack the prominent jaw we associate with that type. He also likely possesses a need for self-aggrandizement—a man of whom more was expected, perhaps, with very likely a prominent forehead. The need for attention suggests a second child or later, so look for a round skull overall—"

"I wasn't aware you could tell birth order," Louverture said, putting the skull in his hand back on the table.

"You haven't been keeping up with the literature. It was in last Pluviôse's Journal—the mother's parts, not yet stretched with birth, pinch the first child's head, rendering it more pointed than later children. All else being equal, of course."

Louverture nodded. "Yes, of course. And—the race—?" He was accustomed to tip-toeing around the subject; most of his colleagues seemed to feel they were doing him a favor by treating him as white to his face and black behind his back.

"A tricky question," Allard said, apparently feeling no discomfort at the topic. In fact he was likely the least prejudiced man in the Corps, genuinely seeing black and white as scientific categories. "What we know shows significant forethought, which suggests a Frank or perhaps an Anglo-Saxon; the apparent motive, however, is irrational, which of course suggests a Negro. On the whole, I would tend to favor one of the European types. Why? Do you suspect . . . "

"It's nothing," Louverture said, letting the unspoken question hang in the air. It was the reason he had been given the case, of course: the fear that this was the work of irrationalists, believers in religion and black magic. The vodoun murders of three years previous had brought him here from Saint-Domingue, and though they had earned him his office and reputation, he had often heard whispers that like follows like.

"I can give you a sketch for each race, if you like," Allard said. "It will take a bit longer, of course."

"Take your time. The sketch will be of little use until we have a suspect to compare it to."

Allard nodded abstractly, his attention returned to the model head in front of him. "As you say."

Louverture tipped his cap in farewell, stepped out into the hallway and headed up the stairs towards his office, wondering how he might conduct an investigation in which he did not have a single lead. A cryptic threat to an unidentified woman, an unmailed letter delivered by an unseen hand . . . Clouthier's canvass would turn up nothing, of course; if the culprit did not want a ransom, he might just as easily take a poor woman, or even a prostitute.

By the time he reached his office Louverture had decided that Allard's delay, as well as the no-doubt slow progress of the graphologist and of Physical Sciences, gave him the excuse to do just what he had first proposed: ignore the whole matter and hope the letter-writer went away, or at least provided him with another clue. He was disappointed, therefore, to open his office door and find the graphologist's report sitting on his desk. Louverture settled into his chair, lit the halogen lamp, and began to read. *Open curves, large space between letters: male. Confident pen-strokes: written cool-headed, without excitement or fear of discovery.* He frowned. That did not square with the notion that the letter-writer was seeking to arouse a reaction from the police, but what other motive made sense? *Correctly-formed letters: well-educated in a good school.* This seemed even more illogical. Anyone who received an education knew that all criminals were eventually caught, save those whose confederates turned on them first. *Neat, precise capitals: a man of some authority.*

Louverture closed his eyes, rubbed at them with thumb and forefinger. A confident man who nevertheless had a pathological need for attention, and felt neither fear nor excitement in taunting the police—as though the message had been composed and written by two different men. The writer, though, had not been coerced, since the letters showed no fear, so what sort of partnership was he looking at? An intelligent criminal with tremendous sang-froid, paired with an insecure, weak-willed . . . but no, it made no sense. The former would restrain the latter from any attention-getting activities, not assist in them; unless a bargain of some sort was involved, the cool-headed man having to gratify the other's needs in order to gain something he required. Access to something he possessed, perhaps—or some*one*—

Well, it was a pretty play he had written: all he needed was a pair of actors to play the parts. Louverture tore a piece of paper from the pad on his desk, uncapped his fountain pen, and wrote *Imagine two criminals—group like faculties* on it. The first criminal, the cool-headed one, would have had little contact with the police, but the second, he very likely could not help it. He opened the bottom drawer of his desk, rummaged inside for a tube labeled LOMBROSOLOGIE; rolled the paper up, tucked it in the tube, and pushed the whole thing into the pneumatic. Standing, he turned the neck of his lamp to point its beam at his bookshelf, then scanned the leather-bound volumes of the Rogues' Gallery there. What would the excitable man's earlier crimes have been? Nothing spectacular, but at the same time something directed at gaining attention. Public nudity, perhaps? Harassment? A man with a wife, a daughter, a sister, perhaps a domestic living in. A man with little self-control, and yet not truly poor, or else how would he have met the educated man he was partnered with? If not poor, though, his neighbors would have complained about the noise that almost certainly came from his house; Louverture took Volume 23, Noise Infractions, off the shelf and added it to the pile on the desk.

He was not sure how much time had passed when he heard the door open. He looked up from the book in front of him, expecting to see Allard with his sketches; instead it was Clouthier. Louverture stood, gave a small salute.

"Officier Principal, what can I do for you?"

Clouthier cleared his throat, brushed at his dark blue jacket with his fingertips. "It's past six. Are we going to see your progress report today?"

"I haven't received anything from Lombrosology or Physical Sciences yet."

"I'm told you haven't given orders to any of the gardiens to search or arrest anyone. Have you spent the whole day reading books?" Clouthier asked, looking around at Louverture's desk and shelves with distaste.

"I've been rounding up known criminals," Louverture said. "Doing it this way saves your men time and energy. Incidentally, are my reports not to go to Commandant Trudeau?"

"To him through me. Public safety is my responsibility, and I must respond quickly to any threat."

"We have almost twenty days," Louverture said mildly.

"If whoever wrote that letter is being truthful. Have you often known criminals to be truthful, Louverture?"

"Why bother to give us the letter and then lie in it? If he wanted to avoid detection, wouldn't it have been better not to alert us at all?"

Clouthier coughed loudly. "It's nonsense to expect him to be logical—if he were a rational man, he'd know better than to be a criminal."

Louverture nodded. "As you say. I'll make sure my report is on your desk before you go—how much longer were you planning on staying tonight?"

"Never mind," Clouthier said. "Just have it there before I get here in the morning."

"Of course. Is there anything else?"

Clouthier seemed to think for a moment, then shook his head, turned to leave. "Just keep me informed."

Louverture waited until Clouthier was out the door, then called to him. "Oh, Officer Principal, I forgot to ask—did your canvass turn anything up?"

With a barely perceptible shake of his head, Clouthier stepped out into the hall. Though he could not help smiling, Louverture wondered whether that had been a miscalculation. It was no secret that Clouthier did not like him, a situation caused as much by his coming from outside the local Corps hierarchy as by his mixed blood. It would be best, he thought, to leave off further teasing of the lion for now. Resolving to restrain himself better, Louverture returned to his desk and began writing his report.

The next morning Louverture was reading over his notes, trying to get them to make sense. He had taken the omnibus instead of his velocipede so that he could read on his way to work, laying the pages on the briefcase on his lap, but the heat and vibration kept him from concentrating. His cap was damp with sweat, but he refused to take it off; he knew from experience how people reacted when they saw his dark, kinked hair emerge from under an officer's hat. Not that there were many people to react this morning, the omnibus being only half-full.

He forced his mind to return to its task. If his theory was right, the second man was undoubtedly the key, but he had not found anyone in the Rogues' Gallery that fit the profile. Could a man with such a need for attention possibly have hidden it all these years? Perhaps he had had another outlet until recently—an actor, for instance, put out of work by the theater closings . . .

A sudden jolt interrupted Louverture's train of thought. He looked up from his notes, saw that the omnibus had stopped in the middle of the street; the driver had already disembarked, and the other passengers were filing off, grumbling.

"Excuse me," he said to the man in front of him, "what has happened?"

"It broke down again," the man said. "Third time this month. I'd do better on foot."

Louverture followed the queue onto the sidewalk. A few of the passengers had gathered to wait for the next omnibus, the rest hailing pedicabs or walking off down the street. The driver had the bonnet open and was looking inside; Louverture tapped him on the shoulder. "What is the matter with it?"

The driver turned his head and opened his mouth to speak, closed it when he saw Louverture's uniform. "It's corroded, sir," he said. "Do you smell that?"

Louverture took a sniff; a sharp smell, like lemon but much more harsh, was emanating from the omnibus' hood. "That is the engine?"

"The battery, sir," the driver said. "That's sulfuric acid inside; eventually it eats away at the whole thing."

"This happens often?"

The driver shook his head. "They break down sometimes, but not usually like this. The scientists think it may be the heat."

"And they're sure it's a natural phenomenon? It hasn't been reported to the Corps."

"I suppose," the driver said, shrugged. "Why in

Reason's name would anyone sabotage an omnibus? What's to gain from it?"

"Well, I hope they solve the problem soon."

The driver laughed. "Me too. Much longer and I'll need another job—there'll be no-one riding them at all."

Louverture tapped the brim of his cap to the man, stepped over to the curb to hail a pedicab. He could hear the other passengers grumbling a bit when one stopped at the sight of his badge, saw the obvious annoyance of the man inside whose cab he had commandeered. He disliked being so high-handed, but he could not afford to be late: after his little dig at Clouthier the night before the man would be looking for reasons to undermine him.

His fears were realized when he arrived at the Cabildo at three-ninety five and the gardien at the desk waved him over. "Officier Principal Clouthier is waiting for you in the interrogation room, sir," he said.

Louverture tapped his cap in acknowledgement and went through the big double doors that led to the interrogation and holding areas, hoping Clouthier had not done anything that would make his job more difficult. When he arrived at the interrogation room he saw the man himself, talking to the gardien at the door to the cell.

"Louverture, nice of you to come in," Clouthier said, bursting with scarcely restrained smugness.

"What's this?" Louverture asked, looked through one of the recessed portholes in the wall; he saw, inside, a dark-skinned Negro sitting at the table. "You have a suspect? How did you find him?"

"He was in possession of another copy of the note, along with paper, pen and ink that precisely matched those used to write the letter, according to Physical Sciences," Clouthier said. "So we brought him in."

Louverture took a long breath in and out. "And just how did you find this particular pen-and-paper owner?"

"I had my men search some of the worse areas of Tremé at dawn this morning. I am not afraid to expend a little time and energy, if it gets results."

"And I suppose he vigorously resisted arrest? I ask only because black skin shows bruises so poorly, I might not know otherwise."

"A little rough handling only. Commandant Trudeau directed that I leave the interrogation to you."

"Gracious thanks," Louverture said. "If you'll excuse me." He nodded to the gardien to open the door and went inside. The suspect was sitting on a light cane chair, his hands chained behind his back; his face, at least, was unmarked. "I am Officier de la Paix Louverture," he said in a calm voice. "What is your name?"

"Duhaime," the man stuttered. "Lucien Duhaime." His eyes darted to the door.

"We are alone," Louverture said. "You may speak freely. Do you know why you have been arrested, Monsieur Duhaime?"

"I didn't—I don't know how that paper got there."

"Someone planted paper, pen and ink in your house, without you knowing?" Duhaime opened his mouth to speak, closed it again. Louverture shook his head. "Well then, how did it get there?"

"I don't. I don't know."

"I see." Louverture sighed. Now there was one man to compose the note, another to write it, a third to deliver it: too large a cast for the play to be believable. Sitting down opposite Duhaime, he realized he still had his briefcase with him; in a sudden inspiration he set it on the table, opened it with the top towards the prisoner, so Duhaime could not see the contents. "I keep the tools of my trade in this case, Lucien. Do you know what they are?"

Duhaime shook his head.

"The most important one is my razor."

Duhaime's eyes widened. Louverture took out his badge, tapped on the image of a razor and metron, crossed. "This razor was given to me by a Monsieur Abelard, but it is not an ordinary razor. Instead of shaving hair, it lets me shave away what is improbable and leaves only the truth." He peered over the open case at Duhaime. "It tells me that you wrote a note with that pen and paper, and placed it on the statue of Reason in Descartes Square, and that we must therefore charge you with suspicion of kidnapping." Duhaime took an involuntary breath, confirming Louverture's suspicion. He took the day's paper from the case, showed the headline to Duhaime. It read *Feu dans le marché: deuxieme du mois.* "Have you seen this? 'Manhunt for kidnapper.' You've cost a lot of time and trouble, Lucien."

"I didn't know anything about a kidnapping. I didn't know!" Duhaime tried to rise to his feet, was restrained by the chain fastening him to the table. "The man, he gave me three pieces of paper, said he'd pay if I delivered them for him. I thought it was a prank."

Louverture leaned back, rubbed his chin. "You've intrigued me, Lucien. Tell me about this man."

Duhaime shrugged, winced as he did so; Louverture saw his right shoulder was probably dislocated. "He was a rich man, well-dressed. A man like you."

"A policier?"

"No, a white."

"A convincing story requires more detail, Lucien," Louverture said, shaking his head sadly.

"He spoke well, though he was trying not to. Clean

shaven, with a narrow face. He wore those little smoke-tinted glasses, so I didn't see his eyes."

"And just where did someone like you meet this wealthy, well-spoken man?"

"I have a pedicab. It's good money since the omnibuses started breaking down." Duhaime looked at Louverture's unbelieving eyes, then down at the table. "I stole it."

"Very well. Where did you pick him up?"

"On Baronne street, just west of the Canal. He was going to the ferry dock."

"Would you recognize him if you saw him again? Or a picture?"

"I'll try," Duhaime said, nodding eagerly.

Louverture closed his briefcase, rose to his feet. "Very well, Lucien, we shall test your theory," he said. "You'll remain our guest for the time being, and I'll see your shoulder gets looked at."

"Thank you, officier."

"It's nothing." Louverture turned to go, paused. "Oh, one thing more. You said you were given three copies: we found the one you planted on the statue, and one more you had. Where is the other?"

"I was to deliver one every night," Duhaime said.

"Where?"

"The statue, first; second the newspaper; and then Reason Cathedral."

"So you delivered the second last night? To the *Père Duchesne*?"

Duhaime shook his head. "No, sir. The other paper."

Louverture swore under his breath, turned to the door and knocked on it harshly. The gardien on the other side opened it and he stepped through; Clouthier was still standing there, by one of the portholes in the wall. "We have a problem," Louverture said. "The *Minerve* has a copy of the letter."

"I'll send a man—"

"It's probably too late. It would have been waiting for them this morning."

Clouthier rolled his eyes. "Assuming your man in there isn't just telling stories."

"He can't read," Louverture said, forcing his voice to stay level. "How do you suppose he wrote the letters? No, he's telling the truth—and by this afternoon everyone will know that 'she dies on the thirteenth.' "

"Perhaps it's a good thing," Clouthier said, shrugged. "It will make people alert; when he strikes, someone will see him and report it to us."

"It will make people panic. With an unfocused threat like this, we'll be sure to get mobs beating anyone they think is suspicious."

"In the poorer neighbourhoods, maybe; we'll set extra patrols in them. But this is not Saint-Domingue, my friend: most of the people here are entirely too rational for that."

"I hope so," Louverture said. Something was nagging at him, some overlooked detail; it slipped away as he probed for it, like a loose tooth.

"At any rate, we still have plenty of time before the thirteenth of Fructidor. Let us hope all the attention doesn't cause our man to move up his time-table."

Louverture nodded, frowned. "Yes, that is strange. Nearly twenty days 'til then, but only three letters." He turned to the gardien by the door. "Have him moved to a holding cell, and see that his shoulder gets looked at."

The gardien looked from him to Clouthier, who gave a small nod.

"I'd best give the Commandant the news," Clouthier said, then tapped his cap and headed for the stairs.

Watching him go, Louverture wondered how much of his theory could be salvaged. If Duhaime was telling the truth—and Louverture felt sure he was—he had been right about the culprit having a confederate, but he was still left with the impossibility of the letter having been written and composed by the same man. He followed his line of thought up the stairs to his office. *When the inescapable conclusion of your assumptions seems impossible*, he thought, *question your assumptions*. His theory depended on at least one of the culprits needing to gain attention for his actions, and the letter to the *Minerve* certainly supported that; the *Père Duchesne* would not print it without approval from the Corps. If that was not the motive, though—or one of the motives—everything that followed from it changed; but what other motive could account for everything?

He opened the door to his office, saw four of Allard's sketches sitting on his desk. Two were the ones they had discussed, assuming a single culprit: one version was white, one black. The other two, both white, were a split version of the first, the one having the physiognomy of a cautious, intelligent man, the second one emotional and impulsive. None of them much resembled anyone he had seen in the Rogues' Gallery volumes the night before. He looked them over, wondering if any of them might be the man Duhaime said had hired him. The first two faces were like nobody he had evercseen, impossible configurations of rationality and impulsiveness; the fourth could be almost anyone. The third, though . . . he narrowed his eyes, imagining that man wearing smoke-tinted glasses. He looked a bit like Allard himself, or perhaps one of the men from Physical Sciences. Someone intelligent, certainly. Louverture tried to imagine what his next move would be. Did he know his messenger had been captured? If so, would he find another one, or would his purpose have been achieved with just the first two letters delivered? Would he be lying low or enjoying the chaos that the story in the *Minerve* would surely spark? No way to know without understanding his motive, and the more Louverture stared at the sketch the more he doubted that this man was seeking a thrill.

Louverture rolled up the sketches, his head starting to feel like a velodrome from the thoughts whizzing around in it. He was missing something, he knew that—some detail, just out of his reach—and he knew that chasing it around and around would not make it appear. Time to do things Clouthier's way: he would have photostats of the sketches made, give them to gardiens assigned to where Baronne crossed the canal and to the ferry dock. Perhaps he could even make some of those snickering stagieres pretend to be pedicab drivers, in hopes the culprit would come to them seeking another messenger. He imagined the man was too smart for that, but all it would cost was time and energy.

Cheered, Louverture headed off to the photostat room. Clouthier could hardly complain about this; just to be sure, he would take part in the stakeout himself—at the docks, he thought, where the breeze off the river would make the heat more tolerable. He would be sure to salute all the pedicab drivers dropping off their passengers.

Early the next morning Louverture sat up suddenly in bed, seized by a sudden thought. Two pieces that had not fit: *the thirteenth* and just three letters to be delivered. If he was right, the two together made up a very important piece indeed, but he could not be sure without a great deal of work—and books that were in the office. He dressed quickly, went downstairs and mounted his velocipede, riding through the empty streets in the dark. Fortunately the rest of the city was still asleep; absorbed as he was by the new lines of thought opening up, he would not have noticed an omnibus bearing down on him. As it was he nearly startled the night guard to death, suddenly appearing in the pool of light cast by the sodium lamps in Descartes square and skidding to a stop mere metres from the door of the Cabildo. He flashed his badge and rushed up to his office. Hours of reading and calculation later he picked up the speaking tube to call Commandant Trudeau.

"Well, Louverture, here we are," Clouthier said when the three of them assembled, some minutes later, in Trudeau's office. "I take it you are going to tell us you've settled the case by doing figures all night?"

"Not the whole case, no, but I think you'll want to hear it. Tell me, Officier principal, do you know the old calendar at all?"

"The royal calendar, you mean? No, I never studied history. Why?"

"What day of the month is it by that reckoning, do you suppose?" Louverture asked.

"What does it matter?"

Trudeau was smiling, nodding to himself. "May I venture a guess, Officier Louverture?" Louverture nodded magnanimously.

"Then if you are right, the timetable has been moved up—or rather, it was further along than we knew."

"What do you mean?" Clouthier said, frowning deeply; then, eyes widening, "Oh—so it is the thirteenth today, by that calendar? Of Thermidor, or of Fructidor?"

"Augustus," Trudeau said, with a glance at the bust on his desk. "Very good, Louverture, though I'm afraid this makes things a great deal more serious."

Clouthier ran his head over his shaved scalp. "But I don't understand. Even the English gave up that calendar years ago. Who would still use such an irrational system?"

"Irrationalists," Louverture said with a faint smile. "And the day is no coincidence, either. Thirteen was a very powerful number to pre-rational minds, associated with disaster. Whatever they have in mind may be bigger than even murder."

"You think it is the vodoun again, then? Is this all part of some irrational magic ritual?" Trudeau asked.

Louverture spread his hands. "I don't know. The number thirteen, the royal calendar—yes, that is common to all of those that hew to the old religions. But the letters, no. The vodoun, the Catholics, the Jews, they all rely on secrecy to go undetected."

"Perhaps the letter-writer is not a threat, but a warning? Someone inside this group who wishes to prevent whatever they are planning to do?"

"Then why not tell us more? And why the letters to the *Minerve*, and the cathedral?" Louverture chewed his lower lip. "If you'll pardon me, that is, Commandant."

Trudeau waved his objection away. "Of course, Officer. Speak freely."

"Moreover, we still have the reports from Graphology and Lombrosology. These tell us the letter-writer is an educated, rational man."

"How can he be a rational irrationalist?" Clouthier put in.

"How indeed?" Trudeau said. "It seems that we resolve one paradox only to create another."

"Commandant, I'm sure I can—"

"I'm sorry, Louverture," Trudeau said, putting up a hand. "Please do not take this as a lack of faith in you, but I am handing this matter over to Officer principal

Clouthier. What you have discovered tells me that we must take immediate action."

"But we have no motive! No suspects!"

"We know where our suspects are," Clouthier said. "All the irrationalists—we know where they live, where they have their secret churches. We found your friend Lucien easily enough, didn't we?"

"But—"

"Officier Louverture, I'm told you've been here since one seventy-five. You've rendered great service to the Corps today, and you deserve a rest."

Louverture clamped his mouth shut, nodded. "Thank you, Commandant," he managed to say. With a nod to each of his superiors he rose and left the room.

The sun was beating down outside, causing Louverture to realize he had forgotten his cap at home; as well, his abandoned velocipede was gone. Shading his eyes with his hands he quick-stepped across the square, then ducked into the Café to pick up a *Minerve* and found a shady spot to wait for the omnibus. The headline, predictably, read *Elle meurt la treizième*; further down the page, another story trumpeted *Une autre sabotage aux théatres: la Comedie Francaise ferme ses portes*. He folded the paper under his arm, unable to cope with any more irrationality. To whose benefit would it be to sabotage all the theaters, without asking for protection money?

"She's not coming," someone said. He turned to see an older black man in a white cotton shirt and pants, sweating profusely; he had obviously been walking a long way in the sun.

"I'm sorry?" Louverture said.

"The omnibus. She's not coming; broke down at Champs Elysées." The man shook his head. "Sorry, son," he said, continued walking.

Louverture mouthed a curse, scanned the empty

street for pedicabs. He supposed that driver had been right in thinking he would be out of a job soon. It was almost like a sort of experiment to see how often buses could break down before people stopped taking them, the way people had stopped going to the theaters . . .

A terrible, inescapable thought hit him. Desperate to disprove it Louverture set out at a run. His face was red by the time he arrived at the theater, a very hot half-kilometre away; he banged on the stage door with a closed fist, catching his breath.

"We're closed," a voice came from inside.

"Corps de commande," Louverture said. He imagined he could hear the man inside sighing as he opened up.

"What can I do for you?" the man said. He was tall, about a hundred eighty centimeters, with a long face and a deeply receding hairline, wearing black pants and turtleneck. He was quite incidentally blocking the doorway he had just opened.

"May I come in?"

The man's eyes narrowed as he stepped aside. "You say you're with the corps?"

Louverture realized that he was wearing neither his cap nor his uniform, and that his hair was showing. He took out his badge, showed it to the man. "Officier de la paix Louverture. And you are?"

"Gaetan. Gaetan Tremblay. I'm the stage manager. At least . . . "

Stepping inside, Louverture nodded, held up his copy of the *Minerve*. "What can you tell me about last night?"

"The cyclorama dropped," Tremblay said. "That's the backdrop that—"

"I know. Was anyone hurt?"

"No—but with all that's happened at the other theaters, people just panicked."

"May I see?"

Tremblay led him down the black, carpeted hallway to the backstage entrance, lit the halogens that hung above. In the pool of light that appeared Louverture could see the fallen cloth, as wide as the stage, gathered around a thick metal pole that sat on the ground. A slackened rope still extended from the far end of the pole to the fly gallery above; the rope from the near end was severed, lying in a loose coil on the floor. "We lowered the intact side so it wouldn't fall unexpectedly," Tremblay said.

Louverture picked up the snapped rope, ran it through his fingers until the end reached him. The strands were all the same length, except for one, and only that one had stretched and frayed. "Has anyone examined this?"

Tremblay shook his head. "I told them it was an accident, but you know how superstitious actors are."

"That will be all I need, then," Louverture said, waited for Tremblay to lead him back out the maze of corridor.

"Officier," Tremblay said when they reached the door, "do you think if we close for a while—the people, will they—"

"Forget?" Louverture pushed the door open, blinked at the light outside. "Of course. With enough time, people can forget anything."

His mind raced as he ran back to the Cabildo. A paradox was not a dead end, he had forgotten that: it was an intersection of two streets you hadn't known existed. He smelled sulphur as he reached the square, saw smoke rising from near the courthouse. The gardien at the door leveled a pistol at him as he neared.

"Keep back, please," the gardien said.

Louverture raised his hands. He could not recall if he had ever seen a gardien draw his gun before. "I'm Officier Louverture," he said, slowly dropping his right hand. "I'm reaching for my badge." He fished it out carefully, extended it at arm's-length.

"Go in, then," the gardien said, "and you might want to get a spare uniform if you're staying."

"What's going on?"

"A bomb. In the courthouse."

"Sweet Reason. Was anyone killed?"

The gardien shook his head. "It missed fire, or else it was just a smoke bomb—but they found two more just like it at the Cathedral and the Academie Scientifique."

"Excuse me," Louverture said, waving his badge at the desk man as he went inside.

"Louverture!" Commandant Trudeau said, looking up from the charts on his desk. "I told Clouthier you wouldn't be able to stay away." Clouthier, his back to Louverture, nodded absently. "Quite a mess, isn't it?"

"Commandant—Officier principal—I think I understand it now," he said. "I think I know who is doing this."

"Which group of irrationalists?

"Not irrationalists; scientists. It's an *experiment*."

Trudeau looked confused, the first time Louverture had seen it on his face. "Explain."

"A series of larger and larger experiments. The theater accidents, the omnibus failures—they were done on purpose, to test how much it takes to change people's behavior. The notes, and the bomb probably too—they were to test us. "

"Test us for what?"

"To see how much it would take to make us react irrationally, see every accident as sabotage, every abandoned briefcase as a bomb. Perhaps we too are just a test for a larger experiment."

"But the notes," Clouthier said, turning to face him. "Who were they threatening?"

Louverture glanced out the window, at the statue in the middle of the square. "Reason," he said. "She dies tonight."

"I'm sorry, Officier, but this makes no sense," Trudeau said. "What would be the motive?"

"I'm not sure. Jealousy, a wish to possess reason for themselves alone? Or perhaps the motive is reason itself. Perhaps they simply want to know."

"This is ridiculous," Clouthier barked. "He wants us chasing phantoms. We know who the irrationalist leaders are; arrest them, and the others will follow soon enough."

"And how will people react when they see the Corps out in force, with pistols? Will they remain rational, do you think?"

"I've ordered a couvre-feu for eight o'clock," Clouthier said. "People will stay inside when they see the lights are out."

Louverture closed his eyes. "As you say."

"Will you join us, Louverture?" Trudeau said, his attention back on the maps on the desk. "We can use another man, especially tonight."

"Is that an order, Commandant?"

There was a long pause; then Trudeau very carefully said, "No, Officier, it isn't. Go home and get your rest—go *quickly*, and show your badge if anyone questions you."

"Thank you, sir."

Louverture went down the stairs, pushed through the gardiens assembling in the lobby; noticed Pelletier, saluted him. Pelletier did not answer his salute; perhaps the boy did not recognize him without his cap and uniform, and at any rate he was talking to the gardiens stagieres around him. Not wanting to interrupt, Louverture stepped outside.

The sun was nearly down, but the air was still hot; Reason's torch cast a weak shadow on the number eight. Heading for Danton Street, Louverture saw a man approaching across the square. He was wearing a dark wool suit, despite the weather; a top hat and smoke-tinted glasses.

Louverture looked the man in the eyes as he neared, trying to read him; the man cocked his head curiously and gazed back at him. The two of them circled each other slowly, eyes locked. When they had exchanged positions the man doffed his hat to Louverture, his perfectly calm face creased with just a hint of a smile, and then turned and did the same to the statue of Reason. Louverture knew that look: it was the one Allard wore while measuring a skull. The man found an empty bench, sat down and waited, as though he expected a show to unfold in front of him at any moment.

The bells in the Cathedral of Reason rang out eight o'clock, and the sodium lamps in the square faded to darkness. The lights were going out all over town; Louverture did not suppose he would see them lit again.

STRAY

———

Benjamin Rosenbaum & David Ackert

She'd found him by the side of the road: Ivan, who had been prince of the immortals, lying in the long grass. Ivan, against whose knees weeping kings had laid their cheeks; who had collected popes, khans, prophets, martyrs, minstrels, whores, revolutionaries, poets, anarchists, and industrial magnates; who could send armies into the sea with a movement of his hand.

She'd stopped her Model T where he lay by the side of the road. He was shell-shocked, marooned at the end of one kind of life, an empty carapace, soul-dry. There were a million drifters and Okies and ruined men cluttering the gutters of Franklin Delano Roosevelt's America; and Muriel had taken him for a white man at first. Colored doctor's daughter stopping for what looked like a white hobo; the wild danger of that. On that improbable fulcrum, his life had turned.

He'd told her what he was. She was a mortal; of course she was afraid. But she'd listened; and at the end of that long, mad tale, she'd gotten up from her cedar kitchen table, cleared the teacups, washed them in the sink and dried her hands.

"I believe you," she'd said, and some strange sweet leviathan had moved through the dark water within him. He'd studied the grain of the polished cedar wood, not meeting her eyes. She was like a glass he was afraid of dropping. But even without looking, every creak of the floorboards, every clink of the dishes told him: stay.

The wedding had been a long Sunday in June. The church was bright, with thick white paint over the boards. It seated forty, squeezed together on pine benches—two rows of out-of-town relatives and Muriel's father's old patients had to stand in the back. There was potato salad and coleslaw and grits and greens on the benches outside. The rich smell of the barbecue, the smoke from the grill. Mosquitoes dancing in the afternoon light.

Muriel smiling and crying and laughing. With Muriel set into the center of his world like a jewel, Ivan was home; when she touched his hand, his enemies became God's wounded children, his centuries of pain and crime a fireside tale to wonder at. In her embrace, Ivan's bitter knowledge was refuted. He was a fool in a garden.

Without her, the world was a desert of evil beings.

And he was full of fear—full of fear, that she would go.

Aunt Gertrude was saying, "No no no, the Monroes, from the *other* side of the family, you know—I think they out in Kansas. Very respectable. Well let me tell you *this*, child—I knew that man was perfect for Muriel *before* she told me he was family. The moment I laid eyes . . . . "

The women fluttered about Ivan and fussed at him. The men tried out their jokes and stories on him. He nodded and laughed, and watched what their bodies told each other. Yes, he was an out-of-towner, strange, his past unknown; drifter, some said, the kind you want to keep on moving past your town. But that kind settled down sometimes—now look how hard he worked at the mill, when there was work. And she was so happy, look how happy she was. And you know that's what Muriel needed to be satisfied: someone with an air of strangeness, like this green-eyed ageless second cousin who had probably been in the Great War.

And he hadn't pulled any of his puppeteer's strings. Not one. All on their own, they had chosen him.

Except Li'l Wallace.

Li'l Wallace was polite. He complimented Muriel's dress and he told the men the one about the sailor and the Dutchman. But to Ivan, the man's thoughts were as loud as a siren: How had this stranger, this high yellow "second cousin" with city manners and slippery ways, won Muriel? Li'l Wallace was strong and good-looking and a steady day-shift man at the mill, and he was from around here. Sure, he was dark, but he couldn't believe all Muriel wanted was a light-skinned man! After ten years of patient and chivalrous wooing, he had a right to the heart of the doctor's daughter. He couldn't fathom how the stranger had gotten by him.

All through the reception, Li'l Wallace's eyes tracked across Ivan's face, hands, clothes, looking for a weakness. Ivan squirmed. It would be so easy: to shift the cadence of his voice to match Li'l Wallace's; to hold his shoulders in a certain way that would remind Li'l Wallace of his dead brother; to be silent at the right moment, then say the words Li'l Wallace was thinking; so that Li'l Wallace would feel suddenly an unreasonable rush of affection for him, would grin, shake his head ruefully, give up his desire for Muriel and love Ivan.

Ivan felt like a cripple. Like a man trying to feed himself with a fork held in his toes. And he was afraid. Eventually, Li'l Wallace would find something out of place. What if he found out enough to hate and fear Ivan? To turn these people against him? Part of Ivan seethed with rage that any human would look at him with those suspicious eyes. How good it would feel to turn that resentment and suspicion, in an instant, to adoration.

But if Ivan was going to be human, to be here, he would have to leave the puppeteer's strings alone.

Ivan had been sitting on a picnic bench in the churchyard, smearing his last piece of cornbread into the cooling dabs of gravy, when Li'l Wallace approached.

"You smoke?"

Ivan blinked up at him. What was this? "I have," he said. He watched the resentment and mistrust brewing in the mortal, calculating its trajectory, aching to banish it.

"Good," Li'l Wallace said, and pressed something small, square, and cold into Ivan's hand. Then nodded, and walked away.

Ivan looked at the lighter. And up at Li'l Wallace's retreating back, and in it, the decision, simple and sweet: that Muriel deserved to be happy.

A shiver raced through Ivan's body. He thought: this human has surprised me. This human has surprised me! Ivan's heart beat large within him and he looked up at Muriel in her white dress, swinging a niece in slow circles in the air. How can this be?

And then Ivan answered himself: because in ten thousand years, this is what you have never seen: what happens, what they choose, if only you leave them alone.

There were moments when he suddenly felt lost in this new life.

Sitting by the pond with Li'l Wallace, a checker-board between them, throwing bread to the ducks, his heart would abruptly begin to race and he would think, what am I doing here? I am wasting time, there is something terribly important I must do, and first of all I must take this human—make sure he is mine, under my control, safe. He'd squeeze his eyes shut and wait for the feeling to pass.

Or he'd be in a church pew singing David's psalms and be overcome with a memory: walking through a walled city to the court of a hillcountry half-nomad potentate, asses braying in the evening, a crowd of slaves falling onto their bellies before him. Scowling at the princes and lords in disgust—this one too passive, this one low and mean, this one dissolute, none of them souls he'd want pressed close to him. And then turning to see the hard eyes and wild grin of the minstrel boy sitting in the corner with a harp in his goatherd's hands. Thinking: ah, yes. You. On you I will build an empire, and a path to God. Whatever you were before, now you are mine; now you are the arrow that pierces Heaven. And seeing the yearning begin in the boy's eyes, the yearning that would never end, that only Ivan could fulfill.

And in the middle of the mill floor, a fifty-pound sack of flour on one shoulder, Ivan would stop, remembering the shadow the roach cast. After he'd feasted on a hundred centuries of human devotion and need, when he was full of power and empty of fear, he'd forced his way past the Last Door of Dream. And beyond the door, where he'd expected answers and angels—in that terrible light, he'd seen a roach skittering across a wall. And he'd known that that automaton, that empty dead machine creeping on and on and on over the bodies of the dead—that insect was Ivan.

He'd burned his castle. Burned his library of relics—the jade knife that killed this one, the lock of that one's hair. Abandoned his living prizes to madness. He'd vanished into a Europe descending into hell: walked through fields of corpses amidst the whistling of shells, on dusty roads by the tinkling and bleating of starving goats. Stared at the blue walls of the sanitorium, seeing the eyes of all those he'd taken. A wall of eyes in darkness. Years which were all one long moment of terror and rage and shame, before he'd crossed the Atlantic.

Now, when it came upon him, he shouldered the bag and moved his feet. One, then the other. Watched the men at their work of stacking, looked at each one, whispering their names. That's Henry. That's Roy. That's Li'l Wallace. Thought of Muriel waiting at home. Of ham and collard greens. Coffee. Checkers. Lucky Strikes.

The eyes still watched him, from their wall.

Ivan loved positioning the checkers, sacrificing one to save another, cornering, crowning, collecting. He loved pretending to make a stupid mistake, giving his last piece to Li'l Wallace with a show of effort and disappointment. And if Ivan kept his eyes carefully on the ducks in the pond and hummed a song from the radio silently to himself, sometimes he could distract himself enough that Li'l Wallace's moves would actually surprise him.

The sun was touching the horizon now. Li'l Wallace finished his smoke and handed the lighter back to Ivan. "How's married life?"

"Can't complain," Ivan said, and looked over at Li'l Wallace. The question was guileless, friendly. But Ivan felt uneasy.

"I guess y'all gon' be working on children now," Li'l Wallace said with an easy smile, his eyes on the lake.

Blood rushed to Ivan's face and he turned away. He

closed his eyes and remembered Muriel crying in the
kitchen. "Shush," she'd said, pushing him away,
"shush, Ivan, yes, I *knew*, I know what life I chose, now
you just let me be, you let me be." Her cheeks
glistening, the bedroom door slamming. (And he could
make her laugh again, make her happy again, instantly,
so easily! He'd closed his eyes, knowing where that
road led: a madman in an empty palace, a lock of hair
in a ribbon, burning.)

Ivan heard Li'l Wallace shift in his chair.

So there you are, you bastard, Ivan thought. You
were right all along. You are the right one for Muriel.
You could have given her a real life, a real family. I can
only give her a parody.

He opened his eyes and saw, in Li'l Wallace's, only
compassion.

And that was too much for Ivan to bear. He pushed
himself out of his chair and headed for the woods. Li'l
Wallace said something; Ivan kept walking. He didn't
speak, he didn't gesture. He didn't trust what he might
do to Li'l Wallace if he did.

Ivan pissed against a tree, buttoned up, and walked
deeper into the woods, toward the abandoned graveyard at its heart. He slowed his heartbeat and watched
the shadows among the leaves. Then, at the graveyard's
edge, he saw the girl.

She had dirty blonde hair and wore a dress stitched
from old calico rags. She was about eleven years old.
She knelt in the dirt, her eyes closed, framed in the
sun's last light filtering green through the trees. She
was praying. Her lips moved, clumsy, honest. There
were tears on her cheeks.

Ivan felt her prayer, like a beam piercing through
the veil. That veil that had been like a wall of stone for
him, that door he had opened at such cost, was like a
cobweb to her. She was whispering in God's ear.

Ivan shifted his posture to become a white man, made himself calm, comforting. He knelt by her and put his hand on her shoulder. She opened her eyes but she was not startled. She smiled at him.

"I'm Ivan. What's your name?"

"Sarah," said the girl.

She bit her lip. The question she was expecting was, what are you doing out in these woods alone? Instead he asked: "What are you praying for?"

Sarah drew in a deep and shuddering breath, but she didn't cry. "I live with my sick grandma. When she dies, I'll be alone. Ain't nobody else to take me in. But I'm not afraid. I'm not afraid. God's gonna' send someone."

Ivan stroked his hand across her hair. This girl's eyes were a speckled blue. And yet their shape was so familiar. Where had he seen them before? He wondered if a little manipulation in a good cause might be permitted him. Surely he could arrange for a family of whites to take her in. Maybe he would ask Muriel to bend their rules. Maybe—

There was a crunch of boots on leaves in the forest behind him. "Ivan?" Li'l Wallace said.

Ivan jumped up. Damn, damn, he'd been lost in the little girl's eyes. Sarah looked wildly around. Li'l Wallace stared at them and frowned. They were both looking at him, and there was no time.

Maybe he could have crafted a way to look that would have set them both at ease. In the old days, when he was powerful. But he was so tired now, and he couldn't risk losing his new home. So he looked as Li'l Wallace expected him to—Negro.

The girl screamed.

"Oh my God!" she shouted. She stumbled back against a gravestone and grabbed at her hair where Ivan had touched it. "You're a *nigger*! Oh my God, no, you're gonna—"

Li'l Wallace hissed in breath, and in it Ivan heard their future. The girl running, crying, found on the road, her imagination feverish. Torches. Guns. Dogs. Crosses of fire. Lil Wallace's feet kicking in the air, kicking, finding no purchase, nowhere to stand.

Sarah drew another breath to scream and —

Ivan took her.

She ran to him and collapsed into his arms, buried her face against his stomach, sobbing. Ivan lifted her up gently, nestled her face against his neck.

For Li'l Wallace's benefit, he said, "Shush now, little miss, you know no one gonna hurt you here, we're decent folk here, no one gonna treat you with any disrespect, come now, Ivan's gonna take you back to your home."

And when he looked up into Li'l Wallace's eyes, suspicion and fear were fading. Li'l Wallace blinked and smiled uneasily and let a breath out. His eyes said: you handled that well. I hope.

Ivan nodded and walked back toward the pond. Li'l Wallace stood behind him, uncertain whether to follow, and Ivan said, "I'll see you tomorrow, brother."

The brown duck quacked at him by the side of the pond. Wanting bread. But he had no bread left. Sarah's little body was warm and light against his. He leaned his head back a little to look in her eyes. She would follow him anywhere. She didn't care if he was white or black. He was her sent angel.

Ivan felt the sting of tears.

Could it be different, this time? What if there was no shaping, no manipulation, no harvesting; what if he gardened her soul, not for himself, but for her? She was his now: very well, he would be hers. His heart was racing; he felt her total attention, the silence in her mind, the way the collected clear themselves away to make room for the master's will, and it sickened him.

He could cherish her, like a daughter. Would it bring her back to herself? He'd freed prizes before, abandoned them to collapse into madness. Not this time. Too late to turn back. He steeled himself: this time there would be only love, a father's love!

He put Sarah on her feet as they approached the porch steps. She leaned in toward him, inhaled the scent of him as it breezed off his shirt, his jacket, his skin. He looked down at her, scratching his jaw, and opened the door.

"Muriel?" he called in, escorting the girl inside. He sat Sarah down at the kitchen table and scooped generous curls of ice cream into a bowl. He heard Muriel coming down the stairs as he handed Sarah a spoon.

Muriel stopped when she saw the girl. She had not expected a third person in the house. The two of them locked eyes.

"This here is our new friend, Sarah," Ivan said.

"Hello, Sarah." Muriel nodded, a nod of extreme politeness, a nod in which no one could find any insolence at all. Her spine was knotted tense. She looked around the room at the chairs, wondering if she should sit down. Smiled broadly. Tried not to wonder where this girl's people were, if they were looking for her, what they would do if they found her here. Trying to trust Ivan. Just a little girl eating ice cream, Ivan saw Muriel tell herself, trying not to think of torches and dogs.

Sarah shrank back a little. She glanced at Ivan, looking for some cue or instruction. She found it in his expression and put down the spoon.

"I don't mean to be any bother, ma'am. Your husband was kind enough to help me after I took a fall on the road. He kept saying nice things about you and so we thought I might like to meet you is all." Sarah sparkled at her hostess. Her smile was warm and innocent, smudged with vanilla.

"Oh," Muriel said, relaxing a little. "Of course." She stepped forward and opened the napkin drawer. "Well, you're certainly welcome here."

Sarah flicked a look back to Ivan. He smiled to reassure her. Well done, little one. We will convince my Muriel. She needs a little time for these fears of hers, fears from the world beyond this house. They don't belong in this house any more; they don't matter now.

Sarah stroked her chin, mock serious.

"Now if I had to guess, I'd say you made this delicious ice cream yourself, am I right, ma'am?"

Muriel laughed and turned back to the girl. "Oh yes, and it's kind of you to . . . . " She stopped and looked at Ivan. He realized he was stroking his chin in exactly the same way, and jerked his hand from his face. Muriel handed the girl a checkered napkin. "Sarah, would you excuse us for a minute?"

Sarah did not move. Not until Ivan dismissed her. Then she collected her bowl, flashed a jealous glance in Muriel's direction, and went out to the porch.

Muriel waited until she heard the screen door swing shut. "Ivan, what in Heaven's name is going on here?"

"I'm sorry, Muriel," he said.

Maybe Muriel hadn't believed Ivan's stories until now, not all the way. She'd listened attentively to all he told her about what he was, what he had been, while she fell in love with him. But for her it was just a bad old life he'd led, as if she'd married a man who had fought his way up from being a back-alley drunk. She hadn't thought too much about the people he'd left behind. "You're *sorry*?"

"I just wanted to talk to her, Muriel—I was curious, and then—she was in a bad way, and I thought we could help her—" He gritted his teeth with the effort of leaving alone the tension knotting the muscles of Muriel's neck, the panic in her eyes. A mortal man

would soothe her, wouldn't he? Li'l Wallace would
soothe her. But where was the line? Did he err, in
keeping his face flat, his movements drained of their
power to unravel her fear? She turned her face away.
"Li'l Wallace came up and I had to be Negro again. The
child panicked, so I . . . I had to . . . . "

"How could you?" Muriel whispered.

"Muriel, it ain't like that. I don't want a prize or a
tool. It's—it was just—the girl's about to be orphaned.
We could . . . she needs us."

"You promised me, Ivan." Muriel whispered. It
burned like a bullet through Ivan's heart.

"Muriel, I know it was wrong. But it's done. We
can do this with love, Muriel, as a family—"

She whipped around to face him. "Ivan, how can
you be what you are and be such a fool? Look in that
little white girl's eyes, look at how she looks at me.
That's not a daughter, Ivan. That's a slave. Is that what
you think I want?"

It would be so easy, so easy. "Oh Ivan," she would
say. "You're right, I'm just shocked is all—but that
poor little girl—bring her back in. Let's make this
work."

And then he'd have lost her. He'd have two slaves.

"This is what I am, Muriel," he hissed. "Should I
just abandon her? I'm responsible for her—"

Muriel walked to the sink and held onto it, seeking
purchase. "You're responsible to me, too, Ivan. You
chose me, too. You said 'I do.' " She wiped at the
corner of her eye a few times as if something was stuck
there. "So what, then? Are we going to run away from
my home and family? Set up a new life for you and
your white daughter, with me as the maid?" She leaned
forward at him, her face flushed dark as wine, her
voice shaking. "Or are you just gonna *change* everybody so they don't mind any that she's white? Or so

they don't know no more? Are you going to just work
some of your tricks on Aunt Gertrude and Li'l Wallace
and the preacher and the police? Are we all gonna end
up as your trained puppies?"

He stood up from his chair, his hands at his sides.
He put his ice cream spoon down on the table. If the
others of his kind had been there, they would have
heard volumes in the clatter of that spoon. Muriel just
looked at him. So he said, "I can never give you what
you want."

Muriel burst out crying.

That surprised him, and for a moment he felt a little
surge of terror from an ancient part of him. What was
he losing, that mortals started surprising him? He
hadn't been paying attention. It had been easy to see
them clearly, in the old days, like dangling string above
a kitten, knowing how the kitten would jump. Now
he'd fallen into a mysterious country.

He put his arms around her, and she bowed her
head to push her forehead into his shoulder.

"You fool, you fool," she sobbed, "I don't need no
baby, I just want you."

Like a fist, some kind of joy or sadness forced its
way from Ivan's chest up through his throat and out
through his face. Its passage was sudden and unexpected, and Ivan sighed. He did not know who he was
anymore.

They held each other. Her tears cooled his shoulder,
and he could feel the tremors dancing through her. And
then he tasted his own tears, unbidden, cool on his
cheeks.

"Ivan," Muriel said in a throaty whisper, "You tell
me straight now. I don't want your good intentions, I
want the truth. Is there any hope for that little girl?
Can you undo what you did?"

It was safe here, in Muriel's arms. In this safe place,

he thought about the plan he'd made on the walk back home, and he could smell its stink of pride—the pride of princes. Muriel felt it in the silence, and she stiffened.

"You mortals," he said, the words muddy in his throat, "you walk around with this huge—emptiness in you, like wanting back into the womb. You think we'll fill it. Once you get that hunger . . . you don't let go. You'll die for us, but you won't leave us. Maybe I can make her forget, but the hunger stays."

"And if you keep her here? Or we go off with her?" She shook her head. "Or you go off with her alone? Is she going to get better?"

"I don't know."

Muriel pulled away. "Good Lord, Ivan! Guess!"

He looked at his hands. "I think she'll be something like a child, and something like a prize, and maybe that'll twist her up." He could feel his cheeks get hot. "No. She won't get better. And I'll have to be . . . what I was."

Muriel shook, her eyes closed. She put her hands over her face. "Oh Jesus, oh Jesus," she said.

Ivan said nothing.

She wiped her tears on her apron. "I can't give you up willingly," she said. "God forgive me. I can't make you stay. And I can't follow you into that."

"I know," he said. He thought of Aunt Gertrude, of Li'l Wallace, of Henry, of the preacher, of Bob Pratchett the white foreman at the mill/ How long before he damned them all? He was a fool.

She saw it in his face. "Ivan. Listen to me. You got to leave folks alone." She reached a hand out to touch her cheek. "And you can, I know you can. You ain't no demon, Ivan. You're just a sinner like everybody else."

He kissed her, and took her close. He squeezed his eyes shut and smelled the salt of her tears, mixed in with dish soap and sweat and vanilla and the spice of cedar wood.

Then he blew his nose into the paper napkin and wiped the sweat from his brow. She looked away from him, down at the table, as he got up and left the kitchen.

Sarah was sitting dutifully in the twilight, looking out onto the dark oval of water and the first eager stars that blinked above it. She heard the screen door swing open and turned, bright with anticipation.

"It's time to go home," Ivan said.

She shook her head, unsure if she had heard him correctly. He offered his hand and she took it. Her fingers were cold from the outside air and the ice cream inside her. They walked through the ragged grass over the hill.

In her face was a wolfish joy—she was soaking him in with her eyes. Somewhere behind that need was that lonely little girl, brave enough to pray in a lonely cemetery. His chest throbbed with pain.

Her lips shivered and her teeth clicked together. He wanted to give her his jacket, but how could she forget him then?

They reached the road. He let go her hand.

He stepped back from her and slouched, scratching his head. He spoke in a new tone that was neither paternal nor comforting, but like that green-eyed nigger who lived in the house by the pond.

"Well, I hope you enjoyed your dessert. Now run along afore anyone sees you hangin' round here."

He saw the arrow of panic as it stabbed through her. Where was her Ivan? Where was her angel sent? Who was this man? "No, no," she said, looking around her. Her head was foggy. She wiped at her eyes. She looked at him: some harmless nigger standing with her under the cold night sky. She stepped away. "What—"

Ivan forced himself to turn and wave respectfully, to walk away.

When he glanced back, Sarah was hugging herself. Her thoughts burned the air. A moment ago she had been saved, she had had a father and a home. Had she been with Jesus? No, she'd eaten with some niggers—shame leapt burning to her cheeks.

She pushed past a fence post and began to run. God had seen her, seen her naked soul, seen everything there was of her to love, and abandoned her. He did not love her at all.

The lost soul fell into the night.

Coldness made a fist in Ivan's belly as he crossed over the hill to his house.

He pulled his jacket around him and stared ahead. Muriel had turned the porch light on so that he would not stumble.

THE COMB

___

Marly Youmans

People always say stories are true stories, and I suppose they believe it, often enough; this one, though, is true—*true as true can be*, as my mother used to say. *Cross my heart and hope to die*, a child says. They do, in the end, all hope to die. Nobody wants to be the moon's immortal lover, who lives on, thousands of years beyond his youth, a husk of a man: Tithonus, the grasshopper, who rasps in the weeds when the moonlight touches him. Or perhaps I'm wrong; perhaps most people don't know that a fate can feel more alien than death.

This tale recounts events that occurred some time ago—it might as well be a century, it seems so long past—when I was living in the pretty hill town of Fincastle, Virginia. Before these things happened, I had been married for several years; my husband left me to chase after another woman. The next year he was sorry, but I refused to let him come home, and after the divorce I had what is commonly called a nervous breakdown.

I was very different then from what I am now. In fact, I feel myself to be so very far from that person that I see her as a second and much younger woman. Poor child! Even after coming home from a "rest cure" in the mountains, she didn't feel any self-pity; she was too engrossed in herself to feel sorry. She wore her hair long and tangled; her eyes were green, with explosive specks of gold around the pupil. She was slim and small and serious, with a rose-colored scar along her wrist where she had tried to bleed to death. Two boys had found her lying in a dirt lane leading into the woods, and it was lucky for her—or unlucky, as she would have thought—that they were chasing after a dog and stumbled across her instead. Lucky, too, that they were Scouts with badges and medals and pins: they leaped on her with glad cries, binding the arm with torn strips of shirt and splinting it for good measure with a stick they had been throwing for the dog.

So that was she, staring up at the sky with eyes like glass.

I feel sad for her, though she would never have felt that way; she believed that one must be proud and cold in the face of what can't be changed. She was a regular player queen, with tragedy in her heart. Outwardly, we look very much the same. But I want to tell her that some day things will make more sense, that after many mistakes, one day she will wake up knowing what matters and what is right and wrong. Such border crossings aren't uncommon.

So she, or I, possessed the unwanted treasure of an entire summer with nothing to do but eat and sleep and walk in the fields and on the hills. My former work and companions had vanished, swept away in the aftermath to the divorce. In a year or two, I promised myself, I would find other pursuits, more meaningful than the old ones that had failed me. I didn't want to visit my father's house, didn't wish to see people. If somebody stopped by, I might go out for a walk—would go, very fast, along the creek, not talking much, picking up fossils at the diggings in the bank. I liked fossils: the old dead life of things. They seemed both profound and simple. I felt a kinship with the leaden press of them against my palms. They were clams, mostly, some sort of mollusk with now and then a confetti of twisted shapes.

Once a friend of my husband's told me their names, but the words skittered and fell through my mind as if through a colander with holes much too large. I couldn't meet his eyes. The syllables, each a solid Latin weight, tumbled apart. They, also, were a kind of fossil.

Usually I hid when people came to call. Afterward, I would peep out of the curtains to see who it had been. Sometimes I didn't even bother to do that. I was never sorry, never cared about missing any of them. I knew the way Fincastle would be gossiping about my "illness": one brown study or willful mood and I'd be branded as a madwoman. But I refused to occupy a niche in the public mind—let the village idiot hold that pedestal. I rarely thought much about my husband any more; I had talked him away in my rest cure in the mountains, and he visited me only as a mood utterly black. Though I knew what it meant, I wasn't interested in naming that state of mind, just as I wasn't interested in knowing the Latin names of things that had lived eons ago. Pieces of me were lifeless and couldn't strike light any more than if they had been two stones in a toddler's hands—two fossil mollusks clapped together to make a noise and nothing else.

When I slipped away from town, I liked to walk in the woods. I stayed away from the streets where I had once strolled, greeting my neighbors. When the rector who lived on the corner came to call, I ducked low to the floor and held still, hiding behind a chair. I had nothing to say, and so I said nothing. After a while, anyone will give up and wander off, especially if there's no light on in the house. I went to bed when it got dark, so I never needed lamps.

My method was to creep out of the back door a little after noon, not long after I woke, taking a handful of dry cereal and a bottle of water with me. I was hardly ever hungry in those days.

My best cure for brooding too much was to traipse on the hills until I grew tired. Sometimes I'd drop asleep on a sunny slope and wake when the shadows touched my face. I liked feeling the sun on my shoulder blades, my hair turning as hot as if it were metal and not merely soft and human—cuttable, like the rest of me.

It was on one of these purposeless outings that I first saw *him*.

I never expected or wanted to see anybody when I was out. I was intent on walking off something. That was all. Occasionally a detail of landscape gave me reason to pause, but not often. A flower, a stone, an oddity: objects on the ground could attract my notice. It seemed to me that some day I might be able to gather these objects together and make a new world for myself—a fanciful idea that led to nothing. I seldom looked at the views that were all around me. They were too dominant, too far away from a downward gaze.

Still, I saw him.

I caught sight of a figure standing in the edge of the trees, and, as I passed by, his eyes caught on mine and then broke away. I had no time to register anything except that he was young-looking, with something golden about his skin and hair.

It gave me a flicker of unease—the reflex of old habits of carefulness—to encounter someone so far from town.

I shrugged. What difference did it make? And thought no more.

Yet that was not the last time I saw him, for I glimpsed the stranger less than a week later, near the same spot, while I was sitting on the remains of a stile.

The second time he rode a horse, and a dog ran at his heels. He nodded at me.

Something in the encounter penetrated my absence: I thought it curious to meet a man on horseback in such a retired place. The moment had the air of being plucked out of time, because there was something courtly about his manner. A slight bow? Some old-fashioned cut to his clothing? The hound and horse were black and gleaming, like creatures from a backcountry ballad. When a crow sliced across the sky, I thought: *It should be midnight, with ice sheathing the trees.* As they passed, I saw that the mare's haunches were splotched, as if by moonlight.

After that meeting, I didn't cross that piece of hillside any more, going out of my way to seek places where I had never been.

Nevertheless, it was on one of these alien walks that he first spoke to me.

I had wandered into a little valley. The landscape was deserted, with nothing but a stream swirling between two hills to make a sound. I felt sleepy and thought of taking a nap, but the site seemed so very still and so unfrequented by birds that I changed my mind. An oak stood near the stream, its canopy more than half-killed by mistletoe. Only a few green leaves dangled from a branch. This ancient was a wonderful-looking tree, even as it stood dying—perhaps because it was dying. The scene reminded me of Caspar David Friedrich's Germanic visions with their decayed boles, processions of monks, ruins, and strange encounters in the sublime. A few years before, I had taken a fancy to Friedrich's paintings and now owned a shelf of books devoted to illustrating and discussing his work. In more energetic times, I had gone on pilgrimage to see a few of the pictures in museums—what is real being so much more alive than a copy.

The romantic tree had caught my attention so completely that I didn't hear him coming down the hillside. When he spoke, I started and had the impulse to flee. I suppose it showed on my face.

"Wait! I'm sorry, I didn't mean to—"

"I'm not—"

"No, of course not. Tired, maybe."

Not frightened, I told myself, *not frightened or even tired, no*. Yet light-headedness came over me, and my pulse was jittery under the scar at my wrist as if the blood were once more seeking a way out. Specks of darkness swarmed before my eyes, and then cleared slowly. He was still standing near me, one hand in the air. Perhaps he had thought that I might fall.

There! I had looked someone full in the face, the first such gaze in a long time. And I was surprised to find that I could still be pleased by another human being's countenance—so pleased that I felt a touch of unreality and wondered whether I had made him up. The eyes were hazel, and nearness showed that he was altogether rather uniform in color, being a golden brown all over—face, arms, shoulder-length hair. The effect was curious. My eyes slid to his fingers. They were large, with pronounced knuckles, knotty and older-looking than the rest of him. Otherwise, he appeared close to my own age. I noticed a comb in his hand.

"Sit," he told me, gesturing toward a flat stone at the brink of the stream.

I couldn't think what to do.

"Go on," he added; "I won't hurt you."

So I sat. Today I sigh at that girl! Why didn't she cry out or tell him to leave? Why didn't she fling herself away? He could have stopped her, of course, but I don't think he would have.

After I had settled myself, he knelt on the grass beside the stone. He didn't begin with the comb but with his fingers. Did I say my hair was uncombed? Had been untended for a long time? Mats that were halfway to dreadlocks hung below my shoulders. Thread by thread, he tugged at the knots. Once he plucked a dried ox-eye daisy from somewhere near the crown of my head. I could smell his skin, the musk of sweat mingled with thyme. At one point I turned to look at the lowered face, the fingers unweaving my hair. For an instant, he shifted his gaze from the task to my eyes. What mood I was in, I hardly know. Under the rose-colored scar at my wrist, the blood flew like a ribbon being unreeled.

He leaned close to untangle a snag above my ear; his breath grazed my neck. The tick of the pulse there felt magnified under his eyes.

The breeze pushed at some loosely balled hair, snared in the grass. Have you ever seen flax pounded and threshed and dragged through hetchels? When wind nudges the clouds of leftover filaments, they roll and catch on the barn floor or on stems in the yard. In an era when everything had its uses, they were gathered for spinning unless birds dared the barnyard and stole some for their nests. But my hair was knotted beyond use, and it was far from flaxen.

When his hands had made the orbit of my head, the stranger reached for the comb. Wielded, the wood shed a fragrance, not quite gardenia—more delicate, less cloying. Afterward he brought water from the stream in his cupped hands and moistened my hair, combing for a long time until once more I began to be sleepy.

"I've always loved this shade of red." His voice sounded low, as if coming from a distance. "I knew it would be wavy when untangled and dried."

His face was near mine. For some moments, I imagined this scene: that I would move toward him, and that he would kiss me. But a cloud passed over the sky, and my thoughts unaccountably drifted away to my ex-husband and how he had betrayed me and wanted to return when it was too late, my heart dead and only grief still springing up with life. When I came back to myself, he was gone. The comb remained, prettily carved from an unfamiliar tree and inset with flowers. Again I felt bewilderment: had it all been a fancy? I remembered the rest cure in the mountains, how my father had given me a queer, puzzled look when he came to visit, saying that I didn't seem entirely present and accounted for. But I had been given my release, my papers signed, and here was a comb that could not be explained away. The heart of each flower appeared to be a chip of ruby; I couldn't identify the wood. Though the grain suggested tiger maple, I had never met with any tree so green at its core. Relaxing, my hand disclosed a row of tooth marks stamped into my palm. Yes, the comb was an undreamt thing, with heft and texture. I hadn't made it up. I jumped to my feet, scanning the forest and the fields. The day was perfectly clear; I could see hills and a cluster or two of distant houses. Until that moment, I had forgotten how lovely the Virginia hill country could be. But I couldn't catch a glimpse of—what was he called? I'd let a man rake his fingers through my hair and never asked his name.

The next morning I failed to use the comb, but I looked in the glass and was not displeased. My hair seemed to have grown since the day prior and to be more luxuriant and floating. I inhaled the scent of the greenwood comb, feeling a moment's giddiness. The sprinkle of freckles on the bridge of my nose, the gold brows and lashes, the mouth that my ex-husband had found lush and sensual when he first met me: I stared at the image as if at a second person. It had been a long time since I had stopped to inspect myself in a mirror.

I bathed and put on a clean white dress. That summer I wore nothing but white. I had five or six old-fashioned cotton dresses with tucks and white embroidery, and I wore them constantly. Perhaps it was a form of mourning. No one had died and deserved black, but I might have been marking the length of a sorrow. Or perhaps I wanted to return to the innocence of childhood, before my husband Hammett had wronged me.

Lashing my hair back with a ribbon, I left for my walk, the comb safe in my pocket. The more I had examined it, the more I had admired the workmanship in the inlay of flowers and tendrils, set in an exotic-seeming wood.

I rambled through places that had imperceptibly become favorites; eventually I found myself in the valley by the stream. I skirted the margin of the water, searching for signs of the stranger, but there was nothing. The Friedrich oak with its few leaves and burden of mistletoe seemed as shrouded in secrecy as before. Slowly I inspected the tree line; I found no sign of a path or any sort of habitation. I considered leaving the comb beside the brook. In the end, I carried it home, and I didn't return to the spot for some days.

In that time, I began to wash my clothes and hair daily, though I still kept to myself. What would it mean if I never saw him again? The glimpse of his face, chin tilted downward and eyes on my hair, haunted my imaginings. My neighbors would have been shocked to know that I had allowed a stranger to touch me so intimately. Yet he hadn't so much as brushed my shoulder with his hand! He had been scrupulously careful not to offend. I thought many things about the man; some of my speculations were monstrous. Yet when I remembered his eyes meeting mine, I couldn't believe any wickedness of him.

After a week had passed, I took to making daily visits to the hillside above the stream, climbing to where I could survey the valley. The old pleasure in landscape, come back to me at last, made me feel more content than I had been in many months. Now and then I would haul the comb through my hair. It was lengthening, faster than was usual in the summertime, and I suspected that it might mean that I was returning to health and getting over my wrecked marriage. In the worst of my depression, strands had fallen whenever I washed my hair. The next time I bathed, I would find that a delicate red bird's nest had collected at the drain. The woven cup would be dry and puffy, easily detached and tossed from the window. These days I seldom saw even a single thread on my shoulder. While I combed, I would forget the dark thoughts linked to my married life and enter a state that felt peaceful and empty. Once or twice I fell asleep in the sun but never woke to find the stranger calling me by name—I half wanted to hear it, until I remembered that he couldn't possibly know mine, just as I didn't know his.

One afternoon, perched on the crest of the hill, I spotted something moving in the west. As I held up a hand to shield my eyes, a shape seemed to flutter indistinctly against the brightness. High summer was a period of occasional mirage and daytime swelter; I blinked, settling the vision. It was a human figure.

Alerted, I slid from my post on a boulder into the shadows. I was frightened at the idea that it might be him and at the reverse—that it might be an even less familiar stranger. And so it proved: the second man charged forward with short, electrical jolts. His progress made me think with a start of Hammett, who had bristled with energy. This man was dressed all wrong for the climate, with heavy layers, some of them already shed and flung over one shoulder. Although the moustache gave the fellow a slightly comic appearance, like a cowboy in a spaghetti western, an authentic malevolence rolled off him. This, too, conjured my former husband, at least as he was in our final months together. For some moments I felt unmoored and dizzy-headed, until I managed to convince myself that this was someone entirely unknown to me.

The landscape seemed resistant to him, or perhaps he had picked a fight with the world; his arms punched through the atmosphere like a boxer's. He appeared to grip a weapon in one hand, but whether a gun or some other instrument, I couldn't tell. I slipped behind a tree, gathering my dress in a bunch at my knees so that it would not billow out and betray me. He paused, his head lifting as if he were scenting the wind, and then loped up and down the stream like a dog, bending to touch the stone where I had sat while my hair was combed. When he snatched something from a patch of weeds, I gasped, sure it was a snarl of my hair. The find must have meant nothing to him, whatever it was, because he jerked his hand outward, casting it away. I remained hiding behind the trunk of the tree until he had been gone for many minutes. Venturing to the rock, I surveyed the trees and meadow.

I might have stayed there until dark, unsure whether I could safely depart, if the stranger with the comb had not come along. He appeared to the west, traveling on foot easily and quickly. Perhaps he caught sight of me as he crossed a low ridge and passed into the valley; his face was turned toward mine. I felt a compulsion to warn him about the other man.

The slope sped my feet; the white dress flew behind me as I spilled out of the woods, racing through the meadow of thyme and wildflowers—I almost collided with him. When he reached an arm to catch me, I blurted out the story, what there was of it. He didn't seem in the least surprised.

"And what's your name? Where have you been?"

He looked around before answering. There wasn't a streak of haze, the view so clear that from the hill-top above I had seen the dots of people moving near a distant clump of farmhouse and outbuildings.

"Far away." He looked serious, adding, "Don't worry about me. I can take care of myself. And Flyn," he told me; "the name is Flyn. Yours is Penelope. Penelope Ophie. Your maiden name, that is." He gave me the merest quirk of a smile. "You knew that, of course."

I was alarmed, wondering how he could know such a thing about me. A thin gold necklace that I had worn when I was a little girl, with Penny in cursive, floated up from memory.

"How do you—"

"I followed you, last time, to make sure you got home all right. And I spoke to one of your neighbors, an old lady with her hair in a twist—or she talked to me—and she told me your name—"

"And probably the story of my life, as she sees it," I said, indignant. So that was how! He would know everything about me, I supposed, including the way the locals were nosing around, checking for any signs of deviation from the norm of Fincastle sanity.

"Yes," he said; "But I wasn't trying to spy. She pinned me to the sidewalk and told me more than I needed to know. She's worried, I'd guess."

I felt in my pocket for the comb. Pressing a fingertip against the teeth and the shapes of the petals had become a habit.

"Here, let me." He took the comb from my hand and began sliding it through my hair. "You've got hair like a sea to drown in."

Half-excited and half-afraid because he had

followed me home, I stood passively, letting the teeth sink through my hair. He would have seen my cottage with the stone foundation and the cherry next to the porch, the hibiscus blooming in the side yard. Mrs. Beklace would've told him about my—about what had happened to me and what a shame it had been and how I had taken on. She couldn't have helped herself.

"Flyn," I whispered.

"Don't worry. I think my own thoughts."

He was combing my hair in long, dreamy strokes, and I had the sense once again that it had grown wildly of late—that it was even now striving to match the sweep of his motion. I put my hand out and touched him on the arm, a bit timidly, because just then he seemed foreign—so peculiar in his first approach to me, so striking in his coloring and height. How incongruous he must have appeared, bending to catch Mrs. Beklace's gossip! My face felt flushed and hot from the rush down the hill, but he seemed cool, and as if he was enjoying the sensation of his arm gliding along my hair. And it was longer then before. Maybe the waves had loosened, uncrinkling in the dry warmth of the day.

I wanted to know plain and simple things: *Who are you? Where do you live, where do you come from? What do you do for a living?* These are the sorts of questions that people ask. But I couldn't bring myself to say them.

When I touched his sleeve, he glanced at me, then gave a little crooked smile before bending to kiss me, one arm pressing me close while the other went on, stroking through my hair.

In one lifetime, there must be only a scattering of memorable kisses. Perhaps most are forgotten, except as they are recalled by an unusual setting or time: a kiss after a return from battle, a kiss by a waterfall under the moon, a single star-crossed kiss from the person for whom one was intended from the foundation of the worlds—one kiss, but no more after.

His skin gave off heat, and where our bodies touched, I felt something that I had never known before: my blood vessels and nerves seemed to have leaped to his. When he leaned away, I felt a sense of deprivation different from anything I had ever felt before. All I wanted was to press against him, to be taken into him. I suppose that sounds strange. I have to remind myself how very little I knew of Flyn—that what I wanted was to let a man I'd barely met thresh away my clothes until I lay naked under the shadow of the trees.

"No." He gathered the sheaf of my hair and tugged. "Come on. He's coming back. I have a feeling that I don't like—"

We jumped the stream and took cover in the woods below.

"Can you go home by yourself?" His eyes were no longer on me but on the high ground.

"Yes, of course, but—"

"Then go."

I turned my face away, not wanting to be rejected; I'd had enough of that.

"Wait. Here." He thrust the comb into my pocket, and I shut my hand over it, feeling the faint trembling life in it subside.

"And this, too." He took a chain from his neck and looped it around mine.

"What's that?"

"Keep it, in case I don't see you for a while. Inside your dress, so no one spies it. Maybe I'll give it to you properly, another time."

He ventured into the clearing and stared at the horizon and tree line before subsiding back into the shade.

"What do you mean, in case you don't see me? I want you to come home with—"

"I want to see you as well; it's not that. Just hard to explain."

In the dark under the trees we kissed again.

"Go on." He pushed me away.

Dusk was drifting over the slope, and sunset gashed the twilight above the crown of the highest hill. I must have paused for a backward glance a dozen times, even though I couldn't see him through the trees. Gold and crimson gouges lingered in the sky. Once I reached the grassy path across the fields, I ran most of the way to town. It was a bright moonlit evening; I hoisted my skirts and raced along the sidewalk toward home, startling Mrs. Beklace, out with her terrier. I gave them a moonstruck smile and laughed as she exclaimed that I had given her "such a fright!" Inside the cottage, I switched on all the lamps. In the mirror my hair fell past my waist. I stared at my flushed reflection for a long time, sure that I had subtly changed during the day. After a while, I sat down on the unmade bed and began combing. It made me sleepy, I noticed, and once I felt half frightened by a tickling sensation in my scalp.

At midnight, I was awakened by a spatter of pebbles striking the window. I glimpsed Flyn's face, the forehead and cheekbone scored by an ugly slash. He wouldn't come in, wouldn't let me come out.

"It's all right. It's not the first time," he whispered. "I have certain—enemies, here and—elsewhere. We've gone on this way for eons—"

"Let me help you," I urged.

Yet I did what he asked and handed out a package of gauze and some ointment, begging him to come inside all the while. I was shameless, but our hands barely touched; he vanished into the dark.

Mechanically I picked up the comb and comforted

myself, drawing the teeth through my hair until I fell asleep, sprawled on the tumble of bedding. In the morning the lamps were still burning. I walked through the six rooms of my house, clicking off switches.

On the slope and valley that morning, there wasn't the least evidence of Flyn or of the other man. I had expected something: blood drops on the grass, a corpse, a weapon. I wouldn't have been startled by anything in the shape of a blunt instrument, but there was nothing to cause surprise.

The afternoon crawled by, and the next—a swath of days, each warm and sunny and empty. I no longer thought about my former husband at all, except to wonder what I had ever seen in him. I had somehow mixed up Hammett with the second stranger. The image of Flyn burned in my thoughts and would not go out. One afternoon I curled up on a sweet-smelling bank of thyme and, like a person enchanted, thought only about him. I didn't plan to leave for home until the first tinge of rose appeared over the hill, and even then I refused to go without a final willing of him to appear.

"Flyn, Flyn, Flyn—"

The name rebounded from the slopes, seeding the air with clamor. Against the sunset, I made out a wavering darkness: it solidified and slid across the field of pink.

I wasn't sure what I had seen. Remembering how the other man had scored Flyn's face, I retreated toward the forest while the sky darkened past cobalt. Near the stream I paused, as gripped by the nocturnal songs of katydids and peepers as I had once been by an unnatural quiet. A nightjar cried out as she swept past and away . . . bats were flittering overhead, hunting for mosquitoes, and the wind made a rushing noise in the tree-tops.

It must have been the breeze that flung away my fear. I didn't stir. My white dress glowed, a beacon showing where I had stopped to listen to the chorus of night.

"Hush. It's me." Flyn's hand found mine. "Anybody else about? You brought the comb?"

Gladness flashed through me. For that instant, I felt my nerves turning to light, and thought: *I am a branch of gold.*

"I always have it." The words trembled on the air. It was true. My skin had even begun to take on the fragrance of the wood. "And there's just the two of us."

"Here. Kneel down." He had dropped to his knees and, as I soon saw, was making a hurried tepee from lint and sticks and shreds of bark. "I want the sun," he murmured. He fished in his pockets for what proved to be a flint stone and a small C-shaped bar of steel. Hurriedly striking sparks, he nursed the fire until it illumined our hands and faces.

"I've never seen anyone do that so quickly—"

"Around your neck—the necklace—do you still have it?"

I fished the string from inside my dress. I had examined the disk repeatedly but could not detect anything through the hard red wax stamped with an image of two trees. Though tempted, I had left it alone.

Flyn heated the covering in the flames until it was soft and could be easily stripped away.

"It's too soon, but I can't help that. I don't have the time." He showed me a pair of rings glinting on his palm. A streak of the coating clung to his skin. "For my family, rings like these have been the sign of union for hundreds of years. Will you take one? Wear it?"

I could have said *no*.

Yet I could no more have uttered the word *no* than

flown to the top of the ash tree at the peak of the hill. Where did he come from? And did he intend to use a ring in the same manner that Hammett had done? I didn't ask.

"What are the letters? It's not English, not any language I recognize." I picked up the smaller of the two and held it close to the firelight. It was surprising how much writing could fit on the inside of a band.

"That is the binding. In the old, almost forgotten tongue."

"But what is it?"

"The binding is—is binding." He stared at the darkness. Light flickering on his cheek made his skin look like the smooth surface of a statue, cast in gold. "Not like other promises. It calls on seven names of God and the corners of the universe and the elements of creation, on the hoop of time and the word that began the world. It is indissoluble. It says that we can't be parted, even if we are very far apart."

"I hardly know—"

I broke off. It was no use to say that I hardly knew him. No, I wouldn't wish for more time, a proper courtship, the perfect moment. I knew that I would let him put the ring on my finger, whatever it meant, if he asked again. The yielding was in me like a desire for annihilation, just as I wanted him to render me to nothing—to dissolve my body into his—by the touch of his hands. "But I don't understand the words."

"It doesn't matter. They'll bind all the same." He reached as if to take hold of my hair, and then drew back. "Only the willingness matters."

"Will it hurt me? Will I be sorry?"

"Sometimes, I suppose," he said; "Is there anything unalloyed? You will be as good as your name, often waiting. My business will call me elsewhere. You'll come to have purposes apart from mine."

"Good as my name—like Penelope with Ulysses, you mean? Penelope with her tapestries? There was a child. A boy, wasn't it?"

"Things appear in patterns," he said, though the words remained oblique to me. "That doesn't mean they aren't different. It's just the nature of lives. There are only so many ways to arrange them. It's the same way with me and the man you saw—as old as Cain and Abel, I suppose."

It was an odd way to answer. He was looking away from me, but when I spoke his name, he turned.

"Will you wear it?"

I nodded, feeling that the ground under me was the lip of an abyss that I could neither fathom nor resist.

The metal was neither yellow gold nor silver. It appeared lustrous, rather like white gold, though the color shifted by the shimmer of firelight. When he slid it home, the band chilled me but in an instant became warm. Until then, I had been alarmed, my fingers trembling so visibly that Flyn had taken my hand between his. I imagined the intricate, tiny words inside the ring slipping through the pores of my skin and flying through the chambers of my heart.

"Now put the other on me."

When I hesitated, he added, "One can't be worn without the other." In each of the rings a twist in the metal made the shape into a Möbius band. I picked up the one remaining and looked through it at the flames.

"Infinite." I hardly knew that I had spoken when he nodded and held out his hand. Though I expected that the ring would never pass the second knuckle, it easily nestled into place.

"Is that all?" If this was a ceremony of marriage, it seemed as crude as a pair of Puritans jumping over a broomstick.

"Simple, isn't it? Just a circle, like a wheel or the

face of a clock." He scattered the fire with his bare fingers, sparks flashing around the ring.

"I don't know." The unaccustomed weight made me uneasy, and I ran a finger over the twist in the metal.

"There's one thing I need to tell you. After tonight, I may not see you for a while. I can't help it. That's why I wanted this to happen now—"

"How long?"

"Oh, I don't know." He tucked a strand of hair behind my ear. "Until your hair touches your knees, perhaps. A good long time."

"I'll use the comb."

"Yes. Use the comb. That will pass the time."

I watched him, fearful that I had done something transgressive, though it did not feel wrong. Flyn reached for my fingers. I felt the same sense of nervous conjunction with his body, worse than before. When he was absent, would the branches of my blood flow in me and elsewhere, joining us in secret?

Just as the sunset was shut out by bars of cloud, a fine rain fell. Afterward the fireflies came out, and the stars. I don't know where we wandered, for I was quickly lost. We seemed to go a long way in the forest, stopping now and then to press close. Again I felt that our blood and nerves made a single circuit. In time we came to a small pavilion. Pavilion may seem a strange choice of word, but I can't think what else to call the roofless place where we made our strange, potent love under the moon. The surge and crest of wanting seemed nothing like anything I had known before: akin to the ocean in depth and mystery and tidal force.

Afterward I would sleep at his side like a shell tossed to the beach, and then wake as the tide wakes, mounting toward the crash of rollers that hurls the seaweed and crystal onto the shore. The silver walls rose up, broken by arches. As the night wore on, they became more and more distinct, as if tugged into being by the moon. When Flyn fell asleep, I stepped to an archway and looked out to see what appeared to be the same stream and the hillside where we had begun, so that our travels through the night seemed also like the pattern of a ring. Once I dreamed as I had never dreamed before: I was a harp, and he the harper; I was the sea, and he a drowned sailor; I was a red tree under three blue moons, and he a bird that cried the name of dawn from my branches as a star rose over the world's edge. We slept and woke a thousand times until the rope of sheets hung from the bed, soaked with salt.

"If there's a child," he told me, "don't call him by name—don't christen him until I see his face."

I knew Flyn in the most ancient sense of the word: knew every inch of his body, the hardness of his chest, the long bones of the legs, the planes of the face, the whorl of hair near the crown of the head. His words became familiar, and his gestures. He liked to laugh; I hadn't thought that he would be so playful. Hours and hours fled while he combed my hair, the two of us sitting in the bed with the hair spilling across us. If I close my eyes, I can feel the stroke of the comb. I picture his gold body and my white one, with the ravel of red sprangling over us.

In that first passion, it never occurred to me to question him, and even now I know that part of what I love in him is a mystery. Since then I have thought about how the Nephilim flew out of eternity to mate with "the daughters of men," according to *Genesis*. I've pondered the medieval and dark age evidence for the northern *aelfes*, friends to mortals. I've lain in a sea of pennyroyal, reading about the People of the Faery Hills. When the wind bedevils the fallen leaves, it means the Sidhe are riding by. Like the White Queen, the figure of Time himself is said to run and to stand still, all at once, under their mounds. There it's the stroke of midnight at the end of December, when the Old Year and the Infant Year are one quivering self. With the comb in my hand, I have a feel for that stopped quickness where one can go clockwise and widdershins at the same time.

Alone in my bed, I've sifted Eros and Psyche, Penelope and Ulysses, the two trees of Baucis and Philemon. Endless romances impinge on mine. I've dreamed of a green couch in a house of earth, with beams that are cedars and rafters that are pines. I've dreamed a manse on fire, a flooded chamber. When I've wakened in the night, I've imagined other worlds, distant or overlapping with our own. I've studied the permutations in the patterns of human stories, said to be limited to nine.

I've even feared that only the first meeting happened, and all since has been the work of the comb. Yet I keep combing . . .

A thousand wild surmises have swept into my thoughts. I have let all of them go.

Whoever wanted a mystery to be unknotted and fully known was mad, and I am sane. Facing it is like stumbling on a grimy, tallow-flecked masterpiece, still alive with the spirit of the dead—the brushstrokes of a moving hand, the captured forms of mortals— evidence and riddle. Or perhaps it is like a story that will not give up its last secret but insists on strangeness.

The vow and the seven names are still pressed against my skin. Our night, like the ring, seemed infinite.

Yet the moment came when I found myself cold on the hillside, dew sprinkled on my nakedness. I had to face the absence of my lover. Then I felt dismay: not that the night had been a dream, for that would be too simple. I feared madness in the vow, feared that I might have jeopardized my very soul in some obscure manner yet to be revealed, feared even that I had bound myself to some white shadow of my former husband—his opposite, his mysteriously-conceived other.

Shivering, I washed my face in the brook and pulled on my dress. The comb lay in the grass, waiting for my hand. I made my way home. What else was there to do?

Forebodings passed, and I began to miss Flyn.

After a few weeks, when I realized that there would, indeed, be a child, I sold my cottage in Fincastle and bought twenty acres of land, including the hillside and valley where we first met. The purchase took much of what I had—cash from the sale, plus an inheritance from my mother—but I had enough left over to live modestly and to pay our local masons for constructing a one-room cottage with arched windows and a stone porch overlooking the stream. Each afternoon I walked from rented rooms stacked with cartons to the valley, watching the progress of the builders. I made amends to Mrs. Beklace and the rector and other neighbors who had cared about me and wished me well. A month ago the house was finished. Already pennyroyal is colonizing the scarred ground beside the porch, and wind flings the odor of thyme through the screens.

The comb stays in or near my hand all day long, and every night I slide its teeth through my hair until I fall asleep. Not a single elf-lock mars the strokes. It makes the time pass, I remind myself. The infant in my belly stops his kicking when I comb. I sing so he'll know my voice when he is born; I remember that my lover said "him," and I believe that the baby will be a boy. Any day now I'll look into his eyes and hold him in my arms. When Flyn sees the face of our child, we'll choose a name.

Ripples of hair can almost tickle my knees.

The time draws near.

Like a night-blooming cereus, a new purpose is budding in the dark, waiting to startle me with its blossom. Seasons alter the landscape, and one day seems to whisper secrets to the next. Twice I've seen the violent man lurking in the trees, watching for Flyn to step into the valley, and once I spied a riderless horse, spangled with moonlight, flying along the stream. If I wake in the night, the arches of the windows look faintly silver, and the stream is silver, too, and all waiting seems about to end.

Until the hour comes, I rest easy in what I don't know. Some day I'll ask this second husband—stranger to whom I have promised myself—to tell me the seven names and the vow.

I am becoming all longing, like a voice prisoned in a shell, but soon I will be changed—as joyous as a tide that hurls treasure to the sands. Something is turning in me, a child and a desire.

On the hills, trees are green that in winter threw patterns of veins onto the sky. Eternity is wrapped around my finger. Breezes whirl in my house of windows, steeping the air with thyme. I am waiting, waiting: will I break into blossom? am I about to be born?

The comb drips its honey into my hair.

All the world is a mystery.

SIR HEREWARD AND MISTER FITZ GO TO WAR

Garth Nix

"Do you ever wonder about the nature of the world, Mister Fitz?" asked the foremost of the two riders, raising the three-barred visor of his helmet so that his words might more clearly cross the several feet of space that separated him from his companion, who rode not quite at his side.

"I take it much as it presents itself, for good or ill, Sir Hereward," replied Mister Fitz. He had no need to raise a visor, for he wore a tall lacquered hat rather than a helmet. It had once been taller and had come to a peak, before encountering something sharp in the last battle but two the pair had found themselves engaged in. This did not particularly bother Mister Fitz, for he was not human. He was a wooden puppet given the semblance of life by an ancient sorcery. By dint of propinquity, over many centuries a considerable essence of humanity had been absorbed into his fine-grained body, but attention to his own appearance or indeed vanity of any sort was still not part of his persona.

Sir Hereward, for the other part, had a good measure of vanity and in fact the raising of the three-barred visor of his helmet almost certainly had more to do with an approaching apple seller of comely appearance than it did with a desire for clear communication to Mister Fitz.

The duo were riding south on a road that had once been paved and gloried in the name of the Southwest Toll Extension of the Lesser Trunk. But its heyday was long ago, the road being even older than Mister Fitz. Few paved stretches remained, but the tightly compacted understructure still provided a better surface than the rough soil of the fields to either side.

The political identification of these fallow pastures and the occasional once-coppiced wood they passed was not clear to either Sir Hereward or Mister Fitz, despite several attempts to ascertain said identification from the few travelers they had encountered since leaving the city of Rhool several days before. To all intents and purposes, the land appeared to be both uninhabited and untroubled by soldiery or tax collectors and was thus a void in the sociopolitical map that Hereward held uneasily, and Fitz exactly, in their respective heads.

A quick exchange with the apple seller provided only a little further information, and also lessened Hereward's hope of some minor flirtation, for her physical beauty was sullied by a surly and depressive manner. In a voice as sullen as a three-day drizzle, the woman told them she was taking the apples to a large house that lay out of sight beyond the nearer overgrown wood. She had come from a town called Lettique or Letiki that was located beyond the lumpy ridge of blackish shale that they could see a mile or so to the south. The apples in question had come from farther south still, and were not in keeping with their carrier, being particularly fine examples of a variety Mister Fitz correctly identified as emerald brights. There was no call for local apples, the young woman reluctantly explained. The fruit and vegetables from

the distant oasis of Shûme were always preferred, if
they could be obtained. Which, for the right price, they
nearly always could be, regardless of season.

Hereward and Fitz rode in silence for a few minutes
after parting company with the apple seller, the young
knight looking back not once but twice as if he could
not believe that such a vision of loveliness could house
such an unfriendly soul. Finding that the young woman
did not bother to look back at all, Hereward cleared his
throat and, without raising his visor, spoke.

"It appears we are on the right road, though she
spoke of Shumey and not Shome."

Fitz looked up at the sky, where the sun was
beginning to lose its distinct shape and ooze red into
the shabby grey clouds that covered the horizon.

"A minor variation in pronunciation," he said.
"Should we stop in Lettique for the night, or ride on?"

"Stop," said Hereward. "My rear is not polished
sandalwood, and it needs soaking in a very hot bath
enhanced with several soothing essences . . . ah . . . that
was one of your leading questions, wasn't it?"

"The newspaper in Rhool spoke of an alliance
against Shûme," said Mister Fitz carefully, in a manner
that confirmed Hereward's suspicion that didactic
discourse had already begun. "It is likely that Lettique
will be one of the towns arrayed against Shûme. Should
the townsfolk discover we ride to Shûme in hope of
employment, we might find ourselves wishing for the
quiet of the fields in the night, the lack of mattresses,
ale and roasted capons there notwithstanding."

"Bah!" exclaimed Hereward, whose youth and
temperament made him tend toward careless
optimism. "Why should they suspect us of seeking to
sign on with the burghers of Shûme?"

Mister Fitz's pumpkin-sized papier-mâché head
rotated on his spindly neck, and the blobs of blue paint

that marked the pupils of his eyes looked up and down, taking in Sir Hereward from toe to head: from his gilt-spurred boots to his gold-chased helmet. In between boots and helm were Hereward's second-best buff coat, the sleeves still embroidered with the complicated silver tracery that proclaimed him as the Master Artillerist of the city of Jeminero. Not that said city was any longer in existence, as for the past three years it had been no more than a mass grave sealed with the rubble of its once-famous walls. Around the coat was a frayed but still quite golden sash, over that a rare and expensive Carnithian leather baldric and belt with two beautifully ornamented (but no less functional for that) wheel-lock pistols thrust through said belt. Hereward's longer-barreled and only slightly less ornamented cavalry pistols were holstered on either side of his saddle horn, his saber with its sharkskin grip and gleaming hilt of gilt brass hung in its scabbard from the rear left quarter of his saddle, and his sighting telescope was secured inside its leather case on the right rear quarter.

Mister Fitz's mount, of course, carried all the more mundane items required by their travels. All three feet six and a half inches of him (four-foot-three with the hat) was perched upon a yoke across his mount's back that secured the two large panniers that were needed to transport tent and bedding, washing and shaving gear and a large assortment of outdoor kitchen utensils. Not to mention the small but surprisingly expandable sewing desk that contained the tools and devices of Mister Fitz's own peculiar art.

"Shûme is a city, and rich," said Fitz patiently. "The surrounding settlements are mere towns, both smaller and poorer, who are reportedly planning to go to war against their wealthy neighbor. You are obviously a soldier for hire, and a self-evidently expensive one at that. Therefore, you must be en route to Shûme."

Hereward did not answer immediately, as was his way, while he worked at overcoming his resentment at being told what to do. He worked at it because Mister Fitz had been telling him what to do since he was four years old and also because he knew that, as usual, Fitz was right. It would be foolish to stop in Lettique.

"I suppose that they might even attempt to hire us," he said, as they topped the low ridge, shale crunching under their mounts' talons.

Hereward looked down at a wasted valley of underperforming pastures filled either with sickly-looking crops or passive groups of too-thin cattle. A town—presumably Lettique—lay at the other end of the valley. It was not an impressive ville, being a collection of perhaps three or four hundred mostly timber and painted-plaster houses within the bounds of a broken-down wall to the west and a dry ravine, that might have once held a river, to the east. An imposing, dozen-spired temple in the middle of the town was the only indication that at some time Lettique had seen more provident days.

"Do you wish to take employment in a poor town?" asked Mister Fitz. One of his responsibilities was to advise and positively influence Hereward, but he did not make decisions for him.

"No, I don't think so," replied the knight slowly. "Though it does make me recall my thought . . . the one that was with me before we were interrupted by that dismal apple seller."

"You asked if I ever wondered at the nature of the world," prompted Fitz.

"I think what I actually intended to say," said Hereward. "Is 'do you ever wonder why we become involved in events that are rather more than less of importance to rather more than less people?' as in the various significant battles, sieges, and so forth in

which we have played no small part. I fully comprehend that in some cases the events have stemmed from
the peculiar responsibilities we shoulder, but not in all
cases. And that being so, and given my desire for a
period of quiet, perhaps I should consider taking service with some poor town."

"Do you really desire a period of quiet?" asked
Mister Fitz.

"Sometimes I think so. I should certainly like a time
where I might reflect upon what it is I do want. It
would also be rather pleasant to meet women who are
not witch-agents, fellow officers or enemies—or who
have been pressed into service as powder monkeys or
are soaked in blood from tending the wounded."

"Perhaps Shûme will offer some relative calm," said
Mister Fitz. "By all accounts it is a fine city, and even if
war is in the offing, it could be soon finished if Shûme's
opponents are of a standard that I can see in Lettique."

"You observe troops?" asked Hereward. He drew
his telescope, and carefully leaning on his mount's neck
to avoid discomfort from the bony ridges (which even
though regularly filed-down and fitted with leather
stocks were not to be ignored), looked through it at the
town. "Ah, I see. Sixty pike and two dozen musketeers
in the square by the temple, of no uniform equipment
or harness. Under the instruction of a portly individual
in a wine-dark tunic who appears as uncertain as his
troops as to the drill."

"I doubt that Shûme has much to fear," said Mister
Fitz. "It is odd, however, that a town like Lettique
would dare to strike against such a powerful neighbor.
I wonder . . ."

"What?" asked Hereward as he replaced his
telescope.

"I wonder if it is a matter of necessity. The river is
dry. The wheat is very thin, too thin this close to

harvest. The cattle show very little flesh on their ribs. I see no sign of any other economic activity. Fear and desperation may be driving this mooted war, not greed or rivalry. Also . . ."

Mister Fitz's long, pale blue tongue darted out to taste the air, the ruby stud in the middle of what had once been a length of stippled leather catching the pallid sunlight.

"Their godlet is either asleep or . . . mmm . . . comatose in this dimension. Very strange."

"Their god is dead?"

"Not dead," said Mister Fitz. "When an other-dimensional entity dies, another always moves in quickly enough. No . . . definitely present, but quiescent."

"Do you wish to make a closer inquiry?"

Hereward had not missed the puppet's hand tapping the pannier that contained his sewing desk, an instinctive movement Mister Fitz made when contemplating sorcerous action.

"Not for the present," said Mister Fitz, lifting his hand to grasp once again his mount's steering chains.

"Then we will skirt the town and continue," announced Hereward. "We'll leave the road near those three dead trees."

"There are many trees that might be fairly described as dead or dying," remarked Fitz. "And several in clumps of three. Do you mean the somewhat orange-barked trio over yonder?"

"I do," said Hereward.

They left the road at the clump of trees and rode in silence through the dry fields, most of which were not even under attempted cultivation. There were also several derelict farmhouses, barns, and cattle yards, the level of decay suggesting that the land had been abandoned only in recent years.

Halfway along the valley, where the land rose to a slight hill that might have its origin in a vast and ancient burial mound, Hereward reined in his mount and looked back at the town through his telescope.

"Still drilling," he remarked. "I had half thought that they might dispatch some cavalry to bicker with us. But I see no mounts."

"I doubt they can afford the meat for battlemounts," said Mister Fitz. "Or grain for horses, for that matter."

"There is an air gate in the northeastern temple spire," said Hereward, rebalancing his telescope to get a steadier view. "There might be a moonshade roost behind it."

"If their god is absent, none of the ancient weapons will serve them," said Mister Fitz. "But it would be best to be careful, come nightfall. Lettique is reportedly not the only town arrayed against Shûme. The others may be in a more vigorous condition, with wakeful gods."

Hereward replaced his telescope and turned his mount to the north, Mister Fitz following his lead. They did not speak further, but rode on, mostly at the steady pace that Hereward's Zowithian riding instructor had called "the lope," occasionally urging their mounts to the faster "jag." In this fashion, several miles passed quickly. As the sun's last third began to slip beneath the horizon, they got back on the old road again, to climb out of the wasted valley of Lettique and across yet another of the shale ridges that erupted out of the land like powder-pitted keloid scars, all grey and humped.

The valley that lay beyond the second ridge was entirely different from the faded fields behind the two travelers. In the warm twilight, they saw a checkerboard of green and gold, full fields of wheat interspersed with meadows heavily stocked with fat cattle. A broad river wound through from the east, spilling its banks in several places into fecund wetlands that were rich with waterfowl. Several small hillocks in the valley were covered in apple trees, dark foliage heavily flecked with the bright green of vast quantities of emerald fruit. There were citrus groves too, stone-walled clumps of smaller trees laden with lemons or limes, and only a hundred yards away, a group of six trees bearing the rare and exquisite blue-skinned fruit known as serqa which was normally only found in drier climes.

"A most pleasant vista," said Hereward. A small smile curled his lip and touched his eyes, the expression of a man who sees something that he likes.

Shûme itself was a mile away, built on a rise in the ground in the northwestern corner of the valley, where the river spread into a broad lake that lapped the city's western walls. From the number of deep-laden boats that were even now rowing home to the jetties that thronged the shore, the lake was as well stocked with fish as the valley was with livestock and produce.

Most of the city's buildings were built of an attractively pale yellow stone, with far fewer timber constructions than was usual for a place that Hereward reckoned must hold at least five thousand citizens.

Shûme was also walled in the same pale stone, but of greater interest to Hereward were the more recent earthworks that had been thrown up in front of the old wall. A zigzag line of revetments encircled the city, with respectably large bastions at each end on the lakeshore. A cursory telescopic examination showed several bronze demicannon on the bastions and various lesser pieces of ordnance clustered in groups at various strong points along the earthworks. Both bastions had small groups of soldiery in attendance on the cannon, and there were pairs of sentries every twenty or thirty yards along the earthen ramparts and a score or more walked the stone walls behind.

"There is certainly a professional in charge here," observed Hereward. "I expect . . . yes . . . a cavalry piquet issues from yonder orchard. Twelve horse troopers under the notional command of a whey-faced cornet."

"Not commonplace troopers," added Mister Fitz. "Dercian keplars."

"Ah," said Hereward. He replaced his telescope, leaned back a little and across and, using his left hand, loosened his saber so that an inch of blade projected from the scabbard. "They are in employment, so they should give us the benefit of truce."

"They should," conceded Mister Fitz, but he reached inside his robe to grasp some small item concealed under the cloth. With his other hand he touched the brim of his hat, releasing a finely woven veil that covered his face. To casual inspection he now looked like a shrouded child, wearing peculiar papery gloves. Self-motivated puppets were not great objects of fear in most quarters of the world. They had once been numerous, and some few score still walked the earth, almost all of them entertainers, some of them long remembered in song and story.

Mister Fitz was not one of those entertainers.

"If it comes to it, spare the cornet," said Hereward, who remembered well what it was like to be a very junior officer, whey-faced or not.

Mister Fitz did not answer. Hereward knew as well as he that if it came to fighting, and the arts the puppet employed, there would be no choosing who among those who opposed them lived or died.

The troop rode toward the duo at a canter, slowing to a walk as they drew nearer and their horses began to balk as they scented the battlemounts. Hereward raised his hand in greeting and the cornet shouted a command, the column extending to a line, then halting within an easy pistol shot. Hereward watched the troop sergeant, who rode forward beyond the line for a better look, then wheeled back at speed toward the cornet. If the Dercians were to break their oath, the sergeant would fell her officer first.

But the sergeant halted without drawing a weapon and spoke to the cornet quietly. Hereward felt a slight easing of his own breath, though he showed no outward sign of it and did not relax. Nor did Mister Fitz withdraw his hand from under his robes. Hereward knew that his companion's molded papier-mâché fingers held an esoteric needle, a sliver of some arcane stuff that no human hand could grasp with impunity.

The cornet listened and spoke quite sharply to the sergeant, turning his horse around so that he could make his point forcefully to the troopers as well. Hereward only caught some of the words, but it seemed that despite his youth, the officer was rather more commanding than he had expected, reminding the Dercians that their oaths of employment overrode any private or societal vendettas they might wish to undertake.

When he had finished, the cornet shouted, "Dismount! Sergeant, walk the horses!"

The officer remained mounted, wheeling back to approach Hereward. He saluted as he reined in a cautious distance from the battlemounts, evidently not trusting either the creatures' blinkers and mouth-cages or his own horse's fears.

"Welcome to Shûme!" he called. "I am Cornet Misolu. May I ask your names and direction, if you please?"

"I am Sir Hereward of the High Pale, artillerist for hire."

"And I am Fitz, also of the High Pale, aide de camp to Sir Hereward."

"Welcome . . . uh . . . sirs," said Misolu. "Be warned that war has been declared upon Shûme, and all who pass through must declare their allegiances and enter certain . . . um . . . "

"I believe the usual term is 'undertakings,' " said Mister Fitz.

"Undertakings," echoed Misolu. He was very young. Two bright spots of embarrassment burned high on his cheekbones, just visible under the four bars of his lobster-tailed helmet, which was a little too large for him, even with the extra padding, some of which had come a little undone around the brow.

"We are free lances, and seek hire in Shûme, Cornet Misolu," said Hereward. "We will give the common undertakings if your city chooses to contract us. For the moment, we swear to hold our peace, reserving the right to defend ourselves should we be attacked."

"Your word is accepted, Sir Hereward, and . . . um . . . "

"Mister Fitz," said Hereward, as the puppet said merely, "Fitz."

"Mister Fitz."

The cornet chivvied his horse diagonally closer to Hereward, and added, "You may rest assured that my Dercians will remain true to *their* word, though Sergeant Xikoliz spoke of some feud their . . . er . . . entire people have with you."

The curiosity in the cornet's voice could not be easily denied, and spoke as much of the remoteness of Shûme as it did of the young officer's naïveté.

"It is a matter arising from a campaign several years

past," said Hereward. "Mister Fitz and I were serving the Heriat of Jhaqa, who sought to redirect the Dercian spring migration elsewhere than through her own prime farmlands. In the last battle of that campaign, a small force penetrated to the Dercians' rolling temple and . . . ah . . . blew it up with a specially made petard. Their godlet, thus discommoded, withdrew to its winter housing in the Dercian steppe, wreaking great destruction among its chosen people as it went."

"I perceive you commanded that force, sir?"

Hereward shook his head.

"No, I am an artillerist. Captain Kasvik commanded. He was slain as we retreated—another few minutes and he would have won clear. However, I did make the petard, and . . . Mister Fitz assisted our entry to the temple and our escape. Hence the Dercians' feud."

Hereward looked sternly at Mister Fitz as he spoke, hoping to make it clear that this was not a time for the puppet to exhibit his tendency for exactitude and truthfulness. Captain Kasvik had in fact been killed before they even reached the rolling temple, but it had served his widow and family better for Kasvik to be a hero, so Hereward had made him one. Only Mister Fitz and one other survivor of the raid knew otherwise.

Not that Hereward and Fitz considered the rolling temple action a victory, as their intent had been to force the Dercian godlet to withdraw a distance unimaginably more vast than the mere five hundred leagues to its winter temple.

The ride to the city was uneventful, though Hereward could not help but notice that Cornet Misolu ordered his troop to remain in place and keep watch, while he alone escorted the visitors, indicating that the young officer was not absolutely certain the Dercians would hold to their vows.

There was a zigzag entry through the earthwork ramparts, where they were held up for several minutes in the business of passwords and responses (all told aside in quiet voices, Hereward noted with approval), their names being recorded in an enormous ledger and passes written out and sealed allowing them to enter the city proper.

These same passes were inspected closely under lanternlight, only twenty yards farther on by the guards outside the city gate—which was closed, as the sun had finally set. However, they were admitted through a sally port and here Misolu took his leave, after giving directions to an inn that met Hereward's requirements: suitable stabling and food for the battlemounts; that it not be the favorite of the Dercians or any other of the mercenary troops who had signed on in preparation for Shûme's impending war; and fine food and wine, not just small beer and ale. The cornet also gave directions to the citadel, not that this was really necessary as its four towers were clearly visible, and advised Hereward and Fitz that there was no point going there until the morning, for the governing council was in session and so no one in authority could hire him until at least the third bell after sunrise.

The streets of Shûme were paved and drained, and Hereward smiled again at the absence of the fetid stench so common to places where large numbers of people dwelt together. He was looking forward to a bath, a proper meal and a fine feather bed, with the prospect of well-paid and not too onerous employment commencing on the morrow.

"There is the inn," remarked Mister Fitz, pointing down one of the narrower side streets, though it was still broad enough for the two battlemounts to stride abreast. "The sign of the golden barleycorn. Appropriate enough for a city with such fine farmland."

They rode into the inn's yard, which was clean and wide and did indeed boast several of the large iron-barred cages used to stable battlemounts complete with meat canisters and feeding chutes rigged in place above the cages. One of the four ostlers present ran ahead to open two cages and lower the chutes, and the other three assisted Hereward to unload the panniers. Mister Fitz took his sewing desk and stood aside, the small rosewood-and-silver box under his arm provoking neither recognition nor alarm. The ostlers were similarly incurious about Fitz himself, almost certainly evidence that self-motivated puppets still came to entertain the townsfolk from time to time.

Hereward led the way into the inn, but halted just before he entered as one of the battlemounts snorted at some annoyance. Glancing back, he saw that it was of no concern, and the gates were closed, but in halting he had kept hold of the door as someone else tried to open it from the other side. Hereward pushed to help and the door flung open, knocking the person on the inside back several paces against a table, knocking over an empty bottle that smashed upon the floor.

"Unfortunate," muttered Mister Fitz, as he saw that the person so inconvenienced was not only a soldier, but wore the red sash of a junior officer, and was a woman.

"I do apolog—" Hereward began to say. He stopped, not only because the woman was talking, but because he had looked at her. She was as tall as he was, with ash-blond hair tied in a queue at the back, her hat in her left hand. She was also very beautiful, at least to Hereward, who had grown up with women who ritually cut their flesh. To others, her attractiveness might be considered marred by the scar that ran from the corner of her left eye out toward the ear and then cut back again toward the lower part of her nose.

"You are clumsy, sir!"

Hereward stared at her for just one second too long before attempting to speak again.

"I am most—"

"You see something you do not like, I think?" interrupted the woman. "Perhaps you have not served with females? Or is it my face you do not care for?"

"You are very beautiful," said Hereward, even as he realized it was entirely the wrong thing to say, either to a woman he had just met or an officer he had just run into.

"You mock me!" swore the woman. Her blue eyes shone more fiercely, but her face paled, and the scar grew more livid. She clapped her broad-brimmed hat on her head and straightened to her full height, with the hat standing perhaps an inch over Hereward. "You shall answer for that!"

"I do not mock you," said Hereward quietly. "I have served with men, women . . . and eunuchs, for that matter. Furthermore, tomorrow morning I shall be signing on as at least colonel of artillery, and a colonel may not fight a duel with a lieutenant. I am most happy to apologize, but I cannot meet you."

"Cannot or will not?" sneered the woman. "You are not yet a colonel in Shûme's service, I believe, but just a mercenary braggart."

Hereward sighed and looked around the common room. Misolu had spoken truly that the inn was not a mercenary favorite. But there were several officers of Shûme's regular service or militia, all of them looking on with great attention.

"Very well," he snapped. "It is foolishness, for I intended no offence. When and where?"

"Immediately," said the woman. "There is a garden a little way behind this inn. It is lit by lanterns in the trees, and has a lawn."

"How pleasant," said Hereward. "What is your name, madam?"

"I am Lieutenant Jessaye of the Temple Guard of Shûme. And you are?"

"I am Sir Hereward of the High Pale."

"And your friends, Sir Hereward?"

"I have only this moment arrived in Shûme, Lieutenant, and so cannot yet name any friends. Perhaps someone in this room will stand by me, should you wish a second. My companion, whom I introduce to you now, is known as Mister Fitz. He is a surgeon—among other things—and I expect he will accompany us."

"I am pleased to meet you, Lieutenant," said Mister Fitz. He doffed his hat and veil, sending a momentary frisson of small twitches among all in the room save Hereward.

Jessaye nodded back but did not answer Fitz. Instead she spoke to Hereward.

"I need no second. Should you wish to employ sabers, I must send for mine."

"I have a sword in my gear," said Hereward. "If you will allow me a few minutes to fetch it?"

"The garden lies behind the stables," said Jessaye. "I will await you there. Pray do not be too long."

Inclining her head but not doffing her hat, she stalked past and out the door.

"An inauspicious beginning," said Fitz.

"Very," said Hereward gloomily. "On several counts. Where is the innkeeper? I must change and fetch my sword."

The garden was very pretty. Railed in iron, it was not gated, and so accessible to all the citizens of Shûme. A wandering path led through a grove of lantern-hung trees to the specified lawn, which was oval and easily fifty yards from end to end, making the center rather a long way from the lanternlight, and hence quite shadowed. A small crowd of persons who had previously been in the inn were gathered on one side of the lawn. Lieutenant Jessaye stood in the middle, naked blade in hand.

"Do be careful, Hereward," said Fitz quietly, observing the woman flex her knees and practice a stamping attack ending in a lunge. "She looks to be very quick."

"She is an officer of their temple guard," said Hereward in a hoarse whisper. "Has their god imbued her with any particular vitality or puissance?"

"No, the godlet does not seem to be a martial entity," said Fitz. "I shall have to undertake some investigations presently, as to exactly what it is—"

"Sir Hereward! Here at last."

Hereward grimaced as Jessaye called out. He had changed as quickly as he could, into a very fine suit of split-sleeved white showing the yellow shirt beneath, with gold ribbons at the cuffs, shoulders and front lacing, with similarly cut bloomers of yellow showing white breeches, with silver ribbons at the knees, artfully displayed through the side-notches of his second-best boots.

Jessaye, in contrast, had merely removed her uniform coat and stood in her shirt, blue waistcoat, leather breeches and unadorned black thigh boots folded over below the knee. Had the circumstances been otherwise, Hereward would have paused to admire the sight she presented and perhaps offer a compliment.

Instead he suppressed a sigh, strode forward, drew his sword and threw the scabbard aside.

"I am here, Lieutenant, and I am ready. Incidentally, is this small matter to be concluded by one or perhaps both of us dying?"

"The city forbids duels to the death, Sir Hereward," replied Jessaye. "Though accidents do occur."

"What, then, is to be the sign for us to cease our remonstrance?"

"Blood," said Jessaye. She flicked her sword towards the onlookers. "Visible to those watching."

Hereward nodded slowly. In this light, there would need to be a lot of blood before the onlookers could see it. He bowed his head but did not lower his eyes, then raised his sword to the guard position.

Jessaye was fast. She immediately thrust at his neck, and though Hereward parried, he had to step back. She carried through to lunge in a different line, forcing him back again with a more awkward parry, removing all opportunity for Hereward to riposte or counter. For a minute they danced, their swords darting up, down and across, clashing together only to move again almost before the sound reached the audience.

In that minute, Hereward took stock of Jessaye's style and action. She was very fast, but so was he, much faster than anyone would expect from his size and build, and, as always, he had not shown just how truly quick he could be. Jessaye's wrist was strong and supple, and she could change both attacking and defensive lines with great ease. But her style was rigid, a variant of an old school Hereward had studied in his youth.

On her next lunge—which came exactly where he anticipated—Hereward didn't parry but stepped aside and past the blade. He felt her sword whisper by his ribs as he angled his own blade over it and with the leading edge of the point, he cut Jessaye above the right elbow to make a long, very shallow slice that he intended should bleed copiously without inflicting any serious harm.

Jessaye stepped back but did not lower her guard. Hereward quickly called out, "Blood!"

Jessaye took a step forward and Hereward stood ready for another attack. Then the lieutenant bit her lip and stopped, holding her arm toward the lanternlight so she could more clearly see the wound. Blood was already soaking through the linen shirt, a dark and spreading stain upon the cloth.

"You have bested me," she said, and thrust her sword point first into the grass before striding forward to offer her gloved hand to Hereward. He too grounded his blade, and took her hand as they bowed to each other.

A slight stinging low on his side caused Hereward to look down. There was a two-inch cut in his shirt, and small beads of blood were blossoming there. He did not let go Jessaye's fingers, but pointed at his ribs with his left hand.

"I believe we are evenly matched. I hope we may have no cause to bicker further?"

"I trust not," said Jessaye quietly. "I regret the incident. Were it not for the presence of some of my fellows, I should not have caviled at your apology, sir. But you understand . . . a reputation is not easily won, nor kept . . . "

"I do understand," said Hereward. "Come, let Mister Fitz attend your cut. Perhaps you will then join me for small repast?"

Jessaye shook her head.

"I go on duty soon. A stitch or two and a bandage is all I have time for. Perhaps we shall meet again."

"It is my earnest hope that we do," said Hereward. Reluctantly, he opened his grasp. Jessaye's hand lingered in his palm for several moments before she slowly raised it, stepped back and doffed her hat to offer a full bow. Hereward returned it, straightening up as Mister Fitz hurried over, carrying a large leather case as if it were almost too heavy for him, one of his standard acts of misdirection, for the puppet was at least as strong as Hereward, if not stronger.

"Attend to Lieutenant Jessaye, if you please, Mister Fitz," said Hereward. "I am going back to the inn to have a cup . . . or two . . . of wine."

"Your own wound needs no attention?" asked Fitz as he set his bag down and indicated to Jessaye to sit by him.

"A scratch," said Hereward. He bowed to Jessaye again and walked away, ignoring the polite applause of the onlookers, who were drifting forward either to talk to Jessaye or gawp at the blood on her sleeve.

"I may take a stroll," called out Mister Fitz after Hereward. "But I shan't be longer than an hour."

Mister Fitz was true to his word, returning a few minutes after the citadel bell had sounded the third hour of the evening. Hereward had bespoken a private chamber and was dining alone there, accompanied only by his thoughts.

"The god of Shûme," said Fitz, without preamble. "Have you heard anyone mention its name?"

Hereward shook his head and poured another measure from the silver jug with the swan's beak spout. Like many things he had found in Shûme, the knight liked the inn's silverware.

"They call their godlet Tanesh," said Fitz. "But its true name is Pralqornrah-Tanish-Kvaxixob."

"As difficult to say or spell, I wager," said Hereward. "I commend the short form, it shows common sense. What of it?"

"It is on the list," said Fitz.

Hereward bit the edge of pewter cup and put it down too hard, slopping wine upon the table.

"You're certain? There can be no question?"

Fitz shook his head. "After I had doctored the young woman, I went down to the lake and took a slide of the god's essence—it was quite concentrated in the water, easily enough to yield a sample. You may compare it with the record, if you wish."

He proffered a finger-long inch-wide strip of glass that was striated in many different bands of color. Hereward accepted it reluctantly, and with it a fat, square book that Fitz slid across the table. The book was open at a hand-tinted color plate, the illustration showing a sequence of color bands.

"It is the same," agreed the knight, his voice heavy with regret. "I suppose it is fortunate we have not yet signed on, though I doubt they will see what we do as being purely a matter of defense."

"They do not know what they harbor here," said Fitz.

"It is a pleasant city." said Hereward, taking up his cup again to take a large gulp of the slightly sweet wine. "In a pretty valley. I had thought I could grow more than accustomed to Shûme—and its people."

"The bounty of Shûme, all its burgeoning crops, its healthy stock and people, is an unintended result of their godlet's predation upon the surrounding lands," said Fitz. "Pralqornrah is one of the class of cross-dimensional parasites that is most dangerous. Unchecked, in time it will suck the vital essence out of all the land beyond its immediate demesne. The deserts of Balkash are the work of a similar being, over six millennia. This one has only been embedded here for two hundred years—you have seen the results beyond this valley."

"Six millennia is a long time," said Hereward, taking yet another gulp. The wine was strong as well as sweet, and he felt the need of it. "A desert might arise in that time without the interference of the gods."

"It is not just the fields and the river that Pralqornrah feeds upon," said Fitz. "The people outside this valley suffer too. Babes unborn, strong men and women declining before their prime . . . this godlet slowly sucks the essence from all life."

"They could leave," said Hereward. The wine was making him feel both sleepy and mulish. "I expect many have already left to seek better lands. The rest could be resettled, the lands left uninhabited to feed the godlet. Shûme could continue as an oasis. What if another desert grows around it? They occur in nature, do they not?"

"I do not think you fully comprehend the matter," said Fitz. "Pralqornrah is a most comprehensive feeder. Its energistic threads will spread farther and faster the longer it exists here, and it in turn will grow more powerful and much more difficult to remove. A few millennia hence, it might be too strong to combat."

"I am only talking," said Hereward, not without some bitterness. "You need not waste your words to bend my reason. I do not even need to understand anything beyond the salient fact: this godlet is on the list."

"Yes," said Mister Fitz. "It is on the list."

Hereward bent his head for a long, silent moment. Then he pushed his chair back and reached across for his saber. Drawing it, he placed the blade across his knees. Mister Fitz handed him a whetstone and a small flask of light, golden oil. The knight oiled the stone and began to hone the saber's blade. A repetitive rasp was the only sound in the room for many minutes, till he finally put the stone aside and wiped the blade clean with a soft piece of deerskin.

"When?"

"Fourteen minutes past the midnight hour is

optimum," replied Mister Fitz. "Presuming I have calculated its intrusion density correctly."

"It is manifest in the temple?"

Fitz nodded.

"Where is the temple, for that matter? Only the citadel stands out above the roofs of the city."

"It is largely underground," said Mister Fitz. "I have found a side entrance, which should not prove difficult. At some point beyond that there is some form of arcane barrier—I have not been able to ascertain its exact nature, but I hope to unpick it without trouble."

"Is the side entrance guarded? And the interior?"

"Both," said Fitz. Something about his tone made Hereward fix the puppet with a inquiring look.

"The side door has two guards," continued Fitz. "The interior watch is of ten or eleven . . . led by the Lieutenant Jessaye you met earlier."

Hereward stood up, the saber loose in his hand, and turned away from Fitz.

"Perhaps we shall not need to fight her . . . or her fellows."

Fitz did not answer, which was answer enough.

The side door to the temple was unmarked and appeared no different than the other simple wooden doors that lined the empty street, most of them adorned with signs marking them as the shops of various tradesmen, with smoke-grimed night lamps burning dimly above the sign. The door Fitz indicated was painted a pale violet and had neither sign nor lamp.

"Time to don the brassards and make the declaration," said the puppet. He looked up and down the street, making sure that all was quiet, before handing Hereward a broad silk armband five fingers wide. It was embroidered with sorcerous thread that shed only a little less light than the smoke-grimed lantern above the neighboring shop door. The symbol the threads wove was one that had once been familiar the world over but was now unlikely to be recognized by anyone save an historian . . . or a god.

Hereward slipped the brassard over his left glove and up his thick coat sleeve, spreading it out above the elbow. The suit of white and yellow was once again packed, and for this expedition the knight had chosen to augment his helmet and buff coat with a dented but still eminently serviceable back- and breastplate, the steel blackened by tannic acid to a dark grey. He had already primed, loaded and spanned his two wheel-lock pistols, which were thrust through his belt; his saber was sheathed at his side; and a lozenge-sectioned, armor-punching bodkin was in his left boot.

Mister Fitz wore his sewing desk upon his back, like a wooden backpack. He had already been through its numerous small drawers and containers and selected particular items that were now tucked into the inside pockets of his coat, ready for immediate use.

"I wonder why we bother with this mummery," grumbled Hereward. But he stood at attention as Fitz put on his own brassard, and the knight carefully repeated the short phrase uttered by his companion. Though both had recited it many times, and it was clear as bright type in their minds, they spoke carefully and with great concentration, in sharp contrast to Hereward's remark about mummery.

"In the name of the Council of the Treaty for the Safety of the World, acting under the authority granted by the Three Empires, the Seven Kingdoms, the Palatine Regency, the Jessar Republic and the Forty Lesser Realms, we declare ourselves agents of the Council. We identify the godlet manifested in this city of Shûme as Pralqornrah-Tanish-Kvaxixob, a listed entity under the Treaty. Consequently, the said godlet and all those who assist it are deemed to be enemies of the World and the Council authorizes us to pursue any and all actions necessary to banish, repel or exterminate the said godlet."

Neither felt it necessary to change this ancient text to reflect the fact that only one of the three empires was still extant in any fashion; that the seven kingdoms were now twenty or more small states; the Palatine Regency was a political fiction, its once broad lands under two fathoms of water; the Jessar Republic was now neither Jessar in ethnicity nor a republic; and perhaps only a handful of the Forty Lesser Realms resembled their antecedent polities in any respect. But for all that the states that had made it were vanished or diminished, the Treaty for the Safety of the World was still held to be in operation, if only by the Council that administered and enforced it.

"Are you ready?" asked Fitz.

Hereward drew his saber and moved into position to the left of the door. Mister Fitz reached into his coat and drew out an esoteric needle. Hereward knew better than to try to look at the needle directly, but in the reflection of his blade, he could see a four-inch line of something intensely violet writhe in Fitz's hand. Even the reflection made him feel as if he might at any moment be unstitched from the world, so he angled the blade away.

At that moment, Fitz touched the door with the needle and made three short plucking motions. On the last motion, without any noise or fuss, the door wasn't there anymore. There was only a wood-paneled corridor leading down into the ground and two very surprised temple guards, who were still leaning on their halberds.

Before Hereward could even begin to move, Fitz's

hand twitched across and up several times. The lanterns on their brass stands every six feet along the corridor flickered and flared violet for a fraction of a second. Hereward blinked, and the guards were gone, as were the closest three lanterns and their stands.

Only a single drop of molten brass, no bigger than a tear, remained. It sizzled on the floor for a second, then all was quiet.

The puppet stalked forward, cupping his left hand over the needle in his right, obscuring its troublesome sight behind his fingers. Hereward followed close behind, alert for any enemy that might be resistant to Fitz's sorcery.

The corridor was a hundred yards long by Hereward's estimation, and slanted sharply down, making him think about having to fight back up it, which would be no easy task, made more difficult as the floor and walls were damp, drops of water oozing out between the floorboards and dripping from the seams of the wall paneling. There was cold, wet stone behind the timber, Hereward knew. He could feel the cold air rippling off it, a chill that no amount of fine timber could cloak.

The corridor ended at what appeared from a distance to be a solid wall, but closer to was merely the dark back of a heavy tapestry. Fitz edged silently around it, had a look, and returned to beckon Hereward in.

There was a large antechamber or waiting room beyond, sparsely furnished with a slim desk and several well-upholstered armchairs. The desk and chairs each had six legs, the extra limbs arranged closely at the back, a fashion Hereward supposed was some homage to the godlet's physical manifestation. The walls were hung with several tapestries depicting the city at various stages in its history.

Given the depth underground and the proximity of the lake, great efforts must have been made to waterproof and beautify the walls, floor and ceiling, but there was still an army of little dots of mold advancing from every corner, blackening the white plaster and tarnishing the gilded cornices and decorations.

Apart from the tapestry-covered exit, there were three doors. Two were of a usual size, though they were elaborately carved with obscure symbols and had brass, or perhaps even gold, handles. The one on the wall opposite the tapestry corridor was entirely different: it was a single ten-foot-by-six-foot slab of ancient marble veined with red lead, and it would have been better situated sitting on top of a significant memorial or some potentate's coffin.

Mister Fitz went to each of the carved doors, his blue tongue flickering in and out, sampling the air.

"No one close," he reported, before approaching the marble slab. He actually licked the gap between the stone and the floor, then sat for a few moments to think about what he had tasted.

Hereward kept clear, checking the other doors to see if they could be locked. Disappointed in that aim as they had neither bar nor keyhole, he sheathed his saber and carefully and quietly picked up a desk to push against the left door and several chairs to pile against the right. They wouldn't hold, but they would give some warning of attempted ingress.

Fitz chuckled as Hereward finished his work, an unexpected noise that made the knight shiver, drop his hand to the hilt of his saber, and quickly look around to see what had made the puppet laugh. Fitz was not easily amused, and often not by anything Hereward would consider funny.

"There is a sorcerous barrier," said Fitz. "It is immensely strong but has not perhaps been as well thought-out as it might have been. Fortuitously, I do not even need to unpick it."

The puppet reached up with his left hand and pushed the marble slab. It slid back silently, revealing another corridor, this one of more honest bare, weeping stone, rapidly turning into rough-hewn steps only a little way along.

"I'm afraid you cannot follow, Hereward," said Fitz. "The barrier is conditional, and you do not meet its requirements. It would forcibly—and perhaps harmfully—repel you if you tried to step over the lintel of this door. But I would ask you to stay here in any case, to secure our line of retreat. I should only be a short time if all goes well. You will, of course, know if all does not go well, and must save yourself as best you can. I have impressed the ostlers to rise at your command and load our gear, as I have impressed instructions into the dull minds of the battlemounts—"

"Enough, Fitz! I shall not leave without you."

"Hereward, you know that in the event of my—"

"Fitz. The quicker it were done—"

"Indeed. Be careful, child."

"Fitz!"

But the puppet had gone almost before that exasperated single word was out of Hereward's mouth.

It quickly grew cold with the passage below open. Chill, wet gusts of wind blew up and followed the knight around the room, no matter where he stood. After a few minutes trying to find a spot where he could avoid the cold breeze, Hereward took to pacing by the doors as quietly as he could. Every dozen steps or so he stopped to listen, either for Fitz's return or the sound of approaching guards.

In the event, he was midpace when he heard something. The sharp beat of hobnailed boots in step, approaching the left-hand door.

Hereward drew his two pistols and moved closer to the door. The handle rattled, the door began to move and encountered the desk he had pushed there. There was an exclamation and several voices spoke all at once. A heavier shove came immediately, toppling the desk as the door came partially open.

Hereward took a pace to the left and fired through the gap. The wheel locks whirred, sparks flew, then there were two deep, simultaneous booms, the resultant echoes flattening down the screams and shouts in the corridor beyond the door, just as the conjoining clouds of blue-white smoke obscured Hereward from the guards, who were already clambering over their wounded or slain companions.

The knight thrust his pistols back through his belt and drew his saber, to make an immediate sweeping cut at the neck of a guard who charged blindly through the smoke, his halberd thrust out in front like a blind man's cane. Man and halberd clattered to the floor. Hereward ducked under a halberd swing and slashed the next guard behind the knees, at the same time picking up one edge of the desk and flipping it upright in the path of the next two guards. They tripped over it, and Hereward stabbed them both in the back of the neck as their helmets fell forward, left-right, three inches of saber point in and out in an instant.

A blade skidded off Hereward's cuirass and would have scored his thigh but for a quick twist away. He parried the next thrust, rolled his wrist and slashed his attacker across the stomach, following it up with a kick as the guard reeled back, sword slack in his hand.

No attack—or any movement save for dulled writhing on the ground—followed. Hereward stepped back and surveyed the situation. Two guards were dead or dying just beyond the door. One was still to his left. Three lay around the desk. Another was hunched over by the wall, his hands pressed uselessly against the gaping wound in his gut, as he moaned the god's name over and over.

None of the guards was Jessaye, but the sound of the pistol shots at the least would undoubtedly bring more defenders of the temple.

"Seven," said Hereward. "Of a possible twelve."

He laid his saber across a chair and reloaded his pistols, taking powder cartridges and shot from the pocket of his coat and a ramrod from under the barrel of one gun. Loaded, he wound their wheel-lock mechanisms with a small spanner that hung from a braided-leather loop on his left wrist.

Just as he replaced the pistols in his belt, the ground trembled beneath his feet, and an even colder wind came howling out of the sunken corridor, accompanied by a cloying but not unpleasant odor of exotic spices that also briefly made Hereward see strange bands of color move through the air, the visions fading as the scent also passed.

Tremors, scent and strange visions were all signs that Fitz had joined battle with Pralqornrah-Tanish-Kvaxixob below. There could well be other portents to come, stranger and more unpleasant to experience.

"Be quick, Fitz," muttered Hereward, his attention momentarily focused on the downwards passage.

Even so, he caught the soft footfall of someone sneaking in, boots left behind in the passage. He turned, pistols in hand, as Jessaye stepped around the half-open door. Two guards came behind her, their own pistols raised.

Before they could aim, Hereward fired and, as the smoke and noise filled the room, threw the empty pistols at the trio, took up his saber and jumped aside.

Jessaye's sword leapt into the space where he'd been. Hereward landed, turned and parried several frenzied stabs at his face, the swift movement of their blades sending the gun smoke eddying in wild roils and coils. Jessaye pushed him back almost to the other door. There, Hereward picked up a chair and used it to fend off several blows, at the same time beginning to make small, fast cuts at Jessaye's sword arm.

Jessaye's frenzied assault slackened as Hereward cut her badly on the shoulder near her neck, then immediately after that on the upper arm, across the wound he'd given her in the duel. She cried out in pain and rage and stepped back, her right arm useless, her sword point trailing on the floor.

Instead of pressing his attack, the knight took a moment to take stock of his situation.

The two pistol-bearing guards were dead or as good as, making the tally nine. That meant there should only be two more, in addition to Jessaye, and those two were not immediately in evidence.

"You may withdraw, if you wish," said Hereward, his voice strangely loud and dull at the same time, a consequence of shooting in enclosed spaces. "I do not wish to kill you, and you cannot hold your sword."

Jessaye transferred her sword to her left hand and took a shuddering breath.

"I fight equally well with my left hand," she said, assuming the guard position as best she could, though her right arm hung at her side, and blood dripped from her fingers to the floor.

She thrust immediately, perhaps hoping for surprise. Hereward ferociously beat her blade down, then stamped on it, forcing it from her grasp. He then raised the point of his saber to her throat.

"No, you don't," he said. "Very few people do. Go, while you still live."

"I cannot," whispered Jessaye. She shut her eyes. "I

have failed in my duty. I shall die with my comrades. Strike quickly."

Hereward raised his elbow and prepared to push the blade through the so-giving flesh, as he had done so many times before. But he did not, instead he lowered his saber and backed away around the wall.

"Quickly, I beg you," said Jessaye. She was shivering, the blood flowing faster down her arm.

"I cannot," muttered Hereward. "Or rather I do not wish to. I have killed enough today."

Jessaye opened her eyes and slowly turned to him, her face paper white, the scar no brighter than the petal of a pink rose. For the first time, she saw that the stone door was open, and she gasped and looked wildly around at the bodies that littered the floor.

"The priestess came forth? You have slain her?"

"No," said Hereward. He continued to watch Jessaye and listen for others, as he bent and picked up his pistols. They were a present from his mother, and he had not lost them yet. "My companion has gone within."

"But that . . . that is not possible! The barrier—"

"Mister Fitz knew of the barrier," said Hereward wearily. He was beginning to feel the aftereffects of violent combat, and strongly desired to be away from the visible signs of it littered around him. "He crossed it without difficulty."

"But only the priestess can pass," said Jessaye wildly. She was shaking more than just shivering now, as shock set in, though she still stood upright. "A woman with child! No one and nothing else! It cannot be . . ."

Her eyes rolled back in her head, she twisted sideways and fell to the floor. Hereward watched her lie there for a few seconds while he attempted to regain the cold temper in which he fought, but it would not return. He hesitated, then wiped his saber clean, sheathed it, then despite all better judgment, bent over Jessaye.

She whispered something and again, and he caught the god's name, "Tanesh" and with it a sudden onslaught of cinnamon and cloves and ginger on his nose. He blinked, and in that blink, she turned and struck at him with a small dagger that had been concealed in her sleeve. Hereward had expected something, but not the god's assistance, for the dagger was in her right hand, which he'd thought useless. He grabbed her wrist but could only slow rather than stop the blow. Jessaye struck true, the dagger entering the armhole of the cuirass, to bite deep into his chest.

Hereward left the dagger there and merely pushed Jessaye back. The smell of spices faded, and her arm was limp once more. She did not resist, but lay there quite still, only her eyes moving as she watched Hereward sit down next to her . He sighed heavily, a few flecks of blood already spraying out with his breath, evidence that her dagger was lodged in his lung though he already knew that from the pain that impaled him with every breath.

"There is no treasure below," said Jessaye quietly. "Only the godlet, and his priestess."

"We did not come for treasure," said Hereward. He spat blood on the floor. "Indeed, I had thought we would winter here, in good employment. But your god is proscribed, and so . . . "

"Proscribed? I don't . . . who . . . "

"By the Council of the Treaty for the Safety of the World," said Hereward. "Not that anyone remembers that name. If we are remembered it is from the stories that tell of . . . god-slayers."

"I know the stories," whispered Jessaye. "And not just stories . . . we were taught to beware the god-slayers. But they are always women, barren women, with witch-scars on their faces. Not a man and a puppet. That is why the barrier . . . the barrier stops all but gravid women . . ."

Hereward paused to wipe a froth of blood from his mouth before he could answer.

"Fitz has been my companion since I was three years old. He was called Mistress Fitz then, as my nurse-bodyguard. When I turned ten, I wanted a male companion, and so I began to call him Mister Fitz. But whether called Mistress or Master, I believe Fitz is nurturing an offshoot of his spiritual essence in some form of pouch upon his person. In time he will make a body for it to inhabit. The process takes several hundred years."

"But you . . . "

Jessaye's whisper was almost too quiet to hear.

"I am a mistake . . . the witches of Har are not barren, that is just a useful tale. But they do only bear daughters . . . save the once. I am the only son of a witch born these thousand years. My mother is one of the Mysterious Three who rule the witches, last remnant of the Council. Fitz was made by that Council, long ago, as a weapon made to fight malignant gods. The more recent unwanted child became a weapon too, puppet and boy flung out to do our duty in the world. A duty that has carried me here . . . to my great regret."

No answer came to this bubbling, blood-infused speech. Hereward looked across at Jessaye and saw that her chest no longer rose and fell, and that there was a dark puddle beneath her that was still spreading, a tide of blood advancing toward him.

He touched the hilt of the dagger in his side, and coughed, and the pain of both things was almost too much to bear; but he only screamed a little, and made it worse by standing up and staggering to the wall to place his back against it. There were still two guards somewhere, and Fitz was surprisingly vulnerable if he was surprised. Or he might be wounded too, from the struggle with the god.

Minutes or perhaps a longer time passed, and Hereward's mind wandered and, in wandering, left his body too long. It slid down the wall to the ground and his blood began to mingle with that of Jessaye, and the others who lay on the floor of a god's antechamber turned slaughterhouse.

Then there was pain again, and Hereward's mind jolted back into his body, in time to make his mouth whimper and his eyes blink at a light that was a color he didn't know, and there was Mister Fitz leaning over him and the dagger wasn't in his side anymore and there was no bloody froth upon his lips. There was still pain. Constant, piercing pain, coming in waves and never subsiding. It stayed with him, uppermost in his thoughts, even as he became dimly aware that he was upright and walking, his legs moving under a direction not his own.

Except that very soon he was lying down again, and Fitz was cross.

"You have to get back up, Hereward."

"I'm tired, Fitzie . . . can't I rest for a little longer?"

"No. Get up."

"Are we going home?"

"No, Hereward. You know we can't go home. We must go onward."

"Onward? Where?"

"Never mind now. Keep walking. Do you see our mounts?"

"Yes . . . but we will never . . . never make it out the gate . . ."

"We will, Hereward . . . leave it to me. Here, I will help you up. Are you steady enough?"

"I will . . . stay on. Fitz . . ."

"Yes, Hereward."

"Don't . . . don't kill them all."

If Fitz answered, Hereward didn't hear, as he faded out of the world for a few seconds. When the world nauseatingly shivered back into sight and hearing, the puppet was nowhere in sight and the two battlemounts were already loping toward the gate, though the leading steed had no rider.

They did not pause at the wall. Though it was past midnight, the gate was open, and the guards who might have barred the way were nowhere to be seen, though there were strange splashes of color upon the earth where they might have stood. There were no guards beyond the gate, on the earthwork bastion either, the only sign of their prior existence a half-melted belt buckle still red with heat.

To Hereward's dim eyes, the city's defenses might as well be deserted, and nothing prevented the battlemounts continuing to lope, out into the warm autumn night.

The leading battlemount finally slowed and stopped a mile beyond the town, at the corner of a lemon grove, its hundreds of trees so laden with yellow fruit they scented the air with a sharp, clean tang that helped bring Hereward closer to full consciousness. Even so, he lacked the strength to shorten the chain of his own mount, but it stopped by its companion without urging.

Fitz swung down from the outlying branch of a lemon tree, onto his saddle, without spilling any of the fruit piled high in his upturned hat.

"We will ride on in a moment. But when we can, I shall make a lemon salve and a soothing drink."

Hereward nodded, finding himself unable to speak. Despite Fitz's repairing sorceries, the wound in his side was still very painful, and he was weak from loss of blood, but neither thing choked his voice. He was made quiet by a cold melancholy that held him tight, coupled with a feeling of terrible loss, the loss of some future, never-to-be happiness that had gone forever.

"I suppose we must head for Fort Yarz," mused Fitz. "It is the closest likely place for employment. There is always some trouble there, though I believe the Gebrak tribes have been largely quiet this past year."

Hereward tried to speak again, and at last found a croak that had some resemblance to a voice.

"No. I am tired of war. Find us somewhere peaceful, where I can rest."

Fitz hopped across to perch on the neck of Hereward's mount and faced the knight, his blue eyes brighter than the moonlight.

"I will try, Hereward. But as you ruminated earlier, the world is as it is, and we are what we were made to be. Even should we find somewhere that seems at peace, I suspect it will not stay so, should we remain. Remember Jeminero."

"Aye." Hereward sighed. He straightened up just a little and took up the chains, as Fitz jumped to his own saddle. "I remember."

"Fort Yarz?" asked Fitz.

Hereward nodded, and slapped the chain, urging his battlemount forward. As it stretched into its stride, the lemons began to fall from the trees in the orchard, playing the soft drumbeat of a funerary march, the first sign of the passing from the world of the god of Shûme.

THE LAST WORDERS

———

Karen Joy Fowler

Charlotta was asleep in the dining car when the train arrived in San Margais. It was tempting to just leave her behind, and I tried to tell myself this wasn't a mean thought, but came to me because I, myself, might want to be left like that, just for the adventure of it. I might want to wake up hours later and miles away, bewildered and alone. I am always on the lookout for those parts of my life that could be the first scene in a movie. Of course, you could start a movie anywhere, but you wouldn't; that's my point. And so this impulse had nothing to do with the way Charlotta had begun to get on my last nerve. That's my other point. If I thought being ditched would be sort of exciting, then so did Charlotta. We felt the same about everything.

"Charlotta," I said. "Charlotta. We're here." I was on my feet, grabbing my backpack, when the train actually stopped. This threw me into the arms of a boy of about fourteen, wearing a T-shirt from the Three Mountains Soccer Camp. It was nice of him to catch me. I probably wouldn't have done that when I was fourteen. What's one tourist more or less? I tried to say some of this to Charlotta when we were on the platform and the train was already puffing fainter and fainter in the distance, winding its way like a great worm up into the Rambles Mountains. The boy hadn't gotten off with us.

It was raining and we tented our heads with our jackets. "He was probably picking your pocket," Charlotta said. "Do you still have your wallet?" Which made me feel I'd been a fool, but when I put my hand in to check I found, instead of taking something out, he'd put something in. I pulled out an orange piece of paper folded like a fan. When opened, flattened, it was a flier in four languages—German, Japanese, French, and English. *Open mike*, the English part said. And then, *Come to the Last Word Cafe. 100 Ruta de los Esclavos by the river. First drink free. Poetry Slam. To the death*.

The rain erased the words even as we read them.

"No city listed," Charlotta noted. She had taken the paper from me to look more closely. Now it was blank and limp. She refolded it, carefully so it wouldn't tear, put it in the back pocket of her pants. "Anyway, can't be here."

The town of San Margais hangs on the edge of a deep chasm. There'd been a river once. We had a geological witness. We had the historical records. But there was no river now.

"And no date for the slam," Charlotta added. "And we don't think fast on our feet. And death. That's not very appealing."

If she'd made only one objection, then she'd no interest. Ditto if she'd made two. But three was defensive; four was obsessive. Four meant that if Charlotta could ever find the Last Word Cafe, she was definitely going. Just because I'd been invited and she hadn't. Try to keep her out! I know this is what she felt because it's what I would have felt.

We took a room in a private house on the edge of the gorge. We had planned to lodge in the city center, more convenient to everything, but we were tired and wanted to get in out of the rain. The guidebook said this place was cheap and clean.

It was ten-thirty in the morning and the proprietress was still in her nightgown. She was a woman of about fifty and the loss of her two front teeth had left a small dip in her upper lip. Her nightgown was imprinted with angels wearing choir robes and haloes on sticks like balloons. She spoke little English; there was a lot of pointing, most of it upwards. Then we had to follow her angel butt up three flights of ladders, hauling our heavy packs. The room was large and had its own sink. There were glass doors opening onto a balcony, rain sheeting down. If you looked out there was nothing to see. Steep nothing. Gray nothing. The dizzying null of the gorge. "You can have the bed by the doors," Charlotta offered. She was already moved in, toweling her hair.

"You," I said. I was nobody's fool.

Charlotta sang. "It is scary, in my aerie."

"Poetry?" the proprietress asked. Her dimpled lip curled slightly. She didn't have to speak the language to know bad poetry when she heard it, that lip said.

"Yes," Charlotta said. "Yes. The Last Word Cafe? Is where?"

"No," she answered. Maybe she'd misunderstood us. Maybe we'd misunderstood her.

A few facts about the gorge: The gorge is very deep and very narrow. A thousand years ago a staircase was cut into the interior of the cliff. According to our guidebook there are 839 stone steps, all worn smooth by traffic. Back when the stairs were made, there was still a river. Slaves carried water from the river up the stairs to the town. They did this all day long, down with an empty clay pitcher, up with a full one, and then different slaves carried water all during the night. The slave owners were noted for their poetry and their cleanliness. They wrote formal erotic poems about how dirty their slaves were.

One day there was an uprising. The slaves on the stairs knew nothing about it. They had their pitchers. They had the long way down and the longer way up. Slaves from the town, ex-slaves now, stood at the top and told each one as he (or she) arrived, that he (or she) was free. Some of the slaves poured their water out onto the stone steps to prove this to themselves. Some emptied their pitchers into the cistern as usual, thinking to have a nice bath later. Later all the pitchers were given to the former slave owners who now were slaves and had to carry water up from the river all day or all night.

Still later there was resentment between the town slaves, who had taken all the risks and made all the plans, and the stair slaves who were handed their freedom. The least grateful of the latter were sent back to the stairs.

Two or three hundred years after the uprising, there was no more water. Over many generations the slaves had finally emptied the river. To honor their long labors, in memory of a job well done, slavery was abolished in San Margais. There is a holiday to commemorate this every year on May 21. May 21 is also our birthday, mine and Charlotta's. Let's not make too much of that.

Among the many factions in San Margais was one that felt there was nothing to celebrate in having once had a river and now not having one. Many bitter poems have been written on this subject, all entitled "May 21."

The shower in our pensione was excellent, the water hot and hard. Charlotta reported this to me. Since I got my choice of bed, she got the first shower. We'd been making these sorts of calculations all our lives; it kept us in balance. As long as everyone played. We were not in San Margais for the poetry.

Five years before, while we were still in high school, Charlotta and I had fallen in love with the same boy. His name was Raphael Kaplinsky. He had an accent, South African, and a motorcycle, American. "I saw him first," Charlotta said, which was true—he was in her second period World Lit class. I hadn't seen him until fifth period Chemistry.

I spoke to him first, though. "Is it supposed to be this color?" I'd asked when we were testing for acids.

"He spoke to me first," Charlotta said, which was also true since he'd answered my acid question with a shrug. And then, several days later, said "Nice boots!" to Charlotta when she came to school in calf-high red Steve Maddens.

My red Steve Maddens.

We quarreled about Raphael for weeks without settling anything. We didn't speak to each other for days at a time. All the while Raphael dated other girls. Loose and easy Deirdre. Bookish Kathy. Spiritual, ethereal Nina. Junco, the Japanese foreign exchange student.

Eventually Charlotta and I agreed that we would both give Raphael up. Charlotta made the offer, but I'd been planning the same; I matched it instantly. There was simply no other way. We met in the yard to formalize the agreement with a ceremony. Each of us wrote the words Ms. Raphael Weldon-Kaplinsky onto a piece of paper. Then we simultaneously tore our papers into twelve little bits. We threw the bits into the fishpond and watched the carp eat them.

I knew that Charlotta would honor our agreement. I knew this because I intended to do so.

———

When we were little, when we were just learning to talk, Mother says Charlotta and I had a secret language. She could watch us, towheaded two-year-olds, talking to each other and she could tell that we knew what we were saying, even if she didn't. Sometimes after telling each other a long story, we would cry. One of us would start and the other would sit struggling for a moment, lip trembling, and eventually we would both be in tears. There was a graduate student in psychology interested in studying this, but we learned English and stopped speaking our secret language before he could get his grant money together.

Mother favors Charlotta. I'm not the only one to think so; Charlotta sees it, too. Mother has learned that it's simply not possible to treat two people with equal love. She would argue that she favors us both—sometimes Charlotta, sometimes me. She would say it all equals out in the end. Maybe she's right. It isn't equal yet, but it probably hasn't ended.

Some facts from our guidebook about the San Margais Civil War. 1932-37: The underlying issues were aesthetic and economic. The trigger was an assassination.

In the middle ages, San Margais was a city-state ruled by a hereditary clergy. Even after annexation, the clergy played the dominant political role. Fra Nando came to power in the 1920s during an important poetic revival known as the Margais Movement. Its premiere voice was the great epistemological poet, Gigo. Fra Nando believed in the lessons of history. Gigo believed in the natural cadence of the street, the impenetrable nature of truth. From Day One these two were headed for a showdown.

Still, for a few years, all was politeness. Gigo

received many grants and honors from the Nando regime. She was given a commission to write a poem celebrating Fra Nando's seventieth birthday. "Yes, I remember," Gigo's poem begins (in translation), "the great cloud of dragonflies grazing the lake . . . " If Fra Nando's name appeared only in the dedication, at least this was accessible stuff. Nostalgic even, elegiac.

Gigo was never nostalgic. Gigo was never elegiac. To be so now expressed only her deep contempt for Fra Nando, but it was all so very rhythmical; he was completely taken in. Fra Nando set the first two lines in stone over the entrance to the city-state library and invited Gigo to be his special guest at the unveiling.

"The nature of the word is not the nature of the stone," Gigo said at the ceremony when it was her turn to speak. This was also accessible. Fra Nando went red in the face as if he'd been slapped, one hand to each cheek.

A cartel of businessmen, angry over the graduated tariff system Nando had instituted, saw the opportunity to assassinate him and have the poets blamed. Gigo was killed at a reading the same night Fra Nando was laid in state in the Catedral Nacionales. Her last words were "blind hill, grave glass," which is all anyone could have hoped. Unless she said "grave grass," and one of her acolytes changed her words in the reporting as her detractors have alleged. Anyone could think up grave grass, especially if they were dying at the time.

All that remains for certain of Gigo's work are the contemptuous two lines in stone. The Margais Movement was outlawed, its poems systematically searched out and destroyed. Attempts were made to memorize the greatest of Gigo's verses, but these had been written so as to defy memorization. A phrase here and there, much contested, survives. Nothing that suggests genius. All the books by or about the Margais Movement were burned. All the poets were imprisoned and tortured until they couldn't remember their own names much less their own words.

There is a narrow bridge across the gorge that Charlotta can see from the doors by her bed. During the civil war, people were thrown from the bridge. There is still a handful of old men and old women here who will tell you they remember seeing that.

Raphael Kaplinsky went to our high school for only one year. We told ourselves it was good we hadn't destroyed our relationship for so short a reward. We dated other boys, boys neither of us liked. The flaws in our reasoning began to come clear.

1) Raphael Kaplinsky was ardent and oracular. You didn't meet a boy like Raphael Kaplinsky in every World Lit, every Chemistry Class you took. He was the very first person to use the word later to end a conversation. Using the word later in this particular way was a promise. It was nothing less than messianic.

2) What if we did, someday, meet a boy we liked as much as Raphael? We were both bound to like him exactly the same. We hadn't solved our problem so much as delayed it. We were doomed to a lifetime of each-otherness unless we came up with a different plan.

We hired an internet detective to find Raphael and he uncovered a recent credit card trail. We had followed this trail all the way to last Sunday in San

Margais. We had come to San Margais to make him choose between us.

It was raining too hard to go out, plus we'd spent the night sitting up on the train. We hadn't been able to sit together, and had had a drunk on one side (Charlotta's) and a shoebox of mice on the other (mine). The mice were headed to the Snake Pit at the State Zoo. There was no way to sleep while their little paws scrabbled desperately, fruitlessly against the cardboard. I had an impulse to set them free, but it seemed unfair to the snakes. How often in this world we are unwillingly forced to take sides! Team Mouse or Team Snake? Team Fly or Team Spider?

Charlotta and I napped during the afternoon while the glass rattled in the doorframes and the rain fell. I woke up when I was too hungry to sleep. "I have got to have something to eat," Charlotta said.

The cuisine of San Margais is nothing to write home about. Charlotta and I each bought an umbrella from a street peddler and ate in a small, dark pizzeria. It was not only wet outside, but cold. The pizzeria had a large oven, which made the room pleasant to linger in, even though there was a group of Italian tourists smoking across the way.

Charlotta and I had a policy never to order the same thing off a menu. This was hard, because the same thing always sounded good to both of us, but it doubled our chances of making the right choice. Charlotta ordered a pizza called El Diablo, which was all theater and annoyed me, as we don't like hot foods. El Diablo brought tears to her eyes and she only ate one piece, picking the olives off the rest and then helping herself to several slices of mine.

She wiped her face with a napkin, which left a

rakish streak of pizza sauce on her cheek. I was irritated enough to say nothing about this. One of the Italians made his way to our table. "So," he said with no preliminaries. "American, yes? I can kiss you?"

We were nothing if not patriots. Charlotta stood at once, moved into his arms, and I saw his tongue go into her mouth. They kissed for several seconds, then Charlotta pushed him away and now the pizza sauce was on him.

"So," she said. "Now. We need directions to the closest internet cafe."

The Italian drew a map on her place mat. He drew well; his map had depth and perspective. The internet cafe appeared to be around many corners and up many flights of stairs. The Italian decorated his map with hopeful little hearts. Charlotta took it away from him or there surely would have been more of these.

The San Margais miracle, an anecdotal account:

About ten years ago, a little boy named Bastien Brunelle was crossing the central plaza when he noticed something strange on the face of the statue of Fra Nando. He looked more closely. Fra Nando was crying large milky tears. Bastien ran home to tell his parents.

The night before, Bastien's father had had a dream. In his dream he was old and crippled, twisted up like a licorice stick. In his dream he had a dream that told him to go and bathe in the river. He woke from the dream dream and made his slow, painful way down the 839 steps. At the bottom of the gorge he waited. He heard a noise in the distance, cars on a freeway. The river arrived like a train and stopped to let him in. Bastien's father woke up and was thirty-two again, which was his proper age.

When he heard about the statue, Bastien's father

remembered the dream. He followed Bastien out to the square where a crowd was gathering, growing. "Fra Nando is crying for the river," Bastien's father told the crowd. "It's a sign to us. We have to put the river back."

Bastien's father had never been a community leader. He ran a small civil war museum for tourists, filled with faked Gigo poems, and rarely bought a round for the house when he went out drinking. But now he had all the conviction of the man who sees clearly amidst the men who are confused. He organized a brigade to carry water down the steps to the bottom of the gorge and his purpose was so absolute, so inspired were his words, that people volunteered their spare hours, their children's spare hours. They signed up for slots in his schedule and carried water down the stairs for almost a week before they all lost interest and remembered Bastien's father was not the mouth of God, but a tightassed cheat.

By this time news of the crying statue had gone out on the internet. Scientists had performed examinations. "Fakery cannot be ruled out," one said, which transformed into the headline, "No Sign of Fakery." Pilgrims began to arrive from wealthy European countries, mostly college kids with buckets, thermoses, used Starbucks cups. They would stay two or three days, two or three weeks, hauling water down, having visions on the stairs and sex.

And then that ended, too. Every time has its task. Ours is to digitalize the world's libraries. This is a big job that will take generations to complete, like the pyramids. No time for filling gorges with water. "Live lightly on the earth," the pilgrims remembered. "Leave no footprint behind." And they all went home again, or at least they left San Margais.

_____

On odd days of the week our people-finder detective emailed Charlotta and copied me. On even, the opposite. Two days earlier Raphael had bought a hat and four postcards. He had dinner at a pricey restaurante and got a fifty-dollar cash advance. That was Charlotta's email.

Mine said that this very night, he was buying fifteen beers at the Last Word Cafe, San Margais.

We googled that name to a single entry. *100 Ruta de los Esclavos by the river,* it said. *Open mike. Underground music and poetry nightly.*

There were other Americans using the computers. I walked through, asking if any of them knew how to get to the Last Word Cafe. To Ruta de los Esclavos? They were paying by the minute. Most of them didn't look up. Those that did shook their heads.

Charlotta and I opened our umbrellas and went back out into the rain. We asked directions from everyone we saw, but very few people were on the street. They didn't know English or they disliked being accosted by tourists or they didn't like the look of our face. They hurried by without speaking. Only a single woman stopped. She took my chin in her hand to make sure she had my full attention. Her eyes were tinged in yellow and she smelled like Irish Spring soap. "No," she said firmly. "*Me entiendes?* No for you."

We walked along the gorge, because this was the closest thing San Margais had to a river. On one side of us, the town. The big yellow I of Tourist Information (closed indefinitely), shops of ceramics and cheeses, postcards, law offices, podiatrists, pubs, our own pensione. On the other the cliff-face, the air. We crossed the narrow bridge and when we came to the 839 steps we started down them just because they were

mostly inside the cliff and therefore covered and
therefore dry. I was the one to point these things out to
Charlotta. I was the one to say we should go down.

The steps were smooth and slippery. Each one had a
dip in the center in just that place where a slave was
most likely to put his (or her) foot. Water dripped from
the walls around us, but we were able to close our
umbrellas, leave them at the top to be picked up later.
For the first stretch there were lights overhead. Then
we were in darkness, except for an occasional turn,
which brought an occasional opening to the outside. A
little light could carry us a long way.

We descended maybe three hundred steps and then,
by one of the openings, we met an American coming
up. In age she was somewhere in that long unidentifi-
able stretch from twenty-two to thirty-five. She was
carrying an empty bucket, plastic, the sort a child takes
to the seashore. She was breathless from the climb.

She stopped beside us and we waited until she was
able to speak. "What the fuck," she said finally, "is the
point of going down empty-handed? What the fuck is
the point of you?"

Charlotta had been asking sort of the same thing.
What was the point of going all the way down the
stairs? Why had she let me talk her into it? She talked
me into going back. We turned and followed the angry
American up and out into the rain. It was only 300
steps, but when we'd done them we were winded and
exhausted. We went to our room, crawled up our three
ladders, and landed in a deep, dispirited sleep.

It was still raining the next morning. We went to the
city center and breakfasted in a little bakery. Just as we
were finishing, our Italian walked in. "We kiss more,
yes?" he asked me. He'd mistaken me for Charlotta. I
stood up. I was always having to do her chores. His
tongue ranged through my mouth as if he were looked

for scraps. I tasted cigarettes, gum, things left in ashtrays.

"So," I said, pushing him away. "Now. We need directions to the Last Word Cafe."

And it turned out we'd almost gotten there last night, after all. The Last Word was the last stop along the 839 steps. It seemed as if I'd known this.

Our Italian said he'd been the night before. No one named Raphael had taken the mic; he was sure of this, but he thought there might have been a South African at the bar. Possibly this South African had bought him a drink. It was a very crowded room. No one had died. That was just—how is it we Americans say? Poem license?

"Raphael probably wanted to get the feel of the place before he spoke," Charlotta said. "That's what I'd do."

And me. That's what I'd do, too.

There was no point in going back before dark. We checked our email, but he was apparently still living on the cash advance; nothing had been added since the Last Word last night. We decided to spend the day as tourists, thinking Raphael might do the same. Because of the rain we had the outdoor sights mostly to ourselves. We saw the ruins of the old baths, long and narrow as lap pools, now with nets of morning glories twisted across them. Here and there the rain had filled them.

There was a Roman arch, a Moorish garden. When we were wetter than we could bear to be we paid the eight euros entrance to the civil war museum. English translation was extra, but we were on a budget; there are no bargains on last-minute tickets to San Margais. We told ourselves it was more in keeping with the spirit of Gigo if we didn't understand a thing.

The museum was small, two rooms only and dimly

lit. We stood awhile beside the wall radiator, drying out and warming up. Even from that spot we could see most of the room we were in. There were three life-size dioramas—mannequins dressed as Gigo might have dressed, meeting with people Gigo might have met. We recognized the mannequin Fra Nando from the statue we'd seen in the city center, although this version was less friendly. His hand was on Gigo's shoulder, his expression enigmatic. She was looking past him up at something tall and transcendent. There was clothing laid out, male and female, in glass cases along with playbills, baptismal certificates, baby pictures. Stapled to the wall were a series of book illustrations—a bandito seizing a woman on a balcony. The woman shaking free, leaping to her death. A story Gigo had written? A family legend? A scene from the civil war? All of the above? The man who sold us our tickets, Senor Brunelle, was conducting a tour for an elderly British couple, but since we hadn't paid it would be wrong to stand where we could hear. We were careful not to do so.

We spoke to Senor Brunelle after. We made polite noises about the museum, so interesting, we said. So unexpected. And then Charlotta asked him what he knew about the Last Word Cafe.

"For tourists," he said. "Myself, my family, we don't go down the steps anymore." He was clearly sad about this. "All tourists now."

"What does it mean?" Charlotta asked first. "Poetry to the death?"

"Which word needs definition? Poetry? Or Death?"

"I know the words."

"Then I am no more help," Senor Brunelle told her.

"Why does it say it's by the river when there's no river?" Charlotta asked second.

"Always a river. In San Margais, always a river.

Sometimes in your mind. Sometimes in the gorge. Either way, a river."

"Is there any reason we shouldn't go?" Charlotta asked third.

"Go. You go. You won't get in," Senor Brunelle said. He said this to Charlotta. He didn't say it to me.

The Last Worders:

On the night Raphael took the open mic at the Last Word Cafe, he did three poems. He spoke ten minutes. He stood on the stage and he didn't try to move; he didn't try to make it sing; he made no effort to sell his words. The light fell in a small circle on his face so that, most of the time, his eyes were closed. He was beautiful. The people listening also closed their eyes and that made him more beautiful still. The women, the men who'd wanted him when he started to talk no longer did so. He was beyond that, unfuckable. For the rest of their lives, they'd be undone by the mere sound of his name. The ones who spoke English tried to write down some part of what he'd said on their napkins, in their travel journals. They made lists of words—childhood, ice, yes. Gleaming, yes, yesterday.

These are the facts. Anyone can figure out this much.

For the rest, you had to be there. What was heard, the things people suddenly knew, the things people suddenly felt—none of that could be said in any way that could be passed along. By the time Raphael had finished, everyone listening, everyone there for those few minutes on that night at the Last Word Cafe, had been set free.

These people climbed the steps afterwards in absolute silence. They did not go back, not a single one of them, to their marriages, their families, their jobs, their lives. They walked to the city center and they sat in the square on the edge of the fountain at the feet of the friendly Fra Nando and they knew where they were in a way they had never known it before. They tried to talk about what to do next. Words came back to them slowly. Between them, they spoke a dozen different languages, all useless now.

You could have started the movie of any one of them there, at the feet of the stone statue. It didn't matter what they could and couldn't say; they all knew the situation. Whatever they did next would be done together. They could not imagine, ever again, being with anyone who had not been there, in the Last Word Cafe, on the night Raphael Kaplinsky spoke.

There were details to be ironed out. How to get the money to eat. Where to live, where to sleep. How to survive now, in a suddenly clueless world.

But there was time to make these decisions. Those who had cars fetched them. Those who did not climbed in, fastened their seat belts. On the night Raphael Kaplinsky spoke at the Last Word Cafe, the patrons caravanned out of town without a last word to anyone. The rest of us would not hear of the Last Worders again until one of them went on Larry King Live and filled a two-hour show with a two-hour silence.

Or else they all died.

Charlotta and I had dinner by ourselves in the converted basement of an old hotel. The candles flickered our shadows about so we were, on all sides, surrounded by us. Charlotta had the trout. It had been cooked dry, and was filled with small bones. Every time she put a bite in her mouth, she pulled the tiny bones out. I had the mussels. The sauce was stiff and gluey. Most of the shells hadn't opened. The food in San Margais is nothing to write home about.

We finished the meal with old apples and young

wine. We were both nervous, now that it came down to it, about seeing Raphael again. Each of us secretly wondered, could we live with Raphael's choice? However it went? Could I be happy for Charlotta, if it came to that? I asked myself. Could I bear watching her forced to be happy for me? I sipped my wine and ran through every moment of my relationship with Raphael for reassurance. That stuff about the acid experiment. How much he liked my boots. "Let's go," Charlotta said and we were a bit unsteady from the wine, which, in retrospect, with an evening of 839 steps ahead of us, was not smart.

We crossed the bridge in a high wind. The rain came in sideways; the wind turned our umbrellas inside out. Charlotta was thrown against the rope rails and grabbed on to me. If she'd fallen, she would have taken me with her. If I saved her, I saved us both. Our umbrellas went together into the gorge.

We reached the steps and began to descend, sometimes with light, sometimes feeling our way in the darkness. About one hundred steps up from the bottom, a room had been carved out of the rock. Once slave owners had sat at their leisure there, washing and rewashing their hands and feet, overseeing the slaves on the stairs. Later the room had been closed off with the addition of a heavy metal door. A posting had been set on a sawhorse outside. The Last Word Cafe, the English part of it said. Not for Everyone.

The door was latched. Charlotta pounded on it with her fist until it opened. A man in a tuxedo with a wide orange cummerbund stepped out. He shook his head. "American?" he asked. "And empty-handed? That's no way to make a river."

"We're here for the poetry," Charlotta told him and he shook his head again.

"Invitation only."

And Charlotta reached into the back pocket of her pants. Charlotta pulled out the orange paper given to me by the boy on the train. The man took it. He threw it into a small basket with many other such papers. He stood aside and let Charlotta enter.

He stepped back to block me. "Invitation only."

"That was my invitation," I told him. "Charlotta!" She looked back at me, over her shoulder without really turning around. "Tell him. Tell him that invitation was for me. Tell him how Senor Brunelle told you you wouldn't get in."

"So?" said Charlotta. "That woman on the street told you you wouldn't get in."

But I had figured that part out. "She mistook me for you," I said.

Beyond the door I could see Raphael climbing onto the dais. I could hear the room growing silent. I could see Charlotta's back sliding into a crowd of people like a knife into water. The door swung toward my face. The latch fell.

I stayed a long time by that door, but no sounds came through. Finally I walked down the last hundred steps. I was alone at the bottom of the gorge where the rain fell and fell and there was no river. I would never have done to Charlotta what she had done to me.

It took me more than an hour to climb back up. I had to stop many, many times to rest, airless, heart throbbing, legs aching, lightheaded in the dark. No one met me at the top.

SINGING OF MOUNT ABORA

Theodora Goss

A hundred years ago, the blind instrument-maker known as Alem Das, or Alem the Master, made a dulcimer whose sound was sweeter, more passionate, and more filled with longing than any instrument that had ever been made. It was carved entirely from the wood of an almond tree that had grown in the garden of Al Meseret, that palace with a thousand rooms where the Empress Nasren had chosen to spend her widowhood. The doors of the palace were shaped like moons, its windows like stars. It was a palace of night, and every night the Empress walked through its thousand rooms, wearing the veil she had worn for her wedding to the Great Khan. If the cooks, who sometimes saw her wandering through the kitchen, had not known who she was, they would have mistaken her for a ghost. The dulcimer was strung with the whiskers of the Cloud Dragon, who wreaths his body around the slopes of Mount Abora. He can always be found there in the early morning, and that is when Alem Das approached him, walking up the path on the arm of his niece Kamora.

"What do you want?" asked the dragon.

"Your whiskers, luminous one," said Alem Das.

"My whiskers! You must be that instrument maker. I've heard of you. You're the reason my cousin, the

River Dragon, no longer has spines along his back, and why my other cousin, the Phoenix, no longer has tail-feathers. Why should I give you my whiskers?"

"Because when I have made my dulcimer, my niece Kamora will come and play for you, and sing to you the secrets of your soul," said Alem Das.

"We dragons have no souls," said the Cloud Dragon, wreathing himself around and around, like a cat.

"You dragons are souls," said Alem Das, and he asked his niece to sing one of the songs that she sang at night, to sooth the Empress Nasren. Kamora sang, and the Cloud Dragon stopped wreathing himself around and around. Instead, he lay at her feet, which disappeared into mist. When she was done, he said, "All right, instrument maker. You may have my whiskers, but on one condition. First, your niece Kamora must marry me. And when you have made your dulcimer, she must sing to me every night the secrets of my soul."

Kamora knew how the Cloud Dragon looked at night, when he took the form of a man, so she said, "I will marry you, if my Empress allows it." And that is my first song.

You can't imagine how cold Boston is in winter, not for someone from a considerably warmer climate. In my apartment, I sat as close as I could to the radiator, sometimes with my back against it. The library at the university was warmer, but the chairs were wooden and hard, so it was a compromise: the comforts of my apartment, where I had to wrap my fingers around incessant cups of chamomile tea to warm them, or the warmth and discomfort of the library. I had been born in Abyssinia, which is now Ethiopia, and had been brought up in so many places that they seemed no place at all, Italy and France and Spain. Finally, I had come to cold, shining North America, where the universities, I told my mother, were the best in the world. And the best of the best universities were in Boston.

My mother was beautiful. I should say rather that she was a beauty, for to her, beauty was not a quality but a state of being. Beauty was her art, her profession. I don't mean that she was anything as vulgar as a model, or even an actress. No, she was simply beautiful, and so life gave her what it gives the beautiful: apartments in Italy, France, and Spain, and an airplane to travel between them, and a diamond called the Robin's Egg, because it was a big as a robin's egg, and as blue.

"Oh, Sabra," she would say to me, "what will we do about you? You look exactly like your father." And it was true. In old photographs, I saw my nose, the bones of my cheeks and jaws on a man who had not needed to be handsome, because he was rich. But his riches had not saved his life. Although he could have bought his way out of the revolution, he had remained loyal to the Emperor. He had died when his airplane was shot down, with the Emperor in it, just before crossing the border. This was after the Generals had taken power and the border had been closed. My mother and I were already on our way to Italy, with the Robin's Egg in her brassiere. "Loyalty is nothing," my mother would say. "If your father had been more sensible, he would still be with us. Loyalty is a breath. It is not worth the ring on my finger."

"But he had courage," I said. "Did he not have courage?"

"Courage, of course. He was, after all, my husband. But it is better to have diamonds."

Her beauty gave her ruthless practicality an indescribable charm.

"You are like him, Sabra. Always with your head in

the clouds. When are you going to get married? When are you going to live properly?" She thought it was foolish that I insisted on living on my stipend, but she approved of my studying literature, which was a decorative discipline. "That Samuel Coleridge whose poem you to read me," she would say, "I am convinced he must have been a handsome man."

I insisted on providing for myself, and living in a city that was too cold for her, because it kept me from feeling the enchantment that she threw over everything around her. She was an enchantress without intention, as a spider gathers flies by instinct. One longed to be in her web. In her presence, one could not help loving her, without judgement. And I was proud of my independence, if of nothing else.

Let me sing about the marriage of Kamora and the Cloud Dragon. Among all the maidens of the Empress Nasren, there was none so clever as Kamora. She knew every song that had ever been sung, since the world was made. When she sang, she could draw the nightingales into the Empress' garden, where they would sit on the branches of the almond trees and sing accompaniment. Each night she followed the Empress through the thousand rooms of the palace, singing her songs. Only Kamora could could soothe the Empress when Nasren sank down on the courtyard stones and wept into her hands with the wild abandon of a storm.

On the night after Alem Das had visited the Cloud Dragon, Kamora said to the Empress, "Lady, whose face is as bright as the moon, there is nothing more wonderful in the world than serving you, except for marrying the one I love. And you know this is true, because you have known the delights of such a marriage."

The Empress, who sat in a chair that Alem Das had carved for her from the horns of Leviathan, stood suddenly, so that the chair fell back, and a figure of Noah broke off from one corner. "Kamora, would you too leave me, as the Great Khan left me to wander among the stars? Some night, it may be this night, he will come back to me. But until that night, you must not leave me!" And she stared at Kamora with eyes that were apprehensive, and a little mad.

"Lady, whose eyes are as dark as the night," said Kamora, in her most soothing voice, "you know that the Great Khan lies in his tomb on Mount Abora. You built it yourself of white marble, stone on stone, and before you placed the last stone, you kissed his lips. Do you think that your husband would leave the bed you made for him? You would not keep me from marrying the one I love."

The Empress turned and walked, out of that room and into another, and another, and through all the thousand rooms of the palace. Kamora followed her, not singing tonight, but silent. When the Empress had reached the last room of the palace, a pantry in which the head cook kept her rose-petal jam, she said, "Very well. You may marry your Cloud Dragon. Do not look surprised that I know whom you love. I am not so insensible as all that. But first, you must complete one task for me. When you have completed it, then you may marry whom you please."

"What is that task?" asked Kamora.

"You must find me someone who amuses me more than you do."

It was Michael who introduced me to Coleridge. "Listen to this," he said.

> "*In Xanadu did Kubla Khan*
> *A stately pleasure-dome decree:*
> *Where Alph, the sacred river, ran*

> *Through caverns measureless to man*
> *Down to a sunless sea."*

"I can't believe you've never read it before. I mean, I learned that in high school."

"Who is this Michael Cavuto you keep talking about?" asked my mother over the telephone. "Where does he come from?"

"Ohio," I said.

She was as silent as though I had said, "The surface of the moon."

We were teaching assistants together, for a class on the Romantics. We read sentences to each other from our students' papers. "A nightingale is a bird that comes out at night to which Keats has written an ode." "William and his wife Dorothy lived together for many years until she died and left him lamenting." "Coleridge smoked a lot of opium, which explains a lot." We laughed, and marked our papers together, and one day, when we were both sitting in the library, making up essay questions for the final exam, we started talking about our families.

"Yours is much more interesting than mine," he told me. "I'd like to meet your mother."

You never will, I told myself. I liked him, with his spiky hair that stood up although he was always trying to gel it down, the angular bones that made him look graceless, as though his joints were not quite knit together, and his humor. I did not want him, too, to fall hopelessly in love. For goodness' sake, the woman was fifty-four. She was in Italy again, with a British rock star. He was twenty-seven. They had been together for two years. I could tell that she was already beginning to get bored.

"There's no one like Coleridge," Michael had said. "You'll see."

———

I have told you that Kamora was clever. Listen to how clever she was. She said to the Empress, "I will bring you what you ask for, but you must give me a month to find it, and a knapsack filled with bread and cheese and dried apricots, and a jar of honey."

"Very well," said the Empress. "You shall have all these things, although I will miss you, Kamora. But at the end of that month you will return to me, won't you?"

"If at the end of that month I have not found someone who amuses you more than I do, then I will return to you, and remain with you as long as you wish," said Kamora.

The Empress said, "Now I can sleep, because I know you will remain with me forever."

The next day, Kamora put her knapsack on her back. "I wish you luck, I do," said the head cook. "It can't be easy, spending every night with Her Craziness upstairs. Though why you would want to marry a dragon is beyond me."

Kamora smiled but did not answer. Then she turned and walked through the palace gates, chewing a dried apricot.

First, Kamora went to the house of her uncle Alem Das, which was built against the wall that surrounded the palace. She found him sitting on the stone floor, carving a bird for the youngest daughter of the River Dragon. When you wound it with a key, it could sing by itself. "Uncle," she said, "They call me clever, but I know that you are more clever than I am. You talked the horns off Leviathan, and once Bilkis, the sun herself, gave you three of her shining hairs. Who can amuse the Empress more than I can?"

Alem Das sat and thought. Kamora was his

favorite niece, and he did not want to disappoint her.
"You might bring her the Laughing Hound, who
dances on his hind legs, and rides a donkey, and tells
jokes all day long, or the Tree of Tales, whose leaves
whisper all the secrets that men do not wish to reveal.
But she would eventually tire of these. You, my dear,
can sing all the songs that were ever sung. If she tires of
a song, you can sing her another. If she is sad, you can
comb her hair with the comb I carved for you, and
cover her with a blanket, and sit by her until she has
fallen asleep. It will be difficult to find anyone as
amusing as you are."

Kamora sighed. "I hoped that you could help me.
Oh, uncle," and for the first time she did not sound
perfectly confident, "I do love him, you know."

"I'm not clever enough to help you," said Alem
Das, "but I know who is. Kamora, I will tell you a
secret. If you climb to the top of Mount Abora, even
higher than the Cloud Dragon, you will find the Stone
Woman. She is the oldest of all things, and I think she
will be able to help you. But you must tell no one where
she lives, and allow no one to follow you, because she
values her privacy. If it grows dark, take out the tail-
feather of the Phoenix, which I gave you for your
fourteenth birthday. It will light your way up the
mountain."

Kamora said, "But uncle, why should the Stone
Woman help me?"

"Take this drum," said Alem Das. "I made it from
the skin that the Sea Serpent sheds once a year. The
Stone Woman is old, and the old always like a
present."

"Thank you, uncle," said Kamora, kissing him on
both cheeks. "There truly is no one in the world as
clever as you."

Kamora walked through the village, chewing a

dried apricot. She walked over the hills, to the foot of Mount Abora. At the foot of the mountain, where the climb begins in earnest, she picked a handful of lilies, which grow by the streams that flow down the mountain to become the Alph. She left them at the tomb of the Great Khan, who had given her sugared almonds when she was a girl. Then she began to climb the path up the mountain. Halfway up, Kamora ate her lunch, bread and cheese and dried apricots. She washed her hands in one of the streams, put her knapsack on her back, and continued to climb. Near the top, she stopped to see the Cloud Dragon and tell him the Empress' condition.

"Well, good luck to you," he said. "If you were anyone else, I would be certain that you would fail, but I've been told that you're almost as clever as your uncle."

"I will not fail," said Kamora, and she gave him a look that made him break into puffs that flew every which way over the mountain. And this is the woman I'm going to marry, he thought. What have I gotten myself into?

In his house by the palace wall, Alem Das thought about his niece and smiled. He said to himself, "Sometimes she is too clever, that girl. First she asked for one of the Phoenix's tail-feathers, then for a comb carved from the shell of the Great Turtle. And now I've given her my drum. Does she really think she's tricked me? Oh, Kamora! It's certainly time you got married."

I'm not sure when we started dating. There was a gradual progression between friend and boyfriend. We were comfortable together, we seemed to fit together like two pieces of a puzzle. But a puzzle that showed what picture? I did not know.

It was a Friday. I remember because we had just

turned back a set of graded papers. I was still taking classes, and for my own class on the Romantics, taught by the same professor for whom I was TAing, I had decided to write a final paper on Coleridge. This will be easy, I thought. Michael and I have talked about him so often.

I was in my apartment. It was cold. It felt like a cave of ice.

And suddenly, I was there.

The Kubla Khan of Coleridge's poem is not the historical Kubla Khan, founder of the Yuan Dynasty, and Xanadu is not Shangdu. Both are dreams or hallucinations. Indeed, if we examine Coleridge's description of the palace itself, we notice that it does not make sense. Here, the river Alph, fed by the streams that flow down Mount Abora, does something strange: it disappears into a series of fissures in the ground, flowing through them until it comes to an underground lake. Coleridge's identification of this lake as a "sunless sea" or "lifeless ocean" is certainly poetic exaggeration, as my experience will show. The palace itself is situated where the river disappears, so that seen from one side, it seems to sit on the river itself. Seen from the other, it is surrounded by an extensive garden, where the Khan has collected specimens from all the fantastical countries, plants from lost Atlantis and Hyperborea and Thule. The palace is built of stone, and rises out of the stone beneath it, so that an outcropping will suddenly turn into a wall. Although Coleridge describes "caves of ice," this is again a poetic exaggeration. He means that since the palace is built of stone, even in summer the rooms are cold, so cold. I was always cold in that palace, as long as I was there.

It was empty. There were silk cushions on the floor, embroidered with dragons and orange trees, but no one to sit on them. There were tables inlaid with tulips and gazelles and chessboards, but no one to play. The curtains that hung in the doorways, filtering the sunlight, rose and fell with the breath of the river. But there was no other breath, and no noise other than a ceaseless rushing as the river swept through the caves below. As I walked, my steps sounded hollow, and I knew that the floors hung over rushing water and empty space. As an architectural feat, the Khan's palace is impossible.

There was water everywhere, in pools where ornamental fish swam, dappled white and orange and black, and basins in which the inhabitants, if there were any, would have washed their hands. The air had the clean, curiously empty smell of sunlight and water.

"I have looked. There is no one but ourselves."

He was dressed as you might expect, in breeches and a waistcoat over a linen shirt which seemed too large for him. He had thick brown hair, and a thin, inquisitive face, and his hands moved nervously. The young poet, already an addict.

I was not sure how to respond. "Have you been here long?"

"Several hours, and I confess that I'm beginning to feel hungry. Surely there is a kitchen? Shall we attempt to find it?"

The kitchen was empty as well, but the pantry was full. We ate sugared almonds, and a sweet cheese studded with raisins, and dried fish that was better than it looked. We drank a wine that tasted like honey.

"Sabra is a pretty name," he said. "Mine is Samuel, not so pretty, you see, but then I'm not as pretty as you." He wiped the corner of his mouth with a handkerchief. "Here we are, Samuel and Sabra, in the palace of the Khan. Where is the Khan, I wonder? Is he out hunting, or in another of his palaces? Perhaps

when he returns he will execute us for being here. Have
you thought of that, Sabra? We are, after all,
trespassers."

"I don't know," I said. "I don't feel like a trespasser.
And anyway, he isn't here now."

"That is true," he said. "Would you like the last of
the almonds? I've never much cared for almonds." He
leaned back against a cushion, his hair spread out over
an apricot tree in bloom, with a phoenix in its boughs.
"Will you sing to me, Sabra? I am tired, and I feel that I
have been speaking inanities. There is an instrument,
on that table. Can you play it, do you think?"

"Yes," I said, and picked up the instrument: a
dulcimer. While my friends in school were at soccer
practice, I was learning to play the dulcimer. It was
another of my mother's charming impracticalities.

"Then sing me something, won't you, pretty Sabra?
I'm so tired, and my head aches, I don't know why."

So I put away the last of the sugared almonds,
picked up the dulcimer, and began to sing.

Kamora could feel blisters forming where her sandals
rubbed against her feet, but she climbed steadily. It was
late afternoon, and the sun was already sinking into
the west, when she reached the summit. The Stone
Woman was waiting for her. She was wrapped in a gray
shawl and hunched over with age, so that she looked
like a part of the mountain itself.

"Back again, are you? And did you ever find your
own true love, the one whose face you saw in my
mirror?"

"I found him, lady who is wiser than the stars,"
said Kamora. "But now I have to win him."

"None of your flattery for me, girl," said the Stone
Woman. "I know exactly how wise I am. What are you
going to give me for my help?"

Kamora took the drum out of her knapsack.

The Stone Woman looked at it appreciatively. "Ah, this is better than that other stuff you gave me. Although the tail-feather of the Phoenix, which you gave me for teaching you all the songs that have ever been sung, burns all night long, so I can weave my tapestries. And every morning I use the comb made from the shell of the Great Turtle, which you gave me for showing you the Cloud Dragon in my mirror, and my hair never tangles." She ran one hand over her braid of gray hair, which was so long that it touched the ground. "But this!" She tapped the drum once with her finger, and Kamora heard a reverberation, not only from the drum itself, but from the stones around her, the scrubby cedars, bent by the wind, and even the air. It seemed to echo over the forested slopes of the mountain, and the hills below, on which she could see the tomb of the Great Khan, as white as the rising moon, and the plains stretching away into the distance.

"What is it?" asked Kamora.

"You uncle didn't tell you? That sound is the beat of the world, which governs everything, even the beating of your heart, and on this drum I can play it slower or faster, more sadly or more joyfully. No one can make an instrument like your uncle Alem, but I think this is his masterpiece. No wonder he wanted you to bring it to me. I'm the only one in whose hands it is perfectly safe. Think, girl, what would a man do who could alter the beat of the world? And by getting you to carry it, he saved himself a trip up the mountain! He is a clever man, your uncle. Now, it's dinnertime, and I'm hungry. Have you brought me any food?"

Kamora took out the honey, of which she knew the Stone Woman was inordinately fond.

"Good girl. Well, come inside, then, and tell me what you want this time."

The walls of the Stone Woman's cave were covered with tapestries. On one you could see the creation of the world by Lilit, and her marriage to the Sea Serpent, in which she wore a veil of stars. On another you could see the flood that resulted from their thrashing when they lay together, so that many of the first creatures she had created, the great dragons with horns like Leviathan's and eyes like rubies and emeralds, and the great turtles that carried mountains and even small lakes on their backs, were drowned. The whole history of the world was there, and on a panel that Kamora had not seen before, she saw Mount Abora, and the marriage of the Empress Nasren, the oldest daughter of the River Dragon, to the Great Khan, with the apricot trees on the mountain blooming around them.

The Stone Woman sat on a cushion and opened the honey-pot. She dipped a wooden spoon into it, tasted the honey, and licked her lips. "Very good, very good. Well, what do you want this time?"

Kamora knew that it was time to be, not clever, but direct. "The Empress, whose hands move like doves, will not let me marry until I have brought her someone who amuses her more than I do."

"So that's how it is," said the Stone Woman. "You can't marry your Cloud Dragon until she lets you, and she won't let you until she has found a substitute. You have been too clever, Kamora. When you asked me to teach you all the songs that have ever been sung, so the Empress would choose you as one of her maidens, to serve her and live in the palace, did you consider that she might want to keep you forever? Getting what you wish for isn't always a good thing, you know."

"If I had not learned all the songs that have ever been sung," said Kamora, "the Cloud Dragon would not have wanted to marry me. And I love him, I can't help loving him, since I saw how he looks at night, when he is a man. Perhaps I should not have looked in your mirror and asked to see my own true love, but when I saw how happy the Empress was with the Great Khan . . . " A tear slid down her cheek, and she wiped it away with her hand.

"Ah, clever Kamora! So you wanted to love and be loved. You have a heart after all," said the Stone Woman. "Just remember that cleverness is not enough to keep a husband, not even the Cloud Dragon, who is less clever than you are. You must show him your heart as well. I warned him about choosing such a clever wife! But how do you expect me to help you?"

Kamora said, "I thought about that, when I walked through the thousand rooms of the palace at night with the Empress. What is more amusing than a person who knows all the songs that have ever been sung? Only a person who can create new songs. Only a poet."

"If you know the answer yourself," said the Stone Woman, "why do you need me?"

"Because I need you to make me a poet. Not one of those poets who sit in the marketplace, selling rhymes so that soldiers, and anyone with a silver coin, can sing them to the Empress' maidens—out of tune! I need a true poet, who can write what has never been sung before."

"A poet?" asked the Stone Woman. "And how to you expect me to make you a poet?"

"In the same way you made the world, Lilit."

Kamora and the Stone Woman stared at each other. Finally the Stone Woman said, "You are as clever as your uncle. How did you know who I was?"

Kamora smiled. "Who else would know all the songs that have ever been sung? Who else would keep the Mirror of Truth in a cave on Mount Abora? And when the Great Khan was laid in his tomb, the Empress put honey on his lips so you would kiss them when he entered the land of the dead. Even songs from the making of the world mention how fond you are of honey. You have created the Sea Serpent, the Lion of the Sun who carries Bilkis on his back, and whose walk across the sky warms the earth, the Silver Stag who summons men to the land of the dead . . . Only you can make a poet."

"Very well," said the Stone Woman. "I will make you a poet, Kamora. But only because I like you. And this is my wedding gift, and the last thing I will do for you. You have had three gifts from me already, and that is enough for anyone." She stood and considered. "But I haven't made a poet for a long time. I wonder if I remember how?"

Have you seen the stone caves beneath the palace of Kubla Khan, called the Lesser Khan because for all his palaces, he could not match the conquests of his grandfather, the Great Khan? Where the stone is thin, it is translucent, so that the caves are filled with a strange, ghostly light. In the dark waters, which are still and no longer rushing, since the river has mingled into the underground lake, there are luminescent fish. When they swim to the surface, they shine like moving stars.

Samuel took off his breeches and swam in the dark water, in just his shirt. I sat on the bank, strumming the dulcimer, thinking of songs that he might like. He floated on his back, his hair spreading around his face like seaweed.

"There seems to be no time here," he said. "At home, I was expecting a person from Porlock. But here, I feel that no person from Porlock will ever come. Time has stopped, and nothing will ever happen. Except that you will keep singing, Sabra. You will keep singing, won't you? Sing to me about how the Stone Woman made a poet." But I did not finish my song, then.

Later, we walked in the garden that surrounded the palace.

"They go on for ten miles," I said.

"How do you know that?" he asked, but I did not answer. It was hot, even in the shade of the almond trees, and the roses, which had been transported at great expense from Nineveh, were releasing their fragrance into the evening. "I think I could stay here forever," he said. "Forget my damned debts. Forget my . . . marriage. Never write again, never write anything else. I'm no good at it anyway. I never finish anything."

"That's not what Lilit said, when she made you."

"What do you mean?"

"Lilit created the poet out of clay. Kamora watched her mold the figure, the height and shape of a man. It was late now. Outside, the moon had risen, and it shone in through the opening of the cave, its pale light meeting the light of the Phoenix's tail-feather. Kamora sat on the floor and watched, but she was so tired that her eyes kept closing, and somehow, between one blink of her eyes and another, the man was complete. He was tall, well-formed, and gray, the color of the clay at the bottom of the river Alph. His mouth was open, as though already speaking a poem.

" 'Now we must awaken him,' said Lilit. 'I will walk around him three times one way, and you must walk around him three times the other. Then I will spread honey on his lips, and you must put honey into his mouth, so that his words will be both nourishing and sweet.'

"Kamora rose. She was so tired that she stumbled as she walked, but three times she stumbled around the poet, and when she had done so, she took the jar from Lilit and put honey into the poet's open mouth.

" 'There,' said Lilit. 'And I really think that this time I have outdone myself. He will be the greatest poet

that ever lived, and every night he will write a poem
that has never been heard before for the Empress
Nasren. He will be like the river Alph, endlessly
replenished by the streams that flow down Mount
Abora.' The poet was no longer the color of clay. Now
he had brown hair hanging down to his shoulders, and
his skin was as white as milk and covered, irregularly,
with brown hair. Lilit took off her gray shawl and
wrapped it around his hipbones. 'Speak, poet. Give us
the gift of your first poem.'

> *"The poet turned to her and said,*
> *'A damsel with a dulcimer*
> *In a vision once I saw:*
> *It was an Abyssinian maid,*
> *And on her dulcimer she played,*
> *Singing of Mount Abora.'*

" 'That's enough for now,' said Lilit. 'You see,
Kamora, your poet works. Now take him to your
Empress, and marry your Cloud Dragon. But don't
visit me again, because the next time you come I won't
be here.' "

"And was he the greatest poet that ever lived?"
asked Samuel. We were sitting on the riverbank, where
the Alph begins to disappear into the fissures below,
surrounded by the scent of roses. The sun was setting,
and the walls of the palace had changed from white to
gold, and then to indigo. I could not see his face, but
his voice sounded sad.

"He was, in the palace of the Empress Nasren," I
said. "He wrote a different poem for her every night,
and she gathered scribes around her to make copies so
they could be taken to every village. They were set to
music, as poems were in those days, and sung at every
village fair. And when her ambassadors traveled to

other countries, they carried the volumes of his poems, fourteen of them, the number of the constellations, on the back of a white elephant, so they could be presented to foreign sultans and caliphs and tzars."

"But elsewhere, in the country of daffodils and mutton and rain? Because I think, Sabra, that you come from outside this dream, as I do."

"In that country, he was a poet who could not finish his poems, and who, for many years, did not write poems at all. How could he, when every night in the palace of the Empress, he wrote a new poem entirely for her? What was left over, after that?"

"Perhaps. Yes, perhaps that is true."

We heard it then: lightening, crashing over the palace, turning the walls again from indigo to white. Once, twice, three times.

"He has come," said Samuel. "He has come, the person from Porlock." And then suddenly, he was gone.

I was staring at my computer screen, on which I had written, "The Kubla Khan of Coleridge's poem is not the historical Kubla Khan, founder of the Yuan Dynasty, and Xanadu is not Shangdu."

Again, I heard three knocks on the apartment door. "Sabra, are you there? It's Michael."

I rose, and went to open the door. "You people!" I said, as Michael walked in, carrying two bags of groceries.

"What do you mean?" he asked, startled.

"You people from Porlock, always interrupting."

He kissed me and put the bags he had been carrying on the table. "I was thinking of making a curry, but— you've had better curry than I can make. Are you going to laugh at my curry?"

"I would never laugh at your curry."

He began unpacking the grocery bags. "So, what

were you thinking about so hard that you didn't hear me knock?"

"Coleridge. About how he never finished anything. And about how I'm not sure I want to finish this PhD. Michael, what would you think if I became a writer?"

"Fine by me, as long as you become famous—and rich, so you can keep me in a style to which I am not accustomed."

Later, after dinner, which was not as disastrous as I had expected, I called my mother. "Nasren Makeda, please."

"Just a moment. Madame Makeda, it's your daughter."

"Sabra! How good it is to hear your voice. I'm in Vienna with Ronnie. Darling, I'm so bored. Won't you come visit your poor mother? You can't imagine these rock and roll people. They have no culture whatsoever. One can't talk to them about anything."

"Mom, I'd like you to come to Boston and meet Michael."

"The one from Ohio? Oh, Sabra. Well, I suppose we can't control whom we fall in love with. It was like that with your father. He was the only man I ever loved, and yet he was shorter than I am by three inches, and that nose—such a pity you inherited it, although you have my ears, thank goodness. But I tell you the truth, I would have married him even if he had not been rich. He was that sort of man. So, I will come and meet your Michael. I can fly over in Ronnie's plane. Is there a month when Boston is warm? I can come then."

Perhaps he would fall in love with her. But sometimes one has to take chances.

For Kamora's marriage to the Cloud Dragon, the Empress' poet Samuel wrote a new poem, one that no one had heard before. It began,

Do you ask what the birds say? The sparrow, the dove,
The linnet and thrush say, "I love and I love."

Alem Das himself sang it, playing a dulcimer strung with the whiskers of the Cloud Dragon, whose sound was sweeter, more passionate, and more filled with longing than any instrument that had ever been made. When he was finished, the Empress Nasren clapped, and Kamora, in the Empress' wedding veil, turned to her husband and blushed.

Later that night, in the cave of the Cloud Dragon, he said to her, "It may be that you are too clever to be my wife."

She stroked his silver hair and looked with wonder at his pale shoulders, shy for once before his human form. "And perhaps you are too beautiful to be my husband."

"Then we are well-matched," he said, "for together there is none in the world more clever or more beautiful than we. And now, my clever wife, are you going to kiss your husband?"

That night, the top of Mount Abora was wreathed in clouds. The Empress Nasren saw it as she walked in the garden of her palace, and she told blind Alem Das, who was walking with her. "Did you know, my friend, that it would end like this?" she asked.

Alem Das laughed in the darkness. "I suspected, from the moment Kamora insisted that my dulcimer should be strung with the whiskers of the Cloud Dragon. She always was a clever girl, although not as clever, I like to think, as her uncle."

"So, your niece is happy," said the Empress. "It is good that she is happy, although we who are old, Alem, know that happiness is fleeing." And she sighed her soft, mad sigh.

"Yes, lady," said Alem Das. "But tonight your roses

are blooming, and I can hear the splashing of fountains. Somewhere inside the palace, your poet is reciting to the wedding guests, who are drunk on honey wine. And we who are old can remember what it was like to be young and foolish and happy, and be content." And they walked on in the moonlight, the instrument-maker and the Empress.

SAVE ME PLZ

———

David Barr Kirtley

Meg hadn't heard from Devon in four months, and she realized that she missed him. So on a whim she tossed her sword and scabbard into the back seat of her car and drove over to campus to visit him.

She'd always thought that she and Devon would be one of those couples who really did stay friends afterward. They'd been close for so long, and things hadn't ended that badly. Actually, the whole incident seemed pretty silly to her now. Still, she'd been telling herself that the split had been for the best—with her working full-time and him still an undergrad. It was like they were in two different worlds. She'd been busy with work, and he'd always been careless about answering email, and now somehow four months had passed without a word.

She parked in the shadow of his dorm, then grabbed her sword and strapped it to her jeans. She approached his building. A spider, dog-sized and iridescent, rappelled toward her, its thorned limbs plucking the air. She dropped a hand to the hilt of her sword. The spider wisely withdrew, back to its webbed lair amid the eaves.

She had no keycard, so she waited for someone to open the door. She checked her reflection. Eyes large, hips slender, ears a bit tapered at the tips. She looked fine. (Though she'd never be a match for the imaginary elf-maid Leena.)

Finally someone exited, an unfamiliar brown-haired girl. Meg caught the door and passed into the lobby. She climbed the stairs and walked down the hall to Devon's door. She knocked.

His roommate Brant answered, looking half-asleep or maybe stoned. "Hey Meg," Brant mumbled—casually, as if he'd just seen her yesterday. "How's the real world?"

"Like college," she said, "but with less Art History. Is Devon here?"

"Devon?" Brant seemed confused. "Oh. You don't know." He hesitated. "He dropped out."

"What?" She was startled.

"Just packed up and left. Weeks ago. He said it didn't matter anymore. He was playing that game all the time." Brant didn't need to say *which* game. Least of all to her. "He said he found something, huge. In the game. Then he went away."

"Went away where? Is he all right?"

Brant shrugged. "I don't know, Meg. He didn't tell me. You could email him, I guess. Or try to find him online. He's always playing that game." Brant shook his head. "And I mean *always*."

Meg strode to her car. She chucked her sword in back, slid into the driver's seat, and slammed the door.

Devon was the smartest guy she'd ever met, and the stupidest. How could he drop out with just one year left? Sadly, she wasn't all that surprised.

She'd met him at an off-campus party her junior year. They'd ended up on the same couch. Before long he was on his third beer and telling her, "I didn't even want to go to college. My parents insisted. I had a whole other plan."

She said, "Which was?"

"To be a prince." He gave a grandiose shrug. "I

think I'd make a pretty good prince." He noted her skeptical expression, and added, "But not prince of, like, England. I'm not greedy. Prince of Monaco would be fine. Wait, is that even a country?"

"Yes," she said.

"Good," he declared, thumping his beer on the endtable. "Prince of Monaco. Or if that's taken . . . "

"Liechtenstein," she suggested.

"Liechtenstein, great!" he agreed, pointing. "Or Trinadad and Tobago."

She shook her head. "It's not a monarchy. No princes."

"No princes?" He feigned outrage. "Well, screw *them* then. Liechtenstein it is."

After that she noticed him everywhere. He seldom went to class or did coursework, so he was always out somewhere—joking with friends in the dining hall, pacing around the pond, or sitting under a tree in the central quad, doodling. His carefree independence was oddly endearing, especially to her who was always so conscientious, though later his indifference to school worried her. She'd ask, "What'll you do after you graduate?"

He'd just shrug and say, "Grades don't matter. Just that you have the degree."

And now he'd dropped out.

Angry, she started her car. She drove back to her apartment.

She emailed him repeatedly, but got no response. Mutual friends hadn't heard from him. His mom thought he was still in school. Meg got really worried. Finally, she resorted to something she'd promised herself she'd never do—she drove over to the mall to buy the game.

It was called *Realms of Eldritch*, a groundbreaking multiplayer online game full of quests and wizards and monsters. Some of the game was based on real life: People carried magic swords, and many of the enemies were real, such as wolves or goblins or giant spiders. And like in real life there was a gnome who sometimes appeared to give you quests or hints or items. But most of it was pure fantasy: dragons and unicorns and walking trees and demon lords.

And elves. In the game store, Meg eyed the box art. Leena, the golden-haired and impossibly buxom elf-maid, grinned teasingly.

Meg had a complicated relationship with Leena (especially considering that Leena wasn't real). The year before, Meg had been riffling through Devon's notebook and had come across a dozen sketches of Leena. The proportions were off, but each sketch came closer and closer to being a perfect representation. Meg had begun teasing Devon that he was in love with Leena. Meg had also once, foolishly, dressed up as Leena in bed, for Devon's twenty-first birthday. It was just a campy gag, but he'd seemed way too into it. He'd even called her "Leena." She'd never worn the costume again, and he'd never brought it up. He'd been pretty drunk that night, and she'd wondered if he even remembered her looking like someone else.

She bought the game (planning to return it the next day) and started home. In the rearview mirror she saw a flock of giant bats tailing her. She tensed, ready to slam the brakes and reach for her sword, but finally the bats veered off and vanished into the west.

Back at her apartment, she opened the game box and dumped its contents out on her coffee table. Half a dozen CDs, a thick manual, some flyers, a question-naire. It seemed so innocuous. Hard to believe that this little box could destroy a relationship. She and Devon had been so happy together for almost a year before he got caught up in this game.

She installed it. As progress bars chugged, she thumbed through the manual, which described the rules in mind-numbing detail—races, classes, attributes, combat, inventory, spells. She'd never understood how someone as smart and talented as Devon could waste so much time on this stuff.

Maybe she could have understood if the game at least featured some brilliant story, but Devon spent all his time doing "level runs"—endlessly repeating the same quest over and over in hopes of attaining some marginally more powerful magical item. And even after he'd become as powerful as the game allowed, he still kept playing, exploiting different bugs so that he could duplicate superpowered items or make himself invincible. How could someone who read Heidegger for fun so immerse himself in a subculture of people too lazy or daft to type out actual words, who instead of "Someone please help" would type "sum1 plz hlp"?

Meg, on the rare occasions that she permitted herself solitary recreation, preferred Jane Austen novels or independent films. She'd once told Devon, "I'm more interested in things that are *real*."

He'd been playing the game. Monitor-glow made his head a silhouette. He said, "What's *real* is just an accident. No one designed reality to be compelling." He gestured to the screen. "But a fantasy world *is* so designed. It takes the most interesting things that ever existed—like knights in armor and pirates on the high seas—and combines them with the most interesting things that anyone ever dreamed up—fire-breathing dragons and blood-drinking vampires. It's the world as it should be, full of wonder and adventure. To privilege reality simply because it *is* reality just represents a kind of mental parochialism."

She knew better than to debate him. But she still thought the game was vaguely silly, and she refused to play it, though he often bugged her to join in. He'd say, "It's something we could do together."

And she'd answer, "I just don't want to."

And he'd say, "Give it a try. I do things *I* don't want to because they're important to you. Sometimes I even end up liking them."

But by then Meg had already spent far too many hours sitting on the couch watching him play the game, or hearing about it over candlelit dinners, and she didn't intend to do anything to justify him spending any more time on it.

It was hard some nights, after they'd made love, to lie there knowing that he was just itching to slip from her embrace and go back to the game. To know that a glowing electronic box full of imaginary carnage beckoned him in a way that her company and conversation and even body no longer could.

Finally, she couldn't take it anymore. Though she knew she might lose him, she announced, "Devon. Look. I don't know how else to say this. It's that game or me. I'm not kidding."

He released the controls and swiveled in his chair. He gave her a wounded look and said, "That's not fair, Meg. I'd never make you give up something you enjoyed."

She stood her ground. "This is something I'm asking you to do. For me."

"You really want me to delete it?"

"Yes," she said. Oh God, yes.

He bit his lip, then said, "Fine." He fiddled with the computer, then turned to her and added, "There, it's gone. All right?"

"All right," she said, euphoric. And for a few weeks things were great again, like they used to be.

But one night she came over and found him playing it again. She stared. "What are you doing?"

He glanced at her and said, "Oh, hi." He noticed her agitation, and explained, "My guild really needed me for this one quest."

"You told me you deleted it."

He turned back to the screen. "Yeah, I had to reinstall the whole thing. Don't worry, I'll delete it again tomorrow."

Meg was furious. "You *promised*."

"Come on," he said, "I haven't played for *three weeks*. It's just this one time."

She stomped away. "I told you, Devon. That game or me. Isn't that what I said?"

"Meg, don't leave, okay? Would you just—" Something happened in the game, and he jumped. "Shit! He got me."

She left, slamming the door. Devon called out, "Meg, wait." But he didn't run after her.

She expected him to call and apologize, beg her forgiveness, but he didn't. Days passed, then she sent him a curt email saying that maybe it would be better if they just stayed friends from now on, and— disappointingly—he had agreed.

The game finished installing. Meg hovered the mouse pointer over the start icon. She felt strangely ambivalent. She'd fought so hard against this damn game, and now she was actually going to run it. She also felt an inexplicable dread, as if the game would suck her in the way it had sucked in Devon, and she'd never escape. But that was silly. She was just using it to contact him. She double-clicked.

The game menu loaded. She created a character and chose all the most basic options—human, female, warrior. The name Meg was taken, so she added a random string of numbers, Meg1274, and logged in. The game displayed a list of servers. Meg did a search for his character, Prince Devonar. He was the only player listed on a server named Citadel of Power. She connected to it.

She typed, "Hi Devon." No response.

She tried again. "Devon? It's me, Meg. Are you there?"

Finally, he answered. "Meg?"

She typed, "Are you OK?"

A long pause. "I found something. In the game. Unbelievable. But now I'm stuck. Need help."

Was this whole situation some elaborate setup to get her to play the game with him? But that was crazy. Not even Devon would drop out of school as part of such a ruse. She typed, "Devon, call me. OK?"

Another pause. "Can't call. Trapped. Plz, Meg, help me. You're the only one who can."

"I can't help," she typed. "I'm only level 1."

"Not in the game," he typed back. "In real life. Ask the gnome. Plz, Meg. I really need you. Can't stay. Meg, save me plz."

She typed frantically. "Devon, wait. What's going on? Where are you???"

But Prince Devonar was gone.

Devon had said to ask the gnome. But that wasn't so easy.

No one really understood what the gnome was. He seemed to wander through time and space. He was usually benevolent, appearing to those in need and offering hints or assistance or powerful items. But he was also fickle and enigmatic. He seemed to only appear after you'd given up hope of finding him. He also seemed to prefer locales with corners that he could pop out from and then disappear around.

So Meg parked downtown and wandered the back alleys. She couldn't stop thinking of Devon's final words: "Save me plz." If only the gnome would show himself. Hours passed.

Forget it. She was going home. She crossed the street—

And then the gnome, before her.

Crimson-robed, white-bearded, flesh like dry sand. One eye brown, kindly. The other blue, inscrutable. In a soft and alien voice he observed, "On a quest."

Finally. She wanted to grab him. "Where's Devon? Tell me."

"This is your path." The gnome pointed to the road at her feet, then westward.

Meg nodded. "I'll follow it."

The gnome turned his kindly brown eye upon her. "Have no fear, though obstacles lie in your way. Your victory is assured, foretold by prophecy: 'When the warrior-maid with love in her heart sets out, sword in her right hand, wand in her left, nothing shall stand before her.' "

"Wand?" she said.

The gnome reached up his sleeve and drew forth a thin black rod, two feet long. He whispered, "The most dire artifact in all the world, the Wand of Reification." He handed it to her. It chilled her fingers, and was so dark that it seemed to have no surface. He said, "Imbued with the power to give form to dreams. It may only be used three times."

Devon had said once that in the game there were items that vanished after you used them. So he never used them. He'd beat quest after quest without them, though they would've aided him considerably. He was always afraid he'd need them later. He'd asked, "What does that say about me?" and she'd said, "You're afraid of commitment?" and he'd laughed. It wasn't so funny now though, as she clutched this wand, so potent yet so ephemeral. How could she ever use it?

When she looked again, the gnome had vanished.

———

Meg retrieved her car and set off the way the gnome had pointed. The road: a double yellow line and two lanes of black asphalt, bordered by sidewalks. She drove. Skyscrapers and then suburbs fell away behind her. She passed clusters of thatched-roof cottages. Men farmed and cows grazed and windmills turned. Sometimes ancient oaks pressed in close to the road. Sometimes she saw castles on distant hills.

The needle on her gas gauge sank, and she hoped to find a station, but there were none. Finally, the engine died. She left her car and set off down the sidewalk.

Twilight came. Then the long line of streetlamps lit up, casting eerie white splotches on the darkened street and creating a tableau somehow dreamlike and unreal. She thought of how Devon and Brant would sometimes smoke pot and then get into long, rambling discourses on the nature of existence. During one such conversation, Devon had said, "Do you know anything about quantum mechanics?"

"Not really," Brant had replied.

So Devon said, "Well, in the everyday world, things exist. If I leave a book on this table, I know for sure that it's there. But when you get down to the subatomic level, things don't exist in the same way. They only exist as *probabilities*, until directly observed. How do you explain that?"

Brant countered, "How do *you* explain it?"

Devon smirked. "Like this: Our world isn't real. It's a *simulation*. An incredibly sophisticated one, but not without limits. It can keep track of every molecule, but not every last subatomic particle. So it estimates, and only starts figuring out where specific particles are when someone goes looking for them."

"That's so weird," Brant had said.

Meg heard a vehicle approaching from behind. Then its headlights lit the street. She glanced back into the glare, then kept walking. The vehicle slowed. It followed, in a way she didn't like. Finally, it pulled even with her. A black SUV, its windows open. From the darkness came a rasping, lascivious voice, "Hey, where you going?"

She ignored it, walked.

"Need a ride?" The voice waited. "Hey, I'm talking to you." A long pause. "What, you too good to talk to us?" When Meg didn't answer, the voice hissed, "Bitch," and the driver gunned the engine. The truck sped off.

Meg watched it go, then watched its taillights flare a sudden red challenge, watched it swing around, its headlights sweeping the trees, watched it come on, two coronas of searing white. Cackles rose from its windows. Meg drew her sword and stepped into the street. The car horn shrieked.

She slashed upward, between the lights, and the truck split. Its two halves swept past on either side. Its right half sped into a tree. Its left half flipped over and rolled thirty yards along the pavement.

Meg followed after. She neared the wreckage. A scraggly vermillion arm reached up through one window, then a face appeared—hairless, dark-eyed, ears like rotting carrots. A goblin. He squirmed free and dropped to the ground. A second goblin crawled from beneath the wreck.

The first drew a long wavy dagger. "Look what you did to my truck!"

But before he could start forward, the second grabbed him and leaned in close. "It's *her*. The Facilitator."

The first goblin studied Meg, and his eyes widened. He sheathed his dagger. "So it is." He touched two knuckles to his gnarled red brow. "I apologize, my lady. We owe you much."

The goblins edged around her, then hurried over to the other half of their vehicle. They dragged out two more goblins, who were seriously injured, and departed together.

And then they were gone. But their words stayed with Meg, and perplexed her, and troubled her greatly.

She had other adventures, vanquished other foes, and the road led ever on. Finally, she came to the peak of a rocky prominence and looked out over a mile-long crater. The street ran downhill until it reached the gates of a dark and forbidding fortress. She knew that this must be the Citadel of Power and that Devon must be within. She hiked down to it.

The drawbridge had been lowered. She eased across, sword in her right hand, Wand of Reification in her left. The portcullis was up and the gate lay open. She slipped into the yard.

Empty. She crept sideways, keeping the wall at her back. She held her breath, heard nothing.

She peeked into the central yard and saw a grand stone altar. She crept closer. An object lay upon it. A wand.

The Wand of Reification.

She glanced at her left hand, which still held *her* wand. She'd thought it unique. She already had a Wand of Reification, and hadn't even used it. She shrugged, took the second wand and tucked it in her belt, then moved on.

She searched bedchambers, kitchens, a great hall, a cavernous ballroom, all empty. She entered an ancient armory. Crossbows, shields, pikes—

Wands.

Rack after rack of wands. Hundreds of wands. A

thousand? Wands of Reification all, she felt sure. She didn't understand.

She went outside and crossed the yard again. The sky had begun to dim, and now she saw faint light in a tower window. She ran toward it.

Which hall? Which way? She dashed through rooms and under arches and up spiral stairs. Finally she found it—a door, shut, wan light spilling from beneath. She hurled herself against the door, and burst into the room with her sword raised.

A bedchamber. Posters on the walls. Devon's posters, from his old dorm room.

Light from a computer monitor. Someone sat before it. He turned. Devon.

He smiled and said, "Meg. Hey!"

She ran to him, enfolded him in her arms along with sword and wand and everything, and said, "Are you all right? I was so worried."

"I'm fine." He squeezed her and chuckled. "Everything's fine." He pulled back, brushed aside a lock of her hair, and kissed her. He was so tall and handsome, tawny-haired and emerald-eyed. He wore a gold medallion over a purple doublet with dagged sleeves. "Come on. You're exhausted." He led her to the bed, and they sat down together. He took her sword and wand and laid them on the nightstand.

She rested her cheek against his shoulder. She stared at the familiar posters (the nearest was an Edmund Leighton print) and whispered, "Aren't you in trouble? I thought you were. Devon, I don't understand what's happening."

"Shhh." He stroked her hair. "Just relax, okay? I'll explain everything."

He said that the real world was just a simulation, like a game. He didn't know who'd made it, but whoever they were they didn't seem to show themselves or ever interfere. Like any game, it had bugs. Many of these involved *Realms of Eldritch,* which was itself a new, fairly sophisticated simulation, and sometimes things got confused, and an item from the game got dumped into the real world. That's how he'd gotten the Wand of Reification, which could be used to alter almost anything. With it he'd set things in motion. He said, "Do you understand so far?"

She nodded, tentatively. It was all so strange.

He said that since the wand could only be used three times, he'd had to go looking for another bug, some way to duplicate the wand. Fortunately, there *was* one. But it was very specific: If a female warrior set out to rescue a man she loved, and was given the wand by the gnome, the game set a quest tag wrong, and let her acquire the wand again at the Citadel of Power, leaving her with two. Devon said, "Ah, speak of the devil." Meg raised her head.

The gnome, his head canted so that his mysterious blue eye watched her. Devon reached toward the nightstand, took the wand, and handed it to the gnome.

Meg murmured, "Why are you giving it to him?"

Devon said, "So he can give it to you again."

The gnome stuck the wand in his sleeve, gave a curt nod, and hobbled from the room.

Meg was mystified. "You said this bug creates an extra wand?"

"Yes."

She thought of the armory. "But you have *hundreds* of wands."

"Over a thousand," Devon said. He took the spare wand from her belt and placed it on the bed. "One for each time you've come here. One thousand two hundred and seventy four wands."

She was stunned. "But . . . I don't remember . . . "

He told her, somewhat cryptically, "When you restart a quest, you lose all your progress."

Meg stood, pulling from his embrace. "Devon, you *lied* to me. You said you were trapped here."

He stood too. "I'm sorry. I had to. You had to be on a quest to save me, otherwise it wouldn't work."

She fumed. "I was in danger. I was attacked!"

He held back a smile. "And what happened?"

"I . . . " She hesitated. "I beat them."

"Of course. Meg, you're level 60. You have the most powerful sword in the game. Nothing can harm you. There was never any danger. Didn't you get my prophecy?"

"Your prophecy?"

"That's why I wrote it," he said. "That's why I made the gnome recite it. So you wouldn't be afraid."

She paced to the window and looked out. This was all too much. "So now you've got a thousand wands. Why? What are you planning to do?"

He came and put his arm around her, and said softly, "To remake the world. To make it what it should have been all along—a place of wonder and adventure, without old age or disease. A place where death is only temporary—like in the game."

"You're going to make the game real," she said.

"Yes."

She felt apprehension. "I don't know, Devon. Maybe you shouldn't be messing around with this. I like the world just fine the way it is."

"Meg." His tone was affectionate. "You always say that."

She felt a sudden alarm. "What?"

Again, he suppressed a smile. "It's already begun. Ages ago. You think the world always had goblins and giant spiders and a gnome running around handing out magic items? That's all from the game. I made that happen."

She felt adrift. "I . . . don't remember."

"No one does," he said. "The wand makes things real. Not just physical, but real. Only I know that things used to be different, and now so do you."

And the goblins, Meg thought. They knew.

Devon kept going: "That's what's so funny, Meg. No matter what I do, no matter what crazy, incongruous reality I create, you always want things to stay exactly the way they are. That's just your personality. But we can't stop now. There's still so much to do. And you'll love it when I'm done, you'll see. You have to trust me."

"I don't know," she said. "I . . . need to think about it."

"Of course," Devon replied. "Take all the time you need."

So she stayed with Devon at the Citadel of Power, and they ate meals together in the dining hall, and danced together in the grand ballroom, and after that first night they slept together again too. She was still in love with him. She always had been. Even the game knew it.

They hiked together around the crater's rim, and he told her of the world as it *had* been, when there'd been no magic at all, and humans were the only race that could speak, and adventure was something that most people only dreamt of. It sounded dismal, and yet Meg wondered, "Could you reverse the process? Put everything back the way it was?"

Devon was silent a while. "It would take a long time. But yes, I could. Is that what you want?"

"I don't know," she said.

That night, Devon told her, "I want to show you

something." He led her to their tower chamber and turned on his computer. Meg was suddenly nervous. The monitor flickered. Icons appeared. Devon said softly, "Look at my background."

It showed two students sitting on a couch at a party. Meg didn't know them. The girl was pear-shaped and frizzy-haired and wore thick glasses. The guy wore glasses too, and was gangly, with thin lank hair and blotchy skin. The two of them looked happy together, in a pathetic sort of way. Meg said, "Who are they?"

Devon said, "That's the night we met."

Meg was horrified. She looked again, and suddenly she *did* recognize traces of themselves in the features of those strangers on the couch.

Devon explained, "I used the wand on us. Nothing drastic. I could do a lot more. I could make us anything we want. But you need to understand, Meg, when you talk about putting things back the way they were, exactly what you're saying."

Meg could accept the way she looked now—merely a pale shadow of Leena. But to think that she might not even be pretty, might be *that* girl . . .

"I thought you should know," Devon said, apologetic.

The next day at lunch, Meg asked him, "What is it you want me to do?"

He lowered his utensils. "Start the quest over."

"How?"

He nodded in the direction of the tower. "On my computer. I can show you."

"So that you'll get another wand?" she said.

"Yes."

"And I won't remember any of this?"

"No," he said.

She leaned back in her seat. "How many more times, Devon? My God, how many more wands?"

"As many as it takes," he said, without equivocation.

She stood up from the table, and said, "I need to think. Alone." He nodded. She went and paced the castle walls.

Devon wanted his new world more than anything. If she went along, then together they could have immortality and adventure and opulence and wonder. What had the old world offered? Crappy jobs and student loans, illness and death. What kind of a choice was that? She'd been here before, even if she didn't remember, and had sided with Devon one thousand two hundred and seventy four times. Who was she now, to doubt the wisdom of all her past choices?

He was still sitting there when she returned and said, "Fine. Show me."

He led her to the tower and loaded the game. He selected a character named Meg, who looked exactly like her. The character was level 60, and carried a Sword of Ultimate Cleaving +100. Devon clicked through a few menus, then stood. "Okay, *you* have to do it."

Meg sat down at the computer. A box on the screen said: "Citadel of Power—Are you sure you want to start this quest over from the beginning?" The mouse pointer hovered over "Yes."

Devon leaned down next to her. "Are you ready?"

"Yes," she whispered.

He kissed her cheek. "I'll see you again soon, okay?"

"Okay," she said, and clicked.

Meg hadn't heard from Devon in four months, and she realized that she missed him. So on a whim she tossed her sword and scabbard into the back seat of her car and drove over to campus to visit him.

Ages passed.

And now Leena the elf-maid is the most beautiful woman in all the world, and her lover is the most handsome man, Prince Devonar. They journey onward together, battling giants, riding dragons to distant lands, and feasting in the halls of dwarven kings. The prince is incandescent with joy. He was born for this, and Leena enjoys seeing him so happy. She loves him.

They ride two white unicorns down a forest path blanketed with fresh snow, and by some strange twist of magic or fate they come upon something that should not exist.

It lies half-buried in the drifts, but Leena can see that it was once a sort of carriage made from black metal. It has a roof, and its underside is all manner of piping, rusted now. Long ago, someone had sliced it in half. Where its other half may now lie, none can say.

The prince leaps from his mount and circles the strange object. "What foul contraption is this?"

Leena drops to the ground too, and staggers forward. A strange feeling passes over her, and a teardrop streaks her cheek. She can't say why. Soon she is sobbing.

The prince takes her in his arms. "My lady, what's the matter?" He scowls at the object. "It's upset you. Here, it shan't trouble us any longer." He pulls the Wand of Reification from his belt and aims.

"No!" She pushes his arm aside. "Leave it! Please."

He shrugs. "As you wish. But come, let's away. I mislike this place." He mounts his unicorn.

Leena stares at the strange carriage, and for a moment she remembers a world where countless such things raced down endless black roads. A world of soaring glass towers, of medallions that spoke in the voices of friends a thousand leagues distant, and where tales were told with light thrown up on walls the size of giants. Film, she remembers. Independent film. Jane Austen.

But the moment passes, and that fantastic world fades, leaving only the present, leaving only this odd, lingering sensation of being trapped in someone else's dream. She mounts her unicorn, and three words stick in her head, an incantation from a forgotten age. She no longer remembers where she heard the words, only that they now seem to express a feeling that surges up from somewhere deep inside her.

Save me plz.

BUFO REX

———

Erik Amundsen

I am called Bufo, I grow fat upon insects. I make my board under leaves, upon logs, and my bed lies in the bogs. My throne is the toadstool, and witch's butter is for my biscuits.

I've never put much stock in humanity, despite what stories might have said of me; I am no great lover of human aesthetics, being, myself, so physically bereft. My hide is olive and warted, my fingers pointed and long, my body flat and fat and swollen around, my face a wide mouth and bulging eyes. Some assume, for all of that, I must want for a bride, something pink and smooth of limb, soft, mammalian, to balance out the whole of my existence. As if, somehow, this will lighten the aesthetic load I place upon the eye of God. Well, I assure you, when the eye of God tires of looking at a creature such as myself—I suspect I shall be the first to know. Until then, I've no use for a bride and no means or place to keep her; I've mates by the score and children by the hundreds with no need to have ever met either; beneath the brown waters, my wedding chamber, they leave of themselves, as do I, without second thought. What could I hope to gain by maintaining one of the warm blooded creatures you men pant and yell to possess that I do not already have, save a lifetime of trouble?

———

That was my testimony in my first kingdom, when they dragged me in chains before the king, and the pink creatures they sought so to protect swooned and then peeked through half lidded eyes at the monster. The sentence was exile, and they frog-marched me to the border, and set me loose on pain of death to never return, but I am called Bufo, I grow fat upon insects. I make my board under leaves, upon logs, and my bed lies in the bogs. My throne is the toadstool, and witch's butter is for my biscuits.

I have no treasure, no hall, nor wealth, nor store, save that the world contains everything that I have ever needed: food, bed, cool mud and warm sun. No gold, but the color of my eyes. But then, there is always some damned fool that must believe that something as swollen and hopping-loathsome as myself must have some use to men, as all things made by God, such as mosquitoes, poison ivy and the clap, are wont to possess. So in this second kingdom of grasping merchants and opportunistic peasants, I learned to my sorrow what every damned fool knows: that toads possess carbuncles in their heads in the space where their brains ought to be. And because my carbuncle taught itself to think and learned that God made, upon the earth, no shortage of damned fools, this time, I showed myself the frontier.

I am called Bufo, I grow fat upon insects. I make my board under leaves, upon logs, and my bed lies in the bogs. My throne is the toadstool, and witch's butter is for my biscuits. I seek out no company, but I'll accept any which treats me decently and which accepts that it is the nature of the toad to eat insects and to lay in the bog. The woman was old, and she might not have been quite right, but I also saw the mounds where her husband and little children had years ago gone, and eaten some of the beetles who had crawled in their bones. Men are a sentimental lot, and sentiment, as any toad knows, rots the carbuncle. Or the brain, whichever it might be. She called me by her children's names and made me clothing; it was perhaps, inappropriate, but mildly charming. I can only apologize for being a poor conversationalist, but to say we were familiar might be characterizing our relationship a little too strongly.

Some men set her on fire so they could have her house. I'm not quite sure I understood what it was all about, but they seemed upset that she'd been talking to me, though I know enough of men to see an excuse when it comes riding up the path, torch in hand. I suspect they would have used me the same way, for sake of consistency, but sentiment is not a burden under which I labor, or not one under which I then labored, and I fled, hopping fast and strong for all my girth.

I am called Bufo, I grow fat upon insects. I make my board under leaves, upon logs and my bed lies in the bogs. My throne is the toadstool, and witch's butter is for my biscuits. I tore my coat and my trousers, but what need have I for the cloth of men? I came to a fourth kingdom and the people here tipped their hats when they saw me come.

"Please, sir," they said. "We've a terrible time with flies and beetles, worms and slugs, and things like that."

"Don't you fear I'll steal your princesses?"

"Our princesses have faces sweet as buttermilk but hearts as cold and dark and wicked as the water under winter ice and voices that make the hens lay weird black eggs, all seven," they said. "Take the lot, and none shall miss them."

"I'll pass," I said. "What about the gem inside my head, I've heard that all toads have them."

"All men know that only damned fools believe that, and we expose damned fools at birth, by law, in this kingdom."

"Better still," said I, "If an old woman talks to me, you won't set her on fire, will you?"

"We've plenty of firewood to keep us warm in the cold months; old women are for stories and spinning."

"I think we may come to an understanding," I said, and I to my new bog went, and began my work. In a few short years, I and my children and grandchildren had the kingdom's pests well in hand, the princesses were all safely married to other countries, to ogres or to pirates, and the people left me to my work.

But man has decreed that good things must not last, and, soon, men came from the kingdom next door; you'll remember them as the ones who set the dotty widow on fire for her house. It seems they'd run out of widows.

In truth, I would have missed the whole thing, if not for a misunderstanding. A young man like the one I first met when I came here, was speaking to a knight from the widow-burning country, with his armor and his surcoat and his heavy cross. The knight asked the young man what God the young man served. The young man replied that, like the knight, he served Christ, but either the knight did not understand his language or misheard, for he shoved the man back.

"Kroaten?" the knight said, which was a name that some people used for me, long ago, and not quite like what the young man said. It got my attention.

"Your God is the same as Kroaten devil!" the knight yelled. Now, I have been called a devil before, fairly often. I'm quite certain no one has ever been feebleminded enough to worship me. But now the knight had my attention, and I was not disappointed if, indeed, I had been expecting a repeat performance of what happened all those years ago at the widow's house on a much grander scale. My children and I hopped off to the bog and waited. When the smoke cleared, only men from the widow-burning nation remained, loudly thanking God for their victory over Kroaten Devil.

Over me.

I am called Bufo, I grow fat upon insects. I make my board under leaves, upon logs, and my bed lies in the bogs. My throne is the toadstool, and witch's butter is for my biscuits. I am an unsentimental being; I was born in a bog and fed first on brothers and sisters. I am not prone to fits or to passions, and I do truly believe to the core of my being that sentiment rots the brain. I sat on my toadstool for days and smelled the smoke of the widow-burning nation, and I felt; the experience was unfamiliar, yet I knew it as it came to me. I have been watching you men for a very long time, and I know what you are all about. I turned my bulbous golden eyes to the castle, where the widow-burning king had unfurled his victory flag, and I decided that I was tired of you men and your killing game.

It's then that I decided you should see how nature plays.

First I went to see scorpion, and he was sitting at the edge of the water.

"Will you ferry me across?" he asked "I cannot find your cousin frog."

"That isn't why I'm here," I said.

I went to visit violin spider, playing his violin in his reclusive cave.

"Have you come to listen to me play my newest funeral march?" he asked.

"In a sense," I said.

I visited black widow in her widow's weeds.

"Let us speak of love and loss," she said. "I shall tell you of my dear husband whom I so miss."

"You shall be reunited," I said.

I visited many others: angry wasp, busy bumblebee and busier honeybee, fire ant, horsefly—all the ones you might expect, and many you might not; some I usually do not visit and never have; some who considered themselves safe from me by their natures, the long-legged spider, certain butterflies; the exact recipe is secondary. That day I swelled to twice my usual size, sloshing with the witch's brew bubbling in the cauldron of my belly. I sat upon my toadstool, terrible pain now coursing through that warted, fat body of mine, skin splitting, suppurating with the strain of all the poisons within, wondering why, in God's name, I would choose to do this to myself.

Perhaps I was tired of moving kingdom to kingdom one hop ahead of the ever-changing idiocy of God's chosen. Perhaps it was to remind man that it was terror that filled Adam's eyes when he fled the garden after he dropped anarchy on the rest of us. I'll never truly remember now.

With veins that pumped the fires of hell, I hopped off toward the castle, the ulcers in my skin burning the ground black where they touched.

The castle's kitchens were well known to me, for it was here that I began my work, years ago, contending with this kingdom's pest problem. In a way, this was more of the same; all things returning to their beginning. Cooks, hastily brought from the widow-

burning nation, were equally hasty in preparing the
victory feast for the king and his men, in situ, and, as
one might imagine from the nation I described, there
was all kinds of cooked flesh. There was also soup—a
great, steaming, bubbling savory cauldron of it. I
watched from the window, a trail of sloughed-off skin
and pus trailing down the outside. I waited, and I
hadn't long to wait, for I was surely dying now, from
all the poison I consumed. But the cooks had ridden
long and hard to get here, and the soup, one of the
opening courses, was not one of their first priorities.
Their attention wandered, and when all of them were
out of the kitchen at once, I leaped. The pain that
followed was a joy compared to the hours that brought
me to that point.

I was called Bufo, I grew fat upon insects. I made my
board under leaves, upon logs, and my bed lay in the
bogs. My throne was the toadstool, and witch's butter
was for my biscuits. I expected to dissolve then, into
brute nature as beasts are wont to do, but I did not.
Instead I hovered over the huge kettle and watched my
body, already made tender with all the venoms, melt
into the soup. The cooks, hearing the splash, returned
and speculated a bubble; no matter, for the soup was
being called for. A stir, a taste; what was it they had
done, this had never been so good; and they set out the
bowls.

The men set out in the stolen hall, the king at his
enemy's throne, and each in turn was given a bowl of
me, which they, amid much boasting and jest, began to
eat, while my shade looked on. Toads, you might
realize, taste horrible, and while the first spoonful of
the soup was sublime, the next was not as good, and
the third not so good as the second and so on; as the
course progressed, the men grew quiet, the compli-

ments and smiles turned to grimaces, but pride, not wanting to be the first to declare the soup awful, drove them to continue. Near the end of the bowl, every spoonful was tongue-spasming torment, and it was near that point that the King lifted his spoon and found, cradled inside of it, a carbuncle, red as hate, big as a goose's egg.

"I'll be damned," I said, to no one in particular. "Those idiots were right after all."

He stared at it for a moment, his face turning red, then purple, and then black; and then he died. His body had swollen out of his clothes and his flesh out of his skin by the time it hit the floor. His men followed his lead a moment later, faithful to the last. His feast, appropriately, burned in the kitchen, and the castle has since become poisoned to the foundations, so that none may touch it and live. With this I am satisfied.

I was called Bufo, I grew fat upon insects. I made my board under leaves, upon logs, and my bed lay in the bogs. My throne was the toadstool, and witch's butter was for my biscuits. Now owner of a man's castle, my shade sits on a throne no less poisonous than a toadstool, waiting for the day when someone retrieves the poisoned stone. Perhaps then, we shall throw down another tyrant. One could grow accustomed to that.

THE MASTER
MILLER'S TALE

———

Ian R. MacLeod

There are only ruins left now on Burlish Hill, a rough circle of stones. The track that once curved up from the village of Stagsby in the valley below is little more than an indentation in the grass, and the sails of the mill that once turned there are forgotten. Time has moved on, and lives have moved with it. Only the wind remains.

Once, the Westovers were millers. They belonged to their mill as much as it belonged to them, and Burlish Hill was so strongly associated with their trade that the words *mill* and *hill* grew blurred in the local dialect until the two became the same. Hill was mill and mill was hill, and one or other of the Westovers, either father or son, was in charge of those turning sails, and that was all the people of Stagsby, and all the workers in the surrounding farms and smallholdings, cared to know. The mill itself, with its four sides of sloped, slatted wood, weather-bleached and limed until they were almost paler than its sails, was of the type known as a post mill. Its upper body, shoulders, middle and skirts, turned about a central pivot from a squat, stone lower floor to meet whichever wind prevailed. There was a tower mill at Alford, and there were overshot water mills at Lough and Screamby, but Burlish Mill on Burlish Hill had long served its purpose. You might get better rates farther afield, but balanced against that had to be the extra journey time, and the tolls on the roads, and the fact that this was Stagsby, and the Westovers had been the millers here for as long as anyone could remember. Generation on generation, the Westovers recemented this relationship by marrying the daughters of the farmers who drove their carts up Burlish Hill, whilst any spare Westovers took to laboring some of the many thousands of acres that the mill surveyed. The Westovers were pale-faced men with sandy hair, plump arms and close-set eyes which, in their near-translucence, seemed to have absorbed something of the sky of their hilltop home. They went bald early—people joked that the winds had blown away their hair—and worked hard, and characteristically saved their breath and said little, and saved their energies for their work.

Although it took him most of his life to know it, Nathan Westover was the last of the master millers on Burlish Hill. Growing up, he never imagined that anything could change. The endless grinding, mumbling sound of the mill in motion was always there, deep within his bones.

He was set to watch a pulley that was threatening to slip.

"See how it sits, and that band of metal helps keep it in place . . ." his mother, who often saw to the lesser workings of the mill, explained. "It's been doing that for longer than I and your father can remember. Now it's getting near the end of its life . . ." The pulley turned, the flour hissed, the windmill rumbled, and this small roller spun on in a slightly stuttering way. " . . . and we can't stop the mill from working when we're this busy just to get it fixed. So we need someone to keep watch—well, more than simply watch—over it. I want

you to sing to that roller to help keep this pulley turning
and in place. Do you understand?"

Nathan nodded, for the windmill was always
chanting its spells from somewhere down in its deep-
throated, many-rumbling voice, and now his mother
took up a small part of the song in her own soft voice,
her lips shaping the phrases of a machine vocabulary,
and he joined in, and the roller and the pulley's entire
mechanism revolved more easily.

Soon, Nathan was performing more and more of
these duties. He even learned how to sing some of the
larger spells that kept the mill turning, and then grew
strong enough to lift a full sack of grain. He worked
the winches, damped the grist, swept the chutes, oiled
the workings. He loved the elegant way in which the
mill always rebalanced itself through weights, lengths,
numbers, quantities. Fifteen men to dig a pit thus wide
down at school in the village meant nothing to him, but
he solved problems that had anything to do with grain,
flour, or especially the wind, in his dreams.

Sometimes there were visits from the rotund men
who represented the county branch of the Millers'
Guild. On these occasions, everything about the mill
had to be just so—the books up to date, the upper
floors brushed and the lower ones waxed and the sails
washed and all the ironwork shiny black as new
boots—but Nathan soon learned that these men liked
the mill to be chocked, braked and disengaged,
brought to a total stop. To them, it was a dead thing
within a frozen sky, and he began to feel the same
contempt for his so-called guild-masters that any self-
respecting miller felt.

On the mill's third floor, above the account books
with their pots of green and red ink, and set back in a
barred recess, leaned a three-volume Thesaurus of
spells. One quiet day at the end of the spring rush when

sails ticked and turned themselves in slow, easy sweeps, his father lifted the heavy boots down, and blew off a coating of the same pale dust which, no matter how often things were swept and aired, soon settled on everything within the mill.

"This, son . . . . " He cleared his throat. "Well, you already know what these are. One day, these books will be yours. In a way, I suppose they already are . . . . "

The yellowed pages rippled and snickered. Just like the mill itself, they didn't seem capable of remaining entirely still, and were inscribed with the same phonetic code that Nathan saw stamped, carved or engraved on its beams, spars and mechanisms. There were diagrams. Hand-written annotations. Darker smudges and creases lay where a particularly useful spell had been thumbed many times. Through the mill's hazy light, Nathan breathed it all in. Here were those first phrases his mother had taught him when he tended that pulley, and the longer and more complex melodies that would keep back those four apocalyptic demons of the milling industry, which were: weevils, woodworm, fire, and rats. As always with things pertaining to the mill, Nathan felt that he was rediscovering something he already knew.

There were slack times and there were busy times. Late August, when the farmers were anxious to get their summer wheat ground and bagged, and when the weather was often cloudless and still, was one of the worst. It was on such late, hot, airless days, with the land spread trembling and brown to every cloudless horizon, and the mill whispering and creaking in dry gasps, that the wind-seller sometimes came to Burlish Hill.

Nathan's father would already be standing and waiting, his arms folded and his fists bunched as he watched a solitary figure emerge from the faded shimmer of the valley. The wind-seller was small and dark, and gauntly pale. He wore creaking boots, and was wrapped in a cloak of a shade of gray almost as thunderous as that of the sack he carried over his thin shoulders, within which he bore his collection of winds.

"So this'll be the next one, eh?" He peered forward to study Nathan with eyes that didn't seem to blink, and Nathan found himself frozen and speechless until his father's hand drew him away.

"Just stick to business, wind-seller, shall we?"

It was plain that his father didn't particularly like this man. After all, every miller worth his salt prided himself on making the best of every kind of weather, come storm or calm, glut or shortage. Still, as the wind-seller unshouldered his sack and tipped out a spill of frayed knots, and especially on such a hot and hopeless day as this, it was impossible not to want to lean forward, not to want to breathe and feel and touch.

"Here, try this one . . . . " Spidery fingers rummaged with a hissing, whispering pile to extract the gray strands of what looked, Nathan thought, exactly like the kind of dirty sheep's wool you saw snagged and fluttering on a bare hedge on the darkest of winter days. " . . . That's a new, fresh wind from the east. Cut through this summer fug clean as a whistle. Sharp as a lemon, and twice as sweet. Delicate, yes, but good and strong as well. Turn these sails easy as ninepence."

Already, Nathan could taste the wind, feel it writhing and alive. Slowly, reluctantly, his father took the strand in his own hands, and the wind-seller's mouth twitched into something that was neither a smile nor a grin. "And this one . . . Now *this* will really get things going. Tail end of a storm, tail end of night, tail end of winter. Can really feel a bite of frost in there, can't you? 'Course, she's a bit capricious, but she's strong as well, and cool and fresh . . . "

It was nothing but some bits of old willow bark, torn loose in a storm and dampened by trembling puddles, but already the windmill's sails gave a yearning creak. Nathan's father might grumble and shake his head, but the haggling that followed all of this conspicuous advertisement was always disappointingly brief. They all knew, had known since before the wind-seller's shape had first untwisted itself from the haze of the valley, that—strange things though they were, the knotted breath of forgotten days—he would have to buy his share of these winds.

Although no one else believed them, master millers swore they could taste the flavor of the particular wind from which any batch of flour had been turned. The weather prevails from the east on Burlish Hill, unrolling with a tang of salt and sea-brightness from the blustery North Sea, but no wind is ever the same, and every moment of every day in which it blows is different, and setting the mill to just the right angle to take it was, to Nathan's mind, the greatest skill a master miller possessed. Even as you sang to your mill and anchored it down, it responded and took up the ever-changing moods of the wind in her sails. But the feelings and flavors that came from the wind-seller's winds were different again. On dead, dry afternoons when the sky was hard as beaten pewter, Nathan's father would finally give up whatever makeweight task he was performing and grumblingly go to unlock the lean-to at the mill's back where he kept the wind-seller's winds.

The things looked as ragged now as they had when they fell from the wind-seller's sack—nothing more than dangling bits of old sea-rope, the tangled vines of some dried-up autumn, the tattered remains of long-forgotten washing—but each was knotted using complex magics, and what else were they to do, on such a day as this? Already writhing and snapping around them—a gray presence, half felt, half seen, and straining to be released—was the longed-for presence of some kind of wind. Up in the creaking stillness of the main millstone floor, and with a shine in his eyes that spoke somehow both of expectation and defeat, his father would break apart the knot with his big miller's hands, and, in a shouting rush, the wind that it contained would be released. Instantly, like the opening of an invisible door, the atmosphere within the mill was transformed. Beams creaked in the changed air and the sails swayed, inching at first as the main axle bit the breakwheel and the breakwheel bore down against the wallower that transported the wind's gathering breath down through all the levels of the mill. The farther sky, the whole spreading world, might remain trapped in the same airless day. But the dry grass on Burlish Hill shifted and silvered, and the mill signaled to every other hilltop that at least here, here on this of all days, there was enough wind to turn its sails.

The winds themselves were often awkward and capricous things; unseasonably hot and dry, awkwardly damp and gray. They seemed to come, in that they came from anywhere at all, from points of the compass that lay beyond north and south, east or west. Even as Nathan and his father began gladly heaving the contents of all the waiting sacks into the chutes, the atmosphere within the mill on those days remained strange. Looking out though the turning sails, Nathan half expected to see changed horizons; to find the world retilted in some odd and awkward way. Lying in his bunk in the still nights afterward when the winds had blown themselves out, he pictured the wind-seller wandering the gray countrysides of some land of perpetual autumn, furtively gathering and knotting the lost pickings of a storm with those strange agile fingers, muttering as he did so his spells over rags and twigs.

The other children at the school down in the village—the sons and daughters of farmers, carpenters, laborers, shopkeepers, who would soon take up or marry into the same trade—had always been an ordinary lot. Perhaps Fiona Smith should have stood out more, as Nathan often reflected afterward, but she was mostly just one of the girls who happened to sit near the back of class, and seemed, in her languorous demeanor, to be on the verge of some unspecified act of bad behavior that she could never quite summon the energy to perform. Nevertheless, she could hold her own in a fight and throw an accurate enough stone, at least for a girl. If he'd bothered to think about it, Nathan would have also known that Fiona Smith lived at Stagsby Hall, a structure far bigger and more set-apart than any other in the village, which had a lake beside it that flashed with the changing sky when you looked down at it from Burlish Hill, but he envied no one the size of their homes; not when he had all of Lincolnshire spread beneath him, and lived in a creaking, turning, breathing mill.

He was surprised at the fuss his parents made when an invitation came for the Westovers and seemingly every other person in Stagsby to attend a party to celebrate Fiona Smith's fourteenth birthday, and at the fussy clothes they found to wear. As they walked on the appointed afternoon toward the open gates of Stagsby Hall, he resented the chafe of his own new collar, the pinch of the boots, and the waste of a decent southerly wind.

It was somewhat interesting, Nathan might have grudgingly admitted, to see such an impressive residence at close hand instead of looking at it from above. Lawns spread green and huge from its many golden windows toward a dark spread of woods, and that lake, which, even down here, reflected the near-cloudless sky in its blue gaze. There were indecently underdressed statues, and there were pathways that meandered amongst them with a will of their own. Of greater importance, though, to Nathan and most of the other villagers, was the food. There was so much of it! There were jellies and sausages. Cheeses and trifles. Cakes and roast meats. There were lurid cordials, sweet wines and varieties of ale. Sticky fingered, crusty faced, the younger children took quarreling turns to pin the tail on a blackboard donkey, and those of Nathan's age soon lost their superiority and joined in, whilst the adults clustered in equal excitement around the beer tent. There was also a real donkey, saddled and be-ribboned and ready to be ridden. But the donkey whinnied and galloped as people attempted to catch it, kicking over a food-laden table and sending a mass of trifles, jellies, and cakes sliding to the grass in a glistening heap. The adults laughed and the children whooped as the donkey careered off toward the trees, watched by the stiff-faced men and women in tight black suits, whom, Nathan had divined by now, were the servants of Stagsby Hall.

The afternoon—for the villagers, at least—passed in a timeless, happy whirl. Much beer and wine was drunk, and the children's livid cordials seemed equally intoxicating. Trees were climbed; many by those old enough to know better. Stones, and a few of the silver trays, were skimmed across the lake. Then, yet more food was borne out from the house in the shape of an almost impossibly large and many-tiered cake. The huge creation was set down in the shade of one of the largest of the oaks that circled the lawns. Nodding, nudging, murmuring, the villagers clustered around it. The thing was ornamented with scrolls and flowers, pillared like a cathedral, then spired with fourteen candles, each of which the servants now solemnly lit.

An even deeper sigh than that which had signaled the lighting of the cake passed through the crowd as Fiona Smith emerged into the space that had formed around it. Nathan hadn't consciously noticed her presence before that moment. Now that he had, though, he was immensely struck by it. He and many of his classmates were already taller and stronger than the parents whose guilds they would soon be joining. Some were already pairing off and *walking the lane together,* as the local phrase went, and even Nathan had noticed that some of the girls were no longer merely girls. But none of them had ever looked anything remotely like Fiona Smith did today.

Although the dress she wore was similar in style to those many of the other women were wearing, it was cut from a substance that made it hard to divine its exact color, such was its shimmer and blaze. Her thick red hair, which Nathan previously dimly remembered as tied back in a ponytail, fell loose around her shoulders, and also possessed a fiery glow. It was as if an entirely different Fiona Smith had suddenly emerged before this cake, and the candle flames seemed to flare as though drawn by an invisible wind even before she had puffed out her cheeks. Then she blew, and all but one of them flattened and died, and their embers sent up thirteen trails of smoke. Smiling, she reached forward as if to pinch out the last remaining flame. But as she raised her hand from it, the flame still flickered there, held like a blazing needle between her finger and thumb. Then, with a click of her fingers, it was gone. The entire oak tree gave a shudder in the spell's aftermath and a few dry leaves and flakes of bark drifted down, some settling on the cake. The villagers were already wandering back across the lawn, muttering and shaking their heads, as the servants began to slice the object up into spongy yellow slices. They were unimpressed by such unwanted displays of guild magic, and by then, no one was feeling particularly hungry.

Without understanding quite how it had happened, Nathan found that he and Fiona Smith were standing alone beside the remains of the cake.

"You're from up there, aren't you?" She nodded through the boughs toward the mill. "Bet you'd rather be there now, eh, with the sails turning? Instead of down here watching a good day go to waste."

Although it was something he wouldn't have readily admitted, Nathan found himself nodding. "It was clever," he said, "what you did with that cake."

She laughed. "All those faces, the way they were staring! I felt I had to do something or I'd explode. Tell you what, why don't we go and have a look at your mill?"

Nathan shifted his feet. "I'm not sure. My father doesn't like strangers hanging around working machinery and it's your birthday party and—"

"I suppose you're right. Tell you what, there's some of my stuff I can show you instead."

Dumbly, Nathan followed Fiona Smith up toward the many-windowed house, and then through a studded door. The air inside was close and warm, and there were more rooms than he could count, or anyone could possibly want to live in, although most of the furniture was covered in sheets. It was as if the whole place had been trapped in some hot and dusty snowfall.

"Here." Fiona creaked open a set of double doors. The room beyond had a high blue ceiling, decorated with cherubs and many-pointed stars. "This . . . " She shook out a huge, crackling coffin of packaging that lay scattered amid many other things on the floor. "*This* is from Father. Ridiculous, isn't it?" A sprawled china corpse stared up at them with dead glass eyes. Nathan had always thought dolls ridiculous, although this one was big and impressive. "At least, I think it's from him. His handwriting's terrible and I can't read the note."

"Your father's not here?"

"Not a chance. He'll be in London at one of his clubs."

"London?"

"It's just another place, you know." Shrugging, Fiona aimed a kick at the doll. "And he's decided I can't stay here at school, either, or even in Stagsby. In fact, I'm sure he'd have decided that long ago if he'd remembered. That's why everyone's here today—and why I'm wearing this stupid dress. It's to remind you of who I'm supposed to be before I get dragged to some ridiculous academy for so-called young ladies."

Fiona crossed the room's considerable space toward the largest of all the sheeted objects which, as she tugged at its dusty coverings, revealed itself to be an enormous bed. Enameled birds fluttered up from its silken turrets as if struggling to join the room's starry sky. Nathan had seen smaller houses.

"This used to be Mother's bedroom. I'd come and just talk to her in here when she was ill from trying to have a son. Of course, it didn't work, so now my father's stuck with a girl for an heir unless he goes and gets married again, which he says will be when Hell freezes."

"All of this will end up as yours?"

Fiona gazed around, hands on hips. "I know what you're thinking, but my father says we're in debt up to our eyeballs. I'm sure that you Westovers have far more money than we Smiths, with that mill of yours. My grandfather, now, *he* was the clever one. Had a real business mind. He was a proper master smithy. He was high up in the guild, but he still knew how to work a forge. He used to show me things. How to stoke a furnace, the best spells for the strongest iron . . . "

"And that trick with the flame?"

Fiona looked at Nathan and smiled. Her eyes were a cool blue-green. He'd never felt such a giddy sense of sharing, not even when he was working hard at the mill. "I'll show you his old room," she murmured.

Up wide, white marble stairways, past more sheeted furniture and shuttered windows, the spaces narrowed. Nathan caught glimpses through windows of the lake, the lawns, Burlish Hill, and then the lake again as they climbed a corkscrew of stairs. Cramped and stuffed with books, papers, cabinets, the attic they finally reached was quite unlike the great rooms below. Fiona struggled with a shutter, flinging sunlight in a narrow blaze. Nathan squinted, blinked, and gave a volcanic sneeze.

She laughed. "You're even dustier than this room!"

Standing in this pillar of light, Nathan saw that he was, indeed, surrounded by a nebulous, floating haze. "It's not dust," he muttered. It was a sore point; the children at school often joked about his powdery aura. "It's flour."

"I know." Something fluttered inside his chest as she reached forward to ruffle his hair, and more of the haze blurred around him. "But you're a master miller—or you will be. It's part of what you are. Now look."

After swiping a space clear on a sunlit table, Fiona creaked open the spines of books that were far bigger and stranger in their language than the mill's Thesaurus of spells. The same warm fingers that he could still feel tingling across his scalp now traveled amid the symbols and diagrams. Guilds kept their secrets, and he knew she shouldn't be showing him these things, but nevertheless he was drawn.

"This is how you temper iron . . . This is an annealing spell, of which there are many . . . " A whisper of pages. "And here, these are the names for fire and flames. Some of them, anyway. For there's always something different every time you charge a furnace, put a spark to a fire, light a candle, even."

Nathan nodded. All of this was strange to him, but he understood enough to realize that flames were like the wind to Fiona Smith, and never stayed the same.

"Not that my father's interested. He likes to joke about how he got through his grandmaster exams just because of the family name. And I'm a woman, so there's no way I can become a smithy . . . " She grew quiet for a moment, the sunlight steaming in copper glints across her hair as she gazed down at the vortex of flame that filled the page.

"What'll you do instead?"

"I don't know." She looked up at him, fists balled on the table, her face ablaze. "That's the frustrating thing, Nathan. *These* of all times. All the old spells, you know, the stupid traditions, the mumbling and the superstitions and the charms and the antique ways of working, all of that's on the way out. Modern spells aren't about traditional craftsmen—not when you can mine the magic right out of the ground. That's what they're doing now, in places up north like Redhouse and Bracebridge, they're drawing it out of the solid earth almost like they extract coal or salt or tar or saltpeter."

Nathan nodded. He knew such things as mere facts, but he'd never heard anyone speak about them—or, indeed many other things—with such passion.

"I'm lucky. That's what my grandfather used to say. I'm lucky, to be living in this time." She shook her head and chuckled. "The future's all around us, just like the world you must be able to see from up on your hill. And this, now *this* . . . " She pushed aside the book, and took down a large and complex-looking mechanism from a shelf. "He made this himself as his apprentice piece."

It took up most of the table, and consisted of a variety of ceramic marbles set upon a complex-looking arrangement of arms and gears, all widely spaced around a larger and even brighter central orb that might have been made of silver, gold, or some yet more dazzling metal.

"It's an orrery—a model of the universe itself. These are the planets, this is the sun. These tiny beads are the major stars. See . . . " As she leaned forward, their blaze was reddened and brightened by the fall of her hair. "This is where we are, Nathan. You and I and everyone else, even the Hottentot heathens. This is our planet and it's called Earth . . . "

Nathan watched as her hands, her hair, fluttered from light to dark amid all this frail and beautiful machinery, and his thoughts, and his lungs and his heart and his stomach, fluttered with them. Although he had no great care for matters of philosophy, he couldn't help feeling that he was witnessing something exotic and forbidden in this strangely Godlike view of the universe that Fiona Smith was describing. But it was thrilling as well.

"Now watch."

Leaning down close to the table, afloat in sunlight, she puffed her cheeks and blew just as she had blown at her birthday cake. But now, smoothly, silently, the planets began to turn.

"You try."

She made a space and Nathan shuffled close. Then, as conscious of the warmth of Fiona's presence beside him as he was of the blaze of the sun, he bent down and he blew.

"Is that how it really works?"

She laughed. "You of all people, Nathan, up on that hill, should understand."

Silently, seemingly with a will of its own, in gleam and flash of planets and their wide-flung shadows, the orerry continued to spin. Nathan watched, willing the moment to continue, willing it never to stop. But, slowly, finally, it did. It felt as if some part of his head was still spinning as, dazed, he helped Fiona close the shutter and followed her back down the stairways and along the corridors of her huge house. Everything, the sheeted furniture, the hot air, seemed changed. Outside, even the sun was lower, and redder, and it threw strange, long shadows as it blazed across the lawn. The world, Nathan thought for one giddy moment, really has turned.

A space of desk near the back of the class at the village school lay empty when Nathan and his classmates returned to school, although there was nothing particularly remarkable in that. Soon, they all were leaving, drawn into the lives, trades, and responsibilities for which they had always been destined, and Fiona Smith's birthday party, if it was remembered at all, was remembered mostly for the drink and the food.

The windmill up on Burlish Hill turned, and the seasons turned with it. More and more, Nathan was in charge, and he sang to the mill the complex spells that his father's voice could no longer carry. The only recreation he consciously took was in the choir at church. Opening his lungs to release the sweet, husky tenor that had developed with the stubble on his cheeks, looking up at the peeling saints and stars, it seemed to him that singing to God the Elder and singing to the mill were much the same thing. Instead of calling in at the pub afterward, or lingering on the green to play football, he hurried straight back up Burlish Hill, scanning the horizon as he did so.

He could always tell exactly how well the mill was grinding, and the type of grain that was being worked, merely from the turn of its sails, but there was a day as he climbed up the hill when something seemed inexplicably wrong. Certainly nothing as serious as a major gear slipping, but the sweep of the sails didn't quite match the sweet feel of the air. He broke into a run, calling to his mother as he climbed up through the stairs and ladders inside the mill. The main sacking floor was engulfed in a gray storm, with flour everywhere, and more and more of it sifting down the chutes. Hunched within these clouds, gasping in wracking breaths, Nathan's father was a weary ghost.

Feeble though he was, the miller resisted Nathan's and his mother's attempts to bear him out into the clear air. He kept muttering that *a miller never leaves his mill*, and struggled to see to the rest of the sacks before the wind gave, even though the batch was already ruined. Finally, though, they persuaded him to take to his bed, which lay on a higher floor of the mill, and he lay there for several days, half-conscious and half-delirious, calling out spells to his machine, which still creaked and turned between periodic, agonizing bouts of coughing.

As poor luck would have it, the winds then fell

away. It grew hot as well. The skies seemed to slam themselves shut. Much more now for the sake of his father than for the mill itself, Nathan longed for a breeze. He searched for the hidden key to the lean-to, and he found it easily in a tin of nails; just the sort of place he'd never before have thought to look. The few knots left inside the small, close space hung like dried-up bats on their iron hooks, and part of Nathan felt that he had never seen anything so weathered and useless, and part of him already felt the strange, joyous surge of the winds that each clever knot contained. There were no spells in the miller's Thesaurus to tell him how to unbind a trapped wind, nor the sounds that he should make as he did it, but doing so came to him easily as laughing and crying as he stood on the millstone floor. The air changed in a clamor of groans. The mill's sails creaked and bit and turned. At last, there was work to be done, and Nathan got on with doing it with a happier heart. He knew without climbing the ladders that his father's breathing would be easier, now that the mill was working properly all around him once again.

Although he was too exhausted to make use of it, Nathan released another wind at twilight purely for the glory of feeling the pull and draft of it through all the mill's leaky slats and floors. More than usually, this one lived up to the wind-seller's tales of bright spring mornings and the shift of grass over cloud-chased hills. When Nathan finally climbed the ladders to see his father, his mother—who had sat all day beside him—was smiling through her tears. He took the old man's hand and felt its hot lightness, and the calluses that years of handling sacks and winches had formed, and the smooth soft gritting of flour that coated every miller's flesh, and he smiled and he cried as well. They sat through the old man's last night together, breathing the moods of the mill, watching the turn of the stars through the hissing swoop of its sails.

Nathan's mother went to live in an old warehouse beside the dunes at Donna Nook, which had once stored southern hops before the channels had silted up. He visited her there on saints' days, taking the early milk wagon and walking the last miles across the salt flats. Although she was wheezy herself now, and easily grew tired, she seemed happy enough there spending her days talking of brighter, breezier hours, and better harvests, to the widows of other millers. In those days, the Guild of Millers still took care of its own, but of course there were no master millers there. Nathan knew, had long known, that a miller never left his mill.

But he was a master miller now—even if the ceremony of his induction that he'd envisaged taking place beneath the golden roof of some great guild chapel had dwindled to a form signed in triplicate—and he gloried in that fact. Heading back from Donna Nook toward Burlish Hill in darkness, he would find his mill waiting for him, ticking, creaking, sighing in its impatience to take hold of the breeze. Often, he sang to it out loud even when no spells were needed. It was only when he was with other people, he sometimes reflected, that he ever felt alone.

The mill was Nathan's now, and that made up for most things, even though there was less and less time for the choir. The spells in those whispering books, and every creak and mood and scent and flavor, every seed of corn and every grain of flour it produced, shaped his life. When he rested at all, it was merely to taste the breeze as he stood on top of Burlish Hill. From there, on the clearest of days, you really could see all of Lincolnshire, and gaze down at the huddled roofs of Stagsby, and the rippling windflash of the lake that lay beside the closed and shuttered windows of Stagsby Hall.

Everyone remarked on Nathan Westover's energy in the seasons that followed. Millers were never known to take an easy bargain, but few drove them as hard as he did. Farmers and grain dealers might have gone elsewhere, but here was a miller who worked to whatever deadline you set him, and never let any of the sacks spoil. On nights of full moon, you could look up and see the sails still turning. It seemed as if he never slept, and then he was to be seen early next morning at the grain markets at Alford and Louth, making deals to buy and sell flour on his own account, driving more and more those notoriously hard bargains, clapping backs and shaking hands in ways that earned money, but also respect.

These were good times across the rich farmlands of Lincolnshire. The big cities of the Midlands were spreading, sucking in labor under their blanket of smoke, and that labor—along with the growing middle classes who drew their profit from it, and the higher guildsmen who speculated in shares, bonds and leases—needed to be fed. Borne in on endless carts, and then increasingly drawn along rails by machines powered by that same heat and steam that drove those burgeoning industries, came supplies of every kind, not least of which was flour for cakes, biscuits, and bread.

Sometimes, although it seemed less often than in the times of Nathan's childhood, the wind-seller still came to Burlish Hill. In rare hot, windless times, the shimmer of something—at first it could have been nothing more than a mirage twirl of dust—would emerge from the valley, and Nathan wondered as he watched where else this man traveled, and what he did on other, less closed-in days. He always bought a few examples of the wind-seller's produce, although in truth he barely needed them, for he made sure that he made efficient use of all the winds that the sky carried to him, and had little need for such old-fashioned methods of enchantment. The world was changing, just as Fiona Smith had once said it would. Magic was being pumped out from the ground beneath northern cities. You could buy oils and new bearings that were infused with it, which was commonly called aether, and which spilled dark hues in daylight, and shone spectrally in the dark. Nathan was happy enough to use the stuff—at least, if it was for the good of his trade. He knew, or surmised, that the hill itself had once been the source of the power that drove the mill's spells, but perhaps that had been wearing thin, and what else could you do but breathe and work through the seasons that time brought to you, and sing, and wait, and smile, and hope for the best?

Few people ever command anything in this world in the way that Nathan Westover then commanded his mill. He even enjoyed the tasks that most millers hated, and loved filling in the reds and greens of profit and loss on the coldest of nights when the sails hung heavy with ice. Numbers had their own climates, their own magics. Even as the inks froze and his fingers burned with the cold, they whispered to him of how far he had come. He was building up savings in a bank account in Louth—which he was then reusing, reinvesting, but still always accumulating, and it sometimes seemed as he stood outside in the bitter air and the night sparkled with motes of frost that the dark shape of the big house twinkled once more with lights.

I'm sure you Westovers have far more money than we Smiths, with that mill of yours . . . . Even if it hadn't been true then, it was almost certainly true now, and the rumor was that Grandmistress Fiona Smith would soon be back at her home in Stagsby Hall. Nathan waited. After all, London and all those other faraway cites were merely places, just like Stagsby, and he was too accustomed to the capriciousness of the Lincolnshire weather to be anything other than patient. He even bought himself a suit, which he never wore after the tailor's fitting, although he often took it out to admire its cut and shake off its gray coating of dust.

There was an even harder edge to the bargains Nathan drove for the following spring's rye and wheat, an even brisker turn to his mill's sails. Then came another summer, and the larks twirled and sang over the ripening corn, and the skies cleared to a blue so deep and changeless that it scarcely seemed blue at all. Then the weather flattened, and there was no rain, and the heat shrank the lake beside Stagsby Hall, and the corn dried and the dogs panted and even the turning of the mill on Burlish Hill finally slowed until there came an afternoon when everything in the world seemed to have stopped—including Burlish Mill.

Nathan was looking out from the mill's top level when he saw a dark shape emerging from the heat-trembling stillness of the valley below. Certainly not a farmer, for the corn was dying and none of them had anything to bring. Skidding down ropes and ladders, he stood squinting and rubbing the sweat from his eyes as he willed the shape to resolve into a dusty silhouette.

The heat was playing tricks. The body wouldn't stay still, and the movement was too swift. Through the thick, flat air, Nathan caught the brisk rattle of hooves. He waited. A rider on a gleaming, sweating, chestnut horse came up, dismounted, and walked quickly over to him. Female, tall and well-dressed, she took off her riding hat and shook out her red hair.

Smiling at his surprise, Grandmistress Fiona Smith took a step closer, and Nathan saw that, whatever else was different about her, the fiery blue-green gleam in her eyes was unchanged. Then her gaze moved up to the sails above him and her smile widened into a wonder that Nathan had only ever seen on the faces of fellow millers. Still smiling, still looking up, she began to walk around the brown summit of Burlish Hill.

Nathan followed. Fiona Smith was wearing dark riding clothes—boots, a jacket, a long skirt—but they were new and sharply cut and trimmed with shining edges of silk. This was nothing like the same girl who'd once stood before the candles of that many-tiered cake. Not that he hadn't dreamed, not that he hadn't dared to wonder—but looking at this woman, watching the way she moved, he marveled at how she'd changed and grown to become something quite unlike the person he'd imagined, yet was still recognizably Fiona Smith . . . All those ridiculous thoughts, all those years, and yet here, real beyond any sense of reality, she was.

"This is where you keep the winds?" Despite the heat of the day, the air around the stone lean-to had a different edge.

"You know about the wind-seller?"

"I've made a small study of your trade." Fiona shivered. Her eyes flashed. "Why don't you use one now?" Her gaze changed shade as she looked at him. "But that's the old way, isn't it?—and no self-respecting miller likes to admit that they can't manage on nature's winds alone. And such winds cost money. That's what I admire about you, Nathan Westover. You're passionate, but you're practical as well. You should hear people talk. Everyone . . . " She turned beneath the still sails, spreading her arms, encompassing every horizon. "From here to here. They all know exactly who you are."

"But probably not by name."

"The miller of Burlish Hill!" She laughed. "But that's what you are, isn't it? Strange, for a man of such substance to have his life founded on a mere breath of air."

Nathan laughed as well, and felt something loosening like a freed cog inside him. He'd never thought of it like that before, but she was right. "I'd always hoped," he said, "that you'd come here."

"And here I am." She gave what he took to be a curtsey. "And I have a proposal to put to you, Nathan. So why don't you show me inside your mill?"

Nathan would have been speechless, but the mill was the one topic about which he was always capable of talking, and pride soon took over from his shock at Fiona's presence. He could even push aside the thought of how he must appear, with his arms bare and his dungarees still gritty from the dust of a long morning's cleaning, and probably reeking of sweat and linseed oil as well. At least all his hard work meant that his mill was in near-perfect condition. Even if Fiona Smith had been one of the guild inspectors who'd used to come in his father's time, he doubted if she'd have been able to find a single fault. Pristine, perched, as ever, on the edge of turning movement, the mill welcomed them through streams of sunlight into its hot, fragrant floors.

"You and I," she murmured as she climbed the last ladder and took his arm to help herself over the lip, "I always used to look up at this mill and wonder if I couldn't become a part of what it does." She was so close to him now that he could feel the quickness of her breath, see how the changed brownness of her skin consisted of the merging of constellations of freckles.

Then they both hunched deliciously close together beside the topmost window, looking down and out at all the world as it was revealed from the combined height of Burlish Hill and Mill. Nathan could feel the warm tickle of Fiona's hair. The world was hazed today, but everything was clear in his head as on the sharpest day as he pointed out the directions of the winds. All Lincolnshire lay before them, and he could feel the soft pressures of her body as she leaned closer. Despite these distractions, he found that talking to her was easy as chanting the simplest spell. When most people looked out from Burlish Hill, they strained for the name of this or that town, a glimpse of the sea, or the tower of Lincoln Cathedral. They saw buildings, places, lives, distances to be traveled, but what Nathan saw and felt was the pull of the sky, the ever-changing moods of the air. And Fiona Smith understood. And she even understood—in fact, already knew—about the demands that different types of grain placed upon a mill. How the millstone had to be geared and leveled differently according to the grist and the weather, and all the complex processes of sifting and sieving, and then of proving and damping, about which even the farmers who produced the stuff, and the bakers who baked it, barely cared. She could have been born to be the wife of a master miller.

Then, as they leaned close, she talked to him of her years away from Stagsby. The school she'd been sent to by her father had been just as dreary as she'd feared, but she'd traveled afterward, fleeing England and heading south and south, toward warm and dusty lands. Looking out, Nathan could smell the air, feel the spice heat of the lives of those darker-skinned people who, as she put it, slept when they felt like sleeping, and danced when they wanted to dance. He'd never cared much for the idea of travel, for the winds of the world always came to him, but now he understood. The mill was turned fully south, facing across the brown weave of England toward other, more distant, shores. Then, although he hadn't spoken a single word of a spell, the whole great machine shook, and its gears moved, and the sails swooped in a single, vast turn. It was a sign.

Helping Fiona back down the levels, lifting her fully in his arms, he felt her amazing warmth and lightness. She laughed and her breathing quickened and she pressed herself closer still. Leaning the whole soft pressure of her body against him as they swayed together on the main millstone floor, she planted a long, hot kiss on his lips.

The mill was entirely at rest again when they stumbled outside, but Nathan's head was spinning.

"It's almost a shame to be back here in England." Fiona sighed, fanning her neck as she pushed back her hair. "I hate London, with its traffic and fog and smell. But here, here—being *here*. You know, I'd almost forgotten. But I feel so at home here in Lincolnshire. And you and I, Nathan, we really could be partners, equals. Let me show you . . . "

Reaching into the pocket of her skirt, she took out something small and round. A coin, a bead, or perhaps merely a pebble. But it had a black aether-glow. Crouching down, she tossed it like a dice onto the brittle brown grass, and the blackness spread. Nathan was reminded of the tumble of the wind-seller's sack of storms, but this was different again, and far more powerful. Grids of fire leapt across the blackness. Dimming even the blaze of the sun, they threw sparks in Fiona's hair. When she looked up at him, that same fire was in her eyes.

"This," she said, "is a map, a plan. It goes far farther than you can see from even this hill. Here are the great cities, the ports and towns and industries, of all of England. See, Nathan, see how they blaze! Even you, up here, must use fire. But think what fire really means. Fire means power. The same power you feel when your body grows hot as you move those arms to work all those clever winches, but magnified, multiplied, almost beyond measure. Then imagine all that power, that heat, controlled." The brightness amid the dark mirror that lay spread before them increased. It spilled and moved and pulsed along quivering veins. Nathan felt like God himself looking down on this different world, for he saw every movement and detail as close and intricate as the fine auburn down on Fiona's bared neck as she leaned beside him. There were shimmers of steam, furnace mouths, endless sliding arms of metal. He tasted coal and smoke.

"The world is changing, Nathan, and you and I—*we*—must change with it. Forget about the old ways, the old songs, the old spells. Already, see here, the arm of the railway is reaching as far as Spalding. Soon it will be here, and here, and here, as well." Fire dripped from her fingers, spilling and spreading between the embers of the towns. "The engines, the rails, will draw everything closer together. People—their trades, their lives."

Nathan blinked. He saw the tiny machines made larger, and enormously powerful, through clever intricacies of iron. But why was she telling him this? He strained to understand.

"I've already had the land down there around Stagsby Hall surveyed. The road itself can easily be widened, and the lake will provide all the water we could ever need—at least, it will when there's a decent drop of rain. And did you know Nottinghamshire's made of nothing but coal? Transportation shouldn't be an obstacle even before we can get a railhead at Stagsby. Right now, the engineers are drawing up the plans for the enginehouse. But they're just *experts*, Nathan, people who work at desks with pens. I need someone who really understands the local markets, and probably knows more than anyone else in this whole county about the grinding of grain. I need someone who has the whole business in his blood."

"You're saying—"

"I'm saying we could work together, down there. We're living at the start of a new age. Forget about the guilds and all the old restrictions, we can make ourselves its kings and queens. As soon as the money is released, straight after the marriage—before, if I get my way—I'll give the order to start digging the steam mill's foundations."

For all that Nathan Westover was a man of business, the conversation was taking a surprising turn. "But what about here, what about this mill?"

"I know, I know, it's a wonderful creation. Of course, it will be months before we can get the steam mill fully commissioned. Even after that, I'm not suggesting that we shut this windmill down immediately. Far from it—I'm sure we'll need it for years to take up the slack and deal with the seasonal rush. But this isn't some dream, Nathan. This isn't about sentiment or imagination. My fiancée's a senior master of the Savants' Guild. He has shares in almost all the major rail companies, and they're developing the latest most powerful magics of steam and iron. Of course, he's old, but he still—"

"What do you mean? You're saying you're *engaged*?"

"Where else do you think I'm getting the money to finance this project?"

Nathan stood up. For all the sun's blaze, the darkness of the map seemed to have spread. Then he started to laugh, taking in great, wracking gulps of air.

"And you thought—you thought that I would give this up? My whole life? Come to work down there . . . " He raised a trembling hand.

"But what *did* you think, Nathan?" She was standing beside him again now, and far too close. He had to turn away.

"All these years. All these *bloody* years. I've hoped . . . . "

"Hoped what, Nathan?" There was a pause. The light gathered. He sensed a change in her breath. "I wish, I *do* wish, that life could be different. But that isn't how it works, Nathan, and even if it did . . . . Even if it did, can you imagine how much money the sort of project I'm talking about needs? It's more than you could ever dream of, wealthy though I'm sure you think you are. My husband will get my name and what little of my companionship he still needs when I'm in the city, and I'll get his money and the freedom to live here. It's a fair enough exchange. But as for the rest. As for the rest. It doesn't mean . . . . I *like* you, Nathan, I truly do, and I felt what we both felt inside the mill. And if we *were* together, if we were business partners, and you were the manager of my mill, who knows . . . . " Her hand was upon his shoulder, kneading the flesh, moving toward his neck, "Who knows—?"

He spun around in a blurring rage. "And you imagined that you could have me as your *employee*—working on some infernal machine! You might as well expect me to go to Hell."

"Hell, is it?" Stumbling back, she stooped to snatch up the stone. Its spell swirled around her in a dark vortex of flame in the moment before the map faded. "You think *that* would be Hell?" She grabbed her mare's reins, mounted, and drew the creature about in a wild and angry lunge. It reared, baring its teeth around the bridle. "There's only one infernal machine,

Nathan Westover," she shouted, "and we're both on it, and so's everyone else in this world!"

With a dig of her heels, Grandmistress Fiona Smith galloped off down Burlish Hill.

The heat finally relented in peals of thunder. Huge skies hurried over Lincolnshire, and what grain there was that year, poor stuff, flattened and wettened, was finally borne up Burlish Hill's puddled track for grinding. If the miller up there seemed even brisker and grumpier in his dealings than he had before, it got little mention, for all the talk was of what was happening down at the big hall. When storms finally blew themselves out, there came a last day of surprising warmth; the last echo of summer cast across the stark horizons of autumn. Sheer luck, although the villagers agreed that the wedding breakfast to which they'd all been invited could scarcely have been bettered. From the few glimpses they'd had of the bride with her flaming hair and pearl-beaded dress, everyone agreed that she made the finest imaginable sight as well. Pity the same couldn't be said of the groom, who looked dried up and old enough to make you shudder at the very thought of him and her . . . Not that much of that was likely, it was agreed, as the wine and the beer flowed, still less a child. Lights were lit as dusk unfurled. A great machine with a greedy furnace and tooting pipes was set chuffing in the middle of the lawns. It gave out steam and smoke and music, and soon everyone began to dance. Amid all these distractions, few would have bothered to look toward Burlish Hill. Still fewer would have noticed that the sails of the mill still turned.

That winter was a hard one. The land whitened and froze, then rang with the iron wheels of the many carts that headed through the gates of Stagsby Hall to scrawl their marks across the ruined lawns. With the thaw came much work as villagers bent their backs to the digging of what seemed like an endlessly complex trench. Sconces and braziers burned as the work continued long into the nights, and the grandmistress herself was often present, offering the sort of smiles and encouragements for which the men were greedy, although few yet comprehended exactly what the work was for. Still, they agreed as they sat afterward in the snug and drank their way though the extra money, it might help put Stagsby on the map. It would never have occurred to them that Stagsby had proclaimed itself across all Lincolnshire for centuries by windmill-topped Burlish Hill.

The huge new contrivance itself, part machine and part factory, looked wholly alien as it squatted amid the spring mud at the brown edges of the filthy lake. The opening of it was cause for yet another party at the hall. People were getting blasé about these occasions by now. They commented on the varieties of cake and beer with the air of connoisseurs, and were cheerfully unsurprised when the first turning of the great cam-wheel failed to occur. Nevertheless, the grandmistress gave a speech up on a podium, and both she and it were more than pretty enough.

Looking down from Burlish Hill through that long winter and into the spring that followed, Nathan absorbed tales and rumors along with the scent of coalsmoke that now drifted on the air. Lights shone now often from the windows of Stagsby Hall, but they were nothing compared to the fume and blaze that glowed beside it. On still days, he heard shouts in odd accents, the toots of whistles, the grumpy huff and turn of a huge and awkward machine, the call of strange spells. The first summer of this new competition, though, went well. Nathan aimed to be as reliable and competitive as ever—in fact, more so. He cut into his savings, reduced his rates, and the crop that year was as good as the previous one had been bad. There was more than enough grist to keep him working night and day, and the winds mostly came when he needed them. Meanwhile, all the machine down in the valley seemed capable of delivering was broken deadlines. If the local farmers took a little of their trade to the new grandmistress, it was more out of curiosity to see the great steambeast at work, and because of her looks, rather than because of the quality of the service she offered. Knowing something of farmers and their nature, Nathan didn't doubt that the novelty would fade. And he was a miller, and there had always been a mill up on Burlish Hill. He was prepared to trust the winds, and the seasons, and be patient.

Nathan was also sanguine about the other changes he noticed in the world. He'd understood long before Grandmistress Smith had laid it out before him on that clever map that one of the main reasons for his success as a miller was the improvement in haulage and communication that the spread of the new steam railways had brought. When a line finally reached as far as the Lincolnshire coast, he was happy to use it to visit his mother at Donna Nook; it saved several hours, and meant he no longer sacrificed an entire day's work. On summer's mornings, the cramped, chattering carriages drawn by those odd new machines were filled with families from the big cities heading for a day out at new resorts. He sometimes even stopped off himself for a stroll along the promenade, although to him the Lincolnshire coast remained essentially a wintry place. This, he thought on a freezing, blustery day when the gaudy new buildings were shuttered and sand gritted the streets, is real weather, brisk and cold and sharp.

The tracks now also ran to the town markets, where the steam and the screech of whistles added to the traditional stink and chaos of the cattle pens, the clamoring baskets of geese and chickens, the shouting and the pipesmoke. There were new animals now, as well. Horses that were too broad and strong and stupid to be called horses, and frighteningly fancy ducks and hens. In this new age of new magic, there were also strange new trades. Still, the tall rooms in which the auctions of grain took place remained places of golden, if bustling, calm. The mass of grain itself was stored in barns or warehouses. All that was here were wicker baskets containing samples, which you could thumb-nail the husks off to taste the soft white meat inside. Nathan relished the whole day, and the entire process. He would, he sometimes reflected, have come to these auctions even if he didn't trade himself. He even enjoyed the conversations, which were invariably about the air, the earth, and the crops.

Market day that September in Louth was busy as ever, and the roar of voices and the jostle of shoulders was entirely familiar. Standing toward the back, Nathan was tall enough to see over the caps and heads of the factors and farmers, and still had a voice that the older millers who clustered at the front had lost. Then, as the bidding commenced, he noticed a shift in the usual ebb and flow. There was a surprising swirl of attention near to the auctioneer's desk, and it was centered around a solitary head of flaming red hair.

It was the same at the next auction, and the one after that. Against all tradition, Grandmistress Fiona Smith—a woman, and no member of any of the recognized agricultural guilds—was bidding on her own behalf. Not only that, but she was far better at getting the auctioneer's attention than anyone else in the room. Worst still, the masculine reserve of these country guildsmen meant that they withdrew from bidding against her at prices that were far too low.

Essentially, she was getting her grain on the cheap because of how she looked.

Nathan was shocked to discover that seemingly sensible men could act like such fools. If a batch of corn or oats was selling at a price he knew to be ridiculous, he made sure he made a better bid. Sometimes, he pushed things too high, and the red head that absorbed so much of the hall's attention would give a negative shake. Still, grain was grain, and he had the stuff stored at his own expense until he found the time and the energy to have it delivered and ground. He'd always thought of himself as hardworking, but in that season and the ones that followed, he surprised even himself. The mill turned as it had never turned, and there was always something more that needed to be done, and even a decent wind wasn't always enough for him. On days when there was a moderate easterly, or a keen breeze from the north, Nathan still found himself looking up in frustration at the slow turn of his mill's sails. Finding a wind hanging hooked in his lean-to that made a close enough match to the one that was already blowing was an entirely new skill, although it was one he did his best to learn. Sometimes, on the right days, the whole mill spun and thrummed with a speed and a vigor that he'd never witnessed. It was thrilling, and the needs of the many mechanisms dragged the songs from his throat until he was exhausted and hoarse. On other days, though, the winds fought angrily, and the mill's beams creaked and its bearings strained and its sails gave aching moans. Such strains inevitably increased the wear on the mill's components, and the costs and demands of its maintenance soared.

On cold winter nights, when there was now still grain in need of grinding, or flour that somehow had to be dried off before it could be sold, he dragged himself to the desk with its books of spells and accounts at which his father and many other generations of Westovers had sat. But the nib trembled, his lungs hurt, and the red and green figures could no longer be persuaded to add up. He'd once never have thought of leaving any job half-completed, but now he staggered off to snatch the few hours' sleep with the colored inks still warring. Then he dreamed of storms of figures, or that the mill was storm itself, and that the air would never stir again across all of Lincolnshire if he didn't work its sails.

Nathan had got little enough in reply on the rare occasions when he'd mentioned the wind-seller to his fellow millers. Did the man come to them on those same still, hot days on which he always seemed to visit Nathan? That hardly seemed possible. Was there just one wind-seller, or were there several of their species or guild? And where exactly did he come from—and what essential substance was it, after all, from which his winds were made?

A flat, hot day. The mill groaning and creaking, and Nathan's bones filled with an ache for the time—it seemed only moments ago—when there was always too much grain, and never enough hours in the day to grind it. This summer, though, he'd had to rein in his bidding in order to keep up his repayments to the bank, whilst the carts had borne their grain less regularly, and in smaller amounts, up Burlish Hill. The farmers never looked Nathan directly in the eye or told him what they were doing, but the evidence was down there in the valley, in a pounding haze of noise and heat. Could people really work in such conditions, when the day itself was already like a furnace? Nathan wiped his face. He hawked and coughed and spat, and worked the bloody phlegm into the dry ground of Burlish Hill with the heel of his boot. Just last week in Gainsborough, he'd been having a bite of lunch at one of the inns beside the market before taking the train that now reached Burwell, only five miles out of Stagsby itself. His bread roll had tasted gritty and sulfurous. He'd spat it out.

A distant engine chuffed across the landscape, trailing its scarf of steam. Somewhere, a whistle blew. Nathan coughed. No grist in need of grinding, but he still had half a mind to unlock the lean-to and take out whatever winds he had left in there, just for the ease they brought to his breathing, and the cool feel of them twisting in his arms . . .

A gray shimmer was emerging from the valley, and it was too stooped and solitary a figure for his heart to begin to race. Nathan remembered his fear and excitement back in the times when his father had been master of this mill, and every spell had been new, every wind fresh and young. Still, it was good to think that some things didn't change, and he almost smiled at the wind-seller; almost wished him a cheery good day.

The man flapped his old cloak. He seemed to give a shiver as he studied the hot, dry horizons. "The hardest of all seasons, eh?"

Nathan shrugged. Almost every farmer said something similar to him when they came up here. It was usually a prelude to their explaining how they couldn't afford his normal rate, and it was scarcely in his interest to agree with them. But Nathan found himself nodding. This really *was* the hardest of all seasons.

"I've a hundred remedies . . . " The wind-seller unshouldered his sack, and there they all were beneath: a knotted multitude of rags, but such beautiful things, especially on a day such as this. Storms and airs and breezes hazed about them in a thousand hurrying tints

of blue and black and gray. Nathan knew how to drive
a bargain, and the Elder knew he wasn't in position for
extravagances, but he couldn't help feeling stirred,
drawn, excited. And was it his own wheezing breath or
the mill itself that gave off that needy groan?

Nathan barely heard the wind-seller's patter about
his products. He of all people didn't need to be told
about the poetry of the skies. He lifted a tarred and
bunched handful of northerly rope that wasn't from
the north at all, and felt the bitter bliss of it swirling
around him, then the soft twine of a southwesterly
blown in from far beyond every southwesterly horizon.
Its breath in his face was the laughing warmth of a kiss.
He bore them all, great stirring armfuls of them, into
his stone lean-to, and hooked them up on their iron
hangers, where they stirred and lifted with a need to be
let loose. It was sweet work, delicious work, to hold
and be taken hold of by this knotted blizzard of winds,
and Nathan found that he no longer cared how many
he really needed, nor what he could afford. By the time
he'd finished, there was nothing left beyond the sack
itself, and, had the wind-seller offered it to him, he'd
have taken that as well.

Nathan was sweating, gasping. He was possessed
by hot spasms, shivers of cold. How much had he
actually paid for this glut? He couldn't recall. Neither
did he particularly care. But as the wind-seller whistled
through thin lips and laid the empty thing of rag across
his back, Nathan felt that today he was owed
something more.

"Tell me, wind-seller," he asked, although he knew
that such questions should never be asked outside
those who belonged to a certain trade or guild,
"exactly how is it that your winds are made?"

"It was your father I used to deal with, wasn't it?"
The man's cold gaze barely shifted, but it took in all of

Nathan, his mill, and his hill. "Although you and he might as well be the same. Same mill, same man, same sacrifices, eh? But it's always slightly behind you, isn't it?—I mean the best of all days, the keenest of winds, the sweetest of grain. It's never quite where you're standing now. And the longer you work, the more you give up, the more time hurries by, the more it seems that the strongest breeze, the whitest clouds, always came yesterday, or the day before."

"You're saying your winds are taken from the past?"

Twisting his neck, the wind-seller gave a shake of his head. "Time was, there were no sails up here, no millstone—and no miller, either. But the winds still came, and the sun rose and fell. Back then, people saw things clearer. You, miller, you've merely given up sweat, and years, and the good state of your lungs to keep this mill turning, but for those people it was the seasons and then the sun itself that had to be turned." The wind-seller laughed. It was a harsh sound. "Imagine—the blood that was let, the sacrifices they made, to ensure that spring arrived, that the next dawn came! But the past is gone, miller—used up. It's as dry and dead as this ground, which has been seeped of all its magic. What we're left with are the husks of our memories. Just like this sky, and this land . . . . "

Nathan watched the wind-seller's shape sink down into the valley's haze. Might as well, he reflected, have tried talking to the winds themselves.

Conversation after the markets in Lincolnshire bars always came free and loud. Nathan had never been one to seek out companionship, but now he found that there was some consolation to be had in sharing a glass or two, and then a few complaints, after another point-less morning at the auctions. Grandmistress Smith was less of a novelty these days, and she won her bids less easily, for there were other steam mills at Woodhall and Cranwell, and an even newer, bigger one in construction at South Ormsby. The world was changing within the giddy scope of one generation, and it wasn't just the wind and water millers who were losing out. Elbowed in with them amid the hot jostle of sticky tables in those bars were hand weavers, carters—even smithies: for all that the Smithies Guild was hand-in-glove with the financiers who constructed these new machines, it was the high-ups, the pen pushers, the ones who wore out their fat buttocks by sitting at desks, who made a nice living, and devil take the old ways and local village businesses founded on decent, traditional skills. It was an odd coalition, both alarming and reassuring, and the talk turned yet more furious as the evenings darkened and business suffered and the drink flowed.

Plans were hatched, then laughingly dismissed as more beer was bought. But the same complaints returned, and with them came the same sense of angry helplessness. Nathan was never a ringleader, but he and everyone else around those tables soon agreed that there were better ways to spend your time and energy than sitting uselessly in a bar. They were *guildsmen*, weren't they? They had their pride. Better to go down fighting. Better still to resist wholeheartedly, and not go down at all.

They met one night at Benniworth. In the morning, the precious furnace that had just been delivered was found transformed into a dented mass of metal as if by a hailstorm of hammerblows. They met again at Little Cawthorpe. A culvert beneath the embankment of the new railway that would bear coal from Nottingham far quicker than the old canals was blown apart, although the damage was far less than might have been expected, considering the amount of explosive that was used. Lincolnshire earth, as any farmer would have attested, was notoriously slow and sticky stuff to move. Something stronger and better was needed, and Nathan brought it with him the next time they met outside Torrington in an owl-hooting wood.

"What you got there, miller?"

Lamplit faces gathered around him, edging and prodding to get a glimpse of the oddly lumpen knot he held in his hand.

"Something alive, is it?"

"Something that'll make them think twice about stealing the living off decent guildsfolk?"

Nathan couldn't bring himself to explain. He merely nodded, and felt the glorious lightness of a wind that had come from a point in the east to be found in no compass. These men didn't really expect to understand. Theirs was a loose alliance, and they remained almost as wary of each others' skills and secrets as of those they were campaigning against.

They called themselves The Men of the Future by now, because that was the opposite of what their wives and neighbors shouted after them, and their target was another mound of earth, although this was far bigger than the railway embankment. Steam mills and their associated machinery were even greedier for water than the watermills they replaced, and a reservoir to supply one such new machine had recently been constructed here in Torrington, taking up good grazing land and creating more aggrieved men. As, shushing each other and stumbling, they came upon it through the moonless dark, the clay bank looked huge. They laid the several caskets at its base. Then they turned toward Nathan.

"Whatever that thing is, might as well use it now, miller."

Nathan nodded, although his movements were slow. The wind that twisted in his hand gave off a sharp scent of spring grass. Leaving it in this marshy spot was like destroying a treasured memory. But what else could he do?

They scrambled back through darkness from the hiss and the flare of the fuse. A long wait. The thing seemed to go out. A dull crump, a heavy pause, then came flame and earth in a sour gale, and a white spume of water lit up the dark.

The men cheered, but the rumbling continued, shaking the ground beneath their feet. Some were knocked over, and all were splattered by a rain of hot earth and stone. There was more fire, and then a boiling, roaring wave. They ran, scattered by the power of all the enraged elements that they had unleashed. It was lucky, it was agreed when heads were finally counted as they stood on a nearby rise, that no one had been buried, burned, drowned, or blown away. It looked as if the dam was entirely wrecked. Several fields had certainly been turned into mire. People would have to listen to Men of the Future now.

It was a long walk home. Drenched, muddied, Nathan kept to the edges of the roads although he scarcely expected to encounter any traffic on a night this black, but then he heard a rumble behind him. He turned and saw what seemed to be a basket of fire approaching. Then he saw that it was some kind of wagon, and that it was powered by steam. For all his increasing familiarity with such engines, he'd never heard of one that ran along an ordinary road, and curiosity made him reluctant to hide entirely from sight.

It rumbled past. Big wheels. A big engine. It really did shake the earth. Then it stopped just a few yards past him, spitting and huffing, and a door at its back flung open.

"I'm guessing you're heading the same way that I am, Nathan Westover," a voice called. "Why don't you give your feet a rest?"

Dazed, Nathan stepped out from the edge of the ditch. He climbed in.

"You look as if you've . . . " Grandmistress Smith's eyes traveled over him.

"It's been a hard season."

"That it has. I'm just back from London, from burying my husband. We'd grown fond of each other, contrary to how people talk, and he was a decent enough man. Neither do I make a habit of picking up men from the roadside on my travels, although I hear that's how the tale is told."

Nathan had heard no such tales, and his chest was proving difficult in the sudden change of air within this hot compartment which was padded with buttoned velvet, and lit from some strange source. The woman who sat opposite was dressed entirely in a shade of black far deeper than that he remembered she had once worn on her sole visit to his mill. No silks or trimmings. Her hair had dimmed as well; trails of gray smoked through it. Only the flame in her eyes was unchanged.

"I suppose," she murmured, "you think we're deadly foes?"

"Isn't that what we are?"

She waved a hand. "Merely competitors, like your fellow millers. And it was never as if—"

"Fellow millers!" Nathan wheezed. He cleared his throat. "There are few enough of us."

"But when you say *us,* Nathan, why must you exclude me? We make the same product. I bid for the same grain in the same halls. And you and I . . . There's a new science. It's called phrenology, and it allows you to determine a man's—I mean a person's—nature merely from studying the bumps on their head. I've had it done myself, and mine reveal me to be stubborn and obstinate, often far beyond my own good interests." She attempted a smile. "And you . . . " She reached across the carriage. Her fingers brushed his bald scalp. "You're an easy subject now, Nathan. One hardly needs to be an expert to understand that you're much the same. And I suppose you remember that offer I made . . . " The steam carriage, which was a clumsy, noisy thing, jolted and jostled. "Of sharing our skills. It could still be done. Of course, I have to employ men from the new guilds to see to the many magics and technicalities of running a steam mill. In all their talk of pressures, recondensing, and strange spells—I can barely understand what they mean even when they're not talking the language of their guilds. Once, I could snap my fingers . . . " She did so now. There was no flame. "And that mill of yours. The dusty air—anyone can see what it's doing to you. We could still . . . "

She trailed off. The machine rumbled on through the night, splashing through puddles, trailing spark and flame.

"There's no point, you know," she said eventually as they neared Stagsby. "You can't resist things that have already happened. Those men, the ones who give themselves that stupid name and are causing such damage. They imagine they're playing some game, but it isn't a game. The Enforcers will—"

"That's not what counts—someone has to put up a fight against steam!"

The lines deepened around her eyes. "You're not fighting steam, Nathan. What you're fighting is time itself."

More than the grain and the flour, more even than the mill, the winds were Nathan's now. Work or no work, whatever the state of the air and the clouds, they encompassed him and the mill. He talked to them in their lean-to, unhooked them, stroked their bruised and swirling atmospheres, drew them out. As the rest of the world beyond his hilltop went on with whatever business it was now engaged in, Nathan's mill turned, and he turned with it. He laughed and he danced. Strident winds from a dark north bit his flesh and froze his heart. Lacy mares' tails of spring kicked and frisked. His winds swirled around him in booming hisses as he sang out the spell that made them unbind, and they took hold of his and the mill's arms. In that moment of joyous release, it seemed to him that he was part of the air as well, and that the horizons had changed. There were glimpses of different Lincolnshires through their prism swirl. He saw the counterglow of brighter sunsets, the sheen of different moons. It reminded him of some time—impossible, he knew, too ridiculous to recall—when, godlike, he'd looked down on the brightly flowing tapestry of the entire universe, which spun like some great machine. He saw the ebb and flow of cities. He saw the coming of flame, and of ice, and the rise of vast mountains pushing aside the oceans. He saw glass towers and the shining movements of swift machines along shimmering highways of light. He believed he glimpsed heaven itself in the sunflash of silver wings amid the clouds. The visions faded as the mill took up the strain of the wind, but they never left him entirely. They and the winds returned to him as he lay on his bunk and snatched at flying fragments of impossible sleep. They came to him more quietly then, not with a scream and a screech and a growl, but in a murmur of forests, a sigh of deserts, a sparkle of waves, a soft frou of skirts. They breathed over him, and he breathed with them, and he let them lift him in their fragrant arms. In and out of his dreams, Nathan laughed and danced.

For all the many winds that he'd bought from wind-seller on his last visit, Nathan knew he'd been less than frugal in their use. Sometimes, on the days of hard sky and mirage earth, he'd look out for that characteristic silhouette climbing up the little-used path from the valley, but the man never came, and part of Nathan already knew that he never would—not because of the indiscreet questions he'd asked, nor for the money he now couldn't afford to give him, but because the man's trade was like that of the millers themselves, and was thus in decline. Why, Nathan had even heard it said that sailors, who were surely the other main market for the produce of the wind-seller's guild, were now installing clever and brassy devices on the decks of their ships that could summon a wind to fill the sails when there was no wind at all. Partly, that sounded like the blurry talk of smoky barrooms, but that, as far as Nathan could see, was how so much of the world had become. He still looked out for the wind-seller on those sour days of bad air that seemed to come all too frequently now, but he knew in his heart that a figure would never shape itself out of the smoke and haze of the valley below. Those last purchases, this marvelous glut, had been like the rush of flour in the chutes when the hoppers were nearly empty. Soon, all that would be left was dust.

Nathan horded his last winds as a starving man hordes his withering supplies. He toyed with them in his mind, carried them about with him, inspected them, sniffed them, sang to them, got the tang of their currents in his mouth. Still, the moment of their release had to come, and it was all over too quickly. And just how were they made—where were they from? The question might now seem immaterial, but it wouldn't let Nathan go. He studied the knots ever more carefully, not only for their feel and bluster, but also the exact nature of their bond. Of course, he'd always known how to undo them—that came to him as easily as winching a sack of grain—but their tying was something else. His fingers traced the long, wavering pattern, which he realized was always the same, no matter from what substance the knot was formed. He followed the kinks that were left in the exhausted scraps once the wind had gone. With so few left, and the wind-seller so absent, it even seemed worth trying to see if he couldn't capture a few small winds himself.

Small they were. He was sure that something vital was lacking even if, as the wind-seller himself had once seemed to say to him, that *something* had already been bled from the very ground. Still, and guilty though he felt, Nathan would sometimes desert his mill for a few hours to gather grasses, or wander the hedgerows of the landscapes below in search of strands of sheep's wool, deer pelt, castings of snake's skin: anything, in fact, that could reasonably be knotted, and through which the winds might once have blown. The knots strained his fingers. They hurt at his heart. They blurred before his eyes. Yet, whatever it was that might once have been trapped within them wasn't entirely lost, for when he undid them, they would let out a sigh, the breath of lost season's air. Never sufficient to drive anything as big as his mill, but enough to bring an ease to his breathing on the most difficult nights when his lungs seemed to close up inside him, and to add some flare and spectacle to the conflagrations wrought by the Men of the Future.

Although the wind-seller never came, Burlish Mill had other visitors now. Men with canes and women with extravagant hats, borne almost all the way to Stagsby from the midland cities, first class, would climb Burlish Hill on summer afternoons and smilingly ask what exactly the cost was for a guided tour. He was slightly less brusque with the painter who lumbered all the way up the slope with his boxes, canvases and easel, but all his talk of *setting down for posterity* was off-putting, and Nathan sent him back down as well. Dismissed, too, was the man who lumbered up with a wooden box set with a staring glass eye, within which, bizarrely, he claimed he could trap and frame light itself.

His trips to Donna Nook had grown less regular, and the last occasion he chose to see his mother was the sort of bitter, windy winter's day when he'd have spilled the hoppers with the sacks of grist he knew his mill longed for, had he any left. After the confinement of the train, he'd hoped that the air along the coast would make his breathing easier, but he felt as if he was fighting some new, alien substance as he hunched toward the old hop warehouse, which now had sand sliding in through its lower windows. His mother wasn't up in her little room, and the fire was out. Stumbling, wandering, he finally found her hunched and gazing seaward from the crest of a dune. Her body was dusted, as if by a coating of the finest and lightest of flours, with a layer of frost.

Now, the nights when he did the work of the Men of the Future were his only escape from the needs of the mill. More and more, he came to think of the world beyond Burlish Hill as a dark and moonless place, erupting with hot iron and black mountains of clinker and coal. The Men of the Future had grown better organized, and the targets of their visitations were kept secret from all but a select inner group to which Nathan had no desire to belong. He was happy, although he knew that happy wasn't really the word, simply to meet in some scrap of wood or of heath, and to take the long, silent march toward another citadel of smoke and fire. There were so many of them now, and with so many purposes. Not just weaving and milling, but threshing, road-making and metal-beating: so many new technologies and spells. Sawmills were powered by steam—printing presses, even—and with each threatened trade came a swelling of their ranks. Pale, slim-faced men from far towns, workers with skills that Nathan couldn't even guess at, were taking charge, and they knew far better than their country colleagues how best to destroy a steam-driven machine. It wasn't about sledgehammers or pickaxes, or even explosives. Such brutal treatments were time-consuming, inefficient, and loud. Far better, they murmured in their slurring accents, to use the powers and magics of the devices themselves. Nathan could appreciate the cunning of setting a millstone turning so its two faces tore and clashed themselves apart. Could see, as well, how clever it was to put lime in a cold furnace, or molasses in a water vat, although some of the more arcane skills that these men then started to use, the muttering of short phrases, the leaving of scrolls of symbols that caused machines and furnaces to break apart when they were restarted, seemed too close to mimicking the work of the new steam guilds themselves. But something had to be done, and they were doing it, and these new Men of the Future continued to encourage the use of the small winds Nathan brought himself. Not that they were essential, he understood, to the work in hand, but their ghostly torrents, which lit up these damnable mills and factories with strange, fresh atmospheres, had become something of a signature of their work across Lincolnshire.

The nights when they met were never ordinary. There was always a similar mix of fear and hopeful excitement. They were, Nathan sometimes reflected, like midnight versions of the summer trips that families from the cities took on the railways to the lakes, the hills, the coast. Some Men of the Future even caught the day's last train to get to their next meeting place, then the morning's milk run to head back home again, and here they all were tonight, gathered once again in some typically remote spot, although the distance of travel had been much shorter than usual for Nathan. He even knew the farmer on whose land they were now standing; he'd once been a good source of trade.

Faces down, backs hunched, the Men of the Future shuffled toward their target in wary silence. As ever, the night was moonlessly dark, but to Nathan these were familiar roads. He didn't count himself a fool, and had long anticipated the night when they would head toward Stagsby. A year or two before, he'd have probably left them to get on with their work and returned to his mill, or perhaps even tried to persuade them to wreck a different machine. Not now. When he was heading home through a gray dawn after one conflagration, a passing grain merchant had halted the hairless beasts drawing his wagon to ask the way to Stagsby's Mill. Nathan knew from the scent of the sacks alone that here were several days' work of good barley, and offered the man an uncharacteristically cheery good morning. The merchant stopped him short when he began his directions. He was looking, of course, for the steam mill down in the valley; not that other thing—just a relic, wasn't it?—up on the hill.

Burlish Hill was nothing more than a presence in the darkness as the Men of the Future passed through the village, where no murmurs were made, no lights were shown. Then came a faint gleam of iron as they met the closed gates of Stagsby Mill. But, just as Nathan had witnessed before, one of the thin-faced men at the head of their procession murmured cooingly to the bolt, and the metal wilted and the gates swung open.

There was no lawn, no trees, only bricks and mud, now at Stagsby Hall. But Nathan, as he turned and blundered into the men around him, couldn't help remembering, couldn't help trying to look. This was the most dangerous time of their work. One night, there would surely be mantraps, men with guns, regiments of Enforcers, or those poisonously fanged beasts like giant dogs, which were called balehounds. Indeed, many of the Men of the Future, especially those of the old kind, would have relished a fight, and there was a brief flurry when the eyes of some living beast were sighted in the pall of dark. Then came suppressed laughter, the glint of smiles. Nothing more than a donkey, old and mangy, tethered to an iron hoop. Once again, their secrecy seemed to have held.

The Men of the Future reached the doors of the machine itself, which gave as easily as had every other barrier. Inside, there was a warmth and a gleam to the dark. The furnace was still murmuring, kept banked up with enough coal to see it through to next morning without the need to relight. There was living heat, too, in the pipes that Nathan's hands touched. He'd been in enough of such buildings by now for some aspects to seem less strange, but this one, especially when the doors of the furnace were thrown open and light gusted out, stirred deeper thoughts. After all, grain was ground here. Although this place was alien to him, aspects of it—the strew of sacks, the smell of half-fermented husks, the barrels of water with their long-handled scoops for damping down—were entirely familiar. But there was something else as well. Nathan sniffed and touched. He was so absorbed in whatever he was thinking that he crashed his head on a beam and let out a surprised shout. Faces glared. Voices shushed him. Rubbing his bare forehead, he realized what it was. This place was cramped, awkward, and messy compared to some of the machines they'd recently targeted. After all, Stagsby Mill had been working down in this valley for almost twenty years, and was getting old.

He watched as the thin men set to their work, quietly shoveling coal into the furnace, stoking up its heat, whilst others of their ilk smirkingly tended to the taps and levers that controlled pressure and heat, murmuring their own secret spells. The heat grew more solid. New energies began to infuse the bricks and irons of the engine house. The main rocker let out a protracted groan. A hiss, a gesture of quick hands, and Nathan was summoned toward the glare of the furnace. The wind that he held in his hands was one of his own best gatherings—just a few looped wisps of seed-headed grass, but it felt soft and sharp as summer sunlight—and he felt sad to release it, much though he knew that it had to be done. Teeth of flame gnashed as he tossed it into the glowing mouth. The furnace gave a deep roar. Coughing and gasping, he was shoved back.

The Men of the Future were in a rush now, but eager and excited as they bustled out. Back in the safety of the cool darkness, they turned and looked, shading their eyes from the open enginehouse door's gathering blaze. There were jeers and moans of disappointment when a shadow blocked the space ahead; some idiot was standing too close and spoiling the show.

"Martin, Arthur, Josh!"

A woman's voice, of all things, although none of them recognized the names she called. When she called them again, and added a few others, along with some hells and goddammits for good measure, it became apparent that she hadn't expected to find herself alone. There was derisory laughter. So much for the hired thugs and the balehounds, although, as Grandmistress

Fiona Smith stepped across the puddled mud toward the gaggle of men who hung back in the deeper darkness, it became apparent that she was holding a gun.

"You're trespassing! I warn you—I'll *use* this thing . . . " The gun was hefted, although it was plainly an old device. "This isn't just filled with swan shot."

The laughter grew louder. This was all simply adding to the show. The grandmistress glanced back when sudden light speared from every aperture of the building behind her.

"What exactly have you done to my—"

Then the entire engine house exploded.

Nathan ran, fighting his way through the searing air, the falling bricks and earth. The blaze was incredible—it was like battling against the sun. A figure lay ahead of him, although it shifted and shimmered in a wild dance of flame and smoke. He grabbed it, drew it up, hauling it and himself across the burning earth that seemed to be turning endlessly against him until, finally, he sensed some diminution of the incredible heat. Coughing, gasping, he laid Fiona Smith down on the rubble and mud beside what had once been the lake of Stagsby Hall. The water was scummed now, licked into rainbow colors by the leaping flames at his back, but he fumblingly attempted to scoop some of it over her blackened and embered flesh before he saw that it was already too late. Little flamelets and puffs of smoke played over Fiona Smith's charred body, but the fire was leaving her eyes. He leaned close, hands moving amid the glowing remains of her hair, and in that last flicker of her gaze, there came what might have been a twinge of recognition, then a final gasping shudder of what felt like release, relief. Nathan's hands still twined. Looking down, he saw that his hands had unconsciously drawn a knot in the last unsinged twine of Fiona Smith's glorious red hair.

The climb uphill had never been harder. His own flesh was burned. His lungs were clogged and charred with flame and soot. As he finally reached, half-crawled, across the summit, he realized that this was the first time he'd ever ascended Burlish Hill without sensing the moods of its air. Now that he did, hauling himself up and looking around at a world which, but for the fire that still blazed in the valley, lay dark at every point of the compass, he realized that there wasn't a single breath of wind—not, at least, apart from whatever was contained within that last knot of hair he'd cut loose with a glowing claw of metal, and that his fingers now held crabbed in his pocket, and was far too precious to be released.

Nathan coughed. With what little breath he had, he tried to call out to his mill. The sound was nothing: the mere whisper of dead leaves from some long-lost autumn. Impossible that this vast machine should respond to anything so puny, but, somehow, groaningly, massively, yet joyful as ever, it did. The sails began to turn. In a way, Nathan had always believed that the winds came as much from the mill itself as they did from the sky-arched landscape, but he'd never witnessed it happen so clearly as it did on that night. Invisibly, far beyond the moon and the stars, clouds uncoiled, horizons opened, and—easy as breathing, easy as dancing, sleeping, and far easier than falling in love—the keen easterly wind that most often prevailed across Burlish Hill, but that was never the same moment by moment, began to blow.

There wasn't a trace of grain in need of grinding, but Nathan still attended to his mill. He released its shackles of winch and brake and pulley to set it turning wildly until all the mechanisms that he'd known and sung to for his entire life became a hot, spinning blur. The sound that the mill made was incredible—as if it were singing every spell in every voice that had ever sung it. He heard his father there within that deep, many-throated rumble, calling to his mill in the strong, clear tones that he had once possessed, and humming as he labored, and sometimes laughing for the sheer joy of his work. And the softer tones of his mother, and all the other mistress millers, were there as well. *See, Nathan, how it sits, and how that band of metal helps keep it in place . . . Now, it's getting near the end of its life . . .* Nathan Westover heard the sound of that stuttering pulley, and then of his own unbroken voice, which had caused its turning to mend. All the winds of this and every other earth sighed with him, and the mill's sails swooped, and the world revolved, and the sky unraveled, and the stars and the planets spun round in dizzy blurs, and the seasons came and went. He saw Fiona Smith, young as she was then, puffing out her cheeks before that huge cake at Stagsby Hall, when the place had still possessed lawns, and its oaks were unfelled. Saw her again at this very mill. *I have a proposal to put to you, Nathan . . .* Saw her as she was at the grain auctions, with the light from the tall windows flaming on her red hair, then sitting in that bizarre machine that rumbled across the countryside, when that same hair was twined with smoke trails of gray. Saw all of these things, but felt, above all, the warm, soft pressures of her body in those few glorious moments when he had once held her on this very millstone floor, and the hot, amazing reality of the taste of her lips and mouth against his own.

The mill roared and Nathan roared with it. Axles smoked, joints screamed, cogs flew, and then, as something final sagged and broke, the top face of the millstone itself bore hugely down on its lower half, screaming a brilliant cascade of sparks.

That memorable night, the villagers of Stagsby were already swirling like ants around what was left of the steam mill when they looked up and saw that the windmill up on Burlish Hill was also burning. Amid the chaos, a ragged line was established to pass hand by hand, slow bucket by bucket, what little was left of the waters of the lake. But the distance was too far, and the mill was already massively ablaze, its flaming sails turning against the night in what seemed to be no wind at all. The heat soon grew far too ferocious to approach, although many stood back to watch, such was the terrible, beautiful sight it made—like some great, mythic bird.

Afterward, there were many rumors. Most popular in Stagsby itself was that the steam mill had long been in decline, and that the grandmistress had been purposefully engineering its destruction to claim on the insurance when she'd been caught out by the suddenness of the blast. Also popular, especially amongst those who had little idea of what insurance was, was that she'd been doing some extra overtime with one of her workers, if you get the meaning, when things had got, well, just a little *too* hot. And as for the old windmill—most likely it had been caught by a spark flown up by the blaze, and everyone knew that the place was half ruined anyway, and doubtless tinder-dry. All assumed, for want of any other sightings, that the miller himself had died inside his mill. The perfunctory official investigations gave people little reason to vary their views. The other theory, which was that the wealthy owners of the latest self-condensing machines had used the so-called Men of the Future as a means of destroying competition, received little credence, and then only amongst those who were in their cups.

Soon, as the wind lifted the ash and bore it westward, and the rain dissolved the charred wood and the grass regrew, nothing but a circle of stone was left on Burlish Hill. Nor was the steam mill down in the valley ever reconstructed. Farmers now sold their harvests on wholesale contract to the big new factories, thus giving up their financial independence for what seemed, for a while, to be a good enough price. Stagsby Hall was acquired by one of the leading families of the steam guilds as a country retreat. Soon, its lawns were reestablished and the lake was dredged and gleamingly refilled; the interiors were extravagantly refurbished in the latest style. The ruins of the steam mill were shored up and prettified with vines and shaggy moss. Five years on, and they could have been a bit of old castle; a relic from an entirely different age. But much of this was hearsay. To judge by all the chuffing, huffing modern carriages that came and went that way through the village, parties were frequently held at Stagsby Hall, but they weren't of the sort to which anyone local would ever be invited. You really had to climb up to the top of Burlish Hill to get any real sense of how fine the big house now looked. From up there you could still watch the clouds chase their reflections across the lake, and see the sunflash of its windows, and breathe the shimmer of its trees, but few ever did, apart from stray couples seeking solitude—for what, otherwise, would be the point?

Weevils, woodworm, fire, and rats are the four apocalyptic demons in a miller's life, and, of these, fire is the worst. But, Nathan reflected as, burned and breathless, he looked back up at the river of flame that steamed westward from Burlish Hill, there were worse things still. At least, he told himself as he walked on, he hadn't left his mill, for there was nothing left to leave.

Following no particular direction, he kept walking until morning, and came across a railway station that he dimly recognized from his journeys as a Man of the Future. He sat and waited there, and took the first train, which bore him all the way to the coast. It was a bright day. Even this early in the summer season, families were camped out on the beach behind colored windbreaks. Laughing children were bathing in the ocean's freezing shallows, or holding the tethers of snapping kites. Nathan watched and felt the bite of the salt against his face, happy to see that the world still turned and the winds still blew, whether or not there was a mill on Burlish Hill.

The rails went everywhere now. They took you places it was hard to imagine had ever existed before the parallels of iron had found them. Even when the timetables ran out and he discovered himself sitting on a empty platform at a time when he knew that no train would be coming, their shining river still seemed ready to bear him on. He traveled. He journeyed. He leaned out of carriage windows, and looked ahead into the fiery, smoking sunset, and licked the salt smuts from his lips. Had he the breath left within him, he might have sung to the teeming air.

Another summer was coming, and the fields were ripening across the wide and heavy land. He sat on the steps beside the bridge of a riverside town where a mother and her daughter were feeding the crusts of their sandwiches to the geese and swans. They were both red-haired. Nathan's fingers bunched the knotted lock he still kept in his pocket. He often longed to release it, and to feel the special giving of a final wind-spell. But he remembered the look in the last embers of Fiona's eyes, and he wondered what he truly had trapped there; what, if released, he might be letting go.

North and south, he traveled on through the many nights, and the landscapes that lay around him in the darkness were stitched in flame. Dawn brought rooftops, chimneys, on every horizon. Swallowed in giant buildings, spat out with the litter and the pigeons onto surging streets, he gawped and wandered. He was cursed, bumped into. Leering offers were made in return for money he no longer had. The sky was solidly gray here, and the airs that rushed up to greet him from the chasms of streets were disgustingly scented. This was a place without seasons, or with seasons that were entirely its own. Nathan had grown accustomed to the tides or delays of departures at stations, but here he was lost.

He wandered the darkening city, taking odd turns as he sought some direction that was neither north nor south, east nor west. Far behind him, the girders of some vast structure were being erected, their black lines gridding the sky, but there were fewer people here, and those who were became furtive in their glances, or ran away at the sight of him with screams and clatters of clogs. Not a place to be, he thought, for anyone who doesn't have business here. But, more and more, he felt that he did. He almost ran, and the bricks rushed by him, whispering with the echo of his dried-out lungs. Whispered, as well, with the glow of all the spells and talismans that were scrawled across them. Some, he was almost sure, belonged to his own guild. Others, he thought, had the taint of the sea about them. And here were the symbols of men who tended the tallest roofs, and of other guilds of those who worked in high places, and breathed the changing airs as they looked down on a different world.

Wheezing, exhausted, light-headed, he stumbled

on. There were gates and walkways. The hidden thrumming of vast machineries ground up through the earth. Dawn, though, brought a different kind of landscape. He was tired beyond exhaustion, and it amazed him that his feet dragged on, that his heart still stuttered, that his lungs raked in some sustenance, but the city had cast itself far behind him—so far that the shifting horizons had smeared it entirely out of memory and existence. Here, puddled and rutted lanes unwound and divided to the lean of empty signposts, bounded by endless hedgerows: fences, gates, railings, snags of string and wire and thorn. And the wind blew everywhere, and from all directions—and the world fluttered with the litter of what seemed like the aftermath of some archetypal storm. Hats and scarves, stray shoes, newspapers, the pages of books, umbrellas, whole lines of washing, the weathered flags of guilds, even the torn sails of ships, fluttered everywhere, or were snatched to tumble in the sky like wild kites.

Nathan's fingers bunched once more around the knot of Fiona's Smith's hair. Here, if anywhere, was the secret of how she might be released. He understood now what all his wanderings had been about, which was to get here, wherever *here* was, and find the spell, the secret, that might unlock that last knot. But he was tired. He was tired beyond believing. Walking, he decided as he leaned against another blank signpost, was an activity he might still just about be able to manage, but he wasn't so sure about breathing, nor sustaining the increasingly weary thud of his heart. But still he pushed on, and the winds, as they came from every and no direction, pushed with him, tearing at his clothing, afflicting him with hot and cold tremors, spiraling around him in moans and whoops. Then he heard another sound—it was a kind of screaming.

Although he now had no idea what it was, it drew him on.

Another fence, its slats torn, flapping and rotting, and another gate, which turned itself closed and then open in the wind, although that wasn't where the screaming came from. Nathan had to smile. It was simply an old weathercock, fixed to a fencepost, and turning madly, happily, this way and that in the wind. So familiar, although he'd never stood this close. The one odd thing about it, he realized, as it screamed and turned on its ancient bearings, was that the four angles of the compass that usually projected beneath such devices were entirely absent, even as rusty stubs. Then the gate reopened, and the weathercock screamed and shifted in directions that lay beyond any compass, and the wind also turned, pushing him along the path that lay beyond.

There was a house, although its windows flapped and its slates and chimneys were in disorder, and there was also a garden of sorts. That blurry sense that he'd felt all morning was even stronger here. There were trees that in one moment seemed to be in blossom, but the next were green, then brown, then gold, then torn to the black bones of their branches in sudden flurries of storm. Roses untwined their red lips and then withered. This was a place of many seasons, Nathan reflected as he gasped his way on, although it belonged more to winter than it did to summer, and more to autumn than to spring.

As much as anything, the hunched figure that lay ahead seemed to be shaped out of the ever-changing territories of the air. Not just windy days, or the sudden bluster of summer thunderstorms, but also the hot stillness of afternoons that seemed to be without prospect of any wind at all, at least until you saw something separate itself from the gray shimmer of the world below. The wind-seller had his sack laid open beside him. He was gathering the tumbled sticks of a nearby willow that shivered and danced its wild arms. Somewhere inside Nathan's head, that weathercock was still screaming, and with it came a sobbing agony in his lungs. He knew he didn't have the strength left to tell the wind-seller what he wanted, and it was a release and a relief to him when the man simply held out his pale fingers, which looked like stripped willow themselves, and took from him that glorious red tress. As Nathan Westover stumbled and fell into the puddled mud, he saw the wind-seller's hands working not to release Fiona Smith's last breath, but looping her hair again to draw another, final, knot.

CONTRIBUTORS

————

DARYL GREGORY writes fiction and computer code in State College, PA, where he lives with his wife and two children. It was while re-reading some of his favorite childhood books to the kids that he first got the idea for "Unpossible." His stories have appeared in *Asimov's, The Magazine of Fantasy & Science Fiction*, and other venues, and some of them are available for free at darylgregory.com. His first novel, *Pandemonium*, will be appearing from Del Rey Books later this year.

KELLY LINK is the author of two collections, *Stranger Things Happen* and *Magic for Beginners*. Recent short stories have appeared in *Tin House, The Restless Dead,* and *Coyote Road*. Her first young adult collection, *Pretty Monsters*, will be published by Viking this fall. Link lives in Northampton, Massachusetts, where she and her husband, Gavin J. Grant, run Small Beer Press. They co-edit the fantasy half of *The Year's Best Fantasy and Horror* as well as *The Best of Lady Churchill's Rosebud Wristlet*, marking the first decade of their occasional zine.

ZORAN ZIVKOVIC was born in Belgrade, former Yugoslavia, and currently lives there, with his wife Mia, their twin sons Uros and Andreja, and their four cats. The author of seventeen books of fiction and five books of nonfiction, Zivkovic continues to push the boundaries of the strange and surreal.

NOREEN DOYLE's fiction has appeared in magazines and anthologies, including *Realms of Fantasy* and *The Mammoth Book of Egyptian Whodunnits*, and she co-edited the World Fantasy Award nominee *The First Heroes: New Tales of the Bronze Age*. With master's degrees in Egyptology and nautical archaeology, she writes historical nonfiction for adult and young readers. Doyle lives in Maine.

WILLIAM ALEXANDER's stories have appeared in *Zahir* and *Weird Tales*, and will soon appear in *Lady Churchill's Rosebud Wristlet* and *Postscripts*. He has been nominated for the Pushcart and selected as a finalist for the Calvino Prize. "Buttons" first took root when Will watched a museum curator explain Picasso's Guernica to several seated kindergartners. She used both hands to carefully pantomime "aerial bombardment." Bagdad was burning at the time.

HOLLY PHILLIPS lives by the Columbia River in the mountains of western Canada. She is the author of the award-winning story collection *In the Palace of Repose*. Her fantasy novel *Engine's Child* will be published by Del Rey in 2008.

ANDY DUNCAN's books include the fiction collection *Beluthahatchie and Other Stories*, the non-fiction guidebook *Alabama Curiosities*, and the fiction anthology *Crossroads: Tales of the Southern Literary Fantastic*, co-edited with F. Brett Cox. By day, he is the senior editor at a business-to-business magazine, and he teaches in the Honors College of the University of Alabama. His fiction has won two World Fantasy Awards and the Theodore Sturgeon Memorial Award.

RACHEL SWIRSKY holds an MFA in fiction from the Iowa Writers Workshop. Her fiction has appeared in numerous magazines and anthologies, including *Subterranean Magazine*, *Interzone*, and *Weird Tales*. She also edits PodCastle, the world's first audio fantasy magazine, which puts up reprints of the best fantasy fiction for free listening online. Her website is www.rachelswirsky.com

CARRIE LABEN lives and writes in Brooklyn, and often allows herself to be distracted by birds. She can be found online at teratologist.livejournal.com.

MATTHEW JOHNSON is a writer and media educator who lives in Ottawa with his wife Megan. His fiction has appeared in places like *Asimov's Science Fiction*, *Fantasy Magazine*, and *Strange Horizons*. He's currently settling into a new job and trying to drum up interest in any of his novels. You can find out more at his website, www.zatrikion.blogspot.com.

BENJAMIN ROSENBAUM lives near Basel, Switzerland, with his wife Esther and his cute and alarming children, Aviva and Noah, who like to cook pancakes, sing recursive songs, and turn people into pigs. His stories have appeared in *Harper's*, *F&SF*, *Asimov's*, *McSweeney's*, *Strange Horizons*, and *Nature*, been nominated for the Hugo, Nebula, World Fantasy, BSFA, and Sturgeon Awards, and been translated into fourteen languages; also, Noah told him he was fancier than Noah's elbow. His collection, *The Ant King and Other Stories*, comes out in August 2008 from Small Beer Press.

DAVID ACKERT co-authored two short stories with Benjamin Rosenbaum. They appeared in *Fantasy & Science Fiction* and *Realms of Fantasy*. He is also an accomplished actor, with roles in over fifty television episodes including "Bones," "CSI: Miami," "Monk," "Six Feet Under" and "The West Wing." His latest film, "La Linea," starring Andy Garcia and Ray Liotta, will be released this year. And he has appeared on numerous stages including The Studio Theater and the Kennedy Center in Washington DC.

A seventh book from **MARLY YOUMANS**, *Val/Orson*, is forthcoming from P. S. Publishing in late 2008. Set among the tree sitters of California's redwoods, the story takes its inspiration from the legendary tale of Valentine and Orson and the forest romances of Shakespeare. Her prior books are: *Ingledove; Claire; The Curse of the Raven Mocker; The Wolf Pit*, winner of The Michael Shaara Award; *Catherwood*; and *Little Jordan*. As she is always playing tug-of-war between time for writing and the needs of a family with three children, she has entirely given up the mad, frolicksome habits that make reading these little biographies so interesting.

In 1963, **GARTH NIX** was born in Melbourne, Australia to the sounds of a brass band. Rather than become a scientist (like his father) or an artist (like his mother), he decided to be a writer. That meant, among other life experiences, attending college, working in a bookshop, and entering the publishing industry. Of course, it's tough to write when you're working all day, so Garth quit his day job to become a full-time writer. The winner of many awards and much acclaim, his novels include *Sabriel, Shade's Children, The Ragwitch, Lirael, The Seventh Tower* series, and *Abhorsen*. Garth currently lives very happily near Coogee Beach in Sydney, Australia, with his wife and child.

KAREN JOY FOWLER is the author of five novels, including *The Jane Austen Book Club*, which was a *New York Times* Bestseller, and two short story collections, including *Black Glass*, which won the World Fantasy Award in 1999. A new novel, *Wit's End*, will be published in April.

THEODORA GOSS is a Hungarian American writer of fantasy short stories. Her stories have been nominated for major awards: "Pip and the Fairies" for the Nebula Award in 2007, and "The Wings of Meister Wilhelm" was nominated for the 2005 World Fantasy Award for Best Short Fiction. She won the 2004 Rhysling Award for Best Long Poem for "Octavia is Lost in the Hall of Masks." Her collection *In the Forest of Forgetting* was published in 2006 by Prime Books. She currently lives in Boston, MA, with her husband, Kendrick, and daughter, Ophelia.

DAVID BARR KIRTLEY's short fiction appears in magazines such as *Realms of Fantasy* and *Weird Tales*, and in anthologies such as *New Voices in Science Fiction*. He lives in Los Angeles, where he is a graduate student in screenwriting and fiction at USC. His website (www.davidbarrkirtley.com) features stories, illustrations, interviews, videos, a podcast, and a blog.

Taken broadly, **ERIK AMUNDSEN** has had an interesting life; he's been a baker, an itinerant schoolteacher, worked for two governments and gotten in bar fights overseas. He now lives at the foot of a cemetery in central Connecticut where he writes nasty little stories and poems that shuffle around in the night when he's not looking. Or at least he hopes it's them; something's got to be making those noises and it's not the furnace.

IAN R MACLEOD lives with his wife and daughter in the riverside town of Bewdley, Worcestershire, England. He's been writing in and around the genre for many years, has been translated into many languages, and, amongst his many awards and nominations, has twice won the World Fantasy Award. He's published four novels and three short story collections and has a new novel, *Song of Time*, out this year from PS Publishing. "The Master Miller's Tale" takes up a theme from two of his novels, *The Light Ages* and *The House of Storms*, which describe with a world which, although in many ways similar to ours, has been changed through the industrial exploitation of magic.

PUBLICATION HISTORY

ABOUT THE EDITOR

Rich Horton is a software engineer in St. Louis. He is a contributing editor to *Locus*, for which he does short fiction reviews and occasional book reviews; and to *Black Gate*, for which he does a continuing series of essays about sf history.